For Linda Sisterson and Claire Stewart

Thank you for giving me strong roots from which I could grow
and explore the world;
for the playful teasing to keep me grounded;
and a lifetime of support, belief and love in times good or tough;
for teaching me that family ties run far deeper than bloodlines or DNA;
for always making me feel lucky to have grown up as I did;
and for holding my hand when it mattered most.

They say 'you can't choose your family'
No matter what, I'd always choose you, and Dad.
Aroha nui ahau ki a koe

DARK DEEDS
DOWN UNDER

VOLUME 2

EDITED BY
CRAIG SISTERSON
& LINDY CAMERON

Clan Destine
PRESS

First published by Clan Destine Press in 2024

PO Box 121,
Bittern Victoria 3918
Australia

National Library of Australia Cataloguing-In-Publication data:

Editors: Craig Sisterson & Lindy Cameron

DARK DEEDS DOWN UNDER, Volume 2

ISBNs: 978-1-922904-28-7 (paperback)
         978-1-922904-29-4 (eBook)

Illustrations:

Kiwi by Māori artist Māhina Bennett

Platypus by Noongar artist Seantelle Walsh

Cover design by Willsin Rowe
Cover Photograph by Liz Olle

Design & Typesetting by Clan Destine Press

Cover image: The Ilparpa Claypans, Central Australia

www.clandestinepress.net

CONTENTS

INTRODUCTION

AHAKOA HE ITI HE POUNAMU

Although it is small, it is greenstone

Kia ora and g'day, welcome to *Dark Deeds Down Under 2*, the second volume of our special anthology series of crime and thriller short stories from a diverse array of fantastic Australian and New Zealand storytellers. It's good to be back.

Last time, I mentioned my love for mysteries and thrillers germinated as a 'sport-loving book nerd' growing up in smalltown New Zealand, and had only grown stronger as an adult, via a serendipitous journey over the past decade and a half as a book critic and features writer, event chair, awards judge, festival founder and more, across both hemispheres. I also mentioned how crime and thriller writing itself had grown over the decades; nowadays it's a rich and wonderful form that delivers not only page-whirring puzzles and thrills but vividly evoked settings, fascinating characters, and explorations of important real-life issues. It can be genre and great literature.

Recent years have only fortified those facts, and my views, with a diverse array of crime writers from many countries producing sublime tales. Alongside their international cohort, Aussie and Kiwi writers have continued to entertain and delight fans, find and encourage new readers, and raise the bar.

In our first *Dark Deeds Down Under* we showcased a mix of legendary figures like Ned Kelly Lifetime Achievement honourees Garry Disher, Kerry Greenwood, and Shane Maloney; the NZ Prime Minister's Award for Literary Achievement recipient Renée; modern crime queens Vanda Symon and Sulari Gentill; newer award-winners bringing fresh perspectives such as RWR McDonald, Fiona Sussman, and Lisa Fuller; and acclaimed stalwarts like David Whish-Wilson, Aoife Clifford, Nikki Crutchley, Katherine Kovacic, Narelle M. Harris, and Alan Carter. Delightfully seasoned with outstanding short story specialists, cross-genre authors, and rising stars like Stephen Ross, Dan Rabarts and Lee Murray, Helen Vivienne Fletcher, and Dinuka McKenzie. The treasure trove that is our local crime and thriller writing keeps glowing brighter.

I recently attended a London launch for debut Kiwi novelist Tom Baragwanath, whose rural noir *Paper Cage* was a 2023 Ngaio Marsh Awards finalist and is now been published in UK and US hardcover. Last year, a full half of the six-book shortlist for the UK's CWA John Creasey (New Blood) Dagger were Aussie authors: Hayley Scrivenor, Emma Styles, and Patricia Wolf. Hayley won for *Dirt Town*, and Scotland-based Kiwi DV Bishop won the Historical Dagger. Emma later went on to win the international Wilbur Smith Adventure Writing Prize for her WA road-trip noir, *No Country for Girls*.

Oscar-nominated Kiwi screenwriter Anthony McCarten was also shortlisted for that prize for his high-concept thriller *Going Zero*. Recently, Michael Bennett's indigenous noir *Better the Blood* won the Beltie Mystery Prize in the United States, having already won a 2023 Ngaio Marsh Award and been the first-ever detective novel shortlisted for the literary-leaning Acorn Prize for Fiction. Anthony, Michael, and *Dark Deeds 1* contributor Vanda Symon were all recently shortlisted for the US-based Barry Awards. And that's just a drop in the bucket, as my parents would say, in terms of growing international attention and success. Or 'go you good thing', as the footie commentators yelped when I was growing up.

So I'm thrilled that I can help provide readers another tasty smorgasbord of Aussie and Kiwi crime and thriller stories with *Dark Deeds Down Under 2*. I'm proud of our first volume (go request a copy from your fave bookseller or local library if you haven't read it), and the wonderful new contributors in this second volume have really taken the baton and run with it. Once again, we have a mix of legendary figures, well-established award-winners and bestsellers, and an array of fresh perspectives and rising stars.

Within these pages you'll travel across an array of urban and rural landscapes – and into times past, present, and future – meeting fascinating and memorable locals.

Some you may recognise from the novels they usually star in, like Robert Gott's failed Shakespearean actor and would-be wartime investigator Will Power, who shares a formative tale from his teenage years; or Jean Bedford's Sydney investigator Anna Southwood, who gets entwined in a missing persons case while holidaying in Nowra. Stephen Johnson brings a new adventure for his body-finding Spotlight TV crew. Emma Viskic's story began as a 'deleted' scene' from her multi-award-winning Caleb Zelic series, before taking on a life of its own.

Other noted series authors deliver intriguing standalone tales for us. Jack Heath eschews the American landscapes of his Timothy Blake books for a deaf cop trapped in a Canberra apartment; after six novels set in southern Africa, Malla Nunn takes readers into a day in the life of a biracial NSW police constable; and Peter Papathanasiou breaks from his DS Manolis and Constable Sparrow series for a deadly game on a suburban golf course.

Elsewhere, Brisbane author Ben Hobson plunges us into the greed and grime of the gold rush era; Ashley Kalagian Blunt explores true events descended from a 'forgotten genocide'; while Hutt Valley writer Andi C Buchanan takes us into the future to examine the generational trauma of violent crime. 2023 Ngaios winner Charity Norman offers a clever confession in a seaside cathedral; and fellow Hawke's Bay writer Shelley Burne-Field (Ngāti Mutunga, Ngāti Rārua) portrays far-right ideology hiding in plain sight. A new policewoman gets a fast lesson in power and politics in Natalie Conyer's story. Anna Downes immerses us in online therapy; Jennifer Lane delivers sizzling drama at a suburban barbecue; and a curious SOCO goes beyond her duties in neo-noir master Chad Taylor's tale. Sydney podcaster Dani Vee has us riding shotgun on a mother's desperate chase; Glasgow-based Helen Fitzgerald returns home with a disturbing child's-eye view on the world; and Northland writer Michael Botur takes us on a revealing Uber ride to a small-town pro wrestling event.

There are a couple of new twists in our new volume. While we're living through a modern golden (opal?) age, the roots of Aussie and Kiwi crime writing run deep. Mary Fortune wrote detective tales decades before Conan Doyle, Dame Ngaio was one of the legendary Golden Age Queens of Crime, and the bestselling detective novel of the 19th century wasn't written in London, Paris, or New York, but 'marvellous Melbourne', as Kiwi lawyer and wannabe playwright Fergus Hume penned *The Mystery of a Hansom Cab.*

So to honour our past as well as our present, in our second volume we're grateful to include stories from two much-missed pioneers of the genre: an excerpt from iconic Australian poet Dorothy Porter's crime-laced verse novel, *El Dorado*; and a terrific Cliff Hardy story from the Godfather of modern Australian crime, Peter Corris.

Finally, I was absolutely thrilled to secure a short story for our first volume from legendary playwright and novelist Renée, a lifelong lover of murder mysteries who wrote her first crime novel aged 89. I was even more stoked to witness Renée's great enthusiasm and support for our project. Sadly, Renée passed away in December.

Kua hinga te totara i te wao nui a Tane, ka tangi hotuhotu nga manu
The great totara tree from the forest of Tane has fallen and the birds cry
    with its passing.

Renée's tremendous legacy, including kicking the door down for under-represented voices in creative fields, will live on in the hearts and minds of so many people she met, and in the words of her stories. So with the blessing of her family, and to honour our friend and mentor, we're breaking our own 'no repeat authors' rules in *Dark Deeds Down Under 2* and concluding our anthology with a bonus story, set on Renée's beloved Ōtaki Beach, that she originally wrote for a collaborative multi-media project for the 2020 New Zealand Festival of the Arts.

As I foreshadowed above, our *Dark Deeds Down Under* anthologies are packed with stories that may be small in size compared to crime and thriller novels but are precious gifts. Pounamu, indeed. Thanks for reading. More treasures to come.

Craig Sisterson, March 2024

THE SNARE

CHARITY NORMAN

'The blood of Christ,' he murmurs, and each of them replies, 'Amen.'

Later, he'll look back on the service and wonder what happened here. Napier Cathedral has always welcomed visitors. Killing them isn't part of the plan.

The congregation kneel at the altar rail – if their knees allow it – or stand, or perch on zimmer frames. Mostly grey heads. The organist and choir arrive first, red-robed druids circling the altar before gliding away to sing the anthem. Something by Byrd today. *Glorious*, that's what Peter will tell them later. Though ... no, no, he doesn't like to be hyper-critical, but one of the altos sounds distinctly flat. The usual suspect.

'The blood of Christ,' he whispers, passing the chalice to Tania what's-her-name, who kneels with her arm around her tiny daughter. He knows her best as Tania Turtle, children's party magician: mid-twenties, redheaded, the star turn at the choristers' Christmas bash when she produced a rabbit out of a top hat. A live rabbit! Astonishing.

'Distraction, misdirection, sleight of hand,' his wife Susie replied, when

Peter wondered how the trick was done. 'I just hope that poor bloody rabbit doesn't mind being shoved into that hat.'

As Tania sips, she lifts her gaze to meet Peter's. People generally keep their heads down, pretending to pray – perhaps actually praying, though he has his doubts. Tania's eyes are an impossibly vivid green. According to Susie she wears tinted lenses, a concept he finds baffling. Peter's not a young, sandal-wearing curate. He's a paunchy, bearded one, who came to the priesthood after thirty years in teaching; but still he's flustered, caught in the gleam of emerald headlights. It's midsummer, and the Dean's off kayaking in the Marlborough Sounds, lucky woman, leaving him to mind the shop.

What's the toddler's name? *Millie.* He's stooping to bless the child when she gives a furious yell and makes a grab for the chalice in his hand. Peter yanks it out of reach in the nick of time, spilling drops of wine – *whoops*!

No harm done. Red wine, red carpet. Tania chuckles. Millie melts into tantrum as her mother carries her back to the pews, her wails drowning the restless cadences of the anthem.

Peter's next customer is a visitor. He kneels awkwardly at the rail, thin as wire in a collared shirt and shorts. A folded handkerchief peeks from his breast pocket, a dapper flourish of cornflower blue; a canvas satchel hangs from one shoulder. According to the greeters at the door, he's a steward from the cruise ship *Southern Dream*. Those floating cities are a feature of the blazing summers, here in the Art Deco city. Tugboats race to guide them through the narrow channel of Napier Port; coaches ferry passengers to wineries and restaurants. They stay for a day or so before steaming away, foghorns blaring farewell.

But here's an odd thing. Like Tania, cruise ship man catches Peter's eye. His stare is intense, quizzical, as if they know one another. *Never seen the guy in my life before.* And ... did he just *wink*?

The stranger is one of the last at the rail. Peter knocks back the remains of the consecrated wine. Then it's a prayer, a couple of notices, a gallop down the aisle during the final hymn. Within minutes the congregation are standing around with their Fairtrade coffee, tucking into home baking. This, Peter likes to think, is where the real work takes place. Susie says it's naked bribery: chocolate brownies used as bait to inculcate people.

He takes up his post near the font, chatting, shaking hands. *Goodbye, thanks for coming. Goodbye, nice to see you.* He's in mid-greet when someone barges into his shoulder, knocking him sideways.

It's cruise ship man. He's mopping his brow with the blue handkerchief, and his face doesn't look right at all. It's puffy, swelling up around his neck and jaw.

'Help me,' he gasps, fumbling in his canvas satchel. 'I can't find my...'

He upends the bag, scattering its contents. People look round as his mug falls, spattering glass and coffee across stone flags. The next moment he's followed it down and is rolling on the marble platform around the font, clawing in silent terror at his throat, his mouth gaping wide – a fish, flapping on the deck of a boat, desperate to live.

Susie drops to her knees beside the stricken man. She's a GP, useful to have around in a crisis. She touches her patient's throat, checks his pulse, his airways – all the while she's yelling instructions: someone's to call 111, tell them to get a move on. Someone else is to help her shift him into a better position.

'He was looking for something,' Peter tells her, gesturing at the satchel, the possessions scattered among glittering shards of glass: sunglasses, wallet, phone, a silver hip flask, the crumpled wrapper of a trendy muesli bar: Z-BOOST™ *Enriched with sunflower and manuka.*

'Maybe an EpiPen,' says Susie. 'I bet he carries one – this looks like anaphylaxis. Check the bag again.'

'He mentioned a peanut allergy,' whimpers Joy Johanssen, who was serving morning coffee. 'He wouldn't touch the brownies, said he never eats *anything* from a kitchen he doesn't know. He even asked about the mugs, but I promised they're fresh out of the dishwasher. Have I killed him?'

It's a good question. Cruise ship man has stopped struggling and turned a disturbing shade of blue. Peter's trying to remember how to administer last rites when the organist comes sprinting down the aisle, brandishing a plastic tube and shouting that it's his own EpiPen. Within seconds Susie has grabbed it, snapped off the top and stabbed the dying visitor in the thigh.

Modern medicine is a miracle. The man's breathing improves within a minute, the battleship tinge to his skin replaced by something more human. By the time an ambulance crew arrives, he's recovered enough to threaten to sue the church.

'That bloody mug must have been contaminated. Place is a death trap.'

Joy bursts into tears. Peter retrieves the muesli bar packet from the floor, scanning its ingredients.

'*Z-Boost* … sunflower, pumpkin seeds, manuka,' he reads aloud. 'May contain nuts. I'd say this is your culprit. Take a look.'

Cruise ship man recoils from the proffered wrapper.

'That's not mine! I never touch those things. Where's my EpiPen?'

The paramedics shift the visitor into a wheelchair. They'll transfer him to hospital, *just for a quick check-up, we'll have you back on your ship by tonight*. Meanwhile, Tania Turtle has retrieved his scattered possessions and replaced them in the canvas satchel: hip flask, sunglasses, wallet, phone. He clutches the bag to his chest, still complaining as he's wheeled outside.

'Ungrateful bastard,' says the organist. 'My EpiPen just saved his life. They cost a fortune.'

Peter spreads the *Z-Boost* wrapper on the edge of the font, feeling its wax-coated smoothness under his fingers. He'll store it in the safe for a while, just in case the visitor makes legal trouble. Around him, normal life is resuming. People are mopping glass and coffee from the floor, tutting at the horror of someone almost dying here. He can hear Tania Turtle reassuring Joy Johanssen as the pair of them fill the dishwasher in the kitchen. *It was that muesli bar, Joy. Not your fault.*

And yet. And yet.

Something is stirring in his memory. A moment of chaos, a rapid movement glimpsed in the periphery of his vision. He's shoving the wrapper into his pocket when he remembers.

The curate's house is tucked into a valley on Napier hill, overlooking the harbour. At dawn the following morning, Peter stands in his garden and watches *Southern Dream* making her way in the limpid early light, leaving a long, curved wake on the glittering sapphire of the Pacific.

Peanut-allergy man is on board. Peter knows this for sure, because last night he called the cruise company to enquire after their steward. The news was good. The visitor – turns out his name was Colin Smith – had recovered, been discharged from hospital, and was already back in his cabin. Colin Smith, who winked at a priest he'd never met before, who nearly choked to death on the steps of the font. He knew nobody in the cathedral community, perhaps nobody in the entire city. He was a stranger here.

But somebody knew him. They knew him well enough to try to kill him.

The ship's funnel is sinking below the horizon when Peter takes out his phone, searching through the contacts ... *yes, here it is* ... summons his courage, and dials a number. It rings only once before he changes his mind, jabbing his thumb to end the call.

The cathedral's vestry is a cave, the air heavy with starch and Brasso. The chalice is locked away in the safe, communion wine in its cupboard. The parish secretary doesn't work on Mondays, so Peter is alone in the echoing building. He's kneeling on the floor with his head inside the ancient photocopier, his hands covered in black ink, his mind still reeling from the events of the day before. *Am I going mad?*

He doesn't hear a quiet opening and shutting of the door between the church and office corridor, nor footsteps on the threadbare carpet.

'Don't pretend you're not expecting me,' says Tania Turtle.

Five minutes later she's sitting in his office, fingers curled around a mug of coffee. Plum-coloured nails.

'I know you rang me at six o'clock this morning,' she says. 'You wanted to talk, but you chickened out. And I know why.'

He doesn't deny it; doesn't admit it either. He rubs his inky hand on a tissue, thinking fast. He's framing his next question: to enquire, not to accuse.

Smiling, she says, 'Take a tip from me: don't ever be a magician. You're an open book. Anyway, I've come to make my confession. An actual one. *Bless me father, for I have sinned.*'

Peter has never heard anyone make an actual confession before, not privately like this. It's more of a Catholic thing. He begins to suggest she waits for the Dean to come back from her holiday, but Tania holds up her hands.

'This one has to be made to you, Peter. Please hear me.'

He ought to stop her. She's about to tell him something he doesn't want to know. It's a matter for the police, surely, not the confessional? But she's come to him, perhaps in trouble. He won't turn her away.

'Go ahead Tania,' he sighs, pulling up a chair opposite hers. 'Let's begin with a prayer.'

He cobbles together a few words of prayer, but she doesn't seem to be listening. Once he's fallen silent she takes a long breath. He has the impression that she's balanced on the edge of a high diving board, teetering, summoning courage. Then she plunges.

'You think of me as 'Tania'. It's not the name my parents gave me. Never mind what that was, I haven't used it in years. They both battled demons, my parents. Rage in his case, alcohol in hers. My baby brother and I fended for ourselves.'

'I'm sorry,' Peter mumbles, but he's baffled. This isn't the confession he expected.

'The point is that by the age of thirteen or so I was sure nobody could ever like me. I was skinny and unwashed, my clothes were grubby hand-me-downs. I had no friends. Plenty of bullies, though. They used to bail me up in the toilets and dunk my head in a sink with bleach in it, 'to wash my hair'. Have you ever been lonely, Peter?'

He shrugs uncertainly, trying to imagine this poised woman as a neglected child.

'I longed for a friend,' she says. 'Just one friend. And my wish was granted. I met her on Facebook. *Gracie*. Oh, Gracie! So much calm and caring in that name, don't you think? She was eighteen, the big sister I never had. I saw lots of photos on her Facebook page: blonde hair, the sweetest of smiles. I lived in Auckland and she was way down in Dunedin so we couldn't meet up but we had long, lovely conversations. All written messages. I never heard her voice, but I knew it would be kind. I poured out my troubles to Gracie; she said those bullies weren't worthy to do up my shoelaces. She gave me tips about how to get rid of nits, paint my nails, what to buy in the op-shop. I loved her so much.'

'But you'd never met her,' Peter objects. 'Not in real life.'

'Nope.'

'Then how could you love her?'

Tania tilts her head, one eyebrow raised. 'Have you ever met God, in real life?'

'Fair point. Go on.'

'Gracie saw me differently to everyone else – *Wow, you could be a fashion model, so beautiful and elegant and thin*. She was an art student, and she said I was her favourite model. Her sketches of me made me feel treasured. She made me into a babyish anime with enormous eyes and a button nose and shining hair. Sounds wholesome, doesn't it? Well, anyway ... one time we were talking about tattoos, and she suggested I might get one when I was older. She offered to design some and draw them onto pictures of me, so I could see how they'd look. She suggested I send her some photos of myself without clothes on, so she could do these sketches.'

'Oh,' Peter breathes. 'Oh no.'

'I wasn't at all keen, but she wrote, *Don't worry, I'll do it first* – and sent photos of herself, half-naked. So I copied her. It started with a bared shoulder but she soon had me revealing more. She kept saying we were just two girls, nobody else would ever see the pictures. She reckoned I'd look amazing with a tattoo on my bottom, and told me how to pose.' Tania shudders. 'I said it didn't feel right, pulling down my pants for the camera. She seemed really hurt – *don't you trust me?* I was sobbing my heart out when I took that horrible picture, but I did it for my friend.'

Her voice splinters. Peter hands her a box of tissues.

'You're wondering why I'd go along with it,' she says, dabbing under her eyes. 'But unless you've hated yourself as much as I did, you can't understand. Gracie was the only friend I'd ever had.'

'A very manipulative friend.'

'That's one word for it. After that, her demands escalated pretty fast. Pornographic. The next time I tried to refuse, her reply came back like a slap in the face. *Do it, or I will send everything, all the slutty photos, to your class at school. Your bullies will love them. I will ruin your life.*'

Peter reels at the shock of it, the stomach-knotted horror of a child reading those words, feeling the jaws of a trap snap shut.

'Couldn't you ask someone for help?' he asks.

'Who? I had nobody. No way out. My only 'friend' was a monster. Gracie assured me that with just one click the images would be all over the internet. I didn't realise they were *already* all over the internet, in the dark, evil spaces – I was quite the sensation on certain websites. So I gave her what she wanted, degrading stuff in front of a webcam, and all the time I was dying inside. The snare pulled ever-more tightly, you see, because the worse the material the more power she had over me. One night, she said I had to ... oh, God. I don't even want to say it.'

Peter is holding his breath. Voices filter through the frosted glass of the window, muffled and diffused. Footsteps, laughter, normal life. A child singing.

'She wanted me to abuse my two-year-old brother,' whispers Tania. 'In front of the webcam. I said I'd rather die, and I meant it, but Gracie didn't care. *Fine. That's your choice.*'

He remembers his own daughter at the same age – her vulnerability, her anxieties. He can scarcely bear to think about thirteen-year-old Tania's suffering.

'What happened, Tania?'

'Gracie gave me one week to deliver. I prayed for a miracle – not that I believed, still don't really, but it seemed worth a try. I planned to lie down on the railway tracks if she carried out her threat. For a week I lived with this terror, but the deadline came and went. Nothing.'

'A miracle?'

'Felt like it. I didn't dare to hope at first. Weeks passed. Months. One day my mum had breakfast TV on full blast and there was a story about a guy who'd just been found guilty in a court in London. Blackmail, sharing indecent images. His name was Carl Simpson, and he'd set up fake personas to snare his victims. I recognised the love-bombing and flattery, the anime sketches, sadistic threats, blackmail, grooming. And the date of his arrest? The same week that Gracie disappeared from my life.'

'You think this Simpson was Gracie?'

'No doubt at all, though in the court case he was Pixie and Yvette. He hid his alias accounts, used different servers, ducked and dived. Clever. The police were sure he had other victims but none came forward. I bet they were all like me, ashamed and broken, trying to hide under their rocks. I followed every word of the press reports. He had dual citizenship, British and Kiwi ... and a life-threatening allergy. His lawyer said he was haunted by a screaming terror of anaphylaxis, so prison would be daily torture for him.'

'Life threatening ...' Peter blinks, not wanting to see where this is going. 'A peanut allergy?'

'Of course. He was sentenced to nine years, served about six. In that time I grew up. Changed my hair, my eyes, my body, my name, my city. I learned how to hack into systems: probation, prison, dark web chatrooms. I even befriended Simpson's mum on Facebook, pretending to be an old schoolmate. She really does live in Dunedin – he really did grow up there. That's the only aspect of Gracie that was true. When he finally ran back home to New Zealand, I was waiting for him.'

'Wasn't he on some kind of sex offenders' register?'

'He was, but years had passed since his release. He called himself Colin Smith. New identity, new country. He still runs rings around the authorities, and I run rings around him. We talk in chatrooms, swapping fantasies. I make mine up. His are horrifying. To him, I am 'Magpie' – a middle-aged bloke as sick as he is. A friend. It took me years to get his trust. When the time was right I baited my trap, just as he once did: I promised him some very, very special material, far too special to be risked online. I arranged to meet him here, among a crowd of churchgoers. Hiding in plain sight. He liked that idea.'

'Sorry,' Peter's holding up his hands. 'Whoa, back up. You arranged to meet a convicted sex offender, here in the cathedral?'

'Well, no. Not me. It wasn't *me* he came here to meet, Peter.' She points with a forefinger, aiming it at his chest. 'It was you.'

He's staring in mute dismay, an awful suspicion beginning to form as she talks.

'Did you spot the blue handkerchief in his pocket? That was the pre-arranged sign. *You* didn't need one of course, because he knew you'd be the guy up the front. Magpie the priest, wearing black and white robes.'

'He thought I ...' Cold sweat gathers on Peter's forehead at the memory of the intense stare, the wink. 'He thought I was like him, had the same obsessions, the same ... how *could* you, Tania?'

Figures kneeling at the rail. Tania holding his gaze as she sipped, embarrassing him. Millie spilling wine. *Distraction, misdirection, sleight of hand.*

'How did you get Millie to make a grab for the chalice?' he asks.

'I told her it was Ribena. She was seriously pissed off when you didn't deliver.'

'You stole his EpiPen from his satchel, didn't you? Swapped it for the *Z-Boost* wrapper. I saw something ... just a flick of your hand, and the satchel wasn't quite closed.'

'Very observant.'

She's watching Peter, the green cat's eyes unblinking. Suddenly, he's afraid. He resists a powerful urge to run screaming out into the sunshine.

'I bet you're wondering about the allergen,' she says.

'No! I don't want to hear any –'

'Powdered peanuts. Simple. I took a mouthful before heading up to the altar, and then –' she pouts, miming herself spitting – 'just like that.'

'You *spat* in the chalice!'

'Really?' She looks genuinely bemused. '*That's* the most shocking aspect of my confession?'

Peter pours water into a glass. His hands are shaking. He's in the presence of a cold-blooded murderer, or at least an attempted one. There's no reason to ask why Tania's here today: he's bound by the seal of the confessional. He must treat what she has told him as absolutely confidential, can never disclose it without her permission. She isn't seeking absolution or redemption; she's here to silence the one witness to her crime. She's done so as effectively as if she'd slit his throat, though a great deal less messily. He can't even tell the Dean, or Susie.

'I was kneeling next to the devil himself,' she says. 'A devil who would certainly prey on other children, destroy other lives. Children like my Millie. I lured him to the altar rail in order to kill him. That's my confession.'

Peter is on his feet, making circuits of the room, dredging up everything he knows about the ethics of confessions. They did a module on it during his training. Seemed simple enough at the time. Not so bloody simple now.

'Look ... you're not telling me about a crime you're planning to commit, are you?' He asks, stopping beside her chair. 'You won't try to attack this man again? Because that wouldn't be a confession, Tania. You can't repent and ask forgiveness for a future sin, no matter how unspeakably wicked your victim. Will you promise me, right now?'

Her mouth twitches. No remorse. She uses her forefinger to sketch the shape of a cross over her chest.

'Cross my heart, hope to die. I've done enough. I will do absolutely nothing else, I promise.'

He wants this woman out of his office, out of the church, out of his life. He mutters a prayer of absolution – though it feels absurd – and walks her to the side door. A group of children and adults are picnicking by the tiered fountains outside. Millie's among them. The toddler comes pelting across to her mum, laughing and holding up her arms.

'Don't look so worried, Peter,' says Tania as she swings her daughter onto her hip, kissing the little girl's cheek. 'There's no evidence. You drank the leftover wine, the chalice was washed. There's nothing to link Colin Smith to me. He'd never in a million years clock me as the skinny kid with brown eyes, mousy hair, a different name.'

'But there's plenty to link him to *me*, isn't there? If they do any digging they'll soon find Magpie. They'll be knocking on my door.'

Tania smiles kindly, as though he's finally guessed the answer to a simple puzzle.

'Well,' she says. 'Let's hope they never have a reason to do any digging.'

Later that week, Susie is scrolling on her phone when she lets out a whistle.

'I don't believe this! Our cruise ship guy – did you say his name was Colin Smith?'

Peter nods silently, dreading what he's about to learn.

'He drowned on Monday night,' says Susie. 'The day after we saved his life. Hopelessly drunk, they assume. He was seen lurching about before toppling over the rail – seems he wasn't popular, nobody was near him. There were big swells and it was pitch black. They've given up the search.' She reads on, shaking her head in disbelief. 'Apparently he had a drink problem, always nipping out on deck to take swigs from his hip flask. He was on his final warning about it. We saw that flask, remember? It fell out when he shook the bag.'

'I do remember.'

She reads out the rest of the article: desperate attempts to find the man overboard, scrambling of the Air Force to comb a vast expanse of open water. Peter's barely listening. Something cold is clutching at his stomach.

I've done enough. I will do absolutely nothing else, I promise.

'How odd,' says Susie. 'Seems his cards were marked. You all right, Peter? You look a bit pale.'

The choir are singing Rutter as the congregation gather at the rail. Zimmer frames, grey heads, plum-coloured nails.

'The blood of Christ,' he whispers.

Tania Turtle smiles as she takes the chalice from his hands. 'Amen.'

SOMETHING TO DO IN THE DARK

ANNA DOWNES

Dear Doctor,

I'm sure that when you suggested I write down my thoughts you didn't intend for me to write you a letter, but I've attempted this exercise a few times now and writing just for me feels too much like talking to myself (and we all know what that means), so, if you don't mind, I think I'll address you directly. However, 'Doctor Snooze' seems silly and Doctor Crispin feels too intimate given that we have not actually met, so I think for now I'll just use Doctor. Dear Doctor. Like Dear Diary. That seems appropriate.

Anyway, many thanks for the program pack which came in the mail today. I have the notebook – that much is obvious because here I am writing in it. I also have the herbs, tea, affirmations, and treatment plan. I'll admit I'm somewhat sceptical; I've never done any online therapy before, and I've certainly never heard of writing as treatment for insomnia. I've always preferred a good strong prescription to anything even remotely woo-woo, and the cost – well, I will confess to balking at that, it's rather steep. But unusual times call for unusual measures, I suppose.

The notebook at least is of fine quality. The paper is pleasant to write on, and the leather binding is very pleasing to the touch. Very soft. It reminds me of something but I can't think what. The inscription strikes a chord, too. *When you put your fears down on paper, you'll see them for what they really are.* Such a simple but revolutionary notion. Catch your worries like fireflies, trap them in a jar and have a good look when the light comes back. Very appealing to my left brain. And of course, it gives me something to do in the dark – something constructive, anyhow. All of which is to say that despite my misgivings I'm prepared to give it a go.

So then. I look forward to pouring out my innermost thoughts and feelings the next time I wake in the night. (Well, no, that's not true. But I do look forward to it helping me sleep!)

Warm Regards,
Mrs Thea Walton.

Dear Doctor,

Last night, I did as you suggested: I ran a bath and added the herbs, made myself a tea, and went to bed early. I read my book as normal (I'm a true crime nut, always have been), but then like clockwork I woke before midnight and just cannot get back off to sleep again. Two hours of wakefulness and counting. My head feels like a badly tuned radio and my limbs are doing that thing I mentioned in my client history form where they fizz and twitch of their own accord. I'm feeling deeply frustrated and angry with myself because sleep is a basic human function, isn't it? Like eating and breathing. Only the critically ill cannot do those things on their own. Am I critically ill? Usually I'd assume not, but the truth is I don't know anymore. I feel defective, like a clock that can't tick, a pen with no ink, ~~a mother who can't~~

Oh dear, I'm spiralling. I can see that. Right, what does your treatment plan say? I'll fetch the notes...

Write it all down, one worry at a time. Lay out your fears like a deck of cards.

Alright, let's see. As I explained in my original email I've been having a rather hard time lately. My husband's death, as you might expect after almost thirty years of marriage, has knocked me sideways, and moving from the family home to a whole new neighbourhood has been quite the culture shock. Initially I was quite excited by the prospect of living alone, which I've never done in my life, if you can believe that. Caring for Brian was very challenging in the end; I was exhausted, and in my quietest moments I dared to believe that life after he passed might not be so bad after all. A blank slate, a fresh start, a taste of true independence – but I was kidding myself. Even without this virus that seems to have the whole world in its grip, even without the bizarre new reality of restrictions and stay-at-home-orders, it was always going to be difficult. I mean, you can never completely start afresh can you? So much of yourself comes along for the ride.

Anyway, I've been putting on a brave face for the sake of Elise and Edward. I don't want them to worry about me, especially not while we're all in lockdown. They need to look after themselves. But I do worry that, now I'm responsible for no one but myself, my body has taken the opportunity to fall apart. Ever since I moved into this apartment, sleep has eluded me. I feel anxious almost constantly and every night when I go to bed my heart beats so fast it feels like a small, frightened animal has taken up residence in my chest. It's all very disconcerting – and entirely new. Besides the odd wakeful night, I've never had a problem with sleeping before, not even when the children were little. I know I should've expected it; insomnia is a common side-effect of grief, isn't it? But I wasn't prepared for how the exhaustion would feel in my body. Achy, like the flu.

Sorry, you already know all of this, but as per your instructions I'm going to write everything down, right from the start, even the small things – because I think you're right, journalling will help me organise my thoughts. Bring them into the light, so to speak. Especially when I wake up in the pitch black with a hammering heart and a monkey brain and I end up pacing around like a lunatic, checking all the locks and listening out for strange noises. Like I have been doing for the past half an hour. As I will probably continue to do for the rest of the night.

But then I suppose that's what happens when your husband dies, you move house, and your life changes beyond recognition. Either that or it's time to cut back on the true crime, ha ha. Ah well. Here's to your program, doctor. I suppose I'd better try that tea.

Best,

Thea Walton.

Dear Doctor,

Well, here I am again, awake in the dark, anxious and writing.

Just moments ago I realised that last night I didn't commit to the exercise properly; I didn't so much write down my fears as explain the situation. And as your website so beautifully explains, it's the fear that keeps us up. So here I go:

Surprisingly enough, I'm *not* afraid of the virus. I'm not at all frightened of being ill. What I am afraid of is sleeplessness. The black stretch of hours ahead, a million minutes until morning, and then the hollow churn of the day. I worry about how I'll function without rest, how fast my brain will deteriorate – which, actually, as fears go, is not unfounded. The cumulative effects of sleep deprivation are myriad. Hypertension, diabetes, obesity, depression, heart attack, the list goes on. You can even give yourself a stroke, did you know that? But of course you did, you're a sleep specialist.

Well, how about this: sea otters hold hands when they sleep so they don't drift away from each other. Found that little pearl on Google. But I digress.

I'm worried about Brian – or rather, the lack of him. We were together so long that his absence is of course emotionally devastating, but it's also unsettling on a more mundane, logistical level. I keep looking around for him, wondering where he's got to. Like that horrible feeling when you think you've lost your passport. And then I remember actually *seeing* him die, watching as his breath left his body – which in turn makes me irrationally afraid that my children will die too, and my grandchildren.

I have to stop myself from texting them all more than once a day just to check that they still exist. Which of course they do, they're always 'fine'. But it doesn't stop me from wondering. I mean, Elise and Edward are grown adults and very capable, but they're both so busy all the time. Even in lockdown it's all go, go, go. And *their* children have just left home for the first time, so that's two more to worry about.

I can't help obsessing over whether Corey is looking after himself properly. Is *he* getting enough sleep? Is he eating right, exercising? Does he have anyone to remind him to take his medication now that he can no longer depend on Elise? What if he has a seizure, will there be anyone there to take care of him? Who knows! At least lockdown means he's confined to the house, but still – sometimes when I close my eyes I see him on the floor of some stranger's room, on the street, in a nightclub, stiff and shaking and alone, biting through his tongue, ~~choking to death on his own blood~~ ...

And Bailey. She's so young and attractive, what if someone takes advantage of her? Again, lockdown is something of a comfort because she's less likely to be dragged into an alleyway on her way back from the pub. But what if someone breaks in? Her flatmates are both doctors, they're still going to work every day so she's often home alone. What if a predator crawls in through a window? You can't tell me that fear is unfounded. Just think of those attacks a few years ago, the Sydney rapist. He cased women's houses, learned their routines, waited for the perfect opportunity, then assaulted them in their own beds. And they never caught him, he's still out there, probably walking around amongst us, pretending to be normal. What an awful thought.

What else? I suppose I'm a little afraid of my new building. All the strangers living above and below. The gadgets in my apartment – the keypad locks, the stove that talks to you, the shower that somehow knows how hot you want the water… how do they even work? All the gleaming white rooms that looked so low maintenance when I first viewed the place now seem cold and clinical. Such a contrast with the comfortable chaos of our old family home. And you should see the windows! Great sheets of glass from floor to ceiling. Impossible to keep clean. And so exposing. Thank goodness I'm all the way up here on the ninth floor.

Fortunately, I don't think anyone can see me from this height. I can see them though. All the apartments in the block opposite, seven floors of little light boxes stacked on top of one another so the whole building looks like the cross section of a beehive. The rows of terraces down on the ground: brick oblongs leading to patchwork squares of decking, a crush of rooves stretching back through Leichhardt towards Lilyfield, Parramatta River and the Iron Cove Bridge. If I step out onto the balcony and look east, I can just about see the long line of red tails lights snaking through Camperdown to Broadway towards the city skyline. From up here, I can look down on it all like an eagle in the sky.

Doctor, you won't believe it but I just paused to read all of that back and the oddest thing happened. I calmed right down. Immediately. It was like all the stress just poured out of my body like dirty water. I felt peaceful for the first time in ages. I suppose you must be right: when the fireflies are trapped, they lose some of their power. I can see my worries for what they are: just words. Black lines against a white background. Harmless, just like you said.

Well, how about that. Who'd have thought it would be so easy? Maybe this online therapy thing is worth the money after all.

Best,
Thea W.

Dear Doctor,

It's 2.37am and I just woke from a nightmare. Someone was in my room, a tall shape, a shadow in the corner, a man, just standing there looking at me. I was so scared I couldn't breathe – and then he started to move. He came towards me, and my heart just about stopped. I sat up and switched on the light, expecting to see... well, I don't know really, but there was nothing there, just the curtain and the window and the mirror. I'd left the sliding door open by accident and the breeze had got caught in the drapes. And now I'm sitting here in the dark with my pulse going berserk, just like a child. Must've been all that fretting about the Sydney rapist.

I feel very alone, Doctor. I feel old. I never used to worry about ageing, but I do now. What will happen when my body packs up, when I can't get out of a chair or get dressed without help? Brian had me, but who will I have? Who? What will become of me?

Thea.

Dear Doctor,

Another terrible dream. Another phantom man standing in the corner of my bedroom – and the door was definitely closed this time, the drapes perfectly still. My mind is playing tricks.

It's probably all the true crime (I'm reading the one about the Golden State Killer at the moment. Do you know it? It's very good) but I can't stop thinking about the rapist. My granddaughter Bailey called earlier and afterwards I couldn't stop imagining a dark figure sliding silently into her room while she sleeps. There's no way that shabby share house of hers is secure; it's very old and the doors look like they're about to fall off their hinges. Not like my building: no one but James Bond could possibly scale the outside, you can't access the front door without a key card or the lifts without a fob, and all the internal doors lock automatically when closed. Well, actually, *my* front door doesn't shut properly unless I shove it. Left to its own devices it gets caught on the frame and I have to lean right against it until the latch clicks. But other than that, I feel safe.

There are some weird noises though. Little thumps and bumps and scratches. Rats, I thought at first. Rodents running around in the walls or the air shafts or whatever other spaces there are. But actually, I think it might be coming from the apartment next door: number 902.

I'm 901. We're the only two on the ninth floor, our front doors stand opposite one another, our balconies are adjoining, but I haven't met the occupant yet so don't want to go over there guns blazing. I don't want a reputation for being a drag. But then again, I might have to pop over at some point. It's very loud. I can hear it right now. A sort of *bumble-tumble*, like when you put shoes in the washing machine. And his front door is always slamming at odd hours of the day and night.

There's a funny smell in the corridor too, did I mention that? Just a faint whiff of something. It could be the bins. There's a small refuse room next to the lifts, which I was told gets emptied daily but perhaps not under current circumstances? I haven't dared go in to check. Or maybe it's the carpets. Either way, it's not pleasant.

Best, Thea.

Dear Doctor,

As per my recent message, I just paid my second installment and am waiting for the next treatment pack. Again, the price does seem to be somewhat steep but I do appreciate the weekly emails and affirmations. And I have to say I'm very much looking forward to more tea. I don't say that sarcastically; I like the taste, very unusual. I enjoy the constant scribbling too, the drag of the pen across the paper, my thoughts and feelings bridled and harnessed... it's rather addictive. Oh, and I realised that the softness of the leather binding reminds me of my babies. I remember their voices calling for me in the night, their velvet little bodies gathered like pillows in my arms... I know that's a strange comparison to make, but it's my notebook and I'll be weird if I want to.

Anyway, Doctor, my point is that I really do think your program is working. The only thing I'd change is maybe an occasional check-in from a real live human being. I get that none of us can go anywhere, I understand that the virtual world is where it's all at these days, and I shouldn't be bothering doctors face-to-face unless I'm at death's door. But, you know, some real company would be nice. Someone to chat to. Just once in a while.

T.

Dear Doctor.

I'm sweltering. The weather is so warm at the moment but I'd rather be out here on the balcony than in the artificial air inside; the apartment is stifling. Seems I'm not the only one who feels that way either: the whole neighbourhood is up and about.

It's interesting, isn't it, how in times of crisis we fall back on routine? Now I'm spending more time outside after dark my sleepless hours feel special, like I'm attending some kind of a concert performed just for me. There's the slide and snap of flyscreens, the odd bark of a dog, the cicadas. The odd flick of a bathroom light, a waft of cigarette smoke. Do you know, one man in the block opposite, fourth floor, regularly gets up at 1am to do push-ups? At 2am, someone on the fifth turns their TV on. Around 3am a baby starts crying. There's a couple in one of the terraces that make toast at 5am and eat it on their roof as the sun comes up. Shortly after that, a middle-aged woman with blonde hair and a high-vis jacket emerges from the house on the corner and heads out for a run. The same sequence, the same dance, these last few nights. Creatures of habit, every one of us.

All except the man in 902. No patterns there, no consistency. In and out of his apartment at all hours. Out at 8pm, back at 2am. Out at 11pm, back at 4am. I know because I can see him coming and going through my peephole. In and out. Back and forth. Morning and night. Now, what do you make of that?

Dear Doctor.

I'm going to have to say something. To the man in 902, I mean. He's so noisy. You should see him: heavy-set with quite womanly hips and long arms like a gorilla. He always wears the same thing: magenta scrubs with training shoes and a baseball cap pulled low over his face. He carries a black duffle bag. I've never seen him without it. And he always lets his front door bang, even in the dead of night, with no thought for anyone else! I've seen him: he just lets it swing closed behind him without even checking that it's closed properly, which it rarely is because it seems he's got the same problem at me, the latch doesn't engage, not even with the force of the slam. Maybe he hasn't noticed. I'd tell him if I wasn't so annoyed.

What's worse is that he does the same thing with his balcony door.

Back and forth, swish and slide. I saw him once but I couldn't tell what he was doing or even see his face. He's white, I know that much. Sandy hair. Anyway, he went straight to the balustrade and looked down at the houses for a few minutes before turning away and heading back inside. I wondered about introducing myself, maybe mentioning the noise, but he went back inside before I got the chance.

Oh, there he goes again! Front door this time. He's going out.

I just checked through the peephole. Definitely leaving, wearing the same magenta scrubs, same baseball cap, same bag. Where on earth could he be going? It's 1.20am!

So, Doctor, this is going to sound rather mad but I was thinking again about that rapist and when I looked up the news reports online here's what I found: 13 women were assaulted in their homes over two years, all break-and-enter attacks, all sexual, all similar in nature. Police think that the same man was responsible, a serial offender with an Australian accent who shines a torch in the faces of his victims so they can't see his face. All the victims lived with partners, but at the time each woman was home alone and asleep. In each instance the rapist appeared to know when the women were alone and gained entry through windows or doors left unlocked due to the warmer weather. Police also believe the women were either stalked or their homes watched before the assaults, suggesting that the rapist is a *shift worker* (the reporter's words, not mine), someone who lives in the area, someone who might be able to see into other people's houses, perhaps a Peeping Tom acting on his fantasies. They also think he's of medium build with a white or European appearance. And guess where all the attacks took place? Summer Hill. Haberfield. Lilyfield. Annandale. Camperdown. Petersham. If you drop a pin right in the middle of those places, where does it fall? Pretty much right on this building.

Now, call me crazy but 902 leaves his apartment at all hours of the night. He wears scrubs; maybe he's a nurse. I haven't seen a torch, but he does go out with a bag. He's definitely of European appearance. He has extensive views out onto the neighbourhood, he can see into people's houses just as well as I can, and he's often out on his balcony. If he spends even half the amount of time I do gazing down at the neighbours, he'd know that the high-vis blonde runner is single, works from home, and always leaves her gate open. Also that the toast-on-the-roof couple eat breakfast at 5am, dinner at 6pm, then go to bed at 9.

And then there are all the noises coming from his apartment and the weird smell in the corridor... I mean, am I losing my mind here or what?

Doctor, I'm logging his movements, tracking his activity. If you read true crime, you'll know that it's important to record *everything*, even things that seem insignificant, because you never know what might make a difference or what the missing puzzle piece might look like. See below: if something happens and the police need assistance with their enquiries, I will have much to produce.

Friday. Out 11.02pm, in 4.12am.

Saturday. Out 1.15pm, in 2.26pm. Out 9.43pm, in 3.19am.

Sunday. Out 6.14pm, in 9.55pm. Out 2.41am, in 5.37am.

Monday. Out 12.52am, in 4.49am.

Tuesday. Noises at 10.13am, 12.24pm, 4.16pm, and 9.11pm.

Wednesday. Bangs and thumps at 6.17pm. Out at 11.56pm. Smell in the corridor worse than usual. Check the refuse room, bins are empty.

Thursday. 9.35pm. 902 is on balcony. Bailey calls but I don't answer, don't want him to hear me; can't call back either, I'm too busy at the peephole. Can't stop or I might miss something.

Friday. 4.22am. Police car in the street below, parked outside the high-vis blonde's house. I can't see what's happening inside but I feel it in my bones. 902. He's done something, I know it. He's been watching from his balcony. He watches everyone. He waits until he thinks no one else is watching, then he goes downstairs, slips in through open windows, drops onto soft carpet and strikes like a viper. ~~I know who he is, what he's doing, I can tell that he~~

Doctor, I'm standing right by my front door, by the peephole, writing up against the wall. I just heard something. In 902. A weird sound like a yawn, a long gaping vowel. You know the kind of noise you make when you're trying to make a point in the presence of others? *Look how tired I am.* Now

I can hear those muffled thumps and crashes again, but coupled with the yawn they seem familiar somehow. It's like déjà vu...

His door is ajar. The latch hasn't engaged. I can still hear the noises. Thumps, moans. I'm going over there, I have to see...

Oh god oh god oh god, Doctor, I don't know what to do, I'm in my bathroom, I've locked myself in, I don't even know if I saw what I saw just now, but I had to get out, I had to hide somewhere, ~~I don't know what to do~~, I can't breathe, ~~I can't~~

~~I don't~~

~~I need~~

Okay. Okay. I'm breathing. I'm breathing. I'm breathing.

Here's what just happened.

After I heard the yawn sound and the thuds, I went out into the corridor. 902's front door was standing slightly ajar. I pushed it open... and I saw blood. It was everywhere, sprays of it on the carpet, up the walls. And he's there, magenta scrubs man, lying on the hallway floor with his head up near the console table, his feet near the welcome mat, convulsing. Oh, it was awful! His limbs were stiff and twitching, his fingers straight, just like Corey does. For a horrible moment I thought it *was* my grandson: I saw his wiry frame and bony shoulders, his baby blue eyes rolling back in his head – and I froze, not because I didn't know what to do, of course I did, I'm no stranger to seizures, I've heard those yawning sounds before, but because there was so much blood. Magenta Man's mouth was slick with it. I thought of vampires, cannibals... but then I understood he'd just bitten through his tongue and the force of his breath had carried it across the hallway in spatters. So then I just stood there, because I knew that touching him wouldn't help, there's no stopping a seizure once it's started and as long as the epileptic is in a safe place there's no need to move them... and that's when I saw it. A high-vis jacket. And several long blonde hairs caught in the zip.

It was on the floor, laying half-in and half-out of a doorway to my right. A sparsely furnished bedroom. I peeked inside and saw Magenta Man's black holdall, sitting on a plain wooden chair pushed up against the wall. Beside it, a torch. A pair of binoculars.

I went further into the room...

And I saw.

I saw.

A grey lump. Waxy skin. A thing that should've been moving but wasn't.

Teeth. Hair. Stone-still eyes. Abstract sculpture. Empty shell. And the smell, the smell…

I stepped back. My foot hit something, my back brushed up against the wall. Not the wall. No. A person.

Magenta Man was no longer on the floor.

He was on his feet.

Standing behind me.

I turned around. He was swaying a little, looking at me through sleepy eyes. *He's tired,* I thought. They do that, seizures. They make people weak. It can take days to recover. I know that. So I shoved him. Right in the chest.

He toppled.

I ran.

I somehow managed to open the door and run into the corridor. At my own door I turned back. 902's door was swinging slowly shut. Through the narrowing gap, I saw Magenta Man go down like a tree, hit his head on the corner of the console table and crash to the floor. I saw the spray of blood. I heard the silence…

Oh god.

Doctor.

I think I just killed my neighbour.

Dear Doctor.

I'm sorry to say that this will be my last letter to you.

I haven't written for two days.

~~I have to tell you~~

~~I need you to know~~

Let me explain. The morning after *the incident,* my daughter Elise knocked on my door. I could hear her calling. *Mum? Mum? Are you alright?* I edged to the door, let her in. I told her what had happened. She was suitably shocked. *He's dead? Are you sure?* She called the police. But when they arrived, they told me that the man next door was fine.

Fine.

Magenta Man was – is – alive and perfectly well.

His name is Pete, they said. Pete Moore. He's a nurse at RPA, lives alone, works nights. *He'd been pushing himself too hard,* they said. *Front line workers are under the pump. He fainted, took a tumble, knocked his head. Lucky he's got a neighbour like you to look out for him.* I asked again and again: could it have been a seizure? Is he epileptic? But they said no. Pete Moore is not epileptic. He's fine. Just exhausted. Just a bump on the head. What's more, they didn't find anything in his apartment. No high-vis jacket, no torch, no binoculars. No blood. No body.

I asked them to check again. I couldn't help it. I told them everything. Elise was appalled. She looked at me like she didn't know who I was.

Everything is normal, love, said the police. *Everything is fine.*

Everything except me.

Elise stayed the weekend. After what happened, she's taking me to the surgery tomorrow morning as a matter of urgency. She says I'm having a nervous breakdown, perhaps even a psychotic break. She says that the grief, nervous exhaustion, the move, the new apartment and sleep deprivation, combined with the isolation of lockdown and the fact that I'm living alone for the first time in years – because of all that, she says, my mind has taken a 'turn'. I have ceased to function. Just like I feared I might.

You know what else, Doctor? She says that you're a crook. A con artist. Not even licensed to practice medicine. She says the 'Doctor Snooze' program is a hoax, that the emails and treatment plan and tea all mean nothing.

It's a thing, Mum, she said. *Scammers are capitalising on the ongoing lockdown, tapping into feelings of anxiety and loneliness, deliberately taking advantage of the vulnerable. It's happening everywhere.* She said that's the *real* crime here: no rapist or dead body or blood on the walls, just a bunch of criminals trying to sell useless 'shit' to people in need. People like me.

I told her she's wrong, you *are* a doctor and the program was – *is* – helping me.

Elise reeled off a list of popular schemes: dating and romance, false billing, fake investments, threats and ransoms, almost anything you can think of. All tricks. I kept telling her she was wrong. But when Elise asked me how much I had money I'd paid, how much time I'd spent online, I didn't know what to say. She told me I can't look after myself, that I shouldn't be living alone after all. And maybe she's right.

Or maybe not. Maybe *I'm* right. Maybe I figured something out, something important. Maybe because I read true crime, because I watch and listen, because I pay attention, I saw the truth in apartment 902. Maybe Magenta Man is actually the Sydney rapist, the one who crawled in through those windows and hurt those women all those years ago. Maybe it's the same man striking again. But no one believes me because I'm a mad old lady, the crazy woman in the attic.

What if 902 *did* have some kind of seizure? What if everything I saw in there was real? What if he covered his tracks after I fled, got rid of the evidence while I was hiding behind my own locked door? I just don't know.

One thing's for certain, though. The journalling isn't helping anymore. It worked at first, and having something to do and someone to talk to has been a lifesaver in many ways – but I think it's safe to say that lately things have got a whole lot worse. Rather than feel more contained, more manageable, my anxiety seems to have metastasized. When I read back through this notebook, all I see is *seizure, blood, rapist, break-in, neighbours, ageing, death...* all my fears, writ larger than life and growing bigger by the day.

And in light of that, and of all that has happened this past month, I can't help but think of what you said. Those words on the website, the weekly emails, the affirmations. *When you put your fears down on paper, you'll see them for what they really are.* Well, I did see them, didn't I, Doctor? And that makes me wonder. Because for all they do to reduce fear, the thing about words is that they are tangible. They give as much power as they take away. They might seem plain and harmless once on the page, but when your innermost thoughts become letters, sentences and paragraphs, they gain shape and form. You can touch them. They become real.

So, as I write what I suspect will be my last lines in this beautiful book, as I stroke its strangely soft baby-skin cover, I can't help but wonder if 'Doctor Snooze' was never about the money. What if this chaos, this very real swarm of uncontained fireflies, was the point all along?

I don't know. I suppose none of that makes any real sense. The only thing I can be sure of now is that this has to stop. I see that now. All of this madness... somehow, it has to end.

So goodbye, Doctor. And for what it's worth – thank you.

Regards,

Mrs Thea Walton.

BAD LISTENER

JACK HEATH

THERE WERE THREE HOLES, EACH THE SIZE OF A DOLLAR COIN. IT looked like someone had wanted to install a floating shelf, but hadn't owned a stud-finder. The neighbour had told the dispatcher she'd heard a hammer, not a drill. 'Mate, it was like three big bangs,' she'd said. 'And someone was screaming bloody murder.'

I'll bet, thought Detective Carol Roper. On closer inspection, these seemed to be bullet holes.

Her phone buzzed in her pocket. She checked the screen. Her sergeant was calling. He should know better. Carol rejected the call and tapped out a message – *Text me, dickhead.*

The plaster had caved in around the edges, and there wasn't much dust on the floor. Carol touched the edge of one of the holes, then wiped her fingertip on her armoured vest. The shooter must have been on this side of the wall. The size of the holes suggested a large calibre, possibly rifle rounds. Forensics would confirm when they cut the plasterboard open to get to the bullets.

It had been two years since Carol last heard the crack of a gun. But she didn't think it would sound like a hammer, even muffled by the wall. Once Carol was done here, she wanted to talk to that neighbour. The speech-to-text app on Carol's phone was useful in more ways than one. Not only would she be able to understand what the neighbour said, but she could compare that to the transcript of the Triple Zero call, after.

All this was assuming Avi didn't take the case off her when he realised how serious it was. Two years ago, he'd wanted her to retire as medically unfit. He never used the D-word –he said she was 'a bad listener'. Carol had convinced him to put her on light duties instead. She'd already given up so much for the Job. In her first year as a cop, her friends had started speaking to her guardedly, then not at all. Some of her dark, curly hair had been ripped out by a tweaker, forcing her to cut the rest short. She'd missed countless dinners with her husband while she was working the two-to-ten shift.

She missed her daughter's singing voice most of all.

Carol turned to face the living room. Who had been shooting at whom? No blood anywhere, and there hadn't been time to clean the scene – she'd arrived less than three minutes after the 000 call, since she'd been at the bottle shop downstairs when it came in. As usual, Avi had sent other officers and told her to stay put. Carol had ignored him and gone upstairs, finding the front door wide open.

A quick search of the apartment had turned up nothing. Three bedrooms, two bathrooms. Carol knew the floor plan because she'd attended several raids on other floors of this building. Over the last year Canberra had been flooded with methamphetamine, and this building was choc-full of tweakers, none of whom seemed inclined to give up their mysterious supplier. Aussie meth-heads weren't smart, but they were loyal.

This didn't strike Carol as a druggie flat, though. Crystal was often mixed with food-dye, and smoking it left stains that were hard to remove. Consequently, users preferred dark furniture. But this apartment had a white leather couch, a soft eggshell-coloured rug, and thick cream curtains framing the open windows, which looked out on another apartment building. Behind that, the Canberra skyline sparkled, and a shimmering half-moon was reflected in Lake Ginninderra. Everything was immaculate, lit by an antique brass lamp. There was even a gas cooktop, which seemed classy to Carol, though it probably just meant the building was old. There was a bottle of olive oil on the island bench, a bowl dripping on the drying rack by the sink and a half-empty bottle of Hahn Light in a stubby holder next to a touristy ceramic ornament. Carol recognised it as a miniature replica of the Shwedagon Pagoda, from Myanmar.

Despite the pleasant decor, something about this place made Carol uneasy. *Something's wrong. Time to leave.* Her guts swam, and her skin prickled, like the air was radioactive.

The explosion that destroyed her eardrums had happened in a warehouse on the outskirts of Fyshwick. The methane leak had been invisible. So was the heat from the faulty charger that ignited it. The warehouse had *looked* unremarkable, but *felt* wrong. Her inner voice had told her to steer clear. Carol had been good at ignoring the voice, back then. These days, it was all she could hear.

As she turned to leave, Carol took a final glance at the damaged wall—and paused. There were four holes, not three. *How did I miss that?* She stooped to peer into the one she'd ignored earlier. Fine dust swirled in the air.

Her phone buzzed again. A text, this time. She checked the screen. The message was from Avi: GET OUT.

Carol dropped to the floor just as the fifth shot came in through the open window. She didn't hear it, but felt the streak of vacuum it left behind, like a tear in the fabric of reality. The bullet struck the wall where her head had been.

Carol lay facedown, heart pounding. Plaster dust stung her nostrils. She couldn't get to the door. Nor could she cross the room to switch off the lamp, which might have helped her hide from the sniper. Instead, she commando-crawled towards the master bedroom, out of the line of fire.

Now she knew why the gun had sounded like a hammer. The neighbour would have heard the bullets hitting the wall, but not the shot itself, which had happened in a different building. The scream would have been the owner of the apartment, realising they were being fired upon, and fleeing in terror.

But why had the sniper taken aim at Carol? Couldn't they tell her apart from whoever lived here?

Her phone buzzed again. Avi, telling her what she already knew in a series of frantic texts:

> *Shots fired bldng opposite.*
>
> *Occupant of apt 515 likely target.*
>
> *Get out and wait for bkup.*

Sound advice, except the sniper was covering the front door. Carol's only option was to wait here, in the bedroom. She reached up, found the cord for the curtains, and drew them so the sniper wouldn't see her. Then she crawled around behind the bed. If the sniper fired through the window, the mattress might slow the bullet down enough to save her.

She texted Avi: *Can't leave shooter has me pinned down hurry*

She wondered if sirens were audible, or if her backup was still on the other side of the lake. When they arrived, they would seal off the area before they entered either of the two buildings, and they'd focus on the one with the shooter. Carol might be stuck here for hours.

She turned off the panicked part of her brain by switching on the calculating part. She thought about the timeline: the sniper had shot at the occupant of the apartment, missed, and presumably seen them escape. So why hadn't the sniper left, too? Why had they stuck around long enough to shoot at Carol?

A terrorist, or any other kind of wacko, would be shooting at cars or pedestrians down on the street. Easier targets. This was something else. Something planned.

A theory started to take shape. There were plenty of valuables in this apartment worth stealing. The motive might be a robbery rather than assassination. In that case, there would be two offenders. A sniper to clear the apartment, and someone else to search it.

If Carol was right, the second offender would be on their way to the apartment right now. They would arrive long before her backup arrived.

She couldn't escape, not with the sniper covering the only exit. Nor could she fight, since she didn't have her service weapon. She looked around frantically for somewhere to hide, but there was nothing. The bed was too low to the floor, and the wardrobe was full of drawers.

A framed photo of a long-haired man hugging a short-haired dog fell off the wall. It thudded on the carpet behind her, the glass cracked.

Most likely, the picture had fallen because someone had slammed the front door of the apartment.

The intruder was already here.

Carol retreated to the ensuite, feeling more and more trapped. She closed the door and braced it with her foot, looking around for something sturdier. There was an electric razor on the vanity, along with a bottle of aftershave and lone bamboo toothbrush in a glass. On a floating shelf—properly mounted—there was a brush, and a hairdryer. Carol guessed the long-haired man lived here, alone. The bathtub was full. Maybe the occupant was saving the water for the hanging fern beside the mirror.

None of these clues seemed useful. Carol could only hope the intruder found whatever they were looking for and left before they reached the bathroom.

She texted Avi again: *2nd offender may be searching apartment. Trapped in bathroom. Need backup!*

For a second, fury washed the fear away. How had she been reduced to this? Letting a burglar search the premises while she cowered in the bathroom? But she didn't seem to have any choice, not unless she wanted to get shot by a sniper and leave her daughter without a mother.

Avi texted her: *Backup coming. 15 mins. Stay put.*

Stay put. Like she wasn't a cop at all – just one more civilian to rescue from the bad guys. That was how they all saw her. Useful only for photoshoots about inclusivity, her head turned slightly to show her cochlear implant. The worst thing was, they were right. She *was* a burden. Helpless.

Or was she? The hairdryer caught her eye.

Thinking quickly, Carol plugged it in and switched it on. Felt the warm air on her palm. Then she threw the hairdryer into the bathtub.

A split-second flash from the power point scarred her retina before the bathroom went dark, along with probably the rest of the apartment, and possibly the rest of the building. Carol didn't know how many floors were controlled by the same circuit breaker.

There were no windows in the bathroom. No light of any kind. Now blind and deaf, Carol might as well have been in a coffin. There was no sensory stimulation at all other than the smell of scorched ozone. Claustrophobia threatened to overwhelm her.

But she'd made progress. The intruder would be confused. It would be hard to search the apartment in the dark. And with no lights on, the sniper couldn't target her.

Arms outstretched, Carol felt her way across the wall until she was back at the ensuite door. She opened it carefully. Quietly too, or so she hoped.

With the curtains closed, the bedroom was pitch black. If the second offender was in this room, Carol wouldn't know it until she bumped into them. She tiptoed across the carpet, holding her breath, her heart thumping. If the floor squeaked, she wouldn't know about it.

She reached the bedroom door and peered out into the combined kitchen and living area. Moonlight streamed through the open curtains, but only seemed to deepen the shadows. Carol could make out the rug, the couch, the winking battery light on the smoke alarm, and not much else.

She squinted towards the front door, which appeared to be closed. She was sure she'd left it open. This confirmed her suspicion about what had caused the picture to fall.

Carol edged sideways out of the doorway, considering her next move. Her backup was still ten minutes away. She could try to get to the door, but the intruder would hear her open it. She was at a huge disadvantage in general. The intruder could hear her, but she couldn't hear them.

It was time to level the playing field. But to do it, she'd have to get to the kitchen – which meant passing the open window.

She told herself the sniper couldn't see her. The moonlight was too faint.

And what if it isn't? Or the shooter has a night vision scope on their rifle?

Ordering herself not to listen to the inner voice, she took a deep breath, and walked into the line of fire.

When she'd first lost her hearing, she'd been tormented by the constant sense that someone was looming behind her. She'd spent weeks looking over her shoulder. Right now, that feeling was magnified by a thousand percent. She took one step. Two steps. The sniper didn't shoot. Three. Still nothing. Four. The fifth step took her into the kitchen area, out of sight of the window.

Rummaging through cupboards would be too noisy, revealing her location to the intruder. Luckily, the olive oil was already on the bench.

At the academy she'd been taught to de-escalate situations, to follow orders, and above all, to obey the law. Her plan probably fell into none of those categories. She did it anyway, uncapping the olive oil and drizzling the fluid all over the stovetop. Then she prodded the ignition button.

For a second, nothing happened—or nothing she could hear. Then there was a rush of heat and a blast of smoke that left her staggering. She dropped to the kitchen floor and crawled away from the burning stovetop, eyes stinging, holding in a cough.

Once she was clear of the smoke, she peeped over the island bench. She was looking for movement, but the flickering glow of the flames made every surface appear to be moving, all shimmers and ripples, like the light in an aquarium. Carol held still, hoping she hadn't miscalculated.

Someone stumbled out of the second bedroom. A big man wearing a hoodie and a COVID-style mask. Too bulky to be the occupant of the apartment. His eyes were wild under bushy brows. He had a finger in one ear, and his opposite ear pressed to his shoulder. The smoke alarm must be screaming. It looked like he was trying to block out the sound, but wasn't willing to let go of the cricket bat in his right hand.

He hadn't seen Carol yet. He was looking at the flames, panicked, not sure what to do. Then he seemed to realise that someone had done this on purpose, and he turned to scan the room. But anything could have been hidden in the flickering shadows, and unlike Carol, he wasn't used to operating without his ears. He didn't sense her creeping up behind him.

'Police!' she yelled, as she grabbed his right wrist.

He reacted immediately, trying to squirm out of her grip, his jaw wide in a scream she couldn't hear. But she had done this a thousand times before. She twisted his arm into a compliance hold behind his spine, forcing him up onto his toes. His hood fell off, revealing a shaved skull with a Southern Cross tattoo on the back.

'Drop the bat!' she roared, but he showed no sign that he understood. The smoke alarm was probably too loud. He kept his right hand clenched around the bat, not that he could swing it while he was bent over backwards like this. He spun, trying to grab her with his left hand. She side-stepped to stay behind him, yelling 'Drop the bat!' over and over. They rotated across the room like ballroom dancers. Too late, Carol realised what the man was doing. Deliberately or not, he was leading her closer to the window. With the flames illuminating the room, the sniper would be able to see her.

The sniper was a lousy shot, and was more likely to hit him than her. Just the same, Carol wasn't willing to risk it. She let the man go, and he spun into the firing line alone.

He whirled to face her and raised the bat, teeth bared, his eyes dark pits. Underlit by flames, he looked like a demon. Carol reached sideways for a weapon. A knife, a bottle—she'd take anything. What she found was the ceramic statue of the Shwedagon Pagoda. Dizzy from the smoke, she hefted it by the spire.

'Back off,' she screamed.

The man swung the bat. Carol swung the statue to block him.

Just as the two weapons were about to connect, the man's bat exploded into splinters. His mate had accidentally shot it out of his hands. The man stared stupidly down at the jagged stump in his grip. Carol seized the opportunity and slammed the statue upwards into his jaw. He was airborne for a second before he thudded to the floor in a halo of broken ceramic and shattered teeth.

Carol grabbed his ankle and dragged him from the line of fire, in case his mate took another shot to shut him up. Now that he wasn't a threat, his safety was her responsibility. She checked his pulse. Strong, but she'd have to get him out of this apartment before the smoke killed them both.

The door burst open and police flooded in, bulked up with armour and waving pistols. *Better late than never*, Carol thought.

'Sniper in the building opposite,' she shouted, waving her arms. 'Get out of the line of fire!'

They ignored this, swarming around her like bees, yelling commands she couldn't hear. Lip-reading was unreliable at the best of times, and impossible in the dark. Carol guessed the sniper had already been arrested, otherwise the cops wouldn't be here.

One officer cuffed the unconscious man while others cleared the bedrooms. Avi appeared, looking aghast – but also a little impressed – at the carnage Carol had wrought. His stubbly jaw hung open, his grey eyes bloodshot. Sweat stained his armpits under the leather jacket he never took off. He asked Carol some kind of question.

'I can't hear you, dickhead,' she said, and then laughed, and then coughed, and then laughed some more.

In slow, clumsily Auslan, he said: *I told you to get out.*

She signed back: *Guess I'm a bad listener.*

Firefighters entered, wielding axes and extinguishers. One squirted foam onto the stove, immediately killing the blaze. He shot Carol an exasperated look, apparently assuming that she lived here, and had started the fire by accident.

Carol shook Avi off as he tried to help her up. 'My legs work just fine, thanks.' As she stood, she looked back at the unconscious man. The whole thing seemed incredible. Using a sniper to scare off the occupant so the apartment could be robbed. What could possibly be worth the risk? The place was more expensively furnished than all the drug flats, but even so –

This last thought snagged in her brain.

Avi was trying to steer her out of the apartment, but she broke free. 'Wait.' She stepped over the unconscious man and crouched over the broken statue. Half of it was still intact, and she peered in.

There they were. Hundreds of Ziploc bags, sticky-taped shut, containing thousands of pills. Pure meth, straight out of the Golden Triangle between Myanmar, Laos, and Thailand.

She turned back to Avi, and held up the remains of the statue. 'That supplier you're looking for?' She couldn't keep the grin off her face. 'He's male, has long hair, and I reckon you'll find him downstairs looking worried.'

THE BARBECUE

JENNIFER LANE

Beatie

'Bet you twenty bucks that shit-heap belongs to Susan.' Jason eased into a parking spot behind an ancient Toyota Corolla. 'She earns around $35k tops. And by the look of her, most of it goes on sausage rolls and make-up.'

Beatie wanted to tell Jason to stop slagging off his workmate in front of the kids, but she lacked the energy. Instead, she gazed across Stanford Park, past a cloud of smoking teenagers and a clump of eucalyptus trees dotted with white cockatoos, to a garishly decorated picnic table and adjacent barbecue. *God help me,* she thought.

'Righto, kids.' Jason turned to their three sleepy-eyed children in the back. 'Ready for the *Stanford Times*' annual Christmas barbecue?'

'Lollies!' Boo's eyes shot open.

'Oh, Boo,' Beatie moaned. 'Remember what happened last time?'

'He'll take it easy today.' Jason opened his car door and climbed out. 'Won't you, Boo?'

Beatie knew Jason was downplaying his excitement. When he reached the footpath he broke into a set of lunges, unaware that she was watching, her face pressed up against the car window. His fitness freak phase was definitely paying off, she thought gloomily. He looked closer to thirty-three than forty-three in his Levis and Country Road t-shirt. The problem was, she wished he didn't. Had he lost his hair and the sight of his toes like most other men his age, she probably wouldn't have lost control of her life.

'I'm starving!' Mitch cried.

Beatie watched as he, Boo and Ally peeled themselves off the sticky vinyl backseat and slid out onto the curb. She then opened her door with a grunt and held onto it while stepping out of the car, steadying her wobbly legs like a newborn foal.

'For you and the kids.' Jason handed Beatie a three-litre bottle of Sprite, and, reaching back into the boot, dug out a six-pack of VB and tucked it under his arm. 'Let's go.'

Beatie lifted the ice-cold bottle, letting the condensation drip down her arm. She pressed it against her forehead, trying to numb her throbbing headache, as she shuffled after Jason in a pair of sandals she only just remembered were too narrow for her wide feet. The kids had already kicked off their Kmart thongs and were running towards the barbecue as if they hadn't eaten in days.

The picnic table shimmered with red, silver, and gold tinsel. Susan must've squeezed every last cent out of the Christmas budget, Beatie figured. The previous year they'd made do with a red and green paper tablecloth which had sailed off the table in a gust of wind, taking the Managing Editor's wife's Christmas cake with it.

Jason forced his beers into a tightly packed esky while the kids circled the table, carefully surveying its contents. Paper plates of cake, Smarties, jellybeans, slices, sausage rolls, fruit pies, crackers and dips lay among the tinsel like offerings to baby Jesus.

'Dead-fly pies,' Boo said. 'Yuck!'

'Shush.' Ally elbowed her younger brother. 'They're sultanas.'

'They're still yuck.'

Next to a tower of Tupperware containers, Susan sat waving a fly away from a bowl of chips and holding a tiny speaker, from which Beatie could hear a muffled *Silent Night*.

'Jason, thank God you're here!' Susan jumped up. 'I came at ten to bags the barbecue. Been busting since quarter past. Will you mind the table?'

Before Jason could answer, Susan handed him the speaker and sprinted towards the toilet block.

The rest of Jason's workmates arrived in a swarm; all sunglasses and hats, bottles clinking and arms straining under the weight of picnic chairs and shopping bags; their whining kids' faces shiny with sunscreen.

'Love the table decorations, Jase.' Brett Stevens cracked open a can of Fosters. 'Who appointed you Santa's little elf?'

Beatie pointed towards the toilet block. 'Actually, it was Su– '

'Thanks, mate.' Jason spoke over Beatie as he hid Susan's speaker between two eskies. 'I knew the role of Santa was already taken. You've obviously been working hard for it all year.'

Brett patted the mound of flab his Ramones t-shirt was struggling to encompass. 'Cheeky bastard.'

'Is Santa coming?' Brett's son asked, wide-eyed.

'No, Sam. This bloke's just having a go at me.'

'Can we go home yet?'

'Come on, mate.' Brett took the boy's hand, opened his tiny fingers to reveal a squashed fruit mince pie, then closed them again. 'Let's go meet some other kids.'

'Smile.' Jason spoke to Beatie out of the corner of his mouth. 'Try to look like you're enjoying yourself.'

'But I'm not. You're ignoring me.'

'It's a *work* Christmas party,' Jason said quietly. 'I've got to talk to *work* people. Just be polite and we'll leave as soon as we can.'

'As soon as we can' was not soon enough for Beatie. She watched the women buzzing around her, their Christmas-themed earrings – candy canes, silver bells and tiny Santa stockings – bobbing about, and tried to imagine ever feeling in the mood for dangling Christmas decorations from her head.

'Oi, Jase!' A woman with a mountain of glossy brown hair waved a pair of tongs at Jason. She wore as much foundation as all the other women at the barbecue put together and a yellowy-red floral maxi dress that made Beatie regret leaving her sunnies in the car. Beatie didn't remember having seen this woman at previous Christmas barbecues.

'Are you man enough to manage the sausages?' the woman asked Jason.

Jason placed his VB on the table and reached for the tongs. 'I think I can rise to the challenge.'

Beatie narrowed her eyes and watched the woman toss Jason a bright green apron, then help him put it on, without any protest from him. As she tied it up at the back, her unnecessarily long red fingernails sparkled in the sun. Beatie glanced at her lemonade wondering whether it was laced with a hallucinogenic. Not only did the apron feature Rudolph the Red Nosed Reindeer, but Rudolph's nose blinked on and off. *Like a lightbulb*. Beatie bet the apron sang the bloody song too. She felt like laughing – Jason in a novelty Christmas apron! – but it actually wasn't funny, and her head still hurt like fuck. She gulped from her plastic cup, felt the bubbles sting her nose. She hated Sprite; it reminded her of the sweet flat lemonade her mum used to give her when she pretended to be too sick to go to school.

She stopped watching Jason make a spectacle of himself and concentrated on maintaining a neutral facial expression – not a smile, that would look weird – to create the impression that she didn't mind standing all alone at her husband's work Christmas barbecue. It's so easy for kids, she thought. Less than five minutes after they'd arrived, a chocolate-faced boy had touched Mitch's arm, and said, 'Tag! You're it', and they'd dispersed into a game of chasings. No alcohol required!

Beatie stole glances at the other women, trying to distinguish the colleagues from the wives to narrow down the suspects. She searched faces as they said, 'What a gorgeous dress!' and 'What are your plans for Christmas?' in between polite sips from plastic wine glasses. She wasn't sure what she was looking for. How do you recognise a woman who's stealing your husband? At least, she presumed it was a woman. She couldn't picture Jason with a man. But then again, standing arm-in-arm on the soft, white sand behind Stanford Surf Club on their wedding day, she never would've imagined him with another woman either.

Which of these women had the power to keep Jason from coming home before seven or eight at night, to compel him to constantly check his phone, even in the middle of the rugby league? The one with the designer glasses and freckly arms? The one who looked like a fat Maggie Thatcher? Surely not the woman who gave him the tongs and helped him into the apron. She was taller than Jason – her hair was only partly responsible – and obviously obsessed with her looks. Jason would think she was shallow and stupid and definitely not his type. But what was his type? Beatie only thought of him as having one type: *Beatie*.

She decided to ignore the hammering inside her head and make an effort to mingle. Talking to the other women could lead Beatie closer to *her* – and finding *her* was the only reason Beatie agreed to come to this tedious barbecue anyway. It'd been six months and five days since she found the note in the pocket of Jason's denim jacket, since she'd read the words: *You set my heart on fire.* It was about time she found out whose heart her husband had enflamed.

While stepping over a tartan picnic rug to approach Susan, Beatie caught a whiff of burning meat and noticed the thick, grey cloud surrounding the barbecue. Jason stood to the left of it, still dressed in that ridiculous apron, its nose flashing like a silent fire alarm. He wasn't 'managing the sausages' at all. All his attention was on *her* – the woman who looked as though she was dressed for a celebrity wedding at the Opera House, rather than the *Stanford Times'* annual Christmas barbecue at Stanford Park. More specifically, his attention seemed to be on her breasts.

She was leaning over the picnic table, baring her enormous pale cleavage to Jason as he passed her a plate of blackened sausages. After selecting a sausage, the woman reached for a slice of white bread, an excuse to expose yet more flesh, wrapped the bread around the sausage and doused it in tomato sauce. She then passed it to a woman in a floppy Rip Curl hat who dropped it onto a paper plate and handed it to the nearest child.

Beatie stood a couple of metres away from the assembly line, not realising her mouth was hanging open until a fly flew inside it, tickled her throat, and made her cough until her eyes watered.

She swallowed two mouthfuls of lemonade before passing the plastic cup down to Boo, who'd just collapsed on the picnic blanket with Mitch and Ally and was panting like a puppy.

'Finish this,' Beatie said, and walked around the table to the line of eskies.

She fished out a cask of Country Dry White Wine and filled a plastic wine glass to the brim. It was icy cold, so much colder than the lemonade Jason had poured for her and far more refreshing. After a few quick gulps, she looked around to check whether anyone was watching before giving herself a top up.

Still holding her glass, she marched over to Jason's boss, a wet leaf of a man called David, who Jason complained about on a nightly basis and who he'd begged her to steer clear of today.

David was standing under a large oak tree, frowning at his watch, and pretending his dog wasn't doing a poo.

'Hi Dave!'

'It's David.' He brushed a few chip crumbs out of his beard. 'You're... Jason's wife?'

'Yes. Beatie.' As Beatie held out her hand, she realised it was sticky with wine but decided she didn't care. Besides, his dog had just done a shit and it stank.

'That's right.' David shook her hand, and then wiped his on his beige trousers.

'Cigarette?' Beatie held out her packet of Benson & Hedges.

David shook his head. 'Gave up years ago.'

'So did I.' Beatie placed a cigarette between her lips and lit it.

Beatie couldn't understand how Jason could be intimidated by this man. Yes, he was the Managing Editor and could sack Jason if he wanted to, but he was also clearly what she would've called a 'drip' around twenty years ago (she couldn't think what the word would be for it now – 'dweeb' didn't quite cut it). She was sure he was blushing behind that beard – why else did men grow beards if not to hide behind? – and his ears stuck out at an alarming angle. He was Dumbo personified! How had he managed to work his way up to Managing Editor of the *Stanford Times*?

Without much encouragement, David launched into a diatribe about the newspaper's readership and how proud he was of its contribution to the community, and even though he was speaking a load of bollocks (no one bought the 'paper' anymore and people only visited the website for the sports results), Beatie nodded and said 'uh huh' in the appropriate places. She knew his rant would eventually come to an end and she could then get down to business and ask him a vital question.

He was listing the journalism awards the *Stanford Times* should've won when Ally cut him off.

'Mum!'

Ally was running so fast her left sneaker skidded on a tree root and she landed on her knees dangerously close to the poo David was pretending his dog hadn't done.

'Can you take Boo to the toilet?'

'Boo?' David asked. 'That's a *child's* name?'

'He's called Boo because he was an accident.' Ally never tired of letting people know. 'Gave Mum the fright of her life.'

'It's just over there.' Beatie pointed to the toilet block, less than two hundred metres away. 'He's big enough to go on his own.'

'Dad said to tell you to take him.' Ally rubbed her grass-stained knees.

'Did he?' Beatie looked over at the barbecue. Jason's angry glare bore through the smoke. 'He probably just wants to get me away from Dave.'

David cleared his throat. 'It's David.'

'Mum! It's urgent. We think Boo's going to be sick.'

'Boo's a big boy. Tell your dad not to worry, I haven't told Dave about him being pulled over by the cops.' Beatie dropped her cigarette butt and extinguished it under her sandal. 'Yet.'

A few minutes later, Mitch was sent on the next rescue mission, complete with a tomato-sauce-smeared mouth and a fresh tear in his t-shirt. Beatie quickly stuffed a scrap of paper she'd been writing on into her handbag.

'Dad said you've got to eat something.' He handed Beatie a bleeding sausage wrapped up in soggy bread. 'It's got lots of sauce so you hardly know it's burnt.'

'What about you, Dave?' Beatie said. 'Want half?'

'No thanks. Better check up on Lisa.' David tugged his dog's lead. 'Come on, Toots.'

'Nice chatting to you,' Beatie said.

She wondered whether David's reply got lost in his beard. Or was he really that much of an arrogant arse? She bit through the sodden bread and into the charcoal grit.

The heat in the car on the drive home – 32 degrees according to the Mazda's thermometer – did little to cool Jason's temper.

'I can't believe you,' he said. 'I asked you not to drink today.'

'Yeah? Well, I was thirsty. And bored shitless.'

'I also *specifically* asked you not to speak to David. You know I've just applied for the Chief Reporter role.'

'I don't know what you're worried about.' Beatie wound down her window, hoping the cool air would ease the tension. 'I was just being friendly.'

'You trod on his dog!' Jason glared at her.

'I didn't see the bloody thing.'

'Dad!' Ally squealed. 'We're going to crash.'

'Shit!' The car swerved, knocking over a black garbage bin as Jason corrected his steering.

'Awesome shot, Dad,' Mitch said.

'I'm gunna ...' Boo whispered. He was squashed in between Ally and Mitch on the backseat.

'What's up, Boo?' Mitch said. 'Your face looks funny.'

'Told you not to have a second sausage.' Ally inched closer to the car door. 'And you gutsed down half the marshmallows.'

'What marshmallows?' Mitch asked. 'I didn't get any.'

'That posh woman Dad was helping dropped them,' Ally told him. 'It was when you were fighting the skinny girl.'

'His dog got under my feet,' Beatie said to Jason. 'I think it was one of those stupid breeds. Or maybe it was blind.'

'And you told him about my speeding ticket!' Jason squeezed the steering wheel.

'Calm down. I was just making conversation. And I left out the bit about your lame attempt to bribe the cop. I'm not thick.'

'It's like you were hitting on him.' Jason's voice was quiet. 'It was embarrassing.'

'Jason.' Beatie rubbed her forehead. She'd been trying to put it – *her* – out of her mind until they'd got home and she'd poured another drink. 'Before you say another word, look at your collar.'

'Don't, Dad!' Ally said. 'We'll crash. I don't want to die.'

'Yeah,' Mitch added. 'Not now. It's the final of *The Voice* tonight.'

'What's on my collar?'

'Tomato sauce!' Beatie yelled. 'Hypocrite.'

'What's a hypocrite?' Mitch asked.

'It's when you say someone's done something wrong, but you've done the exact same thing yourself,' Ally explained. 'So when Dad–'

'How long's it been going on?' Beatie demanded.

'What?' Jason frowned.

'You and her. The *posh woman you were helping*,' Beatie said. 'With her hair piled up like she thinks she's Mary Queen of Scots.'

'Lucinda? Um, she moved here from Perth. Nice enough woman. But nothing's *going on*.'

'David said she started in May.'

'*What* were you talking about with David?' Jason glared at her.

'I'm gunna,' Boo cried. 'Blhhhhhh.'

Beatie turned around to see Boo doubled over and vomit gushing all over his shorts. It slid down his legs onto his grubby bare feet and dripped plop plop plop onto the floor.

Normally seeing someone throw up would make Beatie dry retch, especially in a hot, stuffy car. But she was so consumed with anger she felt distant, as if she was watching Boo on TV.

'Oh my God, Boo!' Ally cried.

'This happened last time,' Mitch said. 'I remember now.'

'But it's black!' Ally wound down her window. 'It's making *me* feel sick.'

'Can you hang on, kids?' Jason quickly turned around to glance at them. 'We'll be home in five minutes.'

'Why don't you hand them your apron?' Beatie asked him. 'In case he throws up again.'

'What apron?' Jason then looked down at his chest and saw Rudolph's bright red flashing nose. 'Shit! You could've told me I still had it on. *Before* I said goodbye to everyone!'

'To *her*, you mean?' Beatie said.

'It's David I'm worried about. He'll think I'm an idiot! That's if he didn't already after talking to you.'

Boo started crying. 'I'm dying.'

'You're not dying. It's burnt sausage,' Mitch said. 'It stinks!'

'Do I need to pull over?' Jason looked in the rear-view mirror.

'Yes, you do,' Beatie said. 'Stop now. I'm getting out.'

'What?' Jason's face was as red as Rudolph's nose. We're nearly home. Don't be pathetic.'

'Pull over! Or I'll throw up too. All over that fucking apron!'

The car skidded to a stop. Beatie scraped her handbag off the floor and slipped the strap onto her shoulder. No one spoke as she stepped out onto the footpath; the kids were shocked into silence. As the car roared away, Beatie noticed them staring at her as if she was standing there stark naked. Boo's chin was slick with vomit. She hoped Jason would have the sense to throw him in the bath when they got home.

A southerly breeze swept through Beatie's hair and cooled the sweat on her forehead. For the first time since she'd lifted her head off the couch that morning, she felt like she could breathe. She reached into her handbag, dug out the scrunched-up piece of paper and flattened it with her fingers. She'd planned to go home first, but why make a special trip? She turned around and began walking back towards town.

Jason

'Morning, Jason.' Susan made a point of glancing over her shoulder at the giant clock hanging on the wall behind her in case he wasn't aware he was over an hour late.

Jason nodded to signal he had no time for small talk. *Bloody nosy Susan*, he thought. *But more to the point, bloody Beatie!* She'd never in a million years be nominated World's Greatest Mum, but at least he could usually rely on her to help get their kids out the front door and onto the school bus. Even if it was only so she could leg it to the bottle-o a few minutes later. That morning Boo had refused to put on his school shoes, crying, 'Mum does it!' Jason ended up resorting to bribery to get them on Boo's feet, one spoonful of Milo per shoe.

The office was quiet, apart from the tap tap tapping of fingers on keyboards. Every *Stanford Times* employee was working like a robot, all programmed to start at 9am on the dot. Meg, Sonia, and a couple of others gave him a quick frown to acknowledge his lateness before looking back at their screens.

'Hiya, Jase.' Brett sat at the desk next to Jason's.

'Hey.' Jason picked up a big tangle of tinsel and grass – who'd dumped it on *his* desk? – and stuffed it into the cupboard behind him.

'You look stressed, mate,' Brett said.

'My kids are a handful at the moment.' Jason dropped his briefcase onto his desk and sat down. 'Boo kept me up all bloody night.'

That was only half true. Boo's whining kept him up until midnight. But he'd also been wondering when Beatie would come home and why Lucinda hadn't replied to his messages. Had he said something wrong at the barbecue? Those worries kept him twisting in his sheets until sometime after 2am.

'Three must do your head in.' Brett leant back in his chair.

'It's mainly Boo.'

Jason wanted to add that the problem was Boo hadn't seen his mum since she'd climbed out of the car on the way home from the barbecue on

Saturday. But, of course, Brett wouldn't understand. He'd ask Jason what the hell he was doing at work. Had he called the police? Why wasn't he driving all over town in a panic like any normal husband would? To avoid looking like a complete arsehole, Jason would then have to reveal his dark secret. It was Beatie's secret really, but his by default. And if he told Brett, everyone would hear (his colleagues were quick to drop the robot facade when there was gossip to be gleaned), and Jason wasn't ready for the world to know what his wife was really like.

What would people think if they knew that every few weeks Beatie went on a week-long bender? And that on a bender she could down enough booze to make an entire university population pass out, often hiding out in that seedy motel by the river? What would that say about him? Even if he explained he'd dragged her to numerous AA meetings and had lost count of the times he'd tried to talk her into coming home to sober up, they'd judge him. Worst of all, Lucinda might decide his life was too messy and call things off.

'Funny, I thought you were pissed about not getting an interview,' Brett whispered.

'What?' Jason moved his briefcase to the floor. 'David finalised the shortlist?'

'Oops.' Brett turned back to his computer. 'Please forget I said that.'

Jason clenched his jaw and ground his teeth, something he'd caught himself doing more and more lately. If he stayed married to Beatie, he'd be toothless before he was fifty. She knew how much he wanted to be Chief Reporter. She didn't know it was mainly so he could share an office with Lucinda, and spend all day breathing in her delicious scent, but still. What had Beatie blabbed to David at the barbecue?

Jason clicked his briefcase open. As he reached inside it for his laptop, the bright green apron slipped out and onto the carpet. It made a tinny sound, which soon turned into a recognisable – if not totally abominable – tune.

'Holy shit,' Brett said. 'It sings!'

'It's Lu's.' Jason nudged it with a shiny black shoe. 'I forgot to give it back on Saturday.'

'Yeah, we saw you getting in your car still wearing it.' Brett smirked. 'Sonia snapped a photo – for the cover of our Christmas Eve issue.'

'You're hilarious.'

'Can you turn that thing off, please Jason?' a robot asked. 'Some of us are working.'

'Sorry, I'm trying.' Jason gave it a kick. 'Why won't it shut up?'

'Morning, chaps,' David said. Of all the moments he could've emerged from his office, David chose the one in which Jason was stomping on Rudolph the Red Nosed Reindeer's face. He stood in front of Jason's desk, hands on his hips, as Rudolph sang on, unperturbed.

'Try pressing the nose?' Brett offered.

Jason picked up the apron and lay it on his desk. He thumped Rudolph's nose and then each of his large, brown eyes before, finally, he felt a switch near the bottom hem. The silence that followed was almost as excruciating as Rudolph's American accent. Jason felt his boss's eyes watching, judging.

'Sorry, David,' Jason said. 'It's just a... silly thing.'

'I think it suits you.' David gave no sign he was joking. What did he mean? Was he implying that Jason was silly too? Is that why he wasn't going to interview him for the job?

Brett cleared his throat. 'Do you need something, David? The cricket write-up will be ready in twenty. Then I'll get the low-down on that house fire.'

'Good work, Brett. Have either of you heard from Lucinda? She missed an important briefing at nine.'

At the sound of her name, spoken by someone other than himself, Jason felt light-headed.

Brett shrugged. 'Thought she was already here.'

'Susan tried calling her at home, but there was no answer.' David frowned, then looked at Jason. 'You two were pretty cosy behind the barbecue on Saturday. Did she seem okay?'

'Um.' What did David mean by cosy? Had it been that obvious that Jason wanted to sweep all the tinsel and food into the bin and take Lucinda on the picnic table? Or had Beatie spouted her suspicions when she was 'making conversation' with David? God, Jason wanted to strangle that woman.

'Yeah. Lucinda seemed fine.' Jason hoped he sounded casual, relaxed, but really he was wondering why she hadn't told him she was going to pull a sickie. He must've upset her somehow.

'Mysterious.' David rubbed his beard. 'This is very unlike her.'

As David headed back to his office, Brett whispered, 'Could've been the sausages. They were lethal, mate.'

Jason decided Brett's comment didn't warrant a reply. He was thinking about Lucinda's beautiful silky hair and long legs, and wondering what he'd done to hurt her.

'Jason?' David was now heading back towards him. 'Perhaps you could check with your wife? She might know where Lucinda is.'

'Beatie?' Jason's voice came out as a squeak. 'She barely knows Lucinda.'

'Are you sure?' David frowned. 'She had a lot to say about her at the barbecue. Even asked me for Lucinda's address. Said she had a surprise for her.'

'Did she?' Jason wasn't sure if the words came out of his mouth.

'I assumed she was dropping off a Christmas present,' David said. 'It was a bit of an odd request, but Beatie's a bit odd, is she not?'

'You must be right.' Jason's mouth was drier than the Great Sandy Desert. 'I'll check with–'

'Excuse me, David!' Susan stopped to catch her breath, as if the distance between her desk and where she was now standing was more than ten metres. 'Sorry to interrupt.'

Jason wished Susan would dust the pastry flakes off her black shirt, but was relieved she'd stolen the attention away from him.

'Lucinda's neighbour just called.' Susan looked down at her notepad. 'Mrs Joan Peters, her name is. Um she thinks ... Well, she reckons there was a big fire at Lucinda's house. Could that be right? She wanted to know if Lucinda's okay. But she sounded really old. Maybe she got it wrong.'

David stared at Jason, before turning to Brett. 'You mentioned a house fire?'

'Yeah.' Brett picked up a folder and flicked through it. 'Arnott Street. House burnt to the ground. I don't have any other details. I was going to call the station after my smoke break. Ha. Get it, *smoke* break. Sorry, bad taste.'

'That's Lucinda's street,' David said. 'When did it happen?'

Jason clenched his jaw so hard he almost pulled a muscle in his neck.

'Saturday evening.' Susan's eyes welled up. 'After the *Stanford Times'* Christmas barbecue. What will I tell Mrs Peters?'

'Wait until we know more.' David stared at the apron on Jason's desk, then lifted his eyes to meet Jason's. 'I'll call the station.'

'All right, thanks,' Brett said. 'You okay, Jase?'

Jason tried to nod, but his head felt cemented to his neck. *This is my fault,* he thought. *Why did I think it'd be fine to bring Beatie to the barbecue?* He closed his eyes, picturing her climbing out of the car after she'd yelled at him to pull over. He'd thought she was bluffing, that she'd cool off and get back in. But then he saw the fire in her eyes. *She was clearly enraged*, he thought. *How long had she suspected something? Should I have forced her back in the car*? She hadn't been herself after Boo's birth, after she'd started drinking heavily, but never did he think she'd be responsible for hurting anyone. For a *house burnt to the ground*. Now she'll go to jail. Their kids will have no mum. He'll lose his job and they'll have to leave town because who'd want to associate with the family of a ... criminal? He bit down hard on his tongue, tasted blood. And all for a bit of fun with ... He pushed Lucinda out of his mind. He couldn't think about her. Not yet. Maybe not ever.

Oh Beatie. What have you done?

SPIKE

ROBERT GOTT

Are introductions necessary? I suppose they are. It would be presumptuous to assume that you've read one, or perhaps all four, of my excellent memoirs; although I can't imagine why you wouldn't have. I call them memoirs although strictly speaking they're more limited in scope than a traditional memoir. They more or less chart the various outrages visited upon my person in the course of simply going about my business. My name is William Power and my business is of course acting. I am a fine actor, but professional opportunities during the war were limited and my attempts to bring Shakespeare to the barbarians in different parts of this country went mostly unappreciated. In the course of this enterprise I was even bombed by the Japanese air force. Well, I suppose the whole of Darwin was bombed, but I was there and I took it personally. But I'm not going to go over ground covered elsewhere.

There is an incident I wish to discuss, and it's an incident I've never spoken about before. Not even my brother, Brian, knows about this, and I've certainly never told my mother, who throughout my childhood showed no interest anyway in encouraging intimacies. At the time this incident took place it would have been helpful if I'd been able to confide in someone, but I knew no one who was interested in hearing the confidences of a fourteen-year-old boy. My father was still alive then. He died when I was sixteen, but my over-riding memory of his opinion of me is of fixed and frank disdain.

I turned fourteen in 1923, and if you check the newspapers for November of that year you should find a flurry of articles about the disappearance of a boy named Peter Spike. He went missing from Wilsons Promontory, in Victoria. This was, and is, an enormous national park with extensive areas of wilderness. This was particularly true in 1923, although even then it was a magnet for people who enjoyed digging a hole and squatting over it. I was not, and am not, one of those people.

My father took pleasure in organising entertainments for me which he knew I would find an endurance. He decided that I might benefit from a few days in the wilderness. Apparently, I stood in peril of becoming soft. Even at fourteen I knew how spurious this reasoning was, and the thought of me spending uncomfortable nights in a tent would give him great pleasure. He'd found a boys' club; I think it must have been some sort of Boy Scouts affiliate. I can't recall its name. Was it the Boys' Brigade, or CHUMS, or perhaps something to do with the Anglican Church? It doesn't matter. I do recall that I was handed a copy of Baden Powell's *Scouting for Boys* and told that I ought to read it in preparation for an adventure. There was no warmth in my father's smile as he handed me the book. There was instead a sort of pre-emptive triumph.

I wasn't attracted to all the hearty manliness and imperial trumpet blowing in the book and was repelled by Baden Powell's warning that masturbation led to the wasteful draining of one's manly sap, and that our reservoir of this sap was of a finite nature. We needed to save our sap for marriage. Feeble children would be the consequence of depleted sap. I began to worry that my allocation had already been severely compromised.

Items began appearing in my bedroom: a knapsack, stout shoes with canvas gaiters, and a foul-smelling oilskin. No explanation came with these articles. Apparently *Scouting for Boys* would answer all my questions. My father certainly wasn't interested in doing so.

Very early on a Saturday morning my father drove me to Spencer Street railway station. I knew at this stage that my adventure was to last four days. My school had granted me two days leave of absence. I was to join a group of eight boys under the supervision of an ex-Army major. These boys were all from good homes. The purpose of this hiking and camping interlude was to instill values of co-operation and to learn some new skills. It wasn't about correcting the recalcitrant behaviour of louts. This was about toughening up, not straightening out. I learned all this in the car on the way to the railway station.

'But who are these boys?' I asked.

'I have no idea,' my father said. 'They're all about your age, and they've all led very comfortable lives.' He paused for effect. 'Until now.'

He dropped me at the appointed place near the station, shook my hand in an awful show of ersatz affection, and drove away. I wondered how he knew that this was the right drop off point, but I saw a truck arrive, and realised that we'd be sitting in the back of this vehicle all the way to Wilson's Promontory, which was a journey of many hours.

I was the first to arrive. Of the other seven, all except one were unceremoniously deposited by an unseen parent. The boy named Peter Spike, the boy who failed to return from this expedition, was accompanied by his mother who stood with him until we were instructed to get into the back of the truck. She clutched her son and began weeping. Peter tried and failed to survive this maternal onslaught with his fledgling manhood intact. By the time he clambered awkwardly into the truck his position at the bottom of the pecking order had been assured.

The truck's suspension made it one step removed from a covered wagon. The canvas flaps at the back were tied securely shut, as if to prevent escape. I don't recall that anyone spoke throughout the entire trip. Each of us was a stranger to the other and there wasn't among us anyone who was garrulous or confident enough to begin talking. Even if there had been, the noise and the exhaust fumes were a discouragement to chat. We would have had to shout to be heard.

The only voice I remember was Peter Spike's, which was surprisingly deep. Despite his small frame his voice had broken early, well ahead of the barely pubescent rest of him. About three hours into the trip he declared loudly that he needed a wee. That was the term he used. The cabin of the truck was separated from its rear end so there was no way of communicating with the driver. Peter Spike was clearly used to having his needs catered to and after another fifteen minutes he stood up and in an amazing feat of dexterity managed to brace himself with one hand against the movement of the truck and relieve himself through a gap in the canvas flaps with the help of the other. By then we'd hit unmade road, so the rising dust may have obscured the spectacle from the driver of the car travelling behind.

We met the ex-Army major when we arrived at the promontory. His name was Alfred Longstaff and he let us know that it was his job to lead us on this hike and harangue us into submission. I thought he cut a ludicrous figure, and he didn't frighten me at all. I saw all of his noisy posturing as akin to an embarrassing tantrum. Most of the other boys were cowed by him, but perhaps they lacked the carapace I'd grown to deal with my father – not that my father ever raised his voice to me, or struck me. I learned early that silence needs to be deflected, just as shouting does.

I'll pass over the hike and the first night of camping. It was unpleasant and dull. There was very little conversation among the boys. None of them presented as potential friends and I was certain that I'd never see any of them again after these few days. Peter Spike continued to make an impression but not in a way that increased his popularity. He did odd things, like eat bark, and a grasshopper, and a grub. He was one of those boys who would drink ink to impress classmates.

Alfred Longstaff had a tent that was slightly larger than any of ours, and I was sure he also had a decent supply of alcohol. By the second night he'd established his routine of shouted instructions, latrine digging allocation, and meal preparation – after which he retired to his tent and drank himself into an early, snore-heavy sleep.

On the third day we plodded through damp forest to Sealer's Cove. It was an enervating, hot day and we arrived at the cove in the mid-afternoon. We were all sweaty, smelly, thirsty, and short-tempered. I feel I ought to delineate the individual characters of the other boys, but I don't remember them as individuals. They were bland and uninteresting and survive in my memory as an amorphous singularity. Only Peter Spike stands out, partly because of his unattractive peculiarities, but mainly because of what happened to him.

We were the only people at the Cove, and we set up our tents among the casuarinas some distance from the beach. Alfred Longstaff unfolded a chair outside his tent and sat lumpenly in it, no longer interested in us. The walk into the Cove had exhausted him or perhaps he was suffering from a hangover. He slumped in the shade and dozed off, providing the mosquitoes with an unchallenged buffet of sinewy flesh, although not much of his flesh was exposed. He wore long trousers and a sweat-stained, long-sleeved shirt. I watched as mosquitoes settled on his hands and ears.

He fell so deeply asleep that he was indifferent to them. Having been tortured by them myself, and believing that I'd contracted malaria, I had no sympathy for him. Drain the bastard dry, I thought.

There was only one thing for us to do and that was to swim. The beach was an arc of clean sand, and the sea looked benign and inviting, although a tumble of clouds was building on the horizon. We walked to the edge of the casuarinas and stripped down to our underpants, except for Peter Spike, who stripped off completely and danced about, whooping like a barbarian. We hurried into the water. He stood at the edge and I guessed that he couldn't swim.

'Come in so we don't have to look at you,' someone said. Spike did a little jig and advanced so that the water came up to his waist. The waves were gentle and there was no evidence of a rip. We swam happily for half an hour, the sea cooling our sunburn. Peter Spike eventually sat in the wet sand, where waves tumbled over his legs and sucked the sand from beneath his buttocks as they withdrew.

At some point Spike walked back to the camp site. I didn't see him do this, but I surfaced after a deep dive and saw him digging a hole well above the tide line with one of the latrine spades. I had no idea what he was doing. He waved the spade above his head, signaling that he wanted someone to leave the water and go to him. I had no intention of doing so, but two of the other boys, who were closer in, left the water and walked to him. I wasn't sure which of the boys they were. I watched as they spoke to Spike, who was laughing, and they joined in. One of them took the spade and began digging in the hole that Peter Spike had begun. Spike kept jumping into it, testing its depth. In no time at all he could stand at shoulder height. He took the spade and dug just a couple more inches, then said something to one of the boys. The boy hesitated, but encouraged by Spike he began shoveling sand back into the hole, until only Spike's head and the top of his shoulders were visible. On the sand beside him was a wide-brimmed straw hat, which Spike wore on the hikes and for which he'd been ridiculed by Alfred Longstaff, who considered it effeminate. Consequently the rest of us felt at liberty to rib him about it too. He was the only one of us not to be suffering sunburn.

One of the boys who'd dug his hole for him placed the hat on Spike's head so that from a distance it looked as if a straw hat had been discarded on the sand.

A few of the boys tired of swimming and left the water. The sky had become overcast and the sea had turned gun metal grey. A distant roll of thunder made me nervous. I'd read in 'The Argus' about a woman who'd been struck by lightning while standing at the water's edge at Apollo Bay. It wasn't the storm though that drove me back to the beach. I was lying on my back so I missed the first cry. Water lapped over my face as someone swam past me. There was something frantic in the movement and when I raised my head I heard someone calling from the beach, 'Fin! Fin!'

It was this moment that secured in me a deep dread of the ocean. People tell me that the sea calls to them. All I hear now in the sound of the waves is a voice saying, 'Come on in and die, land boy.'

I didn't look about me to confirm the sighting of a fin. I swam as quickly as I could, panic jangling every cell in my body. When I reached the shallows I stood and ran up the beach, uncertain that I was safe until my feet burned in the hot, dry sand. There were three of us, and we laughed nervously when we couldn't see the fin.

'I saw it. I swear it was there. It was a shark,' one of them said. A vein of lightning spread across the sky, followed almost simultaneously by a crack of thunder. I quite reasonably thought that my life was in danger. Every schoolboy knows that you count the seconds between the flash and the thunder clap to determine how far away the lightning is. There'd been barely a second. Then the rain started and it fell with monsoonal force. We turned away from the beach and headed back to the camp. Why do we happily immerse ourselves in the sea and run for shelter from rain?

The downpour lasted for an hour. The claims that our tents were waterproof were disproved. Everything was saturated – all our clothes and bedding. Alfred Longstaff's skills as a bushman were exposed as threadbare. When he saw that rain was coming he ought to have gathered enough wood and kindling and kept it dry, to ensure a fire. He didn't. He'd been sleeping, having enjoyed no doubt an afternoon's solitary drinking. We ate cold baked beans and some sort of slimy, foul-smelling canned meat. If it was beef it had come a very long way from the cow slaughtered to produce it. I felt ill after eating it, and retreated through the quagmire of the camp site to my tent. This was a structure I'd come to loathe. We'd each been issued with a one man tent, which was little more than a length of canvas, some props, pegs and rope. It was clumsy, and heavy to carry, and when erected it looked nothing like the tidy structures illustrated in Scouting for Boys. My tent also stank of mould, nurtured and grown over many previous hikes.

I managed to fall asleep, despite being harried by mosquitoes, and wondering if a fourteen year old could develop rheumatism from damp bedding. I didn't own a watch so I don't know what time it was when I heard someone moving about the camp. I didn't stick my head out of the tent. I assumed it was someone on his way to the latrine ditch, the state of which after the rain didn't bear thinking about. I closed my eyes and the image of Peter Spike, trapped in the sand presented itself as if lit by lightning. Had anyone returned to the beach to free him? Had he been at dinner? I wasn't sure. It was dark and I'd been busy slapping away mosquitoes. I wasn't concerned. The thought of him being nibbled by crabs was amusing, and having been stuck in the sand for a few hours might teach him not to be quite such a nong. Nevertheless, I thought I'd better check.

I emerged from my tent into bright moonlight. I'm not afraid of the dark, but I do have a preference for daylight. Walking to the beach was a bit creepy. I wasn't in danger of being attacked by wild animals, although I was concerned about snakes and made my footfalls heavy. This had been one of Alfred Longstaff's bits of bush knowhow. It was probably nonsense, but it made me feel less nervous.

I have a poor sense of direction. I'm not ashamed to admit this. I don't consider that being able to point towards north is a social skill. I knew I was heading in the right direction because I could hear the sea and as I got closer, I could smell it. I recall thinking that there was a different quality to the sound of the water at night. It sounded closer than it had in daylight. I broke from the fringe of casuarinas and stood above the beach. The sea was flat and calm and moonlight bounced on its surface. It took a moment to register that something was very different. The glittering water had advanced up the beach to a point beyond where Peter Spike's head ought to have been visible. Despite the storm it looked to me as if the water had crept, rather than swept to its high position. Peter Spike must have cried out. There was no one to hear him above the noise of the storm. Maybe though, maybe the water had loosened the sand and he'd wriggled free. Surely this must have been what had happened here. I held onto that calming thought until I saw his ridiculous straw hat, bobbing gently at the water's edge. He was out there, the top of his head maybe just an inch beneath the water.

I don't know why, but I looked to my right and saw the silhouette of Alfred Longstaff, sitting, watching the sea. He knew. Had one of the boys realised that Spike hadn't returned and told him? I knew what he was doing. He was waiting for the tide to go out. Should I stay and help him? The thought horrified and repelled me. I didn't want to see Spike's face after small fish and crabs had been tearing at it. Should I at least say something to Alfred Longstaff? I know myself well enough now to be confident that if I'd spoken to him it wouldn't have been to offer reassurance and support, but to declare that I'd had nothing to do with this. I'd seen it happening, and seen that it had been done at Peter Spike's request. This wasn't the action of two bullies; just two boys playing along with another boy's jape. I hadn't seen who those boys were. I'd been too far away and there'd been too much glare.

I didn't speak to Longstaff. I didn't like him, and anyway, he was probably drunk, and I imagined, incandescent with rage that this had happened on his watch. He would ultimately be held responsible.

He stood up, took off his shoes and waded to the place where I imagined Peter Spike's head to be. He didn't have a torch with him, but I could see in the moonlight that he was feeling about in the sand with his feet. He must have made a connection because he leaned over and felt about in the water with both his hands. There was something macabre about this spectacle. I have a feverish imagination and I could feel in my own fingers the sensation of Spike's tattered skin under Longstaff's searching fingertips. I couldn't bear the idea of watching him pull the body out of the sand. I returned to the camp and remained wide awake on my damp bedding, waiting for the sound of Longstaff returning with Peter Spike's body. I hoped he'd have the decency to wrap it in something.

I thought I'd remained awake, but I must have dozed off because one moment it was dark, and the next the tent was awash with limpid light. I strained to hear a sound other than the noisy calls of birds. There was no wind and I could tell that it was going to be oppressively hot. I dreaded the sight that might meet me when I emerged from the tent. I decided not to check first, but came out as if I wasn't expecting to see anything unusual. I certainly didn't want Longstaff to suspect that I'd been watching him during the night.

I stood up and made a ludicrous display of stretching – my acting skills hadn't yet been tuned to their current pitch. To my astonishment Longstaff had somehow managed to coax a fire into boiling the billy, and he sat calmly drinking a mug of tea. He looked at me, his eyes red-rimmed and bleary. There was no sign of Peter Spike's body. Perhaps Longstaff had put it in his tent.

'Get everybody up and out here, will you,' he said. There wasn't a great deal of energy in the demand. He sounded tired – and perhaps I'm superimposing this from a distance – defeated. I went from tent to tent, waking everybody up, and to avoid inevitable rebuffs declared portentously that something had happened. In a few minutes we were all gathered; all except one. I knew now from the looks on the boys' faces who'd helped Peter Spike dig what had turned out to be his grave. Two faces were drawn and puffy around the eyes, and both boys looked scared. It doesn't matter now who they were, and I only recall their first names anyway. One of them was the smallest and least developed of our group – his voice hadn't yet broken – and the other was unmemorably bland. They were staring intently at Longstaff and the smaller boy was shaking slightly. I think only I noticed this.

'Where's Spike?' someone said.

Alfred Longstaff stood up, and with staggering brutality said, 'Peter Spike is dead.'

No one said a word.

'Some of you saw the shark yesterday. I saw it myself. When you'd all run back to the camp I hung around for a bit.'

'So you were watching us' I said.

'I was keeping an eye on you. That's my job, Power.' He managed to summon enough energy to inject some venom into my name.

'Spike was stupidly wriggling about in his little sand pit.' His eyes darted to the two boys, and I knew that a monstrous lie was in the process of being concocted. Had the two boys agreed to this, or were they hearing it for the first time?

'He managed to wriggle free. The silly little bugger was stark naked. That was a sight I didn't want to see so I looked away, and when I looked back he'd gone into the water to wash off the sand. I ran down from where I'd been standing and called out to him, but by then the storm was deafening.'

He paused, and again he looked directly at the boys.

'I saw the shark take him. It happened in a heartbeat. One second his head was visible and the next he was gone. There was no blood. He was just gone. He wouldn't have known what had happened. He wouldn't have felt a thing.'

This was a transparent nicety, which didn't convince me at all. Peter Spike couldn't swim and wouldn't have been sufficiently far out for a shark to take him from beneath. No. I knew what had actually happened, and I knew that Peter Spike must have suffered terribly as the sea lapped into his mouth and over his nose. It was a miserable, appalling way to die.

The smaller of the culprits began to cry, and this set off two other boys, who also began sobbing.

'We need to pack everything up and leave,' Longstaff said. There was no further discussion. As I moved away I saw Longstaff kneel in front of the weeping boy and hold each of his arms close to his body. It was gentle gesture. I heard him say, 'That's what happened. Do you understand? That's exactly how it happened.'

The boy nodded.

Was I the only one who knew for certain that Longstaff was lying? Why didn't I say something? The answer to that is simple. I was fourteen years old. All these years later I don't blame myself for this failure of courage, and I realise that in not blaming myself I must also withhold blame from everybody else. I can't know what Longstaff's motive was. At the time I thought it was self-interest. I suspect it's more complicated, perhaps even nobler than that. Was he protecting those boys from having to pay the heavy price of suspicion and scrutiny if the real nature of the accident was revealed? Was he after all a decent man, and if he was a decent man, what dreadful, personal price did he pay for disposing of Peter Spike's corpse?

I never saw any of the group again. Perhaps they all lived happy, uncomplicated lives, or perhaps for some of them the grip of a drowned boy never loosens.

THE BARBER

SHELLEY BURNE-FIELD

IT'S AN A1 FACT – THE DOORS OF MY BARBER SHOP WILL CLOSE today, and I'll serve information to the people in a new way: my already very popular online channel. It's good. It's so great. Closing my shop is a sacrifice I'm willing to make. My face is getting too well known in the outside world. Too easy to find. The media whores twist a fact just as much as a liquorice strap.

I'm about freedom. It's on my mind constantly, like a migraine drilling in. I don't think freedom is on his mind, this snowflake sitting in my barber's seat. He's said fuck all, yet he's humming like a Disney princess while I shave the back of his neck. Come in for a haircut? I'm not so sure.

In the mirror: notice him. Texting government bosses or wifey. Enjoying a tampon up there. The top of this guy's hair doesn't even need a cut. I trim it anyway. With clippers, not scissors. I'm that good.

His shoes are a giveaway. Canvas or some such. Maybe wool? Expensive, and too clean. I bet he's a researcher. No, an infiltrator. The clippers dig into the back of his right ear, and his humming cuts off real sharp.

'All good, friend?'

His pig eyes get trapped in the mirror. Can he hold it? No! The snowflake nods and laser focuses on his phone. This termite should research how to infiltrate a people's movement and not stick out like dog's balls. His shoes look as washed clean as a nun's front bum – although I've had my run-ins with them, too.

Back in the day, those bitches crushed my little knuckles with their grimaces and the edges of their metre rulers. From their sneers I learned the word 'glee'.

You can tell from this snowflake's buffed fingernails he's only here for me. Did he realise my existence allowed him to wallow in his middle class sink of suds? Under the cape of my protection?

'Did you say it's your last day as a barber?'

'That's right.'

'A big change?'

'You ask a lot of questions, friend.'

'Oh, I... Sorry.'

Why'd he come in today? Hmm? My final day? The very last cut? To get a read on me? Does he give me credit for being a success in this fading paradigm? I started from a few friends and nephews stopping by, to having waiting lists and regulars. I clocked this life more than the clown, my sperm donor, ever did. He was an A1 alcoholic, druggie, exemplar failure.

My shop's been here for years, years! I've existed for the old creased soldiers like Roger, Corporal, retired. He enjoys a yarn. He's a patriot who built bridges for the mugs over in good morning Vietnam. Two tours. Two, the poor bastard. He loves hot towels on his jowls and especially over his eyes, and he doesn't even want his beard shaved. Nothing. He craves the heat and the steam, and the dark.

Then there's the Māori, Harlan, the butcher's apprentice. He reckons he's SāMāori and likes his hair just so, with a frizz mullet. Sāmoan, Māori, they're all the same to me. But man he's huge, and a good guy. A real gentle giant. He's not like those other gorillas or even the dummy Islanders. He told me this joke yesterday.

'Hey Ethan, how would I introduce my wife, when I get one, eh? You know, cos I'm a butcher.'

'How?'

'Meet Pattie.'

Harlan's hair always squeaks when I comb it. Like, it's always primo clean. Countless heads of hair I've scalped: scabby, lice-infected, skin cancered, oily, malodorous, boil covered, sunburned, freckled, flaked, dirty-disgusting and pristine.

Since I started live streaming a year ago, people make appointments just to shake my hand.

Does this snowflake know that donations in my bank account have taken over the income from my barber shop? I'm flush. Over three grand – every week! Money from perfect strangers! And support for live streaming the truth is getting bigger and bigger.

We can't wait for a Trump in New Zealand. Though I'm proud he's actually reached out to my channel. He has his own dynasty to organise. He's a father. I get that. I would kill to protect my kid, too. Hands down it's about the kids.

I've forgiven my filthy slit of a father. I admit it, I probably have dad issues. He's in me.

They'll find out about him soon, but I don't give a rat's arse if they make his past public. I'm an open Wiki leak.

'Do you require a shave? Hot towel?'

'No thanks.'

'Where do you live?'

'What?'

'What street?'

'Ah, Vivian, the flats.'

What a fucking lie.

The snowflake paid with the shiniest credit card you've ever seen! Then he skipped out the door on his fake arse shoes. As he went out, a blobby guy with a camera came in. A female walked in too. This upright baby-oven carried a microphone. I recognised her straight away. She was on television each night. Mainstream.

In the mirror: notice her. Fear. She was skittery. Her radioactive green irises jerked around like a mutant jumping spider.

'Mr Pool?'

'I know you on TV, Mainstream.'

'Yes, that's right. Would you like to comment on your nightly live stream that many feel is spouting dangerous misinformation and conspiracy theories?'

'I know your hack strategy. Why don't you start reporting the truth rather than attacking me? Protect our children?'

She didn't get a chance to answer–

The glass window at the front of the shop exploded inward, glass clattering onto the floor, scattering over the counter tops, and whacking me in the back.

'Whaaaaat!?'

The camera guy grunted and went down on one knee, leaning hard on the camera to stay upright. I dunno, something heroic made me grab her under my armpit. A rod of red and white and blue stripes rolled along the floor.

'What the fork!' hissed the reporter, and she actually said 'fork'– just like that.

The shop was silent and still, except for falling pieces of glass raining off us. I scanned the street but there were only a few suits looking up like meercats, gnawing on wooden sporks.

'Mr Pool? Somebody threw your barber shop pole through the window!'

'Yes, Mainstream. Obviously so.'

'Like who?'

'Find out who the liar is. Who is the lowest common denominator, and you'll find your criminal.'

'Who is the criminal, Mr Pool?'

What a moron. I lifted the pole to look at the scratches underneath. The piece was a rare Marvy. A true stature of American history. I made sure to show a bit of bicep. The camera followed. I moved to the right. The camera followed. This was too good to be true. I remembered: Amy.

'Amy, do you know that the red stripes mean blood? Arteries?'

'No, I didn't know that.'

'Yeah. In the day, barbers weren't just hair cutters. They pulled teeth and stuck leeches, amputated limbs, burned demons away by cupping. The colours signify blood-letting. Did you know that, Mainstream? Like magic. Me, the Barber, encourages the blood flow just as I encourage the flow of information. The white stripes are bandages. The blue for veins.'

'Mr Pool, what do you have to say to the people who think you're bonkers?'

'I'm doing it for the people. They'll thank me one day.'

Blobby guy fixed the camera on my face. Oh yes please. My chance to manifest a singular laser focus into the lens.

'I'm going to destroy your narrative, Mainstream.'

'Mr Pool, what narrative?'

'Your narrative. People want to and will drink from a new source.'

'Do you believe in science?"

'There's science and then there's science truth."

'What about facts?"

'There's your story, my story, then there are the facts. Time to leave, Mainstream.'

In the mirror: notice me. My body definition is A1. I don't even glance at the media puppet and her lapdog walking out.

'Dad? Jesus, what happened?'

Behind me, my boy, crunching over glass. School shirt untucked. Hair tied back.

'Don't blaspheme. No need for it, boy.'

'You okay?'

'Just a low-life. But I'm always winning, bud.'

'Are you online tonight?' He said, kicking the shards.

'Course. Always.'

'Can you... maybe, not mention me?'

'Why? Has someone said something?'

Those a-holes. Basement dwellers. I look up and down the street.

'My teacher asked about your new channel.'

'What'd he say?'

'She.'

'Toxic feminist?'

'No, no Dad. She's okay. Don't worry about it. Alright?'

'I'm doing this for you, mate.'

'I know. Please, Dad. See you at home. Love you.'

'Love you, too.' So much.

My barber doors are closing but the world is ready to burst wide open. The red, the white, the blue. The information bloodletting has begun. Listen to my live stream and let the truth sever the liars and the lies.

They are the disease, and we are the A1 cure.

THE UNIFORM

NATALIE CONYER

THEY CALL PROBATIONARY CONSTABLES *BAGGY-ARSES* BECAUSE new uniforms sag, but Jackie Rose didn't have that problem. She twisted her neck for a back view and from what she could see, her uniform fitted fine. A bit too fine, maybe. A little tight, but that was OK.

She'd only been wearing the uniform a month and didn't feel like she belonged in it yet. She kept checking everything was where it should be: the camera, the baton, the cuffs hanging from her belt. The holster for the Glock she'd collect at the start of her shift. All present and correct. She squared her shoulders. Here she was, a cop. A proper one. And she was going to be a good one.

They'd stationed her at Rose Bay, which covered an area stretching from Point Piper through Vaucluse to Watsons Bay. This was the beating heart of Sydney's rich belt. Here, the religion was real estate; mansions jostled to get at the Harbour and yachts bumped shoulders in marinas. The streets they patrolled were lined with high walls and hedges and were for the most part empty. Not a lot of action in Rose Bay. They were easing her in slowly, she thought, though they'd put her on nights and weekends. She'd heard rookies copped those shifts and she didn't mind. After all, this was just the beginning. She had big plans and you had to start somewhere.

Her partner was Mal McDonald, nickname obviously Macca. In his thirties, he kept himself in shape lifting weights. He had a gap between his two front teeth, shaved his head to hide his bald spot. He started off chatty.

'So,' he said, 'Constable Jacqueline Rose. Bright-eyed and bushy-tailed. What made you become a cop?'

'My dad was a cop.'

Macca's mouth fell open. 'Not – Stanton Rose?'

'Yup.'

'Fuck me.' He sat on this for a while. 'Big shoes to fill,' he said.

He was right. Stanton 'Rosie' Rose, Australian hero. Famous for many things, but most of all for what he did in the 80s, for cleaning up the Cross. Jackie was proud of him and wanted him to be proud of her. 'He's the reason I joined,' she said.

Macca pulled the sides of his mouth down, impressed.

Just after midnight on their third shift together, the radio came alive. *211 Vaucluse Road. Call from inside the house, husband violent, wife fears for her safety.*

Macca took the call. 'On our way.'

They were there in ten. They parked on the street and buzzed at a high wooden gate, Jackie noting the CCTV camera clocking them.

'Who's that?' Male voice, gruff.

'Police. We had a call from this address,' Macca said.

'A mistake.' The voice slurring.

'Nevertheless, sir, we've had a call. We have to investigate.' He was doing the right thing.

After a few seconds the buzzer sounded and the gate clicked open.

The house was wide and flat-roofed and spectacular. Lawns disappearing into darkness, the outline of treetops against a summer night, a high fence around a tennis court.

A man outlined by bright light leaned against the frame of the open front door.

Jackie heard Macca murmur, 'Shit!'

They walked up to him. He was drunk or high or both but coming down from it, his face sweaty, his striped tie loosened, his collar open.

Even so he radiated money and success. He held a phone in one hand and reached out with the other as if this was a meet and greet. His knuckles were smeared with something. Blood?

He peered at Macca's name tag. 'Good evening, Sergeant...McDonald? I'm Henry Vincent.'

'If we could just come in, sir?'

The immortal words, 'Do you know who I am?'

Jackie knew the face but couldn't place it. 'You're... in the government,' she said.

'I'm the Minister of Finance, petal.' Vincent chuckled, a private joke. 'I'm Minister of fucking Finance. Come in. Wife's had a bit of a fall.' He reeled aside to give them room to pass.

The house sloped down to the Harbour. They were on the top level, in a foyer in front of a wide flight of stairs. At the bottom of the stairs on a rucked-up Persian rug a woman half-sat, half-sprawled. She was young, blonde, slim, her hair in a tight pony tail. She wore black leggings, a pink T-shirt and Nike sneakers. She'd propped herself against the stairs and was trying without success to lift herself upright. She held the bottom of her T-shirt against her bloody mouth. Her right eye was shut and already swollen. Jackie ran down to her.

'Don't try to move, there might be damage. I'll call an ambulance.'

The woman used her good eye to see where her husband was. Jackie followed her gaze. Vincent stood at the top of the stairs, hand on the rail, staring down at them. Macca was next to him.

'No ambulance. She'll be fine,' Vincent said.

The woman drew breath, whimpered, lisped through bloody teeth. 'It was an accident.'

Jackie sat next to her, put an arm round her shoulder. 'You don't get hurt like that falling down stairs. He did this to you? Is he your husband?'

Tears streamed down her cheeks. 'Please...'

'He could have killed you.'

Again, the woman looked at her husband. He and Macca had turned away from them. Henry Vincent was clutching Macca's upper arm, speaking fiercely, softly, into Macca's ear, Macca leaning in.

'He could have killed you,' repeated Jackie. Her police training came to her. She said, 'Next time, he... listen, Mrs Vincent, we can get you out of here. We can find you somewhere safe.'

The woman lowered her T-shirt, ran her tongue over her bloody teeth, nodded more to herself than Jackie. 'OK,' she said, softly. 'OK. I...' she didn't finish the thought but straightened her spine, closed her eyes and said as if she'd practised the words many times, 'My name is Moira Vincent and I want to press charges against my husband.'

Macca was suddenly there, looming, big hands under Jackie's armpits, hauling her to her feet. 'We're off. It was an accident.'

Jackie tried to shake loose. 'No way. It wasn't. She says–'

'An accident.' Macca was strong and though Jackie was no lightweight, he lifted her off her feet as if she were a doll. He stood her up, kept his hands on her, brought his head so close she felt the heat of his breath.

'You with me? This woman and her husband were drinking. They got into an argument. She dialled 000, then she fell down the stairs.'

'No! In any case, we have to call an ambulance!' Again, Jackie tried to pull away, couldn't.

'Mr Vincent will see to medical treatment.' Macca kept his grip tight. He forced Jackie up the stairs, blocking her view so she couldn't look back at Moira Vincent.

Henry Vincent was still at the front door. Macca gave him a short nod and shoved Jackie forward so Vincent could close it behind them. Then he let her go and set off for the gate. Jackie, shaken at the speed of it all, didn't move.

'You coming or not? Or you plan on making your own way home?' A minute later, seeing she was still frozen. 'Who's in charge here?'

The rule was the junior cop drove so Jackie started the patrol car on autopilot, swung away from the kerb, made a U-turn. They'd gone a few hundred metres when she said, 'I have to take this further.'

Macca said, 'Pull over.'

They came to a stop. She kept her hands on the wheel.

'What? Go crying to the boss?' His head was turned towards her. A Moreton Bay Fig diffused the street light, striping his face.

She hadn't got that far, but it was the obvious next step. A wave of fury swept over her. She said, 'Damn right, I'm going to the boss. We left a seriously injured woman with her attacker–'

'It was an accident. I'm not even writing it up. And you're not going to say anything.'

'What did he give you? Money?'

He flung himself back in his seat, didn't answer.

'I'm going to make a complaint.'

Suddenly he relaxed, grinned, that gap between his front teeth. 'Try it.'

They drove back to the station in silence. She finished the shift, went home.

Jackie couldn't sleep. She couldn't stop thinking of Moira Vincent and how they'd left her. Next day she got to work early, when she knew the boss would still be there. The boss being Senior Sergeant Pappas, a swarthy old hand with a beard that needed shaving twice a day.

Pappas was bent over his desk, buried in paperwork. Jackie knocked on his open door. When he saw who it was his face blanked and she knew Macca had beaten her to it.

'Can I talk to you, Boss?'

He motioned her in.

He didn't offer her a seat so she stood, cap under her arm, ready to speak. Before she could he held up a palm in a stop sign.

'I heard what happened. I gotta say, Rose, I'm surprised at you.'

She was struck dumb. He sighed, ran a hand over his stubble, said, 'Sit.'

Finally. She pulled out the visitor's chair, perched. Pappas leaned his elbows on the papers on his desk, interlaced his fingers, rested his chin on his knuckles.

'Rose. You're not stupid and I get that you're keen. That's commendable. But you won't get anywhere by doing what you did last night.'

'Um, what do you mean?'

She could see he was getting annoyed. Quickly she repeated, 'I really don't know what you're talking about.'

He clicked his tongue. 'Sergeant McDonald came to me – he doesn't want this to go further, mind you – he felt he had to tell me you intimidated a witness.'

'I *what*?'

'Henry Vincent's wife. Drunk, had a fall. Told you it was an accident and you tried to persuade her to bring charges. Rose, I admire your feminist instincts–'

'Boss.' Jackie was standing now, rigid, clutching her cap in her hand. 'That's not what happened. Macca's lying. The husband bought him off somehow.' She knew she was going too far, couldn't stop herself.

Pappas' eyes went cold. 'You're a probationary constable who's been on the job five minutes. You're accusing a senior, experienced sergeant of accepting a bribe to conceal a crime?'

Jackie knew she'd already said too much. She kept her mouth shut.

Pappas sighed, heavily. He stretched his fingers down the skin of his cheeks. 'Rose,' he said, 'Sit. Some advice?'

She took her seat again, waited. Pappas' voice was kinder now. 'Look. When you're new it's easy to get things wrong. McDonald's been a cop for a long time. He's got a good rep and it's your word against his. As well as Vincent being a cabinet minister. The Minister of Finance, for Christ's sake! The Vincent family! Do you know who they are? Can you imagine the seventeen kinds of shit that'll hit the fan? Oh, my sweet Jesus.'

He screwed his eyes tight against the possibility, opened them wide. 'And think about this. No previous record of problems at that address. Plus, they'd been drinking. Even if the wife says he did it, he'll deny and his lawyers will crucify her in court. They'll crucify you too. Us as well, while they're at it.

'Now. Your options are to chalk this up to experience and move on, or proceed with your complaint. That's your right.' Here Pappas brought up a finger. 'But – and I'm telling you this for your own good, Rose – you'd be killing your career stone dead before it even started.'

'Boss–'

'Not finished yet. This is what we're going to do. You're taking the night off. Sick leave. You're going to have a long hard think about things and you're going to come back tomorrow when you're calmer and we'll discuss it then. OK?'

'Boss, she was hurt–'

'Rose. Did she or did she not tell you it was an accident?'

'Yes, but that was because she was scared of him.'

'Did you or did you not encourage her to lay charges?'

'I...'

Pappas stood, began to gather papers on his desk. 'Think very carefully. You're a promising young policewoman. Don't throw it away on something you don't understand. I'll see you tomorrow. Go home.'

Home was Glebe, had always been Glebe. Jackie was born there, went to school there, hadn't considered anywhere else. Until uni, she'd lived with her father. When she decided they needed space he suggested she take over a terrace he owned in Campbell Street, down the Broadway end. It was cold, dark, and needed skylights, but Jackie couldn't afford them.

Now she stood at the kitchen counter and looked out at her small courtyard. She'd been naive. She knew policing had grey areas, of course she did. But she hadn't imagined anything like this happening to her.

What to do? The obvious person to ask was her father. She didn't want to run to him with every little problem but this was something else, wasn't it? She took up the phone.

'Dad. You there? No, got the night off. Can I come over? I'll explain when I see you.'

Stanton Rose lived in a converted worker's cottage at the bottom of Glebe Point Road. Prime real estate now, with its view of Rozelle Bay.

She used her key. 'Dad? You there?'

'Come through.'

'Got a drink?' She joined him at the back of the house, which had at some stage been opened up as a living and eating area. She threw her bag on the dining table and sat heavily in one of the two cane chairs facing what was now a spectacular sunset.

He came over with a glass of white wine for her, a tumbler of scotch for himself. Stanton Rose was a big man, bluff, silver-haired and still in good shape. He wore elderly blue jeans, a chambray shirt tucked in. He sank into the chair next to her. 'What's up, Jacks?'

She told him what had happened. She found she had to work to stop her voice from quivering. 'I don't know what to do,' she said. 'If I make the complaint, that'll be the end of me as a cop. I might as well leave now. If I don't, then Moira Vincent keeps on getting beaten up until one day he kills her.

'I became a cop because I want to be on the side of justice. I want to make things right, like you did, Dad. And I want to be a good cop, like you were. If I don't raise the alarm now I'm failing that. I'm failing her. Shit, let's be honest, I failed her the moment I let Macca take me out of that house.'

She set her glass down on the floor next to her. 'It isn't *fair*, what Macca did. To me, as well as to her. *It isn't bloody fair!*'

Stanton emptied his drink, crunched an ice cube in his teeth. He walked over to the fridge, got more ice, more scotch – a big slug – came back. Sat down, said, 'Jackie, love, all due respect, but what fucking cloud have you been living on?'

That brought her up short. Her father didn't swear much, especially in front of her. 'I don't understand.'

'You're behaving like a child. It's not *fair*, it's not *fair*. Boohoo.' He knuckled a cheek like a crying toddler.

She was shocked into silence.

He stared at the purple and pink evening, choosing his words. 'Jacks, I know you want to be a good cop. That's what I wanted, too. And I was one, a good cop. I got justice. But I didn't do it by barging in like a crusader. That's not how it works, especially not for whistle-blowers. Pappas is right. If you make a complaint then unless you've got rock-hard evidence plus management on your side, you're stuffed. For good. What you have to do is find another way, and it's not always the nicest way.'

He sculled his drink. 'When they sent me to the Cross, I went in as a sergeant. I was undercover, working for the Feds. I did it because I believed in it. Still do. In the long run, the outcomes were worth it. But to get results, I had to cross lines, do things.'

'What do you mean, *do things*?'

'We knew the cops at the Cross were rotten. We knew they were hand in glove with the real crims but not how the scams worked. I had to learn their secrets and the only way to do that was to become one of them. So I rubbed shoulders with Hakem and Fowler and Saffron and I got brown paper bags full of money and stood over people and verballed witnesses and went to nightclubs and got the same hookers they did.' He shrugged. 'I wasn't proud of it but I had my eye on the long game.'

'You gave the money back, didn't you?'

He looked at her, irritated. 'I was on a cop's salary. How do you think I could afford to buy the house you live in now?' He shook his head in disgust. 'You can't always be lily white. There have to be some perks.'

'Why didn't you tell me this before?'

'I didn't think I had to spell it out. Jesus! You want a lesson in real life? Listen to this. To get those guys, we had to start small. We had to crack the little players and get them to name bigger players and so on. And the first guy, I didn't nail him for being bent. He was having an affair. None of my business but that's what I used to threaten him with. He topped himself not long after. He wasn't the only one. You think that made me happy?'

He got up again, poured scotch, splashed a little on to the dining table, wiped it up with the palm of his hand.

'Would I do it all again? Certainly. We cleaned up the force, *my* force, stopped it from being a laughing stock. Did I do it by the book? No, I didn't. I couldn't have. The Feds knew all about it, by the way. They turned a blind eye because they wanted things right at the other end.

'Did I benefit? Definitely. Paid off this place, made you financially secure. Bought the Campbell Street house. Helped my reputation, too. Got the Cross of Valour, got promotion. Someone wrote a book about me. I'm a TV consultant now.

'You want to be a good cop, Jackie? You want to be more than someone who works a shift and takes a second job? Then think about what you're prepared to do. If you're strong enough to go that route.'

When Jackie got to work the next day Pappas was waiting. 'I've decided not to proceed with the complaint,' she said.

'Good move.'

She turned to go but he called her back. 'Some changes,' he said. 'McDonald's transferring to Homicide. He's taking a few days off before he starts.'

Macca's reward. Not money after all, or not just money. Henry Vincent pulling strings to get him where he wanted to go. Pappas waited for Jackie to comment and when she didn't he added, 'I'm putting you with Durst.'

Her punishment. Payback for making a fuss. Wally Durst – no need for a nickname, the first name said it all – was the station joke, a fat, farting wreck of a man who did as little as possible. Nobody wanted to work with him. Jackie felt a flame of anger, tamped it, said, 'I'll go find him.'

The next month passed uneventfully. The schedule churned and she and Wally were on night shift again when the call came in, same address and almost the same time as before. *211 Vaucluse Road.* From inside the house.

It took them longer to get there because Jackie had to wake Wally up. He was still dozy when they arrived, said, 'You take it, Rose. Lemme know if you need me.' Not the first time Wally had left her alone. So much for the rule about going in pairs.

She buzzed the gate. It rolled aside and, clutching her baton, she made her way down the path. The front door was open as before but this time it was Moira Vincent, standing quietly, waiting. Jackie came close, couldn't tell if Moira recognised her or not.

She knew more about them now, Moira and Henry Vincent. The Vincent family was old-money rich. Henry was the favoured son and he was going places. State cabinet at the moment, but eyes set on Canberra. Moira was Henry's second wife, the trophy one. He'd lifted her out of her PR firm and now she was one of the staples of Sydney's social scene.

Tonight she wore olive green pants and a silky black top. A small black messenger bag, just large enough for phone and lipstick, was slung across her body. Her makeup was overdone, eyes ringed with kohl, foundation thick but not thick enough to hide the cut across her eyebrow and the bruise at her throat.

She said, 'This way.' Jackie followed her down the staircase they'd been on last time, through a huge living area and on to a deck made of concrete, a single slab engineered to look as if it floated in the sky. The effect was emphasised by a low, clear glass railing. There were chairs, tables, an outdoor bar.

Moira walked to the railing at the edge of the deck and bent her head. Jackie followed her gaze. Down below, on a concrete path leading to a harbour mooring, lay a man in a dark suit. He was on his stomach, jacket flared and one arm flung out. The area was lit up and he looked like he was on stage.

'I think he's dead,' Moira said, eerily in control. Or in shock? Jackie didn't have time to check.

'How do I get there?'

Moira showed her and Jackie, with a strong sense of *deja vu*, found herself pounding down stairs again. She reached the man. His head was turned to one side. Henry Vincent, in a small pool of blood. She felt his neck. No pulse. This was the first dead person she'd seen, never mind touched. But they'd covered death in her training.

She lifted one of his arms, put the back of her hand against a cheek. Then she sat on her haunches and looked around her, made her way back to the deck.

'What happened?'

'I need to sit down,' Moira said, pointing to an outdoor table and chairs. She settled in one, her hands in her lap. Jackie angled another to face it.

'We were having a drink,' Moira said. 'One moment he was looking at the water, the next...' she flapped a hand out to the ether.

'When was this?'

'Got a smoke? I wasn't allowed.'

'Sorry, no. Mrs Vincent...

'Moira. My name's Moira.'

'Moira. Tell me in detail what happened.'

Moira raised her head, met Jackie's eyes, blinked. She seemed to focus properly for the first time. Her face too open, her voice too lilting, she said, 'Henry and I were out. We came home late. We were having a drink. He walked to the railing, leaned over... then he was gone. Just like that.'

'And you were here when it happened?'

A slight falter. 'Yes, sure, I told you. I was having a drink with him. I couldn't believe it. I called the police.'

Jackie kept her gaze on Moira. She said, 'I need to clear something up. You say your husband was holding a drink when he went over?'

Moira flicked hair over her shoulder, 'That's what having a drink means, doesn't it?'

'It's just that I didn't see a glass down there, or even pieces of one. Could have missed it, of course, and they might find it later when they go over the crime scene. It's a small thing ...' she leaned forward, elbows on her knees. 'The bigger thing's this. That body down there, it's cooling. Rigor mortis is setting in. Know what that means?'

'No, I don't, but I'm sure you'll explain it.'

'It means your husband's been lying there a good few hours. Which means you didn't phone us until long after he went over. So why don't you tell me what really happened?'

Moira stilled. Behind her black-rimmed eyes, calculations were taking place, odds against odds. After what seemed a long time, she said, 'You were the cop who came before, weren't you? You saw how he hurt me then. You were there and you did nothing. You left me with him. After you went, you know what he did? He beat me up for phoning you. Gave me two broken ribs.' She lifted her top and turned aside so Jackie could see the yellowing bruises, covered them again, rearranged herself.

'And this...' she touched her eyebrow, her neck. 'These are from last night.'

Jackie sat forward. 'They'll take what you went through into consideration.'

Moira's control cracked. Her face twitched, undid itself, broke open. She spat out, '*Take into consideration?* That's – that's not good enough. If the Vincents think I killed him– They'll... I'll lose everything. After what I've been through!

'You have to help me!' she wailed. 'You *owe* me!'

'Tell me what happened.'

Moira spoke haltingly, slowly at first and then faster as she went on. 'I went out to lunch. When I got home I saw Henry's car so I could tell he was here. I came in carefully because I never know – knew – what sort of mood he'd be in. He was at the railing, leaning on it. He must have heard something, me behind him, something like that – he, he sort of jerked in surprise and next thing he went over the railing, just like I said.'

She touched fingers to her mouth. 'I looked over, down at him and he was still moving. He tried to– I watched until it stopped, until it was all over. I had to be sure because if I wasn't...' her voice trailed off and she began to cry.

Was Moira telling the truth? There was no way of knowing. What if she'd found Henry as she claimed, come up from behind, and pushed? If she had, what difference would it make? She thought about Macca, about her father. What was the right thing to do? What did the uniform demand of her?

She took in Moira, her eyebrow, her neck. She leaned in to Moira, who was sobbing for real now, mascara-laden tears coursing down her cheeks.

'Listen to me,' Jackie said. 'Listen!' She clicked her fingers in front of Moira's face to get her attention.

'You can't tell them you came home late because they'll check your alibi. Besides, the camera outside records who comes and goes, and when. You have to say you came back when you did. Tell them you couldn't see Henry although his car was here. You didn't think much of it. You fell asleep and when you woke up he still hadn't appeared. You started to worry, went looking, found him, checked on him, phoned us. Got that?'

Moira began to wipe her cheeks. Jackie reached for her hand and stopped her, 'No, stop. You need to look wrecked.' She repeated, 'Do you understand what you have to say?'

Moira nodded. She took deep, hiccoughing breaths.

'Ok. My partner's in the car outside. I'm going to get him in here and then we'll call Homicide. Ready?'

She took up her radio and waited till Wally, snuffling, came to consciousness. 'Wally! I need you in here now!'

Eventually Wally shambled in. Homicide arrived, in the form of Macca McDonald and another, smaller detective. Jackie wondered if Macca had chosen the case. He looked grim, surveyed the scene, barely listened to her report. The smaller detective, who paid more attention, turned out to be his boss. It was Henry Vincent, after all. This was going to be huge and the big guns were lining up.

Moira repeated what Jackie had told her. Jackie could see Macca was suspicious, but what could he say? After all, no formal record of any trouble at this address, no real reason for doubt.

Forensics came, and called the Homicide guys down to the body. Wally and Jackie were delegated to stay with Moira. Wally went outside for a smoke. Moira and Jackie sat next to each other on the sofa, waiting. There was an awkward silence.

'Thanks,' said Moira, eventually, fiddling with her small messenger bag. She reached into the bag, took out a tagged key, put it in Jackie's hand and closed her fingers round it. 'I mean it. Take this.'

'What is it?'

'My gym locker. It's at *Fit Forever* in Double Bay. I've been saving. Cash, some Krugerrands, jewellery. Nothing traceable.'

Jackie hadn't caught up. 'What do you want me to do with it?'

'Take it. It's yours. I've got all this now.' She waved vaguely at the room. Jackie said, 'I can't...'

The smaller detective, the Inspector, hove into view. 'Mrs Vincent,' he said, 'sorry for your loss. We'll need a statement.'

Outside, the street was a media frenzy. This was big news and Jackie and Wally battled a phalanx of microphones, camera booms, TV vans, even helicopters droning overhead. On the outer fringes Jackie heard a small dark-haired presenter speaking to a camera. She said, 'rumours concerning Mrs Vincent's relationship with restaurant mogul Allan Ignatius...'

Jackie broke stride momentarily, continued walking. Too late now.

By the time she got back to Glebe it was full daylight. She was bone tired. She unlocked her front door and went through to the kitchen. It was gloomy, but skylights would fix that.

She took off her uniform and laid it out, ready for her next shift.

SHOCK WAVES

ASHLEY KALAGIAN BLUNT

'*HAJOGHUTYUN*,' LEVON SAID TO HAGOP AT 1:57 AM ON THE morning of 23 November 1986. *Good luck*. The men's friendship stretched back years.

By week's end, Levon would be charged with Hagop's murder.

Newspaper accounts would later describe Levon as 'well nourished', 'aged about 35', and of 'Middle Eastern appearance' with a heavy accent. 'Ethnic'. Also, an Australian citizen. They didn't describe his full-moon face, his bushy moustache, the tight dark curls styled like a helmet. They didn't describe the way he kept his shoes shined to reflective perfection, or the way his rounded shoulders alluded to his life's burdens.

'*Hajoghutyun*,' Levon repeated, leaning out the car window on a side street in Prahran, the city asleep around them.

Not that his friend would need it. They'd planned everything to the last detail.

Hagop lifted a hand in a casual wave as he pulled away from the kerb. Levon watched the white Holden Torana head north, towards 44 Caroline Street.

Towards the Turkish consulate.

'It all goes back to Gourgen Yanikian,' Levon said. As the Torana's brake lights shrank up the road, Levon sought his son's face in the rear-view mirror. It was time he learned. Time he understood. This was why they were here, in the middle of the night, far away from home and homeland. The branches of the plane trees that lined the street quivered in the wind. A chunk of moon cast weak shadows.

'He was a survivor, you understand. Listen, this is important. In the 1960s, more and more of the world was recognising the Jewish Holocaust. Good news not only for the Jewish people, but for all of humanity, yes. Were we foolish to expect the same? It was Medz Yeghern, the Great Crime of the First World War, that laid the blueprints for the destruction of Europe's Jews. And where is our recognition? Still today the Turkish government denies the Great Crime ever happened!' Levon smacked the steering wheel with his palm, hard.

'Many of us, we are fed up of this. It's a sick, rotting feeling, this lack of justice. It eats away at your guts. Yanikian felt it, of course he did. He was born in Erzurum, at that time part of the Ottoman Empire. His birth came during years of great hatred, bloodshed in the streets and fires set to Armenian homes and businesses. Yanikian's family fled to save themselves. A wise decision. But later, they returned in hopes of retrieving their possessions, and young Yanikian witnessed two Turkish men murder his older brother.'

He had told his son all this before, of course, whispering into his ear as he cradled him to sleep. He wished he could have introduced his son to Yanikian. He'd never met the man, but he lived in his mind, that great sloping forehead, nose like half an avocado, arched eyebrows that remained pitch black, while his snowy hair reached his jacket collar. Levon wished he could have shaken Yanikian's bear-paw hand, just once. To thank him.

'Those years are known as the Hamidian massacres – three hundred thousand dead, and they didn't think the Turks would come for the rest of them? No, no, of course they did. But where could they go? The ones who could leave did, the young men, seeking livelihoods abroad. Journeymen, they were –'

He clamped his mouth abruptly. The headlights of a police sedan stung his eyes as it approached from the opposite direction. He pulled a street directory from the passenger seat, dropped his face into its open pages.

The police car slowed. Levon tensed.

What could they have on him? A fist of anger hardened in his guts. As if his struggle had anything to do with these sun-bleached Australians in their uniforms, men who led comfortable lives knowing nothing of what his people had suffered.

The headlights washed over him. The sedan glided past.

Levon waited. As the police car faded out of sight, he counted to ten.

'Where were we?' He flashed his teeth, a hard smile. 'Ah yes, journeymen. Yanikian left too, of course. He was studying engineering at the University of Moscow when the First World War broke out, Germany allied with the Ottomans, Europe in chaos. Twenty years old, he joined the Russian army and ended up back in Erzurum. There he found the ruins of his family's business, the dead bodies. He lost much of his family in the Great Crime. Like our own family. The men conscripted, then shot. Gendarmes packed the women, children, and elderly into cattle cars. They took thousands by the boatful to be drowned in the Black Sea. They barricaded people inside our churches and set them alight. But mostly, they marched our people into the punishing sun to starve. Even today, you can sink your hands into the sands of northern Syria and bring up bone fragments.'

'Yanikian survived. Finished his education. Moved to Tehran, made a fortune building railroads, then emigrated to California. Life was good, but how could he forget his family? His brother? Memory tortures survivors. They can never live in peace. And then the Turkish government spews their denials.' Acid edged Levon's voice. 'So Yanikian came up with a plan.

'He contacted the Turkish consulate in Los Angeles and claimed he was Iranian. He said a famous painting had come into his possession. This painting had been stolen from the Ottoman sultan's palace in Istanbul a hundred years earlier. Yanikian wanted to return it to the Turkish government, but only if the consul general, Mehmet Baydar, would meet him in person. They arranged to meet at The Biltmore Santa Barbara. Baydar didn't drive, so the vice consul escorted him. Bahadir Demir, his name was.'

Levon twisted his wrist, checking his watch. The second hand seemed to drag towards the next phase of their plan. But it was a new battery. They had really thought of everything.

'It was 27 January, 1973. Years before you were born, my son! Yanikian was a 78-year-old man, white-haired, with a head like a grizzly bear. Baydar and Demir went to his room, believing they were to receive the long-lost painting from an Iranian emigrant. Imagine their faces when Yanikian revealed he was an Armenian, a survivor of the Great Crime! He opened a hollowed-out book and retrieved a Luger. These men believed they were above justice. Yet here it was, come to cut them down.

'And what did Yanikian do, as the two men lay bleeding onto the fine carpet of The Biltmore Santa Barbara? Did he flee? Did he go into hiding? No. He picked up the phone, called hotel reception, and announced that he had killed two evils. Then he took a seat on the patio, under the bright rays of the California sun, and waited for the police.

'It had always been his intention to surrender, you understand. He was re-enacting a great act of justice from five decades earlier, one of the most important chapters in the modern day story of Armenia. That of Soghomon Tehlirian.

'I know you know his name. Another young man who survived the genocide, who witnessed terrible crimes committed against his mother, his sister. After a vicious attack by the Turks, Tehlirian awoke in a pile corpses, left to rot. And yet he restarted his life. This is the resilience of our people! We have faced the very worst of humanity and still we are here, forcing the world to remember us.'

Forcing the world by all means necessary, Levon thought. Sixty years had passed, and nothing else had worked. His people ought to be grateful for the valour of men like himself. Instead, too many of them eschewed their methods.

'In 1921, Tehlirian moved to Berlin, took up engineering studies. But then he made a shocking discovery. One of the leaders of the fallen Ottoman Empire, a primary architect of the destruction ravaged upon the Armenian people, was living in Berlin. This despite the man being sentenced to death in absentia by a military tribunal for those very crimes. The Germans had helped the Ottoman leader escape, and here he was, strolling the streets of Berlin as though he were any ordinary man.'

A man and a boy, about his son's age, approached a car parked a little further along the road, the man carrying a jerry can, shifting it from hand to hand. Levon turned his face as they passed. Later, the boy would be a key prosecution witness at the Victorian Supreme Court. All because he remembered two digits from a number plate.

Levon rechecked the time. By now, Hagop would have parked the Torana at 44 Caroline Street. The work would only take a few minutes. He squeezed the hard plastic of the steering wheel, his knuckles cracking.

'Soghomon Tehlirian could not live knowing this profoundly evil man, who had been sentenced to death by a military tribunal, was walking the streets. He acquired a gun, and in the broadest of daylight, killed the Turk with one clean shot. Tehlirian surrendered to the German police. He went to trial.

'And this trial!' Levon grew animated, palms raised, a hint of delight in his voice. 'He told the judge openly, "I have killed a man. But I am not a murderer." The court heard eyewitness testimony of the Armenian bloodshed during the years of the Great War. The trial made international news! It was not the trial of one man killing another, but a showcase of how a key perpetrator of one of the greatest crimes against humanity had finally been brought to justice. The verdict came back. Not guilty. Tehlirian was set free.

'And this, my son, this is what Yanikian envisioned when he invited the Turkish consul and vice consul to his room at The Biltmore Santa Barbara and, without hesitation or remorse, shot them dead.'

It was time to drive. If they'd planned it right, Levon would turn off Toorak Road onto Caroline Street just as Hagop exited the underground car park.

In six minutes, the bomb would go off.

But that wasn't the plan.

Clenching the gearshift, Levon shifted out of park. He signalled, then pulled smoothly onto Williams Road, heading from Prahran towards South Yarra. At 2.10 am on a Sunday morning, only the occasional vehicle appeared on the roads. Melbourne was asleep.

'People say the Turkish men didn't deserve to die because they weren't alive during the years of the genocide. Rubbish! Demir and Baydar chose to work for that government, chose to perpetuate its lies. They could have had honest careers selling encyclopedias or fixing carburettors, or opened a restaurant like I did. If the genocide had begun in 1973, they would have signed the papers that opened the prison doors and armed the convicts, on the condition those convicts murdered as many Armenians as they could find.'

'Baydar was a man with a wife and children. Yes, yes, but his wife and children went on with their lives. You know what the Turkish gendarmes did to pregnant Armenian women? Never mind. You're too young for such things. The point is that to Yanikian, the pair he shot were not men. They were instruments of the unredressed and ongoing injustice committed against our people. He would go to trial, like Tehlirian in 1921. The death of Demir and Baydar was merely the beginning. Yanikian's grander purpose was to demand justice for the Armenian genocide.'

A red light stopped them, the engine idling quietly. A friend who happened to be a mechanic had gone over the Commodore back in Sydney, topped up the oil, checked the tyre pressure. With all respect to his heroes, Yanikian and Tehlirian, Levon had no intention of surrendering to the Victorian police.

That strategy hadn't worked out so well for Yanikian.

'Time was slogging on, you see. The genocide began in 1915, under the cover of the First World War. By the 1970s, there were fewer and fewer survivors every year. Whether or not you agreed with Yanikian's actions – and many foolish people didn't, mind you – we all had hope that his trial would show the world the historic proof of the genocide.

'But the court didn't agree. Regardless, Yanikian followed in Tehlirian's footsteps. He made no attempt to deny that he had shot the two men. Instead, he took the stand in his defence. His testimony takes up six hundred pages of the trial transcript – I've read them! Throughout everything he'd achieved in his life, the desire for justice for the Armenian people burned at the centre of his soul. He spoke to the court about the twenty-six members of his family who died at the hands of Turkish gendarmes, at the whim of government officials. And what did the court do? Did they acquit him of all charges as with Tehlirian in 1921?

'No! No. Gourgen Yanikian was sentenced to life in prison.'

The speedometer was creeping up, street lamps flashing past. Levon eased his foot off the pedal.

'Still, he rose above the pettiness of the so-called justice system. He rose above his corporeal existence. He declared that he was not Gourgen Yanikian. He was long-denied history returning to claim the bones of one and a half million murdered Armenians.'

Levon pulled the car alongside the kerb across from 44 Caroline Street. Atop the five-storey building, the Turkish flag hung from its pole, flapping in the breeze.

Any moment now, Hagop would stride out of the underground car park, hands in his pockets, the white Holden Torana and its four kilograms of gelignite left to detonate later that day.

'And that is how we came to be here today, my son. Yanikian sent a press release to the Armenian media, explaining his personal war on the evil perpetuated by the Turkish government. He sent individual letters as well, urging others to take action in order to focus world attention on the injustice of the denied genocide. The world has no benevolence. It has no inherent morals. It is up to us to change the course of history before it is too late.'

Levon squinted, twisting his watch face to catch the faint light of the streetlamp. 2:15 am. Hagop was late. Only by a minute, but a minute was a long time when every detail was planned.

No cause for concern, Levon thought. Bad luck with traffic lights could explain the delay.

'We began with the name The Prisoner Gourgen Yanikian Group.' He spoke quietly, with an edge of agitation, his hands tense on the wheel as the engine idled. 'Our allegiances are evident. We have been operating for more than a decade, and are active all around the world.'

His eyes sought the rear-view mirror again, with its lonely view of the empty backseat. His son was not there, of course. He would be sound asleep in his bed in Sydney, dreaming of monster trucks or Super Mario Bros, his current obsessions. Even getting the boy to commit to his Armenian language studies was a daily fight. Nine years old and already he spoke with an Australian accent. But one day Levon would tell him of this night, and the months of planning that went into it. One day, his son would feel their history pulsing in his veins, and look upon Levon as an unknown hero of the Armenian people.

He glanced at his watch, then clamped a thick palm over it, squeezing his wrist, refusing to acknowledge his rising concern. Where was Hagop?

He opened his mouth, trying to distract himself. 'One day –'

The blast drowned his voice. The car rocked, tilting onto the passenger-side tyres before crashing back to the bitumen with a violent impact that jarred Levon's spine. Shattered glass and debris clattered against the Commodore.

Levon pulled his hands from his face. He didn't remember clamping them there. He shook his head, once, twice, but the high-pitched whine in his ears continued. A spiderweb crack spread across the windscreen. He flung the car door open, unsteady on his feet.

Debris littered the street. Tree branches, chunks of concrete, glittering glass, twisted rebar. A brassy alarm blared. Acrid smoke drew his attention to a fire, in what looked to be a neighbouring shop, its plate-glass window now a gaping hole.

The five-storey building was still standing. Curtains hung out its destroyed windows, flapping in the wind.

Hagop. Where was he? They needed to leave, and quickly. Levon could hear nothing but the high-pitched whine in his ears and underscoring that, the blare of an alarm, but soon there would be sirens.

The flames grew, the smoke coiling up towards the Turkish flag. Levon found himself gripping the Commodore's wing mirror.

Where was Hagop? The bomb going off now likely meant he had made an error in setting the trigger mechanism. The horror of it filled Levon. He needed to get out of there before –

Suddenly there was movement in the building. Hagop! Maybe? The main entrance door opened inward, and something must have been blocking it. The person tugged at it, and the door opened inch by inch.

Levon ought to help. He released the wing mirror and took an uncertain step. His knee buckled and he almost went down.

The person continued to struggle with the door. Finally it opened enough for them to squeeze through.

First came a slender leg. Then an arm, a torso.

'*Yes aystegh yem*,' Levon called. I am here. He couldn't hear his own voice.

It was a young woman, blood on her arms and face, a tear in her trousers. She swung her head frantically, arms raised as if to ward off blows, then bolted away from the building, towards a nearby laneway.

Had she seen Levon well enough to describe him?

He couldn't worry about that now. Where was Hagop? They couldn't wait much longer. The police were certainly on their way. Levon stumbled across the street, poorly navigating the glass and debris, thinking of his son, safe in bed, oblivious to what Levon was doing for him. What he might have sacrificed.

Making it to the wedged-open door, he saw the knocked-over filing cabinets that had blocked it. '*Im ynker*,' he called inside, careful not to use Hagop's name. *My friend.*

Hagop should not have been inside the building itself. But then, the bomb should not have gone off for hours, not until he and Levon were far away from Melbourne.

The smoke choked him, and he backed away into the street, wiping his watering eyes. When he pulled his arm from his face, he saw it.

A solitary man's black dress shoe lay near the car park entrance.

No. No, it couldn't be. They had prepared too carefully. Hagop couldn't have made such a terrible mistake. Levon bent toward the shoe. Was that a fine polish reflecting the weak light, or wet blood?

The squall of sirens came closer.

Levon couldn't force himself toward the shoe. He turned his back to it, jogging to the open door of the Commodore and collapsing into the driver's seat. The key waited in the ignition and he struggled with it, his hand not gripping it properly, the key jamming. Maybe the car wouldn't start. Maybe he would be sitting here, a lone Armenian man outside the Turkish consulate, the Commodore's starter screeching in protest, when the police arrived.

But then the engine turned over. Levon shifted the car into drive. Hagop's death meant unanticipated evidence – the thought made him howl, a guttural sound that descended into a sob. Where there should have been glory, there was the shame of failure, and evasion. He would return to Sydney. He would dispose of the 174 sticks of gelignite he had stored in the restaurant. He would book a flight to Beirut. Maybe his wife and son would accompany him.

Maybe not.

In the rear-view mirror, the shoe lay on its side, laces untied. The sirens grew louder.

Author's Note: This is a fictionalised retelling of true events. All facts are drawn from newspaper coverage written at the time of the bombing. Levon Demirian, the co-conspirator of the 1986 South Yarra bombing, was convicted of the murder of Hagop Levonian, in addition to conspiracy. He received a sentence of life imprisonment for murder, and ten years for the conspiracy charge. On appeal, his murder conviction was overturned. After serving ten years in prison in Victoria, he returned to Sydney. To my knowledge, Demirian did not have children.

I KNOW WHERE YOU GO TO, MY LOVELY

JEAN BEDFORD

THE CASE CAME TO ME THROUGH IAN MCNEATH, MY ON-AGAIN, off-again lover. He was a detective in Nowra and I lived in Sydney, so our on-again periods were necessarily brief and infrequent. But I'd taken a few weeks R&R and I was spending part of it at a cottage I'd rented at Shoal Village on the coast near Nowra. McNeath was mostly staying there, too, with occasional forays to his flat in town to get clean shirts and underwear. I suppose we were trying it out – whether the relationship had legs, as he would have said. So far, apart from his atrocious cop working hours, it had been positively idyllic. We'd gone for long moonlight walks along the beach, barbecued chops and sausages on the sandy grass lawn, often to an audience of pelicans, and made love on a mattress we dragged onto the verandah under the stars.

After about a week of this, McNeath was starting to hum refrains from the oldies and goldies that were stacked near the stereo in the living room and the sentimental lyrics were beginning to get into my own synaptic rhythms as well. The owners of the cottage were great Bing Crosby fans, and honeymoon seemed to rhyme with June on an almost atavistic level. I was tempted to drive into Nowra and buy some Guns 'n' Roses tapes, just to clear the air of all the romantic glug, but I didn't. Scratch the most cynical of us and there's a drooling softy underneath, it seems, just waiting to snuggle up and be somebody's cuddle-pie. We did a lot of that too.

So it was almost a relief when McNeath didn't appear for two nights because of a stakeout. It gave me a chance to regain some of my hard-won emotional independence. Sure.

When he did turn up he was exhausted and unshaven, with new lines of fatigue running down his craggy Scottish-Australian face, and shadows under his startling eyes. I found myself humming 'Blue eyes, My baby's got blue eyes' before I knew it, and started laughing.

'What?' he said, smiling tiredly.

'Nothing. I'll make you a sandwich if you like, while you have a shower.'

I scraped together all the leftovers in the fridge and put them between two hunks of bread, then made two strong gin and tonics. I took them out to the deck and sipped at my drink while I waited. The moon was waning now, but still rising early above the sea and large enough to send its gold ripples down to the estuary in front of me. It was late summer, just blending into autumn – my favourite time of year – and the nights were turning cool enough for a cardigan to be slung over my T-shirt.

'So – did you get him?' I asked when he came out smelling fresh and deodorized and bent over my neck to kiss me.

'Nah.' He took a swig of his drink and stared out at the moonlit sea. 'Some fucker tipped him off, I reckon. Hasn't been home for days.' He made a disgusted sound and picked up his sandwich. 'What's in this? Smells great.'

'A little bit of everything, including last Sunday's tandoori chicken.'

'It's terrific.' His mouth was full, but he tried a lopsided grin. 'Especially the whole chilli I just swallowed. Shit.' He practically drained the rest of his glass in one go, then bit into the rest of the sandwich. I could see he was still preoccupied with what he'd been doing the last few days, back to being a cop first and foremost. *The honeymoon's over*, I thought and was aware of a definite lightening of spirits. I really did value that certain distance that was usually between us.

'Oh, I forgot to ask,' he said. 'Did that woman ring? Anderson, or Sanderson?'

'No. No one rang. Who is she?'

He looked sheepish. 'Look, I know you're on holiday, Anna, but–'

'Oh, no.' I gave a groan that was only partly genuine. Was I secretly a bit bored with my vacation? I wondered. 'You arsehole, McNeath. What is it?'

'Missing person.' He ducked the half-hearted slap I aimed at him. 'She's been hassling for weeks, but MP's done everything they can with no result. She got as far as Homicide today, but there's nothing we can do without the scent of a body. She asked me if I knew a private investigator. Well, I do. You don't have to take her on – I just wanted to get her off my back.'

He grabbed my fisted hand and pulled me onto his knees. A few hours later he gave me the background to it, and the next day Ramona Sanderson rang.

I met her in a coffee lounge near where she worked in Nowra. She wasn't at all what I'd expected a Ramona to look like (something dark and smouldering) but was small and ice-blonde, with pointed, cat-like features. She was somewhere in her mid-twenties, I guessed, dressed casual-chic in leggings and a big shirt and wearing very high-heeled strappy black sandals. Her make-up was post-modernist vamp, loads of eyeliner and sharply defined plum-red lipstick against a matt-white face.

When she'd ordered a coffee, I got out my notebook and pen. I gave her the usual preliminaries – what I charged, how I had to work within the law and cooperate with the police, etcetera, and she made an impatient, brushing-away gesture.

'Yeah, that's all okay. Do I have to sign something?'

Her voice was surprisingly deep and resonant and I wondered if she was a singer as well as an office manager, which was what she'd told me on the phone.

'Well, I didn't bring any contracts with me. I'm on holiday. It'll have to be a verbal agreement, if that's all right?'

She gave a brusque little wave again and shrugged. It obviously didn't occur to her to apologise for interrupting my holiday.

'Did that cop tell you anything about it?'

I was starting to dislike her, but then I thought the rudeness might be covering her fear. It was hard to read any emotion into that geisha face.

'I know that your boyfriend's been missing for nearly three months; that he was last seen leaving a pub here in town; he was driving his ute and neither he nor the car have been seen since. Missing Persons have agreed to let me see the file if I take the case on. They say there are no leads – they haven't found any sightings of him or the car anywhere in the state and interstate bulletins haven't produced anything, either.'

'What do you mean, *if* you take the case on? I thought that was organised.' She chewed at a fingernail, and a tear slid slowly down her face. I realised she was holding herself in very hard.

'I have to tell you that there's not much I can do that the police haven't already done,' I said. 'I can go over the same ground, look at the file, see if there's something they might have missed – but they're pretty good at this. Unless there's some element they don't know about?' I paused to give her time to add anything, but she shook her head.

'Also,' I went on, 'I *am* supposed to be on holiday.' But it was a weak protest; I was already intrigued by her blank-faced misery.

I sighed. 'Okay, consider me hired. I'll give it a couple of days, but unless I can come up with a fresh angle, any more'd be wasting your money. How about you tell me all you can? Everything you told the police, and anything else I can think of to ask.'

We went through the usual background questions. Marty Rix was twenty-eight years old. He'd been a bit of a drifter, never settling anywhere until recently, taking odd jobs gardening and building. He'd lived with Ramona for eighteen months and they were talking about settling down, having babies. Her parents had agreed to stake him in a small landscaping business if they got married.

'He was excited about it,' she said stubbornly. 'The cops tried to insinuate he'd just taken off, couldn't face being tied down, but I know him. I was going to help him with the business, do the accounts and that. We'd made the down payment on a couple of acres out of town – we were going to build a house. He'd always wanted to build a house.'

The tears were coming thick and fast now but she made no effort to wipe them away and grey streaks of mascara ran through her white make-up. I fished in my bag for a tissue and handed it to her. She stared at it then started to rub vigorously at her face.

'Tell me about him,' I said. 'Marty. What was – *is* – he like?'

She took a photo from her flat leather wallet. It showed a tall, blonde young man, with an open, tanned face and long shining hair. He was grinning into the sun, his eyes squinted up slightly. He was wearing cut-off denim shorts and a singlet. He looked happy.

'He had a rotten childhood,' she said slowly. 'Foster homes, institutions, all that crap. A bit of abuse here and there. But he rose above it. He had optimism. He wasn't a drifter out of choice, he was always looking for somewhere to settle, somewhere he could make a home and put down roots. It's what he'd wanted most in the world – someone to love who loved him. Some security. A family. He'd found it here, with me. My parents really loved him, too. He was like the son they never had. He said it over and over – that for the first time ever he felt he *belonged* somewhere. He was *happy*. He *was*.'

She was talking about him in the past tense. 'You think he's dead?' I asked softly.

The tears spilled over again and then she was sobbing, her face in her hands, the tissue a shredded mess. I handed her another one and waited.

'He was a lovely man,' she said finally. 'Yes I think he's dead – I know he wouldn't just disappear. I know it.'

She went to the loo and came back with her make-up repaired, only a slight redness round the eyes marring her careful mask. I told her I'd look at what the police had and ring her if I thought of anything more to ask. She nodded and walked out of the café, her back straight and her shoulders back. I'd completely reversed my first impression and now thought she was terrific, a gutsy young woman.

I'd made an appointment with a detective from Missing Persons and I went straight to the police station, peering into doorways to see if McNeath was on the premises. He didn't appear to be.

Lieutenant Charlie Rose was slim and boyish, and looked too young to be a policeman at all, let alone a plainclothes D. He offered me a coffee, which I refused, then left me with a computer, already loaded with the Rix file. I scanned it quickly and then got a print-out – there was nothing new there.

I found the room Rose shared with three other cops and he walked me back to the entrance foyer. I asked him what he thought had become of Marty Rix. He said the opinion around the station was that he'd done a runner. 'See it all the time,' he said wearily. 'They wake up one morning and see their lives laid out in front of them – marriage, kids, the in-laws, boring jobs – and they panic.'

'He doesn't sound like that,' I said. 'I get the impression all that was his idea of heaven.' He shrugged, and opened the front door for me.

'Did you ever get a hint of foul play?' I asked. 'Unsavoury associates, that sort of thing?' There was nothing in the file, but I felt I had to cover it.

'Nah. Nothing. He was clean. Few drinks after work, that's all. Didn't seem to have many friends – just the girlfriend and her family. There were no leads at all. My bet is he's in South Australia or Darwin or somewhere, with a new identity and a new life.'

'What about people he worked for? Did you talk to any of them?' I'd noticed that he was described as 'Part-time gardener' on the sheet.

'Didn't seem any point,' he said. 'He went missing on a Saturday night – hadn't worked since the Thursday, and that was a one-off job for the council, taking down some trees.' He was holding open the door, politely impatient for me to go, so I thanked him and went.

I stood about in the sunlight for a while, trying to think, then I found a public phone and called Ramona's office. She answered the phone and said she was too busy to talk then, so we arranged to meet again after she finished work. I took the print-out of Marty Rix's file to a small park across the road and sat under a tree reading through it again, in case I'd missed something the first time. I hadn't.

I slid down the bench a bit and closed my eyes against the warm dappled sun. I woke up with a half-snore about twenty minutes later and I looked around quickly but no one seemed to have noticed. I sorted myself out a bit and got up rather stiffly. I spent the rest of the time while I waited for Ramona browsing in bookshops and boutiques, but only buying one item – a shirt for McNeath.

We met at the same coffee shop and ordered cappuccinos. I fiddled with my spoon while I wondered how to tell her I didn't think it was worth her while to employ me.

'You think it's useless, don't you?' she said. 'They've convinced you he's pissed off somewhere.'

'No – I don't know. Even if something *has* happened to him, there just doesn't seem to be anywhere to start. No one saw anything. No one heard anything. He didn't have any shady associates, he wasn't into drugs or anything. He wasn't, was he?'

She shook her head. 'No. He used to be, when he was a kid, but he'd been clean for ten years. Just the occasional drink. He said he'd seen too much of how it destroyed people. He said you'd have to really want to die to be on drugs.' She took a gulp of her coffee. 'I just want to know what happened. Otherwise, I'll spend my whole life wondering if perhaps the cops were right, if perhaps he didn't want me and the life we were going to have. That'd just about kill me.'

'Well, the absolutely only thing I can think of that the cops didn't do is talk to some of the people he worked for. I'll give it another day, but if nothing comes up I really think you're going to have to let it go.'

'Okay.' She smiled, and her face suddenly came alive. 'I've got his job book at home – I can ring you tonight with the names. He had a few regulars, but mostly it was just a couple of days here and there, clearing up weeds and stuff.'

'You'd better give me them all for the last few months,' I said, realising I'd involved myself in a lot of running around the next day, or at least a lot of telephoning. I stood up to go but she said she was waiting for a girlfriend so she stayed sitting.

'Anna,' she said as I turned away. 'Thanks very much.' The smile was trembling slightly.

'Don't start crying again,' I said. 'You'll ruin your make-up'. I was feeling a bit tearful myself.

The next day went pretty much as I'd expected, at first. Apart from the council, there were only three people that Marty had worked for with any regularity, and I tried them first. There was a retired couple with an orchard on the outskirts of Nowra, who could barely remember his name, though he'd put in four or five days a month there. There was Trevor the Tree Fella – in fact, a thriving small business run by a bloke called Mike, who'd taken over from the original Trevor a few years ago, and who McNeath had gone to school with. Nowra born and bred, Mike didn't seem like a real lead to the drifter Marty. From what Ramona had said, Marty have never been in this part of the world before. I rang him, anyway.

'No, never met him till a year or so ago,' Mike drawled over the phone. 'He was a good worker, though. I offered him a full-time job but he said his girlfriend's parents were going to set him up in business. I thought that's what must've happened when he stopped ringing to see if there was any work. Disappeared, eh? Bugger me.'

Then there were the Carpenters. A rich couple (he was a lawyer) who'd moved here a few years back; they'd bought a score or so of acres of prime dairy land on the other side of the river, torn down the gracious old verandahed house that went with the property and built a nouveau monstrosity. All this from McNeath who kept a cop's eye on his parish. Marty had recently started doing a day or so a week for them, gardening and clearing.

Mrs Carpenter answered the phone. When I said what it was about there was a dead silence. She recovered quickly but couldn't quite conceal the squeal of panic in her voice when she said, 'Who? Marty who?'

'Can I come out and talk to you?' I asked. Again there was a silence.

'No, I don't know. We employ a lot of people here. I can't remember all their names.'

'I'll bring a photo,' I said. 'How about three o'clock?' I rang off while she was still wavering. I sat staring at the phone for a few minutes, then I dialled the Nowra cop shop. McNeath wasn't in, of course, but I left a message asking him to bring home anything he could dig up on Jennifer Carpenter. I looked at the other names on my list – people Marty had done the odd day's work for, and decided to leave them until I'd spoken to Mrs Carpenter. Her reaction to his name had been interesting, to say the least.

I misjudged the time it would take me to get across to the river property and arrived fifteen minutes early. It was just as well, because as I got out of the car a well-dressed woman came through the front door. She had on a scarlet jacket and carried a handbag as if she was going somewhere, and my suspicious mind immediately jumped to the thought that she was on the way to avoiding me.

'Mrs Carpenter?'

She sighed and took off her dark glasses. She was very beautiful, in that rather degenerate Piaf style, with a snub nose and narrow eyes. Her dark hair was fashionably chopped in punk style and her crimson lipstick was smudged in a way that looked deliberate. She was tiny, like Piaf, and carried herself like a dancer. She stared at me for a moment, then said, 'Shit. You'd better come in.'

I followed her through the mock-Spanish portico into a living room that looked as it if had been furnished from a catalogue. A very expensive catalogue. She flung herself down on a white leather couch and gestured for me to sit as well. Most of the furniture was white leather, and there was a lot of it – couches and armchairs grouped stiffly round marble-topped tables on a sea of moss-green carpet. Floor-length windows looked out at the river over rolling green lawn. To the left, black and white cows grazed peacefully behind white-painted, wooden fences. To the right, a huge kidney-shaped swimming pool glinted aquamarine in the afternoon sun. Clumps of palms stood awkwardly here and there on the grass as if someone had just put them down for a moment and forgotten them. The house was hideous, outside and in, and I stared at her, wondering if she could possibly like it. She seemed like a fragile, exotic orchid in the middle of all this tasteless display.

She caught my eye and her eyes narrowed even further. I hastily delved into my bag for the photo of Marty Rix while she lit a cigarette. I held the picture up to her, but she waved it away.

'I know what he looks like.'

'So you remember him, then?'

'Yeah, vaguely. He did some gardening. I made him coffee or something. You know.'

'Did you know he'd disappeared?'

'Well, I certainly knew he hadn't turned up again when he said he would. I rang him a few times with no answer, then we got someone else out of the paper.' She shrugged as it to say that help was ten a penny for people like her.

'Had you met him before he came to work here?'

'No. Never. We got his number out of the classifieds in the local rag.'

Her tone was casual, dismissive, but she was sitting tensely and her cigarette smouldered to ash in her hand. I had a thought.

'Did he advertise by name, or just occupation?'

'God, I don't know. We wanted an odd-job man, presumably that's how he advertised himself.'

'So, when did you see him last?' She was visibly relaxing and she butted the cigarette out and leaned back.

'I don't know. When did you say he disappeared?'

I gave her the date and she went over to a mock-Regency escritoire in the corner of the room, returning with a white leather-bound appointments diary. She flicked through it, very cool now. 'November, December, December 1st, "Ring MR", that'd be it. That'd be when he hadn't turned up and I wanted to know what was going on. So presumably I last saw him the week before that. Does that help?'

Marty had been last seen by anyone at the pub on November 28th.

'It might,' I said. 'Are you sure you didn't know him from somewhere else?' I was trying to push her back to the state of panic I'd noticed earlier. But she was poise itself, now. Whatever she'd feared from me, I hadn't delivered.

'I said so, didn't I?' she said insolently. 'Now, if you'll excuse me, I have an appointment.'

When I got back to the beach house I rang Ramona.

'Did Marty ever mention Jennifer Carpenter to you?'

'Who? Oh, yeah. Those people out on the river – is that who you mean? I think they were called Carpenter.'

'Did you get the impression he'd ever met her before?'

'No.' Her voice was thoughtful. 'But he did say something… It was about the time he first went out there, hang on I'm trying to remember.'

I hung on, feeling the same excitement as when Jennifer Carpenter had betrayed herself over Marty's name. There was something here, I was sure of it now.

'No.' Her voice was disappointed. 'I don't think it's anything. He just came home one day and said he'd met someone he used to know, then he started laughing. When I asked him about it he said it was a secret – *her* secret. That's all. It's no help, is it?'

'I don't know. Thanks, anyway.' I was still excited when McNeath got home, grinning smugly. He waved a folder at me and said, 'I get lots of points for this, Anna. All the dirt on Jennifer Carpenter. I called in lots of favours for this, so we do everything I want tonight, okay? I mean everything.'

Since I had a pretty fair idea of what his everything might include, I was happy to agree. Especially as it started with oysters he'd bought and fresh fish he grilled on the outside barbecue while I read what he'd found for me.

Jennifer Carpenter, previously Genna Delaney, had a long juvenile record. Soliciting, drugs, dealing, under-age frequenting of licensed premises, purveying of pornographic materials, all by the time she was sixteen. She'd been in state institutions since fourteen – exposed to moral danger – and before that, in foster homes. After she turned eighteen she dropped off the police books, though she was still a possible 'known associate' in some live files. Marriage recorded to Francis Carpenter, solicitor, five years previously when she was twenty-three and he was fifty-one. Her occupation at the time was described as 'company secretary'.

'Foster homes,' I said. 'That must be the connection. Marty went through that stuff as well.'

'Could be,' McNeath said without much interest. 'And now, what I want...'

'It's a leap, Anna,' McNeath said the next morning. 'And YACS'll never give you out those details. It was hard enough for me to pull her sheet.'

'I'm sure it's right,' I said. 'Even if I can't prove it. Perhaps I can confront her and she'll break down and confess and show me where the body's hidden.'

He laughed. 'In your dreams. Do you really think she killed him? Why? Blackmail?'

'I don't know,' I said thoughtfully. 'I feel she's capable of it – killing, that is. Though Marty doesn't sound like a blackmailer. Perhaps he was just too much of a threat to her new way of life. Perhaps it was enough just having someone around who knew where she came from.'

I never really found out, of course. I rang her and suggested she'd known Marty, that they'd shared foster parents, that he knew her past. Perhaps I even let her think I had some evidence. When I went to keep the appointment she'd reluctantly made, the house was empty and a guy from the real estate office was taking photos of the river frontage. The Carpenters had gone abroad, suddenly, he said. They were putting the house up for sale. He vaguely thought there was some illness behind the sudden move – one of them was seeking *medical treatment overseas.*

I gave Ramona back her retainer and told her what I thought. She was pretty calm about it.

'I believe you,' she said. 'It makes me feel better to think he didn't just run out on me. I knew he was dead from the beginning.'

I returned to my holiday and McNeath and I tried to recreate the idyll, but I think both of us were secretly glad when it was over and we resumed our commuting lifestyle.

A month later, when I was back in the thick of things in Sydney, McNeath rang one night and told me they'd found Marty Rix's body, in his ute, at the bottom of the Shoalhaven. He'd been shot by a small-calibre gun.

I drove down to Nowra a few weeks later and made a statement to the cops. Crimson silk fibres vacuumed from the ute might have been from a shirt belonging to Genna Delaney, according to her ex-cleaner. A gun of the same calibre was registered to Francis Delaney.

I rang Ramona while I was there, and she told me that they'd had a night-time scattering of Marty's ashes into the ocean. 'We waited for the full moon,' she said. 'He loved the full moon on the sea.'

The Marty Rix file stays open, with Jennifer Carpenter noted as 'possible perp'. She'll never be able to come back to Australia without facing at least an unpleasant lengthy investigation, but I don't suppose she cares. I'd like to think she does. I'd like to persuade myself that under that momentary panic I saw sorrow and guilt in her face as well, and sometimes I do.

I get some malicious pleasure out of imagining the sticky explaining she would have had to do to her presumably besotted husband; that she's had to tell him the whole story, so that he's become her elderly jailer, the one who knows all, instead of her indulgent sugar-daddy. My favourite scenario is where she tries to kill him too, and she's caught, and spends the rest of her life rotting away in some filthy jail in Venezuela or somewhere.

But mostly I think of her in a deckchair on some tropical beach far away, like Kathleen Turner in the last scene of *Body Heat,* and I don't know if her expression is sad or uncaring. Or perhaps she's standing on a deck under foreign stars, remembering that Marty loved the full moon, and perhaps that's a silver, moonlit tear trickling down her cheek.

And perhaps not.

VACANCY

CHAD TAYLOR

On Sunday morning at approximately 4 am an identified male guest at the Seaview Motel commenced driving his red Mercedes-Benz SL in circles in the carpark turnaround spraying metal against the unit ranch sliders.

The other guests thought it was gangs or something. Some of them got up to see what the ruckus was.

The Mercedes was spewing exhaust in the motel's mock Spanish courtyard. After its wheels dug white doughnuts in the gravel the driver handbraked and got out. When one of the guests asked him what he was doing the driver cursed at them and walked back to the unit where he was staying and slammed the door shut.

The motel manager got out of bed. He came out barefoot in his towelling bathrobe and banged on the front door of the driver's motel unit. There was no response. He shouted for the driver to open up, but there was no reply. The manager went back to his office and got his keys and unlocked the unit and went inside and a minute later came running out white-faced and called the police.

The two investigating uniformed officers arrived at the motel at 4:45 am and parked in the entrance next to the potted ornamental evergreens. One of the police went inside to speak to the manager while the other inspected the abandoned Mercedes. Curtains twitched in the other units as the policeman approached the unit. The policeman leaned in the front door and just as quickly drew back. He turned away and spat on the ground.

When the first policeman and the manager came out of the office the second policeman waved at both men, signalling them to stay back. The manager didn't need to be told.

The first policeman leaned inside the unit door and put his hand to his mouth. After he'd stopped gagging he looked again to confirm that what he'd seen was real.

The scene of crime unit arrived as the sun was pinking over the unseeing rooftops of the coastal town. Delmar parked under one of the Spanish arches opposite the Mercedes and went in first with his camera while Pat and Georgia sat in their rustling paper overalls. Georgia was annoyed that they had to wait.

'Why can't we go in together?'

'Delmar likes to get a clean first impression.'

'We're literally paid to inspect the scene.'

'It's how Delmar does things.'

Georgia scoffed. Pat always did what he was told. Eight years into the job he characterised this as professionalism, but Georgia considered her older colleague skittish. If anyone was entitled to be nervous it was her – she was the newbie. But there was no point in saying more about it. Delmar considered himself an artist of criminal investigation. The last time she challenged him about it he'd torn a strip off.

Twenty minutes later Delmar emerged into the morning light and waved them into the unit as if he'd personally made it safe for non-police to enter. He got in the van to upload his photos to the laptop while Pat and Georgia went in to dust and measure.

As they approached the threshold, Pat paused. Georgia had to poke her head around his shoulder to peek in. But there was no danger inside, only stillness.

The motel unit was a single room with a bathroom. The body of the woman was lying on the bed in a pool of vomit and pills. On the wall opposite the bed was a flat-screen TV and a side table unit containing a mini fridge and electric kettle. One of the two white coffee mugs lay broken on the floor. The body of the man was slumped in the shower unit in an enormous quantity of blood with one wrist cut.

Pat meanwhile had overcome his queasiness and entered the unit as if he'd seen it all before but Georgia thought he probably hadn't.

'Accidental death, and suicide,' Pat said, setting his case down in the middle of the floor.

'Probably.'

'What else would it be?'

Georgia tipped her head at the new Mercedes. 'Look at his car. Look at her clothes. Rich people don't come to a small town to die.'

'That's why we collect evidence.' He lined up his tiny bottles and brushes.

A noise was coming from the bathroom. Someone had left the tap running. Georgia nudged it with her gloved palm to turn it off.

'Don't touch anything,' Pat said.

'I'm not.'

A locked cell phone lay on the tiles. The dead man's slashed left hand draped outside the basin. The razor blade was cupped in his other hand. He was a righty. Georgia picked up the phone and pressed it on his index finger and it unlocked.

'What are you doing?' Pat said.

'Looking.'

But Pat had come into the bathroom. When he saw what she was doing he was horrified. 'Did you open that?'

'No – he did.'

'That's private information.'

'It's in plain sight.'

'What are you, a lawyer? Delmar will kill you.'

'Delmar doesn't want to get his hands dirty. He'll just sit in the van until the detectives come.'

Pat couldn't argue with that. 'Just leave me out of it.'

'I will.'

Pat went back to dusting. Georgia didn't disagree. It was kind of illegal but the man was kind of dead.

The phone's user profile belonged to a man named Claude. Claude worked in a realty office in Ponsonby. Still crouched beside the body of the real estate agent, Georgia unzipped her overalls and fished her phone out of the back pocket of her jeans. When she called the number even at this hour a receptionist answered: they always had someone on. Yes, Claude worked there.

'Are you looking to buy or sell?' the receptionist said.

'I need to sell first.' Georgia said, which technically was true even though she didn't own anything. 'Is Claude a good agent?'

'Of course.'

'But how good?'

The receptionist was effusive. 'Claude's a machine.' His last sale was for $4.1 million. 'Claude's reviewing properties this weekend. Shall I ask him to call you?'

Georgia winced. 'That's okay.'

'It's no trouble.'

'Really – I'll call him.'

A second after she hung up, Claude's mobile whirred. Georgia waited while it went to voicemail. She could feel Pat's reproach from the other room but it was silent and if he wasn't going to say anything then that was too bad.

Georgia looked up house sales in Ponsonby on her phone. Four point one million dollars took five seconds to find. Claude had sold the same property three times in two years. The weatherboard villa was ninety years old with no toilet and holes in the floor. The windows were boarded over with marine ply and there was a sign on the front door warning that the site was not safe for visitors.

A news site carried a little video clip of Claude. The grass on the front lawn reached his waist but as he joked to the camera: I'm not that tall. The real estate agent was proud of selling a property filled with borer and cockroaches and black rot. Flies lay their eggs in the wood. The carpet smelled like piss – that was nothing. He sold a place that had been used as a meth lab. It sells better than a demolition site because the house is still on it. You can do anything with an empty property – that's what scares people off.

Georgia scrolled through Claude's call history.

When she dialled the second-to-last number he called she heard the phone ring in the other room. The dead woman's cell had fallen between the wall and the bed. Georgia fished out the device and pressed it on the corpse's finger to unlock it. The dead woman's name was Bunny.

'You're disturbing evidence,' Pat said.

'I'm examining the scene.'

He glowered at her over his medical mask. Georgia dialled the corpse's work number and held the phone to her ear. 'Oh hey,' Georgia said when Bunny's boss answered. She winked at Pat and he shook his head and went back to dusting.

Georgia introduced herself to Bunny's employer in the vaguest of terms. Bunny managed personnel for call centre placement. Her boss said she'd mentioned something about going away for the weekend, actually. 'What was it you wanted to talk to Bunny about?'

'I was just wondering about what Bunny did,' Georgia said.

'Are you interested in call centre work?'

'I'm not sure I'd be any good at it.'

'Oh, of course you would,' Bunny's boss said. Anyone could work in a call centre. The job required sitting in a booth and reading from a script: you hardly needed English. They paid $12.50 an hour. To qualify applicants had to register at her academy and attend a training course and sit a certificate exam for a total fee of $850, and when they were placed in a call centre she earned a flat fee and a percentage on their first month's salary. If they were fired from the call centre after the 90-day cooling off period, they had to do the course again.

Georgia said she thought that sounded like a very solid business model.

'The hours are very flexible,' Bunny's boss said. 'You can work any shift you want after the first two months.'

'And I'd be reporting to Bunny?'

'Bunny's the personnel manager. You'd report to the shift managers and the shift managers report to Bunny, and Bunny reports to me.'

'So you and Bunny run the company?'

'Oh no.' The boss's chuckle said what a silly idea that was. 'It's my company.'

'How long has Bunny been working there?'

'Years and years. Now, shall we get your details?'

'I'll call you,' Georgia said, and hung up.

Pat had finished dusting and was laying out markers.

'Feel free to join in,' he said.

'I will.'

Georgia scrolled through Bunny's texts. Bunny kept everything. Going through her messages was like reading her diary. What the dead woman didn't say her friends said for her.

The people Bunny hired for the call centre were already in debt. They owe money before they walk in the door. Furniture, food: you need it, but it doesn't make you money. Their debt to me is the first step to profit. A hard worker will be able to pay it off. Everything costs you something. Life is a series of trades. We can't always have the best.

Georgia thought that was probably true.

Bunny mentioned the same man's name over and over: Andrew, Andrew, Andrew. She never said directly what Andrew did to her but she was furious about it. But she wasn't going to waste time thinking about him, she wrote over and over again. She put her energy into her job and the gym and her diet.

She had started drinking at work. The job bored her but drunk it was a challenge. Alcohol made her clumsy and forgetful and when she made a mistake she had to talk her way out of it: she had to charm people. She would touch someone's arm. She would smile. She would make them like her. Afterwards she would go into the restrooms and stick her fingers down her throat.

She had her clothes tailored to flatter her even when she bought them off the rack. She had a woman at the drycleaners who did it: a real find. She hadn't told anyone else at the company about her: they would have taken her away. She knew how it felt to lose things.

She worked to make herself anew. Georgia read email receipts for energy shakes, macrobiotics, exfoliation treatments, pedicures, omega-3 oils, facials, green tea, cycling, wheatgrass, running weights, blood sugar tests, cleansers.

And then one day Andrew's name disappeared and was replaced by Claude.

Bunny told her girlfriends she met Claude at lunchtime in a downtown food hall. She was standing in the queue looking at the fresh foods menu when Claude sidled up to her and said the Chinese is good and she said I hate fried food and moved on. She bought a salad and an apple juice and sat down in the corner as far away from other people as possible and he sat down next to her with two orders of fries and pushed one across at her and said: you need to eat.

Georgia remembered what Claude said in the video clip. There are no obstacles when you start from scratch. The only thing preventing you from succeeding is yourself. A demolished property is a blank page: a blank canvas. It sends people into a panic. But collapse is an opportunity. You should always go for something run-down.

In Bunny's photos Claude was broad and shorter than her. Big head, big hands, thinning scalp. Way past his prime and his prime wouldn't have been that good. He was an unattractive man. She had bright eyes and fine bones. She cut her curls short and starved herself until she was sharpened to a point.

His marriage exploded. His wife took him to court. He wouldn't give her a cent.

Bunny understood that. She weaponised people in debt. Claude sold empty houses to people who then filled them. Later the people moved out again and returned the houses to their empty state. An empty house could be sold and a house with someone inside could not. Her job was about people losing money and his was making people leave. Everything else was an interruption. Claude and Bunny were made for each other.

'What are you reading?' Pat said.

'Her diary.'

'I don't know how you can do that.'

'It's evidence.'

Pat turned to combing the bed, annoyed. He was sick of being left to do all the work to do himself. Georgia thought that was fair enough. She put down the dead woman's phone and started recording personal items.

She went through Claude's luggage. Business shirts, sweatpants, an opened value pack of soap, Polish vodka, earplugs, a sleep mask, breath mints, two power banks.

She shook out the bottles of pills from their plastic bag: Ibuprofen, Paracetamol, Lisinopril, Rogaine, Viagra. She found a Braun Series 7 and a little white plastic cartridge of razor blades individually wrapped in wax paper.

Georgia showed Pat the razor blades: 'He bought these with him.'

'Huh.'

'He also had an electric razor.'

Pat didn't reply. He was sulking.

The razors matched the blade in the dead man's hands. Claude travelled. Hot water, cold water: the salesman prepared for everything.

The day was growing warmer. The motel unit began to smell of human decay.

The detectives arrived at 11. Both men were Delmar's age. They stopped by the forensics van and Delmar walked them to the unit. When the detectives looked inside, they blanched. Delmar asked the team how it was going.

'We're almost done,' Georgia said.

Delmar ignored her and asked Pat if they were finished and Pat said almost. Delmar told Pat to stay on while he briefed the detectives and sent Georgia out to write the report.

Georgia didn't take it personally. Pat would tell her everything they'd talked about later anyway. Pat liked her. It was why he put up with her breaking the rules. He was always trying to impress her.

She rolled down the van's windows and opened the laptop. The internet was slow. Georgia logged into the traffic cams to search for the last hours the couple was alive.

She started with stuttering footage of the street outside the motel. At 2:47 am the headlights of the red Mercedes-Benz SL poked out of the Spanish arches and headed into town along the main road. A sea fog hung over the township. The Mercedes' taillights glowed like a spaceship. The vehicle made a left turn inland and drove for another five minutes. It passed the suburbs dressed in ocean fog. The windows were dark. Everyone was asleep.

The gas station emerged from the haze lit up like a Christmas tree.

Georgia flicked through CCTV feeds. She found one of the Mercedes as it pulled into the garage forecourt. It was the only car at the pumps. The cashier's office was locked with a grille across the window. The camera stared as Claude got out and walked over to the window and spoke to the late-night attendant. He hunched forward as he addressed her over the microphone.

The video footage didn't show how Claude got the attendant to unlock the pump before he paid. The security cam showed him filling the Mercedes and quickly getting back in the car. He drove off fast. The attendant ran out into the forecourt and stood with her arms at her sides, helplessly.

Georgia rang the gas station. The manager had already spoken to the police. He said the attendant had to be in on it. He'd been calling her all day.

'Can you give me her number?' Georgia asked him.

'She's not picking up. That's a sign of guilt. Can you arrest her?'

'I'm not an officer.'

'You said you were with the police.'

'I'm with scene inspection,' Georgia said.

The manager didn't know what that meant. But after a little more cajoling he gave her the number. The manager was right: the attendant wasn't answering. Georgia left the least-threatening message she could and waited for the attendant to listen to it. When she called back the attendant picked up. She sounded all of eighteen.

'I had nothing to do with it,' she said.

She radiated uncertainty. Georgia could see why her boss suspected her.

'How did the man get you to unlock the pump before he paid?' Georgia said.

'He was a good talker.'

'He was a real estate agent.'

'That figures.'

'What else did he talk about?' Georgia said.

'He wanted to know somewhere they could get breakfast. I told them there's nothing open at that hour except the drive-through.' The attendant was stewing. 'I should have called the police. I shouldn't have run away. I panicked.'

Georgia understood. It was hard to work out how you'd gotten yourself into a bad situation.

She told the attendant the man was dead now so she could tell her boss at the gas station any story she liked. The girl didn't seem impressed by that.

Georgia hung up and returned to the laptop, tapping back through the traffic cams.

After Claude stole the gas he drove back towards the motel. She watched as the Mercedes turn right down to the main part of town and right again, backtracking, slowing each time it came to a place that looked like it might be open. The car did a full circle of the central part of the town and then started going along the lanes perpendicular to the main street, behind the warehouse buildings and then it turned around again.

He didn't know where he was going.

Georgia looked back at the motel unit and imagined the couple lying in their togetherness that kept them apart. Bunny was asleep now. She was not snoring. She was lying very still and her skin was clammy and cold.

She and Claude drove down to the coast. They had a wild night. They got slammed on vodka. They went to bed. Claude took one of his little blue pills. She had one too and maybe that triggered a heart attack. Or maybe she'd just coughed and thrown up in her sleep and choked, like a rock star.

And then Claude woke up and rolled over in bed and saw – what? Saw she was dead and she was gone and he was alone in bed again.

Bunny who fought to stay young: she would never get old now.

Claude gets in the car. He drives away. But he has no place to go. He comes back. She is still dead. He is angry. He works it out on the pedal, pushing down on the gas, pushing, always pushing. He can't leave. He can't stay. After everything he's done and been through, he's trapped.

Georgia bit her lip. She could picture it.

Claude who never failed at anything. Claude who never lost a sale, had bad cholesterol, wrecked his marriage, screwed his ex-wife in the divorce, couldn't get it up, was losing his damn hair. He did everything on his phone. He lived out of a suitcase. He crashed in motels.

Bunny and Claude: not quite outlaws. Tough and ruthless and empty and lost.

Claude makes three diagonal cuts in his left wrist, two in his right and then drops the blade on the floor and his eyes widen for a moment and then close.

Pat banged the door of the van as he slid it open. Georgia started like she was waking from a dream.

'The detectives said that guy sold a house without a toilet for four million dollars.' Pat snapped off his rubber gloves. 'Can you believe that? Pretty fucking sweet for a place with no bog.'

Pat grew up on a farm. He used words like bog and lorry and blokes which Georgia ignored to pick out the ones that mattered.

He asked if she was interested in maybe going out for a drink later and she said maybe which meant no. He would work it out eventually.

She typed up the report to be forwarded to the coroner. 41-year-old female, deceased. 54-year-old male, deceased. Not seeking anyone else. No weapon used in the incident.

Accidental death, and suicide.

What else would it be?

Georgia arrived home mid-afternoon so there was a place in the driveway. She shared the house with three flatmates, which meant four cars so they were always jostling for who parked on the street and the kids here who liked to smash side mirrors. The rent for the house was obscene but a quarter was almost respectable.

As she got out of her car she saw their neighbour had unloaded a pile of four-inch beams and bags of cement in the next door's front yard. It was going to be a noisy week.

Her life since she moved to the East Coast was not what she expected. She was born in Auckland but most of her friends had left too. She graduated second to top in her year in science. Her student loan was five figures. She did food product testing for a year but the hours were rotten. There will always be crime work, the job recruiter said.

Georgia wasn't sure about doing police work at first. She was interested in science rather than death. Even if she could have afforded to go to medical school she wasn't sure if she could have stomached dissecting a corpse, but she did know how to put one together. Scene inspection required drawing conclusions. It was all down to what you could see.

The job recruiter told Georgia she was lucky. Forensic work was hard to get in New Zealand. People tended to stay in the job. But a senior man on the coast had just passed away. The recruiter winked at her: dead man's shoes.

Georgia sat reading on the couch that afternoon until her flatmates trickled home from their shifts – fast food, catering, elderly care. It was someone else's turn to make dinner, which suited Georgia after what she'd seen today.

When it got dark she went for a run on the beach. The sea was choppy. The tide had pushed lumps of black seaweed high up the dunes. The wind was against her. She lowered her head to keep the sand out of her eyes.

Three men were line fishing, standing around the portable winch drinking beers. A bored-looking black Labrador was sniffing around. As Georgia ran past the dog took up with her, hopefully. Georgia didn't want to encourage it. She ignored it and kept running and after a hundred yards the animal got bored and turned back.

Across town the motel unit was cordoned off for two days before the police barrier tape was taken down. Commercial cleaners came and scrubbed the surfaces. Decorators replaced the bathroom tiles and painted the bedroom walls. The unit stood empty for eleven days and then new guests arrived, a young couple with a crying red-faced child and the space filled again.

POEMS FROM *EL DORADO*

DOROTHY PORTER

Emma

The killer had buried her
   with her purple octopus
      backpack

Bill fixes on it

someone, her mother perhaps,
   had written her name
      in black texta
along one of the octopus'
   sucker-padded arms –
EMMA.

Not tears,
rather a dehydrating
   bleakness
blasts Bill's eyes
as if some great deadening
   evil
is draining
   his own ocean
and all its resilient purple life
   away.

Thin ice

Bill works on keeping
his face
still
but not cold
as Emma's father,
an academic
from some cool department
at Melbourne Uni,
poignantly dumpy
in his existential jeans
and leather jacket,
growls through his grief.

Bill knows, from experience,
that Tim Farmer
will only stop
when he can bear
the silence.

There is something Bill,
from the Homicide Department
of Hard Fucking Unfair Knocks,
would like to share
with Tim Farmer.

He would like to tell him
at aggrieved length
how all of us
no matter how brave
or timid
are walking on thin ice

that for no good
nor fair reason
could crack under us
at any time.

In the ice's time.
When the cold black water
will receive
and swallow us
leaving nothing
but a passing warm steam
to show briefly
where we had been.

But oh how Bill hated
(he'd rage and bawl
with Tim Farmer if he could)
when the ice
took a child.

As if the ice
didn't get enough
as if the ice
was just cruel and greedy.

We all have so much to bear
the slip, the slide
the sense of the dark
frigid nothing
under our warm-blooded
mortal feet.

But when the ice takes
our young
we know
we will never have
happiness
or find our deluded footing
again.

Give me strength

It was gospel truth
between Cath and Bill
when they were kids
that his beaut
but downtrodden
mum
should run off
with her beaut
but downtrodden
dad.

Also gospel –
his father was a bastard.
her mother was a bitch.

Cath and Bill used to fantasise
about a new life
with his mum
and her dad
happily married to each other.

Cath would openly pray
for some fortuitous
painless bloodless
(Cath always had a weak stomach)
car accident
for the deeply loathed
extraneous parents.

And then the paradise
of life
with two cheerful supportive
accepting adults
who never snarled
give me strength
when you had your hair cut
like an ugly tomboy lout
or stared through you
with cold blank eyes
more bored shitless
than disappointed
you played like a girl
scared of getting her dress dirty
after a bloody and disastrous
school footy match.

Instead
two bad marriages
stayed their inexorable
course –
so Bill and Cath turned to each other
for cheer, support
and blind, unblinking
acceptance.

His kids

All the autopsies
of the murdered children
indicate a gentle death.

Some kind of suffocation,
possibly a hand over the victim's
mouth and nose
at worst El Dorado lying on their chest
to compress their lungs.

Bill won't buy
Cath's floated theory
of a female offender.

Were the kids drugged first?
Part of Bill hopes so,
if it made their deaths
less terrifying.

But there was no trace left
of any likely drug
by the time the bodies
were found.

Bill mulls
over Emma's autopsy report.

Clearly El Dorado
doesn't want to be cruel.
Just lethal.

What is he doing?
How does he see himself?

The Vampire Monster
of the tabloids?

Cath says,
'El Dorado doesn't see him
or herself, Bill,
as a monster at all.
These gentle
even respectful
deaths
seem expressive
of a kind of –
love.'

Bill shudders –
and thinks of Caitlin*
lying sweet
and quiet
in a shallow grave
with a gold thumb print
pressed tenderly
on her dead face.

Does El Dorado dote

on his cherished

victims

so they become

not murdered children –

but his kids?

Bill's daughter.

The dead hand reek

'What does he want
with these kids, Cath?'

Bill rubs his eyes,
slops his beer
and longs for one
of Cath's taunting fags.

'It's clear
he doesn't kill them
straight away.
But he doesn't
molest them.

What does he want?
Does he touch them
at all?'

Cath stares
into the small sour
pool
of spreading beer.

'Bill, even though
he doesn't fuck them
it doesn't mean
these crimes
aren't about sex.

These days
everything's about sex."

Cath shifts up
a gear.
"These murders
stink to me
of a moral crusade.
A sign of these hysterical
times.

Maybe it takes
an alert pervert
like me
to sniff out
the dead hand reek
of righteousness.
After all
I've lived
in its putrid suburban fumes
all my life.

El Dorado doesn't lay
a finger
on his trophy kiddies.

Not even the quickie
of a moist little fondle.
Even if he's unconsciously
dying to.

He's saving them, Bill.
Not only
from the rapacious sexual
fiends
they'll probably grow into
but also
the slavering predators
all around them.
Like their poor mug
teachers and parents.

He keeps them
chaste and innocent
forever.'

Bill noisily finishes
his beer,
and slaps his glass
down.

'So I drag the churches,
I scour the mosques,
for every feral priest
every bearded fanatic
in Melbourne?'

Cath wags a finger.

'Not so bloody fast, mate.
You keep assuming El Dorado's
a bloke.
I always say –
where's there's no semen
there's no bloke smoke.'

'Are you telling me,'
Bill plays along
'that El Dorado
is one of your lot?
A masked kiddie-napping
Dyke on a Byke?'

'Maybe if IVF
keeps knocking her back!'

'Fuck it,' Bill says
'this bastard could be
anyone.

'Not quite.'
Cath smiles
'We're not looking
for WC Fields.
We're looking for someone
whom I'm sure
really *likes* kids.'

'So we can rule out King Herod?'

'Bill, no wonder
you were always teacher's pet
even at Sunday School.'

Bill's nightmare

We're living in the fumes
of a toxic volcano

we're blundering through
the dark streets
caked in hot ash

our children
are gone

our children
have been vaporised

we wring our burnt hands

we run around in black circles

we babble
in mourning sterility
among ourselves.

How dead

Bill stands in the antiseptic
white chill
of the morgue
looking down
at the cleaved body
of another autopsied
child

a small boy
white as a fish

and Bill thinks
with a warm swill
through his own
living heart

a thought
of numbing familiarity

how powerful
the presence
of a corpse
is

how it holds
the living gaze
down
with an abysmal gravity

how dead dead
the dead are.

The ordinary house

This is it.
The street and number
Bill wrangled from the reluctant
Drysdale postmaster.

This is it.
The house. El Dorado's lair.
It must be.

A grey trickle of sweat
courses down Bill's back
despite the clammy cold.

It's an utterly ordinary house.

But its null silent
ordinariness
shivers Bill to his
suddenly full bladder.

Its almost newness.
Its blank aluminium-framed
windows.
Its display-home
fakeness.
Its too many doing-nothing
rooms.

Most horrible of all
the brutally crew-cut
brown-grassed hill
on which the ordinary house
stands –
with a sprinkle
of cheeky thistles
that the mower missed –
like an antiseptic pimple.

And Bill knows
that El Dorado
must have slaughtered
all the trees.

THE BALANCE

MALLA NUNN

7.56 am – Moving violation

A DICKHEAD IN A RANGE ROVER CHUCKED A U-TURN ACROSS
double lines in a designated school zone one metre away from a busy cross
walk. Probationary Constable Ayah Ryan hit the flashing lights and threw
in a siren blast. The luxury four-wheel drive had committed three moving
violations in under one minute.

The Range Rover pulled over and the tinted window slid down. School
kids gawked from the sidewalk.

'Go earn us some money, Ryan,' said Senior Constable Dean Lewis,
her Field Training and Assessment Officer. The combined fine for the
violations was over four hundred bucks – an ace first catch of the day.
Lewis gulped his double shot espresso from the Greek café on Frommer
Road and leaned back. His job was to train and assess, which he could do
perfectly well from the passenger seat of the patrol car. Let the nipper cut
her teeth.

Ayah tucked a loose curl of hair under her cap and prepared herself for the inevitable 'are you shitting me?' expression on the driver's face. No matter how many PR pamphlets the New South Wales Police Force printed with beaming Arabic, Vietnamese, and 'mixed ethnicity' officers on the front, no-one seemed prepared for a lean, half-Kenyan, half-English Australian constable in uniform blues. Ayah's freckled nose, full mouth, and lack of a penis gave the general public pause. Their discomfort was *their* issue to deal with, not hers. She was the future of law enforcement.

'Yes?' the driver of the Range Rover leaned out of the open window, gold bracelets jangling against sun-tanned skin. A sculpted eyebrow raised in surprise.

'May I see your licence please?' Ayah kept a neutral expression and held out her hand, rock steady. Smiling was a mistake. Smiling made her look young and soft. Unprofessional.

'I have another school drop-off to make and the traffic is hell.' The woman rifled through an oversized Gucci hobo bag and pulled out a matching red wallet with two intertwined G's stamped into the leather. 'How long will this take?'

'As long as it takes,' Ayah said with her legs hip-width apart and her feet grounded. The power pose, Lewis called it. A chunky boy in a private school uniform sat in the back seat of the Rover, the buttons of his blazer ready to pop. For his sake, Ayah hoped the kid was smart. His mother liked fashionable accessories and overweight kids were out of style.

'Here.' The woman flipped out her licence and Ayah took it to the patrol car to run the details. All clear. She let the minutes build up while Senior Constable Lewis sipped coffee. 'Vindictive little thing, aren't you?' he said. 'You'd never know it at first glance.'

'Well...' Ayah had the grace to blush. 'She asked for it.'

'No skin off my nose, Ryan. Hit her with the full fine. Make her wallet cry.'

'Happy to,' Ayah said and walked back to the Rover. Certain people rubbed her the wrong way and brought back memories of being Ayah the hippie kid with a Kenyan mother and a blonde, two-bongs-a-day surfie father who chased waves from one end of Australia to the other. Ayah the outcast, who burned with the secret desire to live in a plain suburban house with a mailbox and a metal sprinkler ticking in the front lawn. Ayah the skinny kid, who shied away from the yoga pants mummies with the latest tech strapped to their wrists and their hair pulled into high ponytails. Those women side-stepped her in shopping malls and looked down at her from electric four-wheel drives that never left the tarred road. Namaste, my arse.

That was Ayah, past tense. Ayah Ryan, present tense, was a probationary constable with a Glock 22 on her hip to prove it. She wrote up the ticket and the stunned expression on the woman's face sent a jolt of pure joy through her heart. Her crunchy granola, "peace be with you" parents would be appalled at the pleasure she took in punishing the over-privileged. Patriarchal power tripping, they'd have called it. Subjugation of the masses through brute force, they'd say. They'd be ashamed of the thrill that issuing the ticket gave her.

But *she* wasn't.

9.43am – Rabbit Run

Ayah turned the patrol car onto Broadbend, a wide street flanked by a mix of old tin-roofed weatherboard houses, red brick bungalows, and two story modern behemoths with glass balconies and acres of terracotta urns leading to grand entrance doors. She slowed the car to a walking pace and counted down the numbers to 425.

A minute before, she and Lewis had caught a call to a break and enter in progress at this address.

'That's the likely little bastard.' Lewis jabbed a finger at a skinny man dressed in baggy track pants and a sweatshirt with the hood pulled up to hide his face. He walked fast and with a limp, his thin arms wrapped around his midriff like he'd burst his appendix. Ayah accelerated and pulled two houses ahead of him. The front of his hoodie bulged. The little bastard saw the patrol car and bolted toward a park on the corner, his elbows flapping like a chicken.

'Floor it,' Lewis said. Ayah mashed the accelerator and rocketed the car to the corner. She was only a split second behind the thief who sprinted into the park with his limp miraculously healed.

Lewis gave chase and Ayah followed after locking the vehicle. A sign to her right read, 'Bentwood Valley Parklands'. Not a park, but parklands. Shit. The little bugger knew his patch. The parkland was a long finger of dense green that ran through three suburbs. Dozens of streets radiated off the park, each with hundreds of places to hide. Ayah jumped over a fallen branch and sprinted to close the gap with Lewis. It wouldn't take long. Lewis had his strengths but sustained speed wasn't one of them.

The land sloped down to a creek at the bottom of the valley. Birds sang from a eucalypt forest growing along the ridge. A lawnmower whined in a backyard. Ayah gained speed on the descent. Her boots crushed freshly mown grass and sticks.

'Go right!' Lewis called over his shoulder as he disappeared to the left of a path that ran along a dirty creek. Ayah sprinted right through dappled sunlight. A piece of silver glinted in the dirt. She slowed to scoop it up. A child's teething ring, of all bloody things. Ayah clutched it in her fist and ran till the path disappeared into a golfing green; another outrage according to her parents who preferred wild places to stay wild and, on this topic, Ayah agreed with them. A woman in pink plaid wrestled a golf bag across a wooden bridge that spanned the creek.

'He ran back there!' She pointed in the direction of the clubhouse. 'To the parking lot...'

A car door slammed and tyres squealed. Ayah sprinted to the nearly empty lot and spun in a circle. She saw a clapped out Volvo, trees, and houses. Smoke hung in the air and the smell of burned rubber tickled her throat. She picked up a smashed CD from a vacant parking space. It must have fallen when Mr. Hoodie got into his car to flee the scene. 'Pan Flute Lullabies.' Ayah grimaced. And the former owners of this disc wondered why their baby screamed itself to sleep every night.

Ayah walked to the clubhouse and checked for security cameras. She found two of them pointing towards the front door. No eyes on the parking lot. Mr. Hoodie was long gone. Ayah swivelled her head and spoke into the radio on her shoulder.

'Ryan. Over.'

'Get the bastard?' Lewis asked.

'Nah.' Ayah's breath came quick from the run. 'Slippery bugger got away.'

Failure to apprehend was aggravating but the blow by blow report she'd have to write on a five-minute chase to nowhere pissed her off even more. The job came with a crap-tonne of paperwork and she hated it. Her parents would say that the detailed report she'd have to write on a failed arrest was instant karma for enjoying working for the man.

Ayah saw it differently. Her patriarchal power trip was a reward for doing the paperwork and it was more than worth the trouble.

10. 58 am – Siam Sensation

Gilt carvings of Thai dancers with delicate hands and elongated arms framed the entrance to the Siam Sensation massage parlour on Frommer Road. A 'Massage Only. No Sex!' sign was displayed in the front window and underlined in red. Twice. Lewis opened the door and a bell chimed overhead. They entered the reception area lit by a fake candle chandelier that cast a low light over the vibrating massage chairs and silk cushions. A petite woman in traditional Thai costume waved them inside.

'I'm Constable Ryan and this is Senior Constable Lewis.' Ayah did the intros. Part of her training. 'And you are?'

'Hom,' the women said. 'Hom… that means fragrant. Sweet.'

The room smelled of sandalwood incense and sweet tea. The scent of Ayah's tie-dyed childhood.

'You reported a disturbance?' Ayah said.

'Massage finished,' Hom whispered. 'Man won't leave.'

A bloke who missed the 'Massage Only!' sign in the window or just thought he deserved more than what was advertised, Ayah guessed.

'Is he armed?' *Assess the level of threat before engaging* the instructors at the Academy had taught her.

'No,' Hom said. 'Angry. Sad.'

Ayah tried to imagine what angry/sad might look like.

'Where is he?' Senior Constable Lewis stood taller as if to assure the tiny masseuse that he was on the job and that problems would be solved and justice would be done. At six foot plus and in his uniform, Lewis looked like the genuine article, while Ayah, in contrast, was slim, with dark skin and just normal woman size.

'Come…' Hom led them down a short corridor with silk-curtained massage rooms on the left side. She stopped at the third compartment and mouthed the words, 'Inside here'.

Ayah nodded and motioned Hom out of the way. A part of her, the part that doubted her strength and confidence, that didn't quite believe she belonged in the job, hoped that Lewis would go first but he stood back and waited for her to lead.

He looked at her and tilted his head at the purple silk curtain.

'Police,' Ayah said through the slit, her hands loose by her sides. 'Cover up, mate. We're coming in.'

She jerked the curtain wide and searched the dim room. An old white man with a plaster band aid stuck to his forehead lay on the massage table with a blue sheet clutched to his chin. A dwindling erection made a sluggish bump under the thin cotton cover. Ayah put him at north of seventy hard years if his crooked fingers and frail arms were any indication.

'Name?' Ayah asked.

'Marco Baldini. I live... just here. Around the corner. What have I done wrong?' He seemed genuinely confused, even embarrassed by his nakedness.

'Massage is over, Marco. Time to go home,' Ayah said. The old codger thought $55 bucks stretched to a happy ending, a foot massage and a cup of jasmine tea. Thirty years ago, maybe. 'Get dressed. We'll see you out.'

'I have done nothing wrong,' he insisted. 'I pay for the company of a woman. Is that a crime?'

'No, but you paid for a massage. No bells and whistles. Didn't you read the sign in the window?'

'Yes, but...' he pointed to a backpack in the corner of the room. 'If I pay for another hour. I have money.'

Ayah groaned. 'You're in the wrong place, mate. Massage only. Like the sign says.'

'Jesus...' Lewis moved into the room, impatient. 'You can't get your rocks off here, matey. Pull on your daks and find a knock shop.'

Marco frowned and clutched the sheet closer. 'What is a knock shop?'

This time, Lewis groaned. 'A brothel. A house of ill-repute. A bordello. A place where ladies will do whatever it is that you want.'

Marco nodded, took in the information and processed it. 'These women will lie with me like I did with my wife and then, afterwards, they will sing to me and comb their fingers through my hair?'

'Can't make promises about the singing, champ, but the rest will work out fine,' Lewis said and clapped his hand on Marco's shoulder. 'Get dressed, hey? We'll wait for you in the corridor.'

'Am I in trouble?' the old man asked and a sudden sadness pierced Ayah. The strength of the feeling took her breath away. Jesus, being in the same room with the old man's loneliness hurt her. It physically hurt. She pushed the feelings down and refocused. Fucking bleeding heart hippy. Toughen up. Grow a pair.

'We'll talk to the lady at the front and explain the mix-up,' Lewis said. 'But you can't come here again. Understand?'

'Yes, thank you,' Marco said and Ayah moved into the corridor.

Lewis joined her and leaned back against the wall to wait for the old man to finish dressing. Ayah copied Lewis's relaxed posture and looked at him. His kindness in dealing with the old man was a pleasant surprise.

'You're a softie,' she said.

'There are plenty of police who think kindness is weakness. Don't be one of them if you can help it, Ryan.'

'Noted,' she said.

11.25 am – Random Traffic Stop
'That one.' Lewis jabbed a finger at a blue campervan with a topless mermaid painted across the side. An invitation to, *Dive in. The water's fine*, was scrawled above the mermaid's wild and tangled hair. Ayah liked the brightly painted campers all the backpackers drove around in. Lewis did not.

'Guilty, officer.' The driver of the camper van said in an Irish accent. He gave Ayah his licence before she asked for it. 'How will I be punished?'

'Depends on what you've done wrong.' Ayah peered at the man in the passenger seat and shook her head. Sunburned did not begin to describe the red ruin of the man's face. His lips were cracked and he had the blinding white outline of sunglasses banded across his eyes. A bad day at the beach that would take a week to repair. Tourists...

'Are you qualified to take confessions, officer?' The grinning driver said.

'Confessions? No. I mostly dish out punishment,' she said, straight-faced.

'And what sin do I have to commit to get myself handcuffed by you, officer?'

Ayah's eyes narrowed in mock warning. 'Being saucy with the law is a good start.'

'I can't help myself, officer. Women in uniform and all that.'

Ayah walked to the patrol car and ran the rental plates and provisional driver's licence through the system. All clear, much to Lewis's annoyance. If he made the laws, driving a campervan with mermaids painted on the side while sunburned and Irish would be an offence.

'Buy some sunscreen and keep off the beach between noon and 3 pm,' she said to the driver, who gave her a mock salute and drove away at thirty miles an hour, taking the piss. Ayah smiled, happy to be happy after the scene at Siam Sensation. The job swayed her, took her from high to low and back up again without warning. Emotionally unstable, the senior officers *could* say about her. They'd be half-right.

'Good looking, was he?' Lewis said when Ayah dropped into the driver's seat and flicked on the engine.

'Just young and optimistic.'

12.17 pm – Banh Mi

They picked up three Banh mi rolls from a Vietnamese bakery squeezed between a failed gym and a barber shop that specialized in brute haircuts for men with apprehended violence orders against them. Ayah ordered chicken with chilli and coriander. Lewis doubled-down with two pork rolls, no onion, no chilli. Ayah found a parking spot in a back street connected to the main drag by a shabby arcade with a toilet. A clean place to pee. Gold.

They ate in silence. Ayah was hungrier than she'd realised. A multicultural parade passed by the patrol car window: a woman in a hijab with three children running behind her; a redheaded bloke in khaki work shorts, Blundstone boots, and a hi-vis vest; and a gangly Chinese teenager with his arm over the shoulders of a green-eyed brunette with wide hips.

Ayah chewed and picked through the highs and lows of the morning. She thought about the sad old man. She thought about the thrill of writing out a ticket to a walking billboard for Gucci. Despite her parents' relentless disapproval, for her, the job had meaning and dimension. She *liked* it. She allowed herself to entertain the possibility that she might actually be good at it, too.

Pop. Pop. Pop. Pop.

The quiet of the suburban neighbourhood shattered and dragged Ayah into the present in an instant. Her heart pounded and the roots of her hair itched.

'That's a gun.' Lewis swung his door open. 'Call it in, Ryan.'

'On your left, Lewis!' Ayah yelled as a blue Holden Commodore with flashing chrome mags roared past the patrol car, blew through a crosswalk, and swung left onto Frommer Road. Horns beeped. Tyres screeched. Ayah picked up the radio, 'Shots fired. Shots fired. Albyn Street. Between Harlow Road and Moorebank Street North. Backup required. Blue Holden Commodore with silver rims seen fleeing the scene southwest on Frommer Road. Over.'

The operator followed up with a broadcast for immediate assistance and Ayah flipped the door handle, her fingers clumsy against the silver metal. She jumped out of the parked patrol car, her boots hitting the sidewalk with a thud. A man wailed, 'Kayla! Kayla...' from a public parking lot in the middle of the block. The desperate keening set Ayah's teeth on edge.

She ran toward the voice. Lewis surged a half pace in front, Ayah right behind him. A café owner peeked into the street with a mobile phone glued to his ear, the emergency services on the line, no doubt.

A jet black Humvee with personalized *BADMFKR* plates blocked the exit to the half-empty lot. A dark-haired man with tatts inked across his neck and arms lay in a pool of blood. Ayah could see a gunshot wound to his shoulder and another on the right side of his chest. His hands clawed and flexed towards the Humvee, his voice collapsing to a whisper.

"Kayla... baby..." The man groaned as blood gushed from his wounds.

Ayah ran to the Humvee, mouth dry, her hand firmly on the grip of her Glock 22. Two bullet holes had ripped into the side of the Humvee, the metal curled inward like dead sunflower petals. The top half of a baby seat was visible through the tinted window. Lewis kneeled by the man and put pressure on the chest wound to stem the bleeding. Ayah pulled the door of the Humvee open with sweaty palms, her breath suspended in her chest, a vague Goddess prayer spinning through her mind. *Be well. Be happy. Live free of pain and suffering...*

A little girl, maybe a year old, in a blue onesie slumped in the car seat. A stream of bright red blood pumped from her right arm. Ayah checked for a pulse. Weak, but there. Barely. Forget a life free of suffering and pain. Life. Just life itself would do. Ayah grabbed Kayla's bunny blanket and pressed it hard against the hole on her arm. Blood soaked the cotton and warmed Ayah's fingers. She kept pressure on the wound. More red. More heat. An endless flow from such a tiny source.

Ayah lifted her attention from her hands to the girl. A toddler, still in nappies. The daughter of a BADMFKR who believed his shit couldn't touch his kids. Christ knows Ayah's own parents had made strange choices on their endless search for Utopia but this little girl with gold hoops through her tiny pink ear lobes and a bleeding gunshot wound – this was unforgivable.

'Stay with me, Kayla, stay,' Ayah whispered to the unconscious little girl.

The short scream of police sirens weaved into the undulating wails of an ambulance. Red and blue lights strobed across the shiny cars in the parking lot. Time got longer and shorter at the same time. The sounds of the chaos around Ayah faded as she concentrated on the little girl. She blinked in the eye of the storm. Her calm voice called out orders to the paramedics.

'Priority one. Over here. An infant. Gunshot wound.'

Ayah's focus was so intense that she couldn't hear the voices of the paramedics telling her to get out of the way. She pressed against the wound, with her hand, her heart, and her mind.

'Stop bleeding,' she said. 'Breathe for me, Kayla.'

A paramedic pulled Ayah away and leaned into the Humvee. Ayah sucked in a deep breath and stepped back to watch as a female paramedic lifted Kayla's body from the car seat. She wrapped the toddler in an emergency blanket and carried her to the ambulance. Still alive. Still breathing. Thank the Goddess.

Paramedics rushed to attend the injured man, lying unconscious at the back entrance to the Top Fadez barber shop. Ayah clenched her fists and bit down a surge of rage. She wanted to lean into the man's face and scream. *Hey dickhead! Thought you could be a bad motherfucker and keep your kids safe at the same time? Fuck you!*

A para pushed his palms to the man's chest and pressed once, twice, three times. No response. BADMFKR's body went limp. One second he was there. The next, he was gone. Just gone. Ayah's knees buckled and she dropped into a crouch. Her chest ached. It was hard to breathe. To think.

To do anything but rock back and forth. It was too late to change what happened. She shut her eyes.

The world became sounds. A police radio. Footsteps. Disjointed words. An ambulance siren. The tiny drip of her own tears hitting the ground.

A hand pressed on her shoulder. Lewis. She forced her eyes open.

Lewis crouched next to her and said nothing. The adrenalin high that kept them focused through the initial response to the crisis slowly drained away to leave an unsettled numbness in its place. Ayah gripped her hands to her knees to stop them shaking. She caught the metallic scent of blood. She was covered in it. It was under her fingernails and in the grooves of her knuckles. Long streaks of it stained the front of her pants from where she'd wiped her palms to clean them. Drops of blood had splashed on her boots, too.

'We're in the suburbs.' She waved at the sedate apartment blocks and the Anglican church on the corner with its steeple shooting into the sky. An old man with a tartan shopping trolley sat on a low fence across the street to watch the police work the crime scene. The ordinariness of it all hit her.

Lewis said, 'People live in those apartments. Where people live, there's always trouble. The villains have to live somewhere, too, Ryan. It's not all speedboats and harbour-side mansions with topless dancers like on telly. Bad men have families. They have wives and kindergarten drop-offs. Like our friend, Howard Kelly, here.'

Ayah looked up at Lewis, surprised they'd already IDed the victim.

'He was a well-known bad guy. He has the names of his wife and kids tattooed on his left arm.'

'How many kids?' The number didn't matter but Ayah needed to know.

'Three.'

Three kids. No dad. Bills still to pay. She lay her right cheek on her drawn-up knees and imagined the rolling waves of Cronulla beach pulling her out beyond the white foam breakers and into the cool water. That's what she'd do later. Wash herself clean in the ocean. Let the sun warm her face. Taste salt on her lips.

'I can't do this job,' she said suddenly.

'Why's that?' Lewis asked.

'Are you taking the piss?'

'Nah. Just want to know why you want to leave the job.'

Two paramedics kneeled beside Howard Kelly's body; their shoulders slumped in defeat. He was dead and he'd stay that way forever.

'I've got a shot up kid's blood on my hands. And her father dead on ground over there.'

Lewis said, 'Can you not see the moment of grace, here, Ryan?'

She looked at the mess around her. The aftermath of the horror. People all around her were doing what they could to restore peace, calm, safety and order. They worked to balance the bad with the good. Hard work; vital and necessary.

Ayah realised she was part of it.

THE CADAVER CREW

STEPHEN JOHNSON

'Stab him if he stops the car.'

Jo Trescowthick didn't lift her eyes from thumbing a phone keypad in the rear of the Channel 5 crew SUV. Kim Prescott half turned in the shotgun seat. 'With what?'

'Your pen. Keys. Fingernails. Anything lethal. Just don't let him stop at that fish and chip shop.'

The target, camera operator Ken Withers, sniffed loudly as they cruised through Queenscliff's main street. 'Aaaah! Fried dim sims and soy sauce.'

The car slowed. Jo didn't wait for the front seat assassin; she whacked the driver in the left ear.

'Yow! You can't do that. I'll tell Mac you're assaulting his crew – there'll be no more freebies.'

'Shut up and turn right at the roundabout. I'm not going to put up with smelly farts all night.'

Withers rubbed his ear and obeyed. Kim smirked. Romance, of a sort, occasionally flickered between the petite production assistant and the two-metre-tall cameraman. Jo's love tap indicated the on-again, off-again companionship was on-again. For now.

Kim was grateful to be saved from Withers' fried food diet. Asphyxiation in the crew car was a constant fear on road trips with the perpetually hungry Withers. Ironically, death of a different kind was on the agenda for their current *Spotlight* assignment – a murder in Queenscliff. Not a real one, for a change. Kim and Withers had a habit of finding bodies while on the job. Men stabbed or dissected by deranged killers. So, no other reporter or camera operator were considered when the Murder Mystery weekend invite landed in front of the program producer.

'Send the cadaver crew,' Mac told the Friday production meeting. 'Their body count is too low.'

A shiver ran through Kim as the vehicle stopped at a Victorian mansion on Gellibrand Street. She had seen enough gore to last a lifetime. All she wanted was an entertaining story for Monday night. They were going to record paying guests dressed in nineteenth century-style finery pretending to be Sherlock Holmes.

'Looks creepy.' Jo checked her phone. 'Perfect for hiding a body – or two.'

The trio stared at the three-storey bluestone building with its rounded turrets on the seaward corners. Ivy covered the facade between. A brass plate by the entrance revealed its heritage – Prospector House. The first owner struck it rich at the gold fields in Ballarat.

'Not bad for a weekender, though it's out of place among these white cottages.' Withers jerked a thumb over his shoulder. 'And Fort Queenscliff.' It was red brick. 'This looks like it's been plucked from somewhere in England.'

Kim opened the door. 'I'm half expecting the ghosts of Agatha Christie or Ngaio Marsh to greet us.'

'Who?' Withers hadn't moved.

Jo shook her head as she joined Kim on the pavement; it would be a waste of time educating the cameraman about the Queens of Crime. 'Those turrets look interesting. The views over Port Phillip Bay would be spectacular.'

'We'll check in and explore. Kenny, get some set-up shots of Queenscliff for an opening montage. Do Dutch tilts on the mansions, cottages, street signs. I'll grade them to look sinister. Meet you back here in an hour.'

'Okay.' Withers turned on the engine as Jo leaned in the window.

'If I get a whiff of a fried dim sim when you return, you'll be sleeping on the beach.'

'We're so excited to have *Spotlight* filming here, although we weren't expecting you this early. I'm Vickee.'

The Victorian styling didn't extend to the attractive, dark-haired, mid-20s receptionist. Her navy mini skirt would have caused blushes among the gentry when the mansion was constructed. The white blouse with name tag added more decorum.

'Rochelle, was going to greet you, but she dashed out the door about 15 minutes ago.' Vickee shrugged off the hostess faux pas. 'Magnus is here – somewhere. The Murder Mystery weekend is his idea anyway.'

'That's alright,' said Kim. 'I wanted to look around before the guests arrived, see which rooms work better for filming. I'll probably bump into Magnus. Can you sort out the check in Jo?

Jo snapped a salute which the reporter ignored. 'What time do the amateur detectives arrive – and how many are there?'

'Fourteen – six couples, two singles. Check-in is from two o'clock. The cocktail party is at six. That's when they get the briefing from Magnus. The fun begins with dinner at 7.30.'

'Sounds good.' Kim retrieved a notebook and pen from her shoulder bag.

'Just a warning. Magnus said he was going to arrange some surprises. I don't know what they are. He's been secret squirrel about the plans. We don't even know who is going to get killed. Or where or when. That's annoyed Rochelle a bit.' A sly grin, another shrug from Vickee.

'Easy peasy,' said Jo. 'Professor Plum with a knife in the library.'

Kim turned from Jo and Vickee chattering at the reception desk in the wide central hallway to explore Prospector House. Herringbone parquet flooring stretched to the rear, contrasted by oak panelling to half room height. Above were red painted panels, several featuring crossed swords. The blades were thin. Rapiers? Hopefully they were not part of the planned pantomime.

A carpeted staircase with a carved banister started beyond the first doorway on the right. Would a bloody victim be splayed on the landing by dessert to send the amateur sleuths into a frenzy?

Kim chuckled. Her fertile imagination confirmed it was a great setting for a murder mystery. She entered the room at the foot of the stairs. It was a guest lounge with two large chesterfields supported by half a dozen club chairs and tables for tumblers of whisky. The walls featured half-height timber panelling, broken by four sash windows. Blue panels, without weapons, continued to the intricate plasterwork on the ceiling. Kim wondered how much appeal the nineteenth century setting had for modern tourists at the seaside. Was the themed weekend with a television crew a bid to revive a flagging business?

Jo and Vickee could be heard laughing from the upper floors as Kim crossed the hallway. She entered the dining room; the décor was more suited to a gentlemen's club. She didn't linger; it was unlikely to feature in the post dinner action. Unless the *victim* was poisoned.

The next door on the left, the library, was closed. She had the freedom of the house for the next 24 hours, apart from the ten guest bedrooms. Kim turned the brass handle. There was no timber panelling inside; the floor to ceiling shelves were stacked with ancient tomes. They bracketed another tall sash window. She pushed the door wider, stepped inside – and saw the body.

It was a slender, dark-haired man in a suit, face down, one arm resting close to his head, the other tucked into his body. It was the classic crime scene pose that stopped Kim from screaming, although her heart pounded as she chewed on a knuckle. There was no blood spreading on the carpet, no protruding knife, no bullet holes, no obvious head wound. Was it really a dead person, or one of the surprises Magnus was preparing?

Kim's fingers were white on the handle; she hadn't seen all the room. Should she retreat – loudly attracting Jo and Vickee's attention – or check the library properly? Fear of embarrassment won the debate; the *victim* could be a prop for the amateur detectives. Kim took half a step and peeked around the door – nothing. No Colonel Mustard cleaning a smoking pistol on the sideboard. Just a TV reporter and – what?

It was early to be displaying bodies. The guests could be exploring the property for several hours before the mystery evening started. Or were they meant to be teased by this victim? Would guests want to report a crime, or wait until Magnus set them loose to solve the mystery? Who would be a party pooper?

Her eyes stayed on the body as the thoughts whirled. She wished Jo was there to help decide the next move. The PA would probably kick the man in the ribs. If he grunted, they could laugh and walk away from the charade.

There was no practical Jo to rely on. And no sign of life from the man on the floor. An actor would know how to disguise his breathing. If he's faking, would there be a smirk on his face, trying not to laugh at the gullible reporter who thinks she's found a real body at a murder mystery party? That helped her resolve.

Kim released the door handle, edged closer. The face was turned towards the shelves. The hand obscured his eyes; she guessed he was in his 40s. No movement. She nudged a leg with her right foot. No response. She tried again against the rib cage. No grunt.

Her recent history with dead bodies taught Kim to never touch them. She had experienced the wrath of forensic officers grumpy that reporters had tread all over their crime scenes. But how did she know if it was a crime scene without establishing if the body was a dead body? She needed an independent witness. Vickee might be a better alternative; she wouldn't have to listen to Jo hoot as she repeatedly told the *Spotlight* crew about Kim's latest victim, who wasn't dead.

Kim backed away, looked at the handle. That was all she had touched, apart from nudges with her Skechers. She looked down the hallway, hoping Vickee was back at reception. Empty seat. Vickee should have returned from escorting Jo to her room. There was no laughter from the upper floors. The whole building was strangely quiet. And still no sign of the proprietor, Magnus.

Oh! Is that him?

Kim stepped back inside the library. No change. Could it be Magnus? Kim had briefly checked the Prospector House website at Channel 5, although it displayed no photo of Magnus or Rochelle. Not much research was required as the story would unfold with the guest attempts to solve the mystery. It would be action driven. Perhaps more drama than anyone expected.

Come on Kim, time to act.

First step was to confirm if the man was dead. If he was, Ken Withers and his camera had to be urgently recalled. Get some vision before the cops arrived. But the plan depended on Kim checking for a pulse.

The stillness was spooking her. No actor was that good. She looked at the wrist. It was too close to the face, no chance of checking for life that way. There was a small gap between the arm and throat. She slid her fingers between, probing for a heartbeat. Ten seconds; nothing. Change positions. Another 10 seconds; no reaction. She tried a third time. The man was not going to roll onto his back and laugh at her. He was a real victim at a fun murder weekend.

Kim snatched her phone, tapped a message to Withers.

RETURN NOW WITH CAMERA ROLLING!

Kim had biffed Withers, yelled at him, but never shouted at him in text. He would understand the urgency. She hoped he was nearby as the cops would need to be called within a few minutes. She could explain Withers being on scene, but not arriving after the first patrol car and wanting footage.

Another thought struck Kim as she paced the hallway. Was this a murder, or had she jumped to the wrong conclusion? Did the guy have a heart attack, or an aneurysm? There were no obvious signs of injuries. Perhaps she should have done CPR rather than dial her cameraman. Guilt kicked in despite not knowing anything about resuscitation techniques.

Would Vickee be able to help? She might know the man. Kim looked up the stairs, no sign of the chatty pair. She debated whether to call for an ambulance as she climbed to the first floor. Stupidly, Kim hadn't waited to hear her room allocation. Were the *Spotlight* guests on the first or second floor?

'Jo! Vickee! I need help'

Kim ran along the hallway that mirrored the downstairs grand entrance. No doors flew open. She returned to the staircase and climbed.

'Jo! Where are you? Vickee? Anyone? There's a body in the library.'

Kim hammered on every door as she raced to the front of the building. No humourists poked their heads out to inquire if the body was Miss Scarlett or Mrs Peacock. And no Jo or Vickee. She returned to the staircase, there was nowhere else they could be. Perhaps Kim had missed them returning to the ground floor while agonising in the library. They might be outside, admiring the architecture or garden. She stumbled down the stairs, lucky not to twist an ankle.

Her spirits lifted at the reception desk; Withers was standing on the path between the street and the veranda with his camera in hand. But he was laughing at the roof.

'Kenny. Get in here, quick. I have to call the cops – and an ambulance. I need you filming because the stations are close.'

Withers shrugged, hoisted the camera to his shoulder and lumbered onto the veranda.

'I hardly see the urgency. We can leave her there for a while – give me a chance to brush my teeth first. Hide the aroma of the dim sims.' Withers rubbed his stomach.

'What are you talking about? I can't find Jo. Or the receptionist.'

'They're in the left turret.'

'How did they get up there?'

'I don't know. I saw them waving frantically when I returned. I thought that's why you called me back – poke some fun at Jo. And I can't see why we need cops or ambulance.'

Kim hauled him by the arm down the hallway. 'Because of the body in the library.'

Withers stopped, making Kim slip on the polished parquet.

'Another body?'

'Yes. In there.' Kim pointed to the library doorway.

'Who?'

'I don't know.'

'How did they die?'

'No idea. There's no obvious injuries – or blood.'

'You sure they're dead?'

'Yes. I checked for a pulse.'

Withers rubbed his face. Walked to the entrance and poked his head through for 20 seconds. He returned to the stairs.

'Jeezus, Kim. Could be a heart attack – or anything.'

Kim shrugged. 'I know. I thought it was a prop for the party. Vickee – the receptionist – said the organiser was arranging a few *surprises* for the guests. But he looked so real – and he wasn't moving. I had to check. When I couldn't find a pulse ... I guess I assumed he had been murdered. Given the circumstances – it was almost logical.'

'Or he could be a guest who popped his clogs with an exciting book.'

'Yeah. I might have been carried away.' Kim's shoulders slumped.

Withers checked the settings on his camera. 'That's understandable, given our history. Okay, you go rescue the maidens in the tower and I'll film. I'll do the old trick with the discs – swapping the first one in case the cops confiscate it when they arrive.'

'You'll only have a few minutes. I'll call them as I go upstairs.'

Kim felt pride as her colleague nodded, pressed record and went to work, not much rattled Kenny. The emergency number was dialled as she climbed the stairs. Cops first, there wasn't much an ambulance could do – apart from confirm Kim's diagnosis.

Experience from previous cases taught Kim to keep her communication short, otherwise the operator would hold her on the line to assess the risk level for first responders. And possibly keep an offender on site. She reported a death at Prospector House, reassuring the operator there was no danger – as far as she knew – to police or public. She disconnected with the excuse an ambulance crew might be able to produce a miracle.

Kim wondered how long the body had been in the library – 10, 15, 20 minutes? There weren't many staff around the building. It could have been there for hours. She was making a big presumption that, if the man had been murdered, the killer was long gone.

Kim reached the second floor still clueless about the body, and why Jo was trapped in the turret – or where to access it? There was no ladder in the hallway, or hatches in the roof. Maybe there were stairs from one of the bedrooms?

Kim returned to the front of the building. Jo was probably having a hissy fit that Withers had not released them. He had seen her in the window several minutes ago, yet no sign of a rescuer. That made Kim smile despite the tension. A sneaky dim sim – or half dozen – and a delayed rescue was not going to encourage a romantic night. Kim stuttered at the final doorway; it meant she would be sharing with Jo instead.

The door to the bedroom below the left turret was unlocked. It opened to a massive room with a four poster bed. The darker tones were left on the ground floor; the room was elegant, with views to the water from the curtained sash windows. Kim had to look carefully for the turret entrance, which was set flush with the wall. There was no handle, or lock. She pushed near the crack, hoping it would spring open. It didn't budge. She tried again in several different places, same result. Strange. She knocked.

'Jo! Vickee! Are you up there?'

Footsteps thundered on hidden stairs.

'Kim – what took you so long? What happened to Kenny? Someone is playing silly buggers. Let us out.'

'There's no handle. I've been pushing against it – but nothing is happening. Is there a secret lock Vickee?'

'The door is on a snib. But there's a wedge around somewhere in case it blows open in a storm. Have a look on the floor.'

There was an ottoman in the corner which Kim hadn't bothered to move. She lifted the corner fold; there was the offending timber that trapped them.

'Found it.'

Kim had to wiggle it back and forth. Had their pushing wedged it tighter, or was it deliberate? Finally, it came free.

'Push now.'

Both prisoners were red-faced from the sunlit turret and the wait.

'What's going on Kim? Was this your idea of a joke?'

'Me?' Kim flung her arms wide. 'I had nothing to do with it. Who just set you free?'

Vickee fanned her face with a hand and picked up the wedge. 'I don't see how that could accidentally get stuck. Maybe Magnus was checking the bedrooms. He saw the door open and wedged it to make it look tidy.'

It was a logical explanation to Kim. On any other day. 'Maybe.'

Jo caught the vibe. 'What do you mean? And why didn't Kenny come straight up to rescue me?'

'He's downstairs getting vision of the body in the library.'

Vickee was incredulous, Jo snorted.

'What – Professor Plum getting into trouble already?'

'No. There really is a dead man.'

'Oh. Who?'

'I don't know.' Kim turned to Vickee whose jaw had dropped. 'I'm sorry to shock you. I found a man lying face down. No pulse and no obvious injuries. I've called the cops and ambulance. They'll be here soon. I hate to ask – but can you describe Magnus?'

Tears rolled down both cheeks, Vickee slumped onto the ottoman.

'That's terrible. Poor Magnus – he's been working so hard to make Prospector House successful. Rochelle worried about the stress it was causing. They spent a lot of money remodelling to make it look like an authentic nineteenth century country house rather than a hotel.'

Jo dropped to her knees and comforted the receptionist. She looked at Kim. 'I don't think Kim is sure that the body is Magnus. How old is he? What was he wearing today?'

'Magnus always wears a suit. Loves to look dapper.'

Kim winced, which Vickee missed. She didn't interrupt.

'Apparently he got his first suit for his tenth birthday – that was almost 50 years ago.'

Kim blinked. Magnus was about 60, that didn't fit the age of the body in the library.

'Ah, Vickee. I don't think that matches the age of the man downstairs. He looks to be in his 40s. He was in a suit, and quite fit.'

Vickee smiled, wiped away the tears. 'That can't be Magnus. You would never call him slim – he was an ex-heavyweight boxer.'

Jo stood. 'Who is it then? No guests have arrived.'

'Let's go check on Kenny. The cops will be here soon. Perhaps you might be able to identify him Vickee.'

The trio scampered down the staircase, arriving on the ground floor as a constable with his hand on his holster stood at the entrance.

'Stay right there, ladies. What do you know about reports of a body in the hotel?'

Vickee clutched Jo, who shuffled behind Kim. The *Spotlight* colleagues were no strangers to guns, Kim still bore the scars from a 9mm.

'It's okay officer. I found the body of a man in the library.' She slowly pointed to her right. 'I don't know how he died. There's no sign of any weapons.'

Kim saw the officer relax, then another emerged from behind him.

'Okay, please step this way, slowly. You can stand with my colleague while I look.'

A siren could be heard approaching. More cops, or the ambulance?

'I have to tell you that we're a television crew doing a story. If you didn't see our cameraman out by the crew car, he's likely to be inside the library.'

The cop grimaced. 'You know that's not allowed.' He stepped forward, hand still on the Glock on his hip.

Kim wanted to say they've been in similar situations with bodies – twice – and knew not to contaminate the scene. Hard-earned wisdom kept her silent.

The trio passed the cop mid-hall. They stopped at the reception desk when he reached the library entrance.

'Armed police. Come out ...' The cop turned to Kim. 'What's his name?'

'Ken Withers.'

They waited. Withers didn't appear. A low moan reached the entrance. The cop dashed inside. His colleague raised an arm to halt the trio, while moving forward to support his mate. He disappeared as well. A few seconds later he returned.

'Tell the paramedics to come inside.'

'Kenny!' Jo shot forward before Kim could restrain her. The cop in the doorway gently caught the anxious PA.

'Vickee, can you pass the message to the paramedics? I need to find out what's happened to Kenny.'

Kim's legs were turning to jelly as she approached the library. Jo had been allowed inside. A good sign or a bad sign? She clutched the door frame, what danger had she unwittingly created for her colleague?

Withers was flat on his back, Jo shedding a waterfall over him, the cops glancing between the cameraman and the first body.

'Is he ...'

The constable nodded. 'He'll be okay. Knocked out while filming the body, I think.' He pointed to the first victim. 'Not sure what happened to him – that will be up to the pathologist and detectives to solve.'

Kim sagged against the frame, grateful for Wither's hard head. He'll live to earn a few pints boasting about the attack at his favourite pubs. She looked at his camera – the record light was on.

'Officer. If you pass me the camera, I might be able to help you.'

Kim watched the officer weigh his options: leave everything in place, or disturb the crime scene and potentially identify the offender. A career saviour, or enhancer. Fortunately, the constable was ambitious.

He watched Kim cue the footage; less than a minute had been recorded. The camera was focused on a low shot of the body when it tilted, accompanied by the smack of something hitting flesh.

Withers was a veteran newsman; protect your gear at all costs, even when being belted around the head. Instinctively, he had clutched the camera to his chest; the lens angled upwards. It revealed the face of an angry, grey-haired man in a boiler suit. Kim would have bet the house on it being Magnus; the traditional attire swapped for workman's clothes to remove evidence of his earlier crime?

Kim paused the vision on the clearest frame. 'If you show this to Vickee, the receptionist, I think she will confirm this is the proprietor, Magnus.'

It was probably the most important vision of Withers' career, but it would be many months before *Spotlight* could ever hope to broadcast it. That would take delicate negotiations by Mac, their program producer, to get the footage returned after the prosecution. Kim should have been frustrated by that prospect; here they were at the heart of another homicide investigation, and the detectives would take away their best vision. However, she knew from the few shots on the camera that Withers had been bashed after changing the discs. The first was somewhere safe, Withers just needed to wake up and tell them.

Jo had been shunted aside while the paramedics worked on the cameraman felled in the line of duty. That's the story that would become a legend in all the bars around Channel 5. They stood in the hallway, listening to an occasional grunt from Withers and the cops working their phones. Vickee had confirmed the likely offender was Magnus.

'He's going to get such a bollocking.' Jo bounced on her toes with pent up energy, arms folded. Kim wondered if she might take a swipe at poor Withers when they carried him out.

'Solving a crime isn't going to save him?'

'Nope. I smelled the dim sim breath as soon as I entered the library.'

Kim laughed. 'Look on the bright side – the hospital will have to put up with his farts tonight.'

Jo barely suppressed a grin.

Kim looked back towards reception. More cops had arrived outside. A crowd was gathering on the street. It would take a while for detectives to drive from Geelong. Kim had solved half their case – they knew the likely killer. A description and details of his car were already being circulated. Could she earn extra kudos by identifying the victim and the reason for his death?

First, she had to alert Channel 5's weekend news; the story couldn't be held until *Spotlight's* next program on Monday. Chief of staff, Ciaran O'Malley, would be cock-o-hoop that the cadaver crew had delivered again from inside a crime scene. Kim scrolled for O'Malley's number as she walked towards the guest lounge. Inside was a sobbing middle-aged woman.

'Excuse me, I didn't know any guests had arrived.'

The blonde-haired woman waved a hand but didn't raise her eyes. 'I'm not a guest.'

'Oh. Are you Rochelle? I'm Kim Prescott, part of the television crew.'

A nod was the confirmation.

Kim wondered how much the co-proprietor knew about the death. The woman couldn't be dangerous, not if the cops had left her sitting alone. She had O'Malley's phone number in hand, but didn't dial. Could Rochelle fill in the gaps?

Kim sat at the far end of the chesterfield. 'Forgive my bluntness, but my cameraman has been knocked unconscious and there is a dead man in your library. We know your husband committed one crime – is he responsible for both?'

It was one of the most brutal questions Kim had ever asked, she was perched on the edge of the sofa ready to flee. The sad, slow lift of Rochelle's head indicated it wouldn't be necessary.

'Yes. Magnus killed him.' Rochelle used a handkerchief to wipe her eyes.

'How? There were no obvious injuries.'

'He punched him.'

Kim nodded. There had been more than 120 one-punch fatalities in Australia since the start of the millennium. Alcohol was the major factor in three quarters of the cases. Kim knew there had been no hint of booze on the victim in the library.

'Pádraig never stood a chance.'

'You knew the victim?'

'We ... were lovers.'

'Oh. I'm sorry for your loss. What happened?'

'Pádraig is... was our accountant. He was always here during the remodelling.' Rochelle managed a smile. 'He was a charming, gentle man. Always ready with a joke and smile. Such a contrast to Magnus.' A shrug. 'A harmless fling developed into something much deeper.'

Kim nodded. 'Did Pádraig want you to leave your husband?'

'Yes.' Tears fell again. 'He knew I couldn't tell Magnus. I begged Pádraig not to confront him. Magnus has been so stressed by the cost of the renovations and marketing the murder mystery weekends. It wasn't the right time.'

Kim read between the lines. 'You and Pádraig were arguing about it in the library?'

A nod.

'Magnus heard?'

A sniffle.

'He hit Pádraig – and you fled?'

A head shake. 'No. Magnus is a former heavyweight boxer. I had to check Pádraig.'

'But nothing could be done?'

'No. he was gone.' A heavy sob.

'What did Magnus do?'

Rochelle twisted the handkerchief in her fingers, dabbed both eyes. 'He wanted to dump Pádraig's body. Too much had been invested in all this.' Rochelle waved an arm at the walls. 'He wasn't going to let Pádraig's death ruin his plans. That's when I ran.'

There it was: a murder mystery and an assault – all wrapped up inside an hour. Magnus probably trapped Jo and Vickee in the turret so he could move the body. The killer was still free, but Kim didn't expect Magnus to escape the Bellarine Peninsula.

The mobile ring tone ended the conversation. Kim answered.

'Hello Ciaran.'

'Kim! We're hearing there's heavy police activity in Queenscliff. That's where you Kenny and the toe crusher are staying – right?'

Kim smiled. 'Yes.'

'Do you know what's happening? We need a lead story for the news. Can you help us?'

'Two seconds Ciaran.'

Kim walked to the hallway where Withers was being wheeled towards the entrance. He was awake, smiling. No cops could hear her.

'Kenny, where's the first disc?'

'Top drawer in reception desk.'

Kim patted him on the shoulder; the speech was slurred but Withers still had all his marbles. She walked behind the stretcher, opened the drawer, retrieved the precious footage, slipped it into her shoulder bag. Jo smiled as she followed Withers to the ambulance.

'Ciaran. Get the live truck on the road to Queenscliff. We've got another exclusive crime story for you – and we've solved it already.'

CLICK

PETER PAPATHANASIOU

I'm not leaving until this man is dead.

Anna had been stalking him for some time now. Over a month.

She was now sitting in her car, a Nissan Leaf Electric, what had become her second home, watching him through the windscreen as he unloaded golf clubs from the boot of his eight-cylinder Holden Commodore. Rain droplets began to polka dot the glass. She reached forward and flicked on the wipers. The controller slipped through her fingers, still oily from her last drive-through meal. The used wrappers formed an extra layer of carpet on the car floor.

An ocean of green stretched out before her. She had decided, after careful deliberation, that it was the perfect location. Manicured fairways and subtle undulating greens would be the last thing he would ever see. What a way to go.

He didn't deserve such a glorious exit. Not for what he'd done. As a senior cardiologist at St Vincent's Hospital, Anna knew the last thing so many people saw was the inside of a speeding ambulance or the lights of an operating theatre or a squalid flat and a needle. Those were the people she couldn't save. Their faces stayed with her; some of their organs, too, on donating their bodies to research.

Over the weeks, she had carefully considered the options as she tracked his movements across Sydney's lush eastern suburbs. He ran daily errands, did weekly shopping with his wife, went for a swim at Bondi, and every Thursday met his friend for a schnitzel and beer lunch at a nearby bowling club in South Coogee.

As an observer, it was excruciatingly boring. Anna desperately wanted him to detour from his regular route and visit a seedy brothel or see a secret gay lover in a cold toilet block. A location where she could both kill and disgrace him.

The blackest part of her wanted to do it in the park when he was playing with his granddaughter. She was all pigtails and everything pink, his fairy princess. Have her little hand slip from his grasp as he collapsed. Uncertain, she would lean in slowly, tap him gently on the shoulder, imagine he was playing. *Poppy, are you okay?* She was waiting for the moment he reared to life and took her in his arms, laughing, cuddling. But then he wouldn't. He would just lie there, face down, unresponsive, until she started bawling and a passerby noticed, called an ambulance. Being so young, the memory would stay with her always.

Anna had considered all that. But she was a mother herself, and a daughter, too. So, the golf course was her gift to him.

'Bit of rain today, Harry.'

It was his playing partner in his burgundy BMW 3 Series saloon, arriving right on time for their Wednesday afternoon round. Tee time was always two o'clock sharp.

'Yep, might be a wet one. But I checked the radar earlier and it said the worst is going to miss us. I'm up for nine holes if you are.'

'Maybe even eighteen,' he replied. 'Just so long as I'm out of the house!'

They laughed as only old friends could.

Anna sneered. He had been taunting her like that for weeks. Living the good life.

Moore Park was a public course, for which Anna was thankful. A private club would've been out of her reach. It was a choice that surprised her since he was a man with money, who had made a lucrative career. Yet he had retained simple tastes. He drove a new but modest car, and lived in an unassuming house, albeit in one of the more exclusive beachside suburbs within earshot of the roaring Pacific Ocean. His adult children appeared the same – respectable, but not extravagant, in their clothes and cars and demeanour. Anna had watched him do his own gardening, walk his own dog, pick up its poop with a rubbr glove.

She put it down to not having come from money, from being a self-made man who remained grounded. It was a redeeming feature, that was unquestionable. But not enough to save his skin.

She once thought he'd caught sight of her, parked across the street as he exited the front door of his house. She sped away before he could approach, and was more careful in future.

Anna gathered her hair at the back, bunched it together, and fastened it with a large hairpin from her handbag. There were more grey strands each day and she had no time to keep dyeing them. A black cap with a prominent golf sponsor concealed her shame from the world and aided in her overall camouflage. Her tartan trews did the same, even though their garish red and white pattern would have done the opposite anywhere else. She had bought them online with a set of second-half golf clubs that the owner had assured her would lower her handicap in weeks. As if she cared about that.

Sydney's changeable autumn weather had conspired with the time of week to ensure the dirt car park was near empty; the course, too. Anna smiled at the thought of fewer potential witnesses. It was another reason why she'd chosen the location. A café or shopping centre or airport or library risked CCTV.

Anna got out of her car and collected the clubs from the back seat. She skipped swiftly across the car park, shoes sinking in the soft clay, clubs rattling in her bag. Her quarry lay ahead, collecting his push cart from the clubhouse, walking to the first hole, a straight par three.

She kept her distance and did all the expected things of an amateur golfer. She collected a scorecard and half-sized pencil, and paid for the hire of a cart. She thanked a disinterested teenage attendant from behind a big pair of black sunglasses that concealed most of her face. He did not respond and returned to absently scrolling away on his mobile phone.

Anna strode to the first teeing ground with purpose. Two lessons with an ex-pro and practice on the driving range meant she could now handle the equipment well enough to avoid suspicion. It helped her hand-eye coordination that she'd once played softball in high school, and been rather good at it, too. She retrieved her titanium driver, placed her tee, addressed the ball, and rotated her shoulders. Her drive found the middle of the fairway. She smiled at the tiny white dot sitting comfortably in the emerald expanse encircled by soaring eucalypts. Beyond it, the two men had now christened their respective six-packs of lager, the first of which would be emptied before the first green. Steady nerves and low heart rates were crucial for lower scores.

Now she just needed to wait until they separated. That was when she would strike.

Dark thunderheads hovered in the distance, to the west, Penrith and beyond. Pockets of blue sky peeked through, revealing thin shafts of watery sunlight. At the end of the fairway, the arch of a rainbow appeared from behind a row of old, dependable oaks. The storm was passing, leaving in its wake a loose rain that quickly dissipated, and a lushness that made Anna want to take off her shoes and walk barefoot across the velvet lawn.

She kept him in her sights. It was why she carried a pair of folding binoculars in her bag, checking on him after every swing. He was no hacker. His technique was honed over years of regular rounds with work colleagues, discussing their latest client file in between club selections. But he was still prone to dubbed shots that flew crooked, which made him scream blue bloody murder. He really needed to calm down, thought Anna, or was at risk of having a heart attack.

Naturally, he was completely oblivious to it being anything other than an ordinary round of golf. It was just another afternoon in the fresh air; himself against the course and sobriety. He would go home to his wife later, tell her all about it, eat a delicious home-cooked meal, and fall asleep in his comfortable armchair to the sound of rugby league commentary, and dreaming of a hole-in-one. Anna loathed him for it. She walked faster, determined not to let her chance slip.

Putting was not Anna's forte. She allowed herself only one attempt at the hole before either kicking the ball in or simply picking it up and pretending to mark her scorecard. She wasn't there to experience the thrill of finding the green from a bunker or draining a forty-footer. She was there for something far more intoxicating.

The second hole was a par four with a dogleg left. Anna found the water hazard once and the rough twice. By the time she had retrieved a new ball from her bag and tossed it onto the green, she was starting to better understand the madness of golf. She turned and looked back up the fairway from where she had walked. It was empty, there was no one following her, wanting to play through. And the safety of the clubhouse was getting further and further away.

Anna checked her binoculars again at the third teeing ground; still no chance. The playing partners were similarly aged and skilled, invariably going shot for shot on every hole. Fourth hole, a long par five; fifth, a short par three; sixth, a bottleneck par four; seventh, a par five with dogleg right; eighth, a par four with water. Anna was frustrated and getting tired and had only limited time. By the ninth, they were almost back at the clubhouse. Anna feared they'd called it a day after nine holes, deciding it was enough. Fortunately, they didn't.

It wasn't until the par five thirteenth that the men ended up on opposite sides of the fairway, about fifty metres apart, lining up their next beer and their next shot on the course's longest par five. But they were still too close together for her liking. Ideally, she wanted him in the rough, away from view altogether.

And then it happened. As she watched through the eyepieces, he scuffed his shot and sent a heavy clod of earth flying. It went almost as far as his ball, which disappeared into a nearby thicket of pine trees and underbrush. She heard him curse and his playing partner laugh before saying: 'See you at the next hole!' and walking off towards the green.

Anna had practiced. She was ready. Now, she did not hesitate.

Pushing her cart and clubs to one side, she concealed them behind a row of bushes and walked with resolute footsteps down the dead centre of the fairway. She would return to collect them after her work was complete. She did, however, take one item with her, which she removed from the front zipper of the golf bag – her weapon of choice. It was the only thing she needed. She carried it in her right hand for the world to see. There was no turning back now. Automatic pilot.

The wind picked up, blowing the storm clouds east and freshening the dry skin on Anna's face just as she arrived at the conifers. A whiff of sweetness hung in the air, amplified by the recent rain.

She expected to find him rustling through the long grass, searching for his misplaced white dot with a twisted iron and bent back. That was to be her story, too, if he happened to see her before she got to him. That she'd also fallen afoul of the golfing gods, damn them.

But he wasn't looking around at all. He was standing perfectly still with his back to the fairway. Anna approached him with trepidation, unsure of what game he was playing. Then she noticed his trousers were hanging loose at the back, his hands around the front, and she knew the only game he was playing was waiting for his enlarged prostate to cooperate. He really needed to see a good urologist, Anna thought. She knew a few.

Anna circled him from behind, maintaining a safe distance. She peered through the trees, stepping carefully sideways to avoid cracking a twig or rolling an ankle. His hearing aid made it unlikely he'd hear her, but she was careful, nonetheless. As much as she wanted to witness his final breath, she also wanted to watch him a moment longer.

A decade working busy Sydney emergency departments and cardiac wards had taught Anna that a person's last seconds on earth were sacred, to be cherished. They were particularly telling when a person knew they were about to die. But this moment would not have such drama.

She desperately wanted to confront him, to tell him why she was doing what she was doing, to make him understand. The only problem was if she did that, she feared she might blink. She might fail her task or be seen, and not have another opportunity or risk getting caught. She reluctantly decided to forego the satisfaction of revealing her motivation for the sake of completing her mission. That was ultimately more important.

Anna put a palm to her chest to slow her breathing. She felt her lungs moving up and down, inflating and deflating. A plunging feeling burnt a hole in the pit of her stomach. She thought she was ready, but in fact she was terrified. This was a death, like so many others she had witnessed. But by her own hand.

He adjusted his stance and let his trousers and oversized Y-fronts fall. They descended his thin chicken legs with minimal effort, slipping to his ankles. His bony white bum greeted Anna in a decidedly helpless way. He was a little boy again, free and unashamed, letting the cool breeze touch his pale skin in places not normally touched.

It's time, Anna willed herself. Do it.

She looked down at her hand, at the hard, heavy metal object.

She had already estimated the distance and knew he was well within range. Like her golf, she'd practiced this as well, alone over many hours. She had painstakingly optimised her approach, learning from her mistakes to ensure her techniques were robust and repeatable for when it mattered most. It was the scientist in her, her analytical brain, calculating and recalculating, testing, fine tuning. The fact he wasn't moving only made her task easier and minimised the chance of error. All she needed to do now was execute.

The wind stopped blowing. The flickering pine needles went limp. Anna bounced the cold, weighty item in her hand nervously, examining its shape. She only looked up again when she heard the patter of a weak, uneven stream on wet dirt. His prostate had finally relaxed. Now, the clock was ticking, he wouldn't be still for much longer.

Her fingers clicked it open. The weapon woke from its slumber, its slick black screen alive with colour and light. Having previously sent out a raw packet of data on an earlier stalk, Anna had already extracted the relevant model and serial numbers. Now all she needed to do was deliver the deadly command.

It only took a few keystrokes, delivered with swift precision. A text message to a friend, if you will. A work e-mail to a colleague. So mundane, so ordinary. And yet...

The final blow was one click. Not a trigger. Not a gash. A muted sound.

Click.

Almost instantly, he slumped to the ground, his knees landing in the warm puddle of urine. He clutched his left shoulder with his right hand and let out a light whimper of distress. He turned to look behind him, desperate for help, for his playing partner, for anybody.

But all he saw was a woman in a golf cap and tartan trews who only stood staring, silent, watching as his organs starved and shut down.

Their eyes locked for a second before hers narrowed and his rolled back into his head. It all went unsaid. He fell forward, headfirst into the dirt with a fleshy thump, his organs and cells starved of oxygen, the life evaporating from his body.

Anna lingered for a moment, admiring her work, her data, her art. She spun around to make sure she was still alone. There was no need to examine the unmoving body, no one could possibly have survived the jolt she had just delivered. The hint of a smile crept across her lips.

She turned and walked back up the fairway, left her push cart by the clubhouse, threw her clubs in her car and drove away.

FRACTURES THROUGH TIME

ANDI C BUCHANAN

I STRETCH MYSELF OUT ON THE LONG-DISTANCE, DRIVERLESS eco-rail up to Tauranga. The seats are comfy, and it's not too busy, not on a Thursday at the start of spring. I've watched a movie and had a coffee from the hover-cart, and it almost feels like it could be a holiday, almost feels like I could be chasing sun and ambling on riverside walks, rather than trying to understand something that has fractured more than one family over the generations.

Emma tries to call me, and I ignore her. She sends me a message and I delete it unread. I look out of the window for a while, watching the small towns with flaking paint on their weatherboard houses, children and chickens running loose and happy.

I look back at my tablet, open a file. I press a few filters and my grandfather's picture smooths into high definition. It's not quite three dimensional – they weren't the standard back then in the 2020s – but I can tilt the angle a little, see him turn towards me, catch a hint of a smile in his eyes. He, Jack Allard, is twenty four in this photo, recently married. I think his parents chose this one for the media. Early on they'd used the most recent one, even though it wasn't the best angle and was slightly out of focus, hoping someone would recognise him, that it would trigger someone's memory, hoping he might be found alive.

I open the other pictures I've found from other articles, arrange them side by side. In one he's tired – it will have been from when my dad was a baby, so perhaps a result of many sleepless nights. His mouth is asymmetrical, as if the camera caught him just as he was starting to speak. He looks more real, as if I could almost reach through and get to know him. That image was taken when he had just turned twenty four. He didn't know he wouldn't live past the end of that year.

My grandmother remarried four years later, and by all accounts my father was considered less a child and a victim than an ugly reminder of the past. He bounced unhappily between his paternal grandparents and his mother's new family. Too young to remember his father, he never really felt at home with either.

I totally understand why my father never wants to talk of this. Too young to properly remember, and yet his whole life was shaped by it. I said it fractured our family, but most of the fractures are hairline, too small for the outsider to notice, but permeating everything we are. Now I've prodded at it, at barely closed wounds, and he feels more distant from me than he ever did. We could break at our weakest point, and everything could smash to pieces.

I catch a driverless shuttle to my hotel and get Chinese takeaways, eating it on the tiny third-floor balcony. I'm inexplicably tired from the long journey. That night I dream of experiences I never had, worlds I never knew.

I dream of cells and lockdowns, of lights that were never turned off.

I've been to a prison once, a guided tour we did back when I was at school. I did hybrid school, one week in person, one virtual, and on the last day of each in-person week we did an educational trip. I much preferred the wildlife based ones, the trips to the bird sanctuary or to the engineered habitats around the coast to replace ecosystems devastated by global warming. I've always loved being outside, clambering over rocks and hillsides, or walking by the sea with the wind heavy in my hair. I was less excited by the day trips into Wellington to tour the museum where all the animals were dead, or the parliament buildings restored after the earthquake. But the prison trip was something else.

The prison had been fully decommissioned and was awaiting demolition; it was one of the last ones to close and had been operating at a fraction of its capacity for well over a decade before that. But you could still feel what it had once been. It's the lighting I remember most. That harsh, shallow lighting that made it clear always that you were away from the world.

I remember wondering, as we finally emerged into the sunlight, how anyone could have expected anyone to change after locking them away in there?

That's why, when a woman contacted me wanting to prove the innocence of the man convicted and imprisoned for killing my grandfather, I agreed to talk to her.

Her name was Emma Blaese and she was the daughter of Barnaby Williams, a man in his thirties at the time of the murder with a history of drug use, low level crime, and mental illness.

Faced with the evidence he admitted to the crime – people back then were often given a little less time in prison if they said they'd done it, to encourage them to save the courts time and expense. The flaws in this are obvious. He spent fifteen years in prison; a life sentence didn't mean you were in prison for the rest of your life, but you were never truly free. Once paroled, you lived under strict conditions and could be sent back if you broke them.

Barnaby moved to a small settlement in the Bay of Plenty where he lived off the newly introduced UBI and odd jobs before dying before he reached sixty.

I hadn't known about Emma before she arrived, but it didn't surprise me Barnaby had children. The effect on her – a small child at the time of sentencing, like my father – was obvious. I hadn't thought too much, growing up, about how many other people must have been affected. All I knew was my father's emotional distance, how he used to spend whole weekends sleeping, his refusal to ever go to funerals.

I didn't tell him about Emma, not at first. Probably I should have done, but the old wounds were so deep I was scared to re-open them.

I told Emma to come out to my place next time she was in Wellington – it's not far out of the city if you get the train, and it's hardly the sort of conversation you want to have in a cafe. She told me she had a KiwiChip, rare for someone her age, so I put her ID number into the system so she could use the implant to go through the gates and up the lift without me needing to go down for her. This development is two five storey blocks, 50 apartments in all, with balconies and a central grassy courtyard with swings for the kids and some bench sets and barbeques at one end. I share the apartment with my partner and a friend. It's a little pokey, but otherwise nice.

Emma was exactly on time. I'd calculated she was in her early sixties, but she didn't look it. She was wearing a yellow blouse, with a blazer under her arm – she'd clearly had a day of business meetings. She brought some lemon biscuits from an indie bakery near her house, and take-away coffee, hers in her own bright-pink cup, and mine in one of the off-white rental cups you return to the cafe for your deposit back. Very normal for discussing a murder.

She was well prepared, and got straight to the point. 'In his papers he said he helped dispose of the body but didn't kill him,' she said, looking at me for a reaction. 'That was where the DNA evidence and everything came from.'

I wasn't sure how I was meant to feel about this. I had feelings about my grandfather's murder, and the effect it had had on my father, but on some level it didn't matter who killed him. It was all long in the past. Not like we could bring anything back. But I swallowed my obvious commentary.

'Why else would he do it? Money?'

'Perhaps. Or misguided loyalty. Or they had something else on him, they were blackmailing him or threatening him. Look, I'm not saying he was a good guy, but I really don't think he killed your grandfather. It was really rare, in those days, to get a murder conviction without a body being found.'

'Why does it bother you?' I said. 'And why is it me you've come to?'

'Because people don't rest until the answer's been found,' she said, looking at me. I turned my head. Eye contact has always been difficult for me. 'And because you were exactly the one who'd understand that. Okay, okay, I also need your permission as a family member to get some files opened.'

I knew, even then, that it wasn't the whole story.

I wake up early on my first day in Tauranga, almost a year after that fateful first meeting with Emma. I am used to taking self-driving podcars when public transport isn't available, but they don't go this far outside the main settlements. Instead I have to find a driver with a big car, a four-wheel drive, the sort that carry spare batteries for long trips.

'Got family up here?' the driver asks. I choose my words carefully, knowing that she likely knows many of the locals, the changing hands of land and property. She'll be the sort who keeps track of who taught at the local schools, who used to be the local doctors.

'Used to,' I say. 'Bit of a nostalgia trip. Settle some old ghosts.'

The landscape has changed around the coast, predictably enough. The Wellington earthquake shifted land even this far north, and the sea level rises that came with climate change warped it even more.

It must have been another world, then, back when my grandfather was alive. On November 20th, 2025 he dropped his son – my father – off at his parents' house, and was never seen again. A friend who he'd previously made a failed attempt to go into business with named Ryan Ward was the main 'suspect' – see how easily I use the language of the adversarial justice system of a bygone era. There seemed to be a financial motive, and several people testified he had a quick temper; a euphemism, I think, for a history of violence.

But it was Barnaby Williams who had left his DNA on the body, and it was Barnaby Williams who confessed.

'Full of ghosts round these parts,' my driver tells me, snapping me back to the future. 'Are you sure this is where you want me to leave you?'

'Yeah, here's good, thank you.'

'Do you want to book in a ride back, or just message me? It's not too busy at the moment, but I warn you there might be a wait.'

'I'll message you, thank you. I don't mind a wait.'

'Right-e-o. Hope you enjoy your walk.'

I look out at the landscape, the undulating land mostly given to sheep or cows, and the orchards that are the mainstay of the region. A few houses cluster down towards what my phone tells me is North, but it is nothing you'd call a settlement, not really.

There is a bit of a chill in the air but I am comfortable enough without my coat. I wonder why I'd felt the need to come here, if it was just to add some dimension of reality to what was going round and round and round in my head.

I start to walk, uphill, the landscape laying itself out in front of me.

There was no evidence here that Barnaby Williams had ever existed. The shed in which he made his home was likely demolished years ago, that or it collapsed in upon itself. The only picture I've ever come across, from a young journalist hoping for more of a story than there was, showed it in wretched condition.

I never thought I would end up anywhere near here. I never thought it would consume a year of my life. When Emma showed up at my apartment in need of my help I thought I'd approve her access on a few things, once I'd had chance to meet her, and that would be the end of it. Instead, it sucked me in.

We set about it like a project. Neither of us had much idea what we were doing – she worked in tech, but had a history masters that gave her some solid research skills, though her actual speciality was interracial relations in the early Chinese goldmining settlements, about 150 years before the murder in question. I worked in data analysis for solar energy, so I had some idea how to spot patterns. We went in fine detail through files that had been unopened for decades. We retraced the known movements from the police report, as best we could given all the changes in the city since then.

Once we had structures in place, we got through the information much more quickly than I would have expected. It was almost comforting – being able to work in such a methodical way with all the data gave a quick and easy sense of achievement. But there was more to it than that, there was a sense of thrill of being on the cusp of revelation.

Slowly, we started to unpick the case and create a new one. Everything started to become clear. Or at least it seemed to.

Emma shows up just as I am beginning to suspect she won't. I wish I could say I don't care about the money, but my partner and I want to have children. The state payments are barely enough, and I want to give a child more.

Emma is on an electric bicycle, ill-suited to the roads. I'm not sympathetic; she has a lot more money than me, and will have had no trouble finding a driver.

'You know I could have brought these to you,' she says, catching her breath. 'Couriered them even.'

I know that. I always knew I didn't have to meet her – the law only requires me to view the original documents, and that only because of their age. Everything else could have been done electronically.

'I sent you my research,' I say.

'Thank you,' she replies, coldly, but I can see she is almost shaking.

I had worked on the premise that Barnaby had been telling the truth, that he had helped dispose of the body. His motivation was unclear though, perhaps he was paid, perhaps he was threatened, hey, perhaps he really liked disposing of bodies. I'm glib, but I felt like anything was possible at that point. That left several more questions, most notably: if he didn't kill my grandfather, did Ryan Ward?

I didn't find information that wholly implicated him, but I found enough. I learned to get my head round the alternative currencies they were using, cryptocurrencies they called them. It seemed the police of the time found the concept even trickier than I did. I got to the point where I understood enough that I could read their records, and compare them with some historical records.

My grandfather was on the verge of bankrupting Ryan. The police back then hadn't investigated that angle enough, not when they had the sort of evidence they were used to, the DNA and the fingerprints of Barnaby.

It might not have been enough proof for the courts then, but it was enough proof for me. The person who murdered my grandfather was not Barnaby Williams, but Ryan Ward.

'Why did you have me come up here,' Emma says.

'It's where Barnaby Williams lived out his days,' I said. 'Guess I wanted to pay my respects.'

'He's long dead,' she replies. 'Does it matter?'

'I'm here to settle the past,' I said. 'You were the one who opened these old wounds. Why would you do that, if not to put things to rest.'

But I already knew the answer to my question.

Now I look at her, the rage in her eyes, as she clenches her fists and her hair – dyed very well, I assume, or else she's been lucky, because it doesn't look dyed – blows out in the wind.

Ryan's daughter, not Barnaby's. She wasn't trying to clear her father's name; she was trying to implicate him. I don't know what to say. I don't know exactly what point she's angry at, having a father who was a murderer?

Or angry on behalf of my grandfather? So I just stand there, helplessly. Eventually she looks at me, sees the questioning on my face, and begins to explain.

'It's hard to explain what it was like. This whole memory of seeing him, his clothes covered with blood, standing in the laundry, and then being told, year after year, that I'd made it up. Everything changed from then: it was all arguments, objects being thrown. I was made to feel like an imposition. The terror that hung through the house, even though none of us knew what we were scared of.

And I know what you're going to say, you young people, that this was the problem with the carceral system: punishment, punishment and the fear of punishment, it didn't just punish the perpetrator, it punished their families. Well you're right. But you know what else punished my family, and could have been better, could have made a better decision? Him. That fucking man.'

I'd thought, the whole time, that we were on the side of an innocent man harmed by the carceral system – not a guilty one who escaped it. Still, is it not always best for the truth to emerge?

'Why did you lie to me?' I ask.

'Would it have motivated you? My rage and spite?'

I shrugged. 'Maybe.'

'Seriously? You'd have helped me if you knew my motivation?'

'Maybe you could have done it yourself and not dragged me into it.' I know I am coming across sullen, and her being old enough to be my grandmother is decidedly adding a whole tone to it. I am resentful though, and not very sure how to aim it.

She nods, though, conceding the point. 'It's a better world this one. Not perfect, but we're learning. Doing things better. Calling people in and keeping them in communities rather than casting them out and locking them away. But what am I? I was born in a different time? I want to be better but there's rage still burning in me. Are you going to tell me I can't direct that at the one person who deserves it?'

I clench my fists, pull them behind my back.

'You think it's a game to me? It's my grandfather who was murdered, in case you've forgotten.'

She looks at me, curious.

'Of course. I know. And this isn't a game to me either.'

'Good. Because you have all these feelings and you seem to be barely recognising that maybe this has had an impact on me just as much as on you.'

'I… I thought it was so obvious it didn't need to be said.' She's stumbling over her words now.

'Well it does.' I say, surprised at my own forcefulness. 'Because we don't talk about it enough. In fact, we never talk about it and I thought, I thought if…'

I don't continue the sentence. We've reached as far as things are going to go, so we just stand there, facing each other on this rural road, for what seems like hours. I can feel tears welling in my eyes, but mercifully they do not fall.

'I'm sorry,' she says eventually. Her voice is little more than a whisper.

So is mine. 'Thank you.'

'You'll get your money. It's locked in a family trust for now, but I'll get it when he dies. It's the least I can give you – call it a thanks for helping me out, or an apology from my family to yours. Whichever helps you sleep at night.'

'And you?'

'I'm going back home and I'm going to tell everyone it was him. I'm going to destroy his name as the last thing I do. They'll walk away – there'll be no pretence any more – and he can die sad and alone. I don't care if he only has hours left, I don't care if he doesn't need to live with it – the point is it's finally coming back to him. After all these decades, he's going to have to face the consequences of his actions.'

Emma trundles off on her bike. I'm thinking about us moving to a bigger apartment, with room for a couple of kids. I'm thinking about parenting in the way my father couldn't. I'm thinking about my father and feeling all broken and heartsick for the child he was. Emma wanted to see consequences, but I can see nothing but consequences, fracturing out endlessly through time and families.

There isn't a grave for Barnaby Williams. There isn't a headstone. He was cremated, which has always been the cheapest option, and now – with space so short – is almost always done, unless there's a religious reason not to. Some of those still have markers, little holes in a wall where their ashes are kept or they are commemorated, but even though he appears to have family, there's no sign of them. I like to think they took him somewhere far better than a memorial wall in a cemetery on the edge of town. I like to think it's what he wanted. I'm hardly religious, but I'd like to think he found some kind of peace.

I know Emma acted like my generation, and the next, think we're smug, think we've got it all worked out, that we judge hers for what they did. And perhaps I do a little – or at least I found her rage repellent – but I'm more sorry she's so obviously wrapped in trauma, than I am judging her position as right or wrong. I don't think we've got it sorted out at all. I think we're growing a bit better, every day. And that sometimes, to go forwards, we have to delve into the unpleasantness of the past once again.

Before I go home, I'll visit my father. I'll tell him what I found out. I don't know if it will tear open old wounds or finally give us a sense of peace, but he has the right to know. And maybe, if I'm honest, I need to tell him, need to tell him that it's affected me to see how much this has affected him. In my imagination he will start crying and we'll be free to deal with everything.

That probably isn't how it will go. Things don't get resolved just like that, and my father never cries, at least in front of me. The curse of this whole situation is that we've never been able to talk about things properly, and this isn't a movie. But maybe we'll sit for a while, out on the deck. He'll pour me some whiskey. I'll help dig up some potatoes or feed the chickens. He'll talk about repainting the fence.

GOD BLESS THOSE WHO NOBLY TOIL

BEN HOBSON

God bless all those who nobly toil,

Or mid the fierce war strives,

May each their foeman's prowess fail;

God bless their babes and wives.

Ellen F Young, Ballarat

Published in the *Geelong Advertiser* and *Intelligencer* in 1854

HE WAS CROUCHED DOWN ON HIS HAUNCHES SURROUNDED BY THE tents and the men working their claims, the women and the kids at play in a waterhole on the rise nearby, a metal bowl full of nothing rested on his lap. The sound of slopping earth, of rattling gold sieves desperate for the colour, of men grunting. And there was the cat in the darkness.

The last of his food was in his hand. A small lump of damper no wider than his thumb. He held it up, praying it would grow larger, and popped it in his maw. His throat, having not been slaked since it had rained those days ago, made the morsel feel like he'd swallowed dirt. He dropped the plate onto the earth, the sound of its banging making the cat's ears startle, making it turn its head to look at him. The rain had mottled its fur with dust and mud. He grabbed at his shirt, at his trousers. His clothes were dense with it, too. The two of them were united, tumbledown and worn. The cat had no purpose either. It licked its arse and did nothing else. For all the good he was, he might as well do likewise. The cat turned from him suddenly, scurrying away over the sodden earth, retreating into its owner's tent.

It had been days since somebody had found something worth getting up in the stirrups. You always knew when it happened not from the shouting but from the hushed way the diggers stopped their digging and the hurried efforts of a crew rushing from their site, taking whatever small patch of fortune they'd dug up in their hands straight to the shop for measurement. They were quiet and hurried to ward off would-be thieves.

They were wise to keep their secrecy. The coppers had arrived in Ballarat some months prior and they'd had little impact on the petty thieving or on the men playing their illegal games of two-up. Wilfred had seen them come, building their little hut, taking fees from these blokes just bloody struggling to feed themselves. They'd take their money alright, but do nothing to earn it. They'd soon start charging him for waking up in the morning, charge the cat for its fur. He looked at the building now perched atop the hill they'd chosen, little more than a large canvas tent.

The smell of cooking stew and burning wood nearby struck him and made his lips water. Somebody was always cooking in the camp. He looked down at the plate he'd dropped and ran his tongue over his lips and teeth searching for the remaining crumbs.

He shifted his feet in the dirt and looked up with his hands on his hips and there was the cat, looking out at him from the confines of its tent, the noise of its owner farting awake from within. He retreated up a rise and walked from the camp, the sound of mining equipment and blokes shitting and water and the smell of the wet earth, the smell of their work and sweat, all of them shitting and pissing in one big bowl. They were in the slop of it, this mess they'd created.

He walked up the rise and sat beneath one of the eucalypts and felt how wet his pants were and felt his bones shaking. He looked down at the camp and waited for the sun.

A few days later the hunger was upon him in earnest. As he walked through the tent village the smells from the cooking drove him wild, making him see in colours he didn't know existed.

A pot full of stew and the person tending it with her back to him and before he'd made the decision his hand was in there and it was too hot but he didn't care. He was lowering his hand again into the stew when he felt somebody shove him. He fell down and the shover was upon him then, a man.

'You old bugger,' he said. The man's nose shrivelled up at the smell now beneath him.

'I'm hungry. I'm sorry.'

'That's my kids' food.'

'I'm sorry.'

The man's eyes moved down to Wilfred's chest and he said, 'You should sell that if you're hungry.'

The man grasped at the wooden pendant. 'That's my boy's.'

'It would get you something.'

'I can't sell it.'

'You can't take what's not yours either. You hear me?' His nose puckered up once more. 'You stink, old man. You should wash and work like the rest of us.'

The man rose and offered a hand down for Wilfred to take but Wilfred only lay there. The man shrugged and wiped the hand on his shirt front and strode back to his tent. Wilfred saw children there and the woman from earlier. As the man returned to his tent one of the children said, 'What's wrong with him?'

Wilfred looked at the pendant on his chest and ran a finger over the wood, felt the way his son's small knife had etched in the pattern. He remembered watching him do it, his son hiding his little efforts from him each time he'd asked. For days he'd been at it. Until one morning he had felt his son's small fingers clutch his own in his sleep and then he'd woken up and seen him standing there over him and then he'd felt it, the pendant, placed into his palm.

Wilfred nodded. He was breathing hard. The pleasant feeling in his gut as the food wormed its way through him gave him no reason to regret what he'd done. He put his elbows back and tried to stand but could not. The least he could do was roll over so he could no longer see the family looking at him. So he did.

Days later he woke with the hunger in him deeper, his stomach sitting somewhere in his feet. He stood looking down at the camp. It was still daylight and he estimated it to be near midday judging by the arc of the sun. He was sleeping longer into each day and staying awake later. He wiped the back of his hands over his eyes and then wiped his hands on his trousers. He went into the camp and felt swallowed by its noise.

He came upon a family of Wadawurrung. The man was holding court surrounded by diggers, women holding their children, as he hefted his spear in the air; shouting his words. His skin painted in ochre, large white dots on his legs, and a series of stripes up his chest.

Wilfred knew the lines meant things to the Wadawurrung, but he didn't know what. His hand went to his pendant, to the lines his son had etched in, and wondered, not for the first time, what it was saying to him.

The man has small children who went around the circle holding out a hat upturned, collecting coins and gifts. Most of the diggers were as poor as he and only crossed their arms, but some of the small children watching had little trinkets they deposited into the hat. He stood back as the hat came to him, but the Aboriginal boy holding it saw him and pushed through the crowd to beckon him, to invite whatever offering he could manage. His hand went to the pendant around his neck.

'I'm sorry,' he said. 'I'm useless. I don't have anything.'

The young boy's smile never left his face, only nodding at Wilfred. He toddled back to his family. The Aboriginal man now hefted his spear and pointed at a tree in the distance, a young sapling as wide as a fist. He looked at the hat and, in a showy gesture, shook his head, waved his hands. The Wadawurrung boy circled the group again and collected more money from some of the diggers, who were not keen on giving it up but were keen enough to see what the man would do.

Wilfred should go and steal the hat, run up there in a frenzy and grab it and run. But he'd only muck it up somehow and then he'd be in jail and be worse off than he was already.

The man, finally satisfied with the offering, in one quick movement aimed the spear and hurled it. It flew through the air and around him Wilfred heard the children gasping and then it sunk itself into the tree.

The *thunk* of it and then the wobble of the shaft. The crowd cheered, the children especially.

Wilfred moved on.

He walked by a man sloshing dirt into a pan and felt the thirst for gold again but knew there was nothing he could do. He remembered all those useless months he'd spent scratching feebly at the dirt, working claims long ago abandoned by others. The man had his pan and was swirling the red and brown earth, looking down and then swirling it again, trying to shake the colour loose. The man did this in a hurried way and was quick to discard what he had and lift up more earth with his shovel. He looked up and saw Wilfred watching.

'You want something?' he said, sloshing his dirt into his pan.

Wilfred shook his head.

'Get outta here then.'

'You finding much?'

The man said, 'Get outta here.'

'I'm not a copper.'

'No, you're not.'

The man looked back down and swirled again but now Wilfred felt one of his eyes on him even if he wasn't looking. So he walked away but as he did so he fell down near the lip of the dig. He made it seem as though he'd fallen because he was clumsy or old or weak and the man shook his head and laughed but didn't see Wilfred take one of the small picks he had resting there for more delicate work. As he stood he held it up behind his back and wobbled to make the man laugh some more and when he was a distance from the scene of his crime he turned back. The man had not noticed and was still busy lusting for the colour in his pan. Wilfred smiled to himself and looked at the small pick and walked away.

He stood then for a while studying the tent of the owner of the cat. The cat was nowhere in sight. There were men nearby in their tents and a nearby family had two children who were playing out the front with a ball crafted from wood. Wilfred remembered their game, remembered playing it with his son. One of them had to hide the ball and the other had to find it. One with their eyes shut counting loud. He saw the small boy place the ball under a bucket at the front of a stranger's tent and then dash away and the ball looked all the world just like one he had owned many years ago.

He turned back to the tent of the man with the cat. He knew the man took the cat with him when he dug and so its absence meant his absence too. Wilfred stood a moment and saw the little girl find the ball and shout her victory, holding it aloft over her head and running after the boy, both of them laughing, and then ventured forward.

He swung back the front of the canvas and crouched his way in and the flap lowered and he was in that muffled dark of a tent. He had in front of him the pick held ready but found no quarry. He ducked low down and began rummaging through the trunk at the foot of the mattress. This bloke bloody in it enough to afford a proper mattress. There were papers Wilfred lifted and squinted at in the dark. They seemed to be correspondence but there were no statements of property. He kept looking and lifted the mattress and saw beneath even in the dimmed light of the musty canvas there was a small patch of recently disturbed dirt.

He got down on his knees and left the mattress leaning up against the canvas. He started going at the earth with the pick and had soon emptied a hole and found what was stored. There was a small wooden box with ornate carvings of two ducks on top and inside this were five little flecks of gold alongside a bunch of coins and the man's gold licence. He rubbed his fingertips over the gold and pocketed them and put the rest back in the box and placed the box back in the hole. They were not much but they would feed him for a month.

He felt near his ankles a disturbance, a creature moving, and then felt the creature latch itself around his calf muscle. He cried out and in his haste tried to stand but found the canvas topple. He muffled against the fabric but the thing around his ankle did not let go and he knew it was the cat. He kept kicking at it and trying to scrape it off with his free foot but in his confusion and panic he could not manage it. He heard the low growl of it.

Then he felt the man tackle him around his middle through the tent and then he was down in it. All muffled fury and confusion. He felt the man strike him through the fabric and lost his breath because of it, a fist right in his ribs. The canvas began suffocating him and he felt the man kicking at him and there was shouting somewhere too.

He struggled his hand free of tent and struck out with the pick in a hasty arc, striking nothing but air and then earth. He swung it again in the hope of warding off attack while he tried to shuffle free from his confines. The cat still attached to his leg, digging its claws in, drawing blood. He was old and he was weak and he wondered if he had any blood at all and wondered if the cat's claws had sunk straight through him somehow and he wondered all this while swinging the pick and stumbling to his feet.

Shrugging off the canvas and then he was free in the open. A crowd had gathered and had given him a wide circle and the man he was trying to steal from had taken a few steps back. The two little children he had noticed before were watching him, terror in their eyes, clutching hold of their mum. He saw no animosity in any of them, even in the man, the cat owner. They only regarded him with pity, a creature.

He dashed forward. The man hadn't seen it coming and took a step back and tripped and he was down on his arse. Wilfred lifted the pick and swung it down with the man panicking, scurrying backward, and sank it into the man's shin. The man cried out in the mud and dust and kicked at Wilfred who fell to his side and then as the crowd gathered around the fallen bloke, he was up and running. Some who had been watching gave pursuit. He ran through the tent village, past a mess of people who barely took any notice of him.

He ran up the hill and turned back and saw the men still struggling through the tent village. He was old and breathing hard. He felt the cat still attached to his calf muscle and finally looked down at it. Its claws adjusted and sank into him and he cried out and grabbed it by the scruff of its neck. He yanked it and yanked it until he'd wrenched it free and then it was hissing and spitting and clawing. He stuffed it into his shirt front and thought maybe he might negotiate with the man he injured for the return of his cat. Maybe he would let the whole thing go if he returned the cat and the gold. The cat immediately went to work on his chest and was yowling and crying. He sank into the tree line and then fought his way through the bush and kept going.

Shouting behind him. He kept running and was soon up a hill. He looked back. Three men giving pursuit. He felt tired and knew if he stopped too long he would sink down. There came a new pain in his chest and it made him shout. The cat had sunk its teeth into the meat near one of his nipples. He batted it with his free hand and saw the pick in the other and saw there was blood on the tip of it.

Moving up, over fallen trees, through the bush. Breathing hard, the cat making it harder. Put your hand out, that's it, use the tree, pull yourself forward. The smell of the eucalyptus and the sound of their noise oncoming.

Rounding a corner there was a stream and he ran along its bank. There were fewer trees near and then it widened. As he stepped over stone he looked back and then he was falling. He felt himself go deep and then it was black and then he collided with the earth.

Breathing. Something buried against him. He coughed and felt wet and cold and looked up and saw black and dirt. Dirt in his eyes covering his mouth. Something sticky. He lifted his fingers and felt down around near his ankle. A deep throbbing heartbeat in his left knee. Unrepentant dark.

He coughed and the noise startled him. He was on his back. Looking up he could see stars and he knew then he had fallen into a mine. One of the old ones without any type of support. Just diggers lusting for gold carving their way into the earth without care. He coughed again and felt a warmth flush over his chest. He lifted his hand up and felt the sleeping creature there nestled beneath his shirt, on top of the pendant. He put a hand under his shirt and lifted it and felt its muddy fur. The cat felt as though it was asleep. He lowered his hand.

He sat up on his elbows and blinked and tried to look at the mess he knew his legs were in. Impossible in the dark. There were no noises above of the men still looking for him. He knew he couldn't go back.

He strained and sat up and felt the pain in his legs freshen. There was no specificity to it. Just a big throbbing pain. He leaned down and felt with his fingers. His right foot was at an impossible angle and through his trousers on his left leg he felt a sticky mess near his kneecap.

He fell back onto his back and looked up at the hole and breathed in the stars.

It grew to be morning. The cat stirred against him and then he felt it pushing against his chest, its claws sticking into the bones of his ribs. He felt it yowling even if it wasn't doing so audibly. He looked up at the hole.

Half want someone to find me, he said to the cat.

He levered himself up to his elbows. Though the mine swallowed most of the available light he could see his legs a little better. His right foot was a wet noodle. It still throbbed with pain. He tried rolling his left pant leg up but after leaning forward the pain grew so sharp he had to lean back and then he was yelling and cussing and flailing his useless old limbs against the earth. His whole face sticky with blood and dust. He must look a corpse.

He rolled to his front and the pain in his legs heightened and he remembered sticking the man with the pick in his leg and looked down at his own and almost laughed. On his hands and elbows he attempted crawling back up the hole in which he'd fallen. He'd tumbled quite a way. Each inch sent pain rippling through his body. After what felt years he looked up and saw he'd almost not travelled any distance at all. The cat at his front clawing at him and now yowling audibly, fighting for freedom against the confines of his shirt.

He stopped in his efforts and just lay there breathing. He felt around in his pockets quickly and found no trace of the little box with the carved ducks. He must have dropped it. He rolled back over and then on his back he laughed and laughed. The cat stopped clawing at him as he started to sob and then he was just there breathing with a cat resting on top of him and this was now what remained of his life.

As he calmed he realised how hungry he was now, how thirsty. He felt drawn in, like his skin had sucked itself in over his stomach like the pegged-out canvas of a tent.

It came upon him then the idea that he should eat the cat. He moved a hand over his shirt front. It was warm and breathing and it had been the cause of his harm. Without the cat he would not have stumbled and would not have been caught. He felt the warmth of its blood already gushing through his insides. He might get a few more days out of that. It would be easy. He'd hold it and twist its neck and then tear it open with his fingers. His legs were a mess but he might survive long enough that somebody could stumble over the mine and he'd call out and then he'd be saved.

Saved for what though. Saved for what. He felt the cat through the shirt and as soon as he'd clasped hold of its fur it started its yowling and clawing at him. He yanked it from him and held it in its impotent fury clawing at his wrist. He grabbed it by the head and looked it in the eye and said, 'I better let you go back to him'.

The cat decided it would still, and it looked at him and he felt that maybe he could feel its beating heart through his fingertips.

With one hand he took the pendant he had worn the last ten years from around his neck. He undid the clasp with difficulty, hands shaking. He brought it around and put it over the cat and saw the loop of it was too wide, that it would soon shake off. So he tied a knot around it twice and tried not to choke the cat. The cat started immediately clawing at it, but he'd tied it well.

'That was my boy's,' he said. 'That's all he left me with when he ran off.'

The cat kept clawing at it. Wilfred looked at it one last time. Ran his fingers over its shape, felt the warmth of his son's hand in his.

Bugger it.

And he threw the cat down. It did not look back as it scurried up the mine wall with ease. As it was halfway up the mine he saw and heard the small pendant he'd tied to it fall. Then the cat was gone and he was all alone.

He lay back against the earth and felt where the cat had been warm against him and put a hand there until the warmth was gone. He looked up the passage of the mine and knew he'd never reach the pendant. He was too weak and too broken. He moved his hand up and felt where the pendant had been. He had hoped the cat would leave the mine with it and the owner would find it and wear the pendant and in some way he would have continued on. But it was just a pendant and the whole thing was foolish. He imagined his chest was still warm and placed a hand there and imagined his son there instead of the cat, the small body of his baby boy warming him, the feel of his new skin, the soft dark of his hair. Breathing out slowly, letting his breath touch the top of his boy's head, watching his hair gently flutter like butterfly wings. Returning to the last moment he had truly been whole.

WEB DESIGN

EMMA VISKIC

LISA WAS SINGING *EENCY WEENCY SPIDER* FOR THE HUNDREDTH time when she saw the car. A white Commodore a couple of car lengths back. Something about the way it had swung around the corner, was tailing her up the hill. Her foot pressed harder on the accelerator.

'Eency Spider, Eency Spider,' Abby's voice rose from the back seat.

'Shhh,' Hamish said. 'Mummy's worried.'

He was watching her in the mirror. Old-man eyes in the face of a four-year-old. She'd done that to him – her and bloody Billy.

'I'm just concentrating, sweetie.' She kept her voice light, light, light.

The Commodore was metres from her bumper now. She could see the driver. A fleshy face half-hidden by a baseball cap and dark glasses. Familiar. One of Billy's mates? She gripped the wheel with damp hands. OK, get off the highway and lose him in the back roads. A vision of dirt-track emptiness, her bleeding body.

'Eency Spider, Eency Spider!'

Lisa slipped her hand beside the seat and felt for the pry bar.

'Eency Weency Spider,' she sang as her fingers closed around the cold metal. 'Climbed up the waterspout.' She straightened, keeping her hand low. 'Down came the rain and washed poor Eency out.'

She'd smash his windscreen, his face, his kneecaps. She stomped on the brake and pulled over in a squeal of tyres, had the door open, one foot on the road before he drew level.

He didn't stop.

Didn't slow down.

A glimpse of a *Hawks* bumper sticker as he flew by. Just a local, the guy who'd flirted with her in the supermarket car park yesterday. He'd commented on her dress, made a joke about Abby's curls.

God, what an idiot. She lowered herself to her seat with trembling legs. Abby was screaming; her dumpling cheeks streaked with snot and tears. Bad mother. Bad, terrible, horrible mother. Lisa dropped the bar onto the passenger seat and started the car.

'Out came the sunshine and dried up all the rain. And Eency Weency Spider climbed up the spout again.'

She put Abby straight to bed and carried the toolbox out to the back yard. Hamish shadowed her, one hand clutching Blue Bear, the other tucked down his pants. He'd started wetting the bed after their third move. She gave him the toolbox to mind and got to work on the back step. Each cat-piss rental house was filled with lurking dangers. She lay awake each night cataloguing the ways the kids could die: a loose step, an old fuse box, an unearthed lamp. Their house, their real house, had been perfect.

'*My little homebody,*' Billy used to say, running a thumb along her calloused palm. '*My heart and hearth.*'

But there was no more beautiful house, no more beautiful Billy, no more beautiful money.

'Are we moving again?' Hamish asked.

'Not yet.'

His hand fossicked deeper in his pants. 'It's nice here.'

'I like it, too. Can you pass me a Phillips head screw?' Funny, she'd never thought of herself as a country girl, but this town had everything going for it.

She tightened the screw and sat back. 'Okay apprentice, give it a go.'

Hamish stomped up and down the steps and gave her solemn thumbs up. 'Solid as a rock.'

Billy's saying, only the rocks he meant were sold by the gram and turned out not to be such a solid investment after all. Crack cocaine, for God's sake. He'd cried when he told her how much he owed. Half a million. If he hadn't done a runner, she probably would have killed him herself.

She pulled out her notepad and checked her list. Stupid to spend so much time on the house, on getting Hamish settled at kindy, on meeting the neighbours; putting down roots that they'd just have to rip out again.

'OK, apprentice, let's have a look at that lamp.'

She was counting out the coins for the kids' ice creams when someone came up behind her. A large, tanned hand slid a ten dollar note across the milk bar counter.

'I've got it, Leese,' a man's voice said. 'My treat for the kids.'

The guy from the supermarket smiled down at her. His cap and sunglasses were gone, revealing dark eyes and short, blond hair. Something reptilian about the eyes.

'Thanks,' she said. Steady voice, easy smile. 'That's kind of you.'

She swung the stroller around and strode out. It was a small town; not that weird she kept seeing him. Except that Billy was the only person who'd ever called her *Leese*.

She started stuffing bedding into suitcases as soon as they got back to the house. Hamish followed, his hand toying with the waistband of his shorts.

'Are we going?'

'Yes.'

The emergency bags were in the boot, her hard-earned savings in the spare wheel. She'd replace everything else when they got to Adelaide/ Perth/Broome. She picked up the suitcases and ushered the kids down the hallway.

He was standing in the open doorway.

She snatched up Abby and pulled Hamish to her side.

'Nice house you got here, Leese. Not as flash as your last one, though.'

Pity that burned down. Glad you and the kids got out – be a fucken horrible way to die.'

Couldn't run with the kids. A weapon, something heavy. She scanned the hallway.

He smiled down at Hamish. 'This one's a good little footy player isn't he? I've been watching him play at kindy.'

Jesus, fuck. Heart hammering so hard she might vomit it up.

'Where's Billy, Leese? I've been hoping he'd turn up.'

'I don't know. He took everything and ran.'

'That's a bad habit of his, isn't it?' He stroked Abby's plump cheek. 'Your daddy's a naughty, naughty man, isn't he Abby? Stealing things that don't belong to him.' His snake eyes fixed on Lisa. 'Tell Billy that Detective Sergeant Manning wants his money by Sunday. All five hundred, plus an extra ten for fucking me around.'

'I don't know where he is.'

'Then I guess I'll be paying you a visit on Sunday. You and the kiddies.' He gave Abby's cheek a pinch and sauntered away.

Lisa slammed the door and turned the deadlock. Detective Sergeant. There was no getting away from a cop: a trail of electronic breadcrumbs showing their every move. Bloody Billy – ripping off a cop. The stupid bastard.

'Are we going now?' Hamish asked.

'Not yet, sweetie.'

The dog hadn't died easily: there were burnt patches on its flanks, foam around its mouth. Sick. Just fucking sick. Poor old fella. This is where trusting men had got her – dead dogs in the backyard. She sobbed as she swaddled its limp form in an old sheet. Please God, let it be a stray, let her bury it deep enough before the kids woke up.

On Saturday night, she parked the car in the backyard and put the kids to bed in it. Hamish had been dubious at first, but she'd brought him around with tales of camping and adventure. When they were asleep, she slipped back inside the house to wait. He came in the dull-witted hours before dawn. Not there one minute, in the darkened living room the next. She clambered to her feet, the streetlight glinting on the knife as she whipped it behind her back. Just a flash, but it was enough.

'Leese, Leese, I thought you were smarter than that.'

'I've got the money.' Her voice was too high. 'It's all there. Over by the table.'

'Glad to hear it.' He patted the wall and found the light switch. A click, but no light.

'Bulb's gone,' she said.

'I'm sure it is.' A tone as dry as kindling.

She took a step towards him. 'I'll turn the lamp on.'

'Stay the fuck where you are, sweetheart.'

He shuffled towards the lamp, his hand reaching for the switch. She stood poised, not breathing. A burst of light, a bang, and he thudded face-down on the floor. The smell of charred meat and piss. She edged closer, the squeak of her rubber-soled shoes loud in the silence. The old lamp had blown a fuse, but she kept well away from its exposed wiring as she knelt to feel for his pulse. Nothing. And she breathed again. She hadn't been sure if the wire she'd run from the unearthed switch to the power point would hold enough current, but it had worked perfectly. Wetting the floor had been a good idea, too – he'd died a lot faster than the dog.

Hamish blinked sleepily as she opened the car door.

'Go back to sleep,' she said. 'I'm just putting something in the boot.'

'Are we going?'

She paused with her hand on the boot lever. She'd known as soon as she pulled off the highway that this was the place. Couldn't say why, just that it seemed like a town where they could flourish. She'd been right, too – she'd built up a nice little trade in eccies and ice. And there'd be no stopping her now Billy and his fuck-ups were gone. They could settle in properly, let their roots grow deep.

'No, sweetheart,' she said. 'I think we'll stay.'

Author's note: This short story started off as a chapter I'd deleted from my first Caleb Zelic novel, *Resurrection Bay*, but quickly took on a life of its own. By the time I'd finished writing it, only one word of the original chapter remained – the iconic Aussie car, the Holden Commodore.

NOT MY DAUGHTER

DANI VEE

'You're not taking my children, Neil.'

It was hard to breathe with a gun sticking into the back of her neck. If it wasn't for the kids, she would probably have hung herself from a tree branch by now. A part of her didn't give a shit whether he pulled the trigger, she just wanted it to end. A mother could never choose between their children, could they?

'I'm not going to kill you, Emma. I just want to even things up.'

An eye for an eye. Isn't that what he used to say in his sermons? A tooth for a tooth. A life for a life. She liked the rhythms of the words, the simplicity of religious law, the justice. It had taken most of her adult life to undo her faith and realise the church's real work was shame and control. Come as you are, they said. Just don't stay that way.

'I'm not an unreasonable man, Emma. You get to choose which one I take.' His mouth was against her ear. 'Eeny, meeny, miny, moe. Do you have a least favourite, Emma?'

She recoiled at the heat of his breath and remembered the last time he'd gotten this close to her. 'Don't do this, Neil.' He was nothing, she reminded herself, nothing but a God-fearing misogynist prick who'd spent his life preying on the weak. Always under the guise of religion.

'The death of Charlie meant nothing to you,' he spat.

'We've all suffered.'

'I've suffered,' he snapped. 'Maryanne suffered, but you kept going as if nothing happened.' His face was close to hers.

'What do you want from me?'

'Accountability? Empathy?' He shook his head. 'You could've been a friend to Maryanne. It's the least you could've done. Even Brent figured out who you really are.'

Neil had been watching her. He never would've forced his way into her home at this hour if Brent had been there. 'What do you know about Brent?'

Neil laughed. 'It was inevitable, don't you think?'

Emma knew about her husband's affair. Men were incapable of hiding such things, she just didn't have the bandwidth to confront him. A single indiscretion shouldn't end a marriage, she told herself. She loved him enough to turn a blind eye to his mid-life crisis and when it was over, they would get on with their lives. She didn't think he'd fall in love with someone else.

'It was unstoppable,' he told her the day he left. She watched him pack a suitcase, as if it were happening to someone else. 'I feel alive for the first time in years.'

'Do you mean your dick was unstoppable and your dick feels alive?' Maybe if you spent more time being a good father, you'd have been too exhausted to fuck someone else.

Emma saw her world disintegrating and couldn't do a damn thing about it.

He shook his head at the glass of wine in her hand. 'Try not to drink yourself to death.'

She'd stood at the door and watched him pull out of the driveway; she was a pathetic sight made worse by her belief that he was coming back. Becoming a single mother at her age was akin to being the mouldy piece of bread at the end of a loaf.

'And now all this time later, here Neil was, with a gun pressed against her neck. 'Who's it going to be, Emma? Or do I put a bullet in all your heads.'

'Punish me, Neil, not the kids.'

'I am punishing you. I've thought about this for five years. Choose.'

'You're crazy,' she cried. 'Jack has anxiety, ADHD, anger management. He needs me.'

'Clarabel, she must be five by now?'

'She's a baby.' The words caught in her throat. 'She wouldn't survive.'

'Ivy then. Your little loose cannon, just like you.' He smiled. 'I knew you'd do it.'

'I didn't–'

'Choosing through a process of elimination is still a choice.' He lifted his arm in the air and looked smug as he smacked the butt of the gun into her face. She felt a blinding pain, then nothing.

Emma tasted blood as she lifted herself off the carpet. She tried to figure out how long she'd been unconscious. It was getting light, so a few hours at least. She pushed open her oldest daughter's bedroom door. Ivy was gone. Fuck. She checked on her other kids, Jack was in his bedroom with the covers cocooned around him, and Clarabel was stretched across her bed like a starfish.

She couldn't think in a straight line. The police were not an option, Neil knew things about her that would make the authorities question whether she was fit to be among society, let alone a mother. She called Brent but his phone went straight to voicemail. Ever since he became a father again, he found himself incapable of answering a phone.

She texted him. URGENT. Call me asap.

Think, she told herself, but her thoughts scrambled in her head. Millie. Relieved that she'd finally had a half decent idea, she ran outside and tapped on her next-door neighbour's front door.

'Ivy's been taken to hospital,' she lied, 'appendicitis, probably.'

Millie yawned and pulled her into a hug. 'I'm sorry. I'll look after the kids.'

Emma arrived at Sunnyside Psychiatric Facility in 50 minutes. The woman at the desk was a young brunette, who looked like she might still be in school. It was almost eight am, visiting hours were in less than hour.

'I'm early,' Emma said, 'but is there any chance I can see Maryanne Carter? It's urgent.'

The woman tapped away on the keyboard and shook her head. 'Mrs Carter was discharged three weeks ago.'

'What? Three weeks ago? Are you sure?'

The woman nodded.

'Are they still living in Surry Hills?'

'I can't release that information.' She was apologetic but jittery.

'Her husband is a dangerous man.' Emma whispered. 'I want to check that everything's okay.' She paused. 'Did you meet him?'

The woman nodded and from the expression on her face, she agreed.

'A real misogynist,' she said, trying to appeal to the young woman. They were all feminists these days.

The woman hesitated and leant over the counter. 'Their address hasn't changed since she was admitted.'

Emma smiled broadly. She might just find them before they do anything too stupid.

It had been five years since Emma had been to the Carters' house. Not much had changed: the weeds were still overgrown, the brown brick house stood like a cold sore at the end of the street. The surrounding houses were new builds that rose like white castles from the ground. Their neighbours must've despised them. Knocking on the front door, Emma thought she heard voices, but no-one answered. The blinds were shut and there was no way of looking inside from the front yard. Unlatching the side gate, she let herself into the backyard. Through the glass sliding door, Emma saw Maryanne staring right at her. She tried yanking open the door, but it was locked.

'What do you want?' Maryanne mouthed.

'We need to talk.' Emma shouted, making sure she was heard through the glass.

Maryane came closer. 'Did he do that to your face?'

Emma nodded. 'He's taken Ivy.'

Maryanne opened the sliding door a crack. 'After all these years, you want to talk?'

'I need you to help me.'

Maryanne rolled her eyes then moved aside to let her in.

The house was dark and smelt like wet socks. The furniture was worn, the carpet stained. Maryanne and Neil had never been obsessed with aesthetics, but the place was filthy. Dirty dishes were strewn across the sink, empty coffee mugs or their rings left behind on most surfaces. There was a breakfast tray on the bench with two rashers of burnt bacon and a tomato.

'Sorry for the mess. I wasn't expecting company.'

Emma explained why she was there. 'What would Neil want with Ivy?'

Maryanne stared out into her barren backyard. 'Charlie's death destroyed him. Us. Everything, really.'

'I didn't know you'd been discharged from the facility.'

Maryanne shrugged. 'I've become very good at pretending to be what everyone wants.'

'Where is he, Maryanne?' Emma leant towards her. 'I can never understand what you've been through, but as a mother–'

'Who am I a mother to, Emma?' There was acid in her voice. 'My only son is dead.'

'Surely, you wouldn't wish this on anyone.' Emma's voice cracked; she was getting desperate.

Maryanne straightened her spine. 'You think I'm supposed to tell you that I care what happens to your daughter? I lost my son, I don't go outside, I take more sleeping pills than most people eat breakfasts, and I've been on suicide watch for five years. I'm not apologising.'

Emma swallowed the lump in her throat. 'I think he's going to kill her!'

Maryanne picked up a pipe that looked like it was used for medicinal marijuana. 'He has a place out at Eden. He's involved with the church and Pastor Nicholas Hemmingway.'

Emma froze. She hadn't seen Pastor Nicholas since Charlie was alive. 'He doesn't live here anymore?' Emma asked. It was odd because Neil had adored his wife.

'I'm not much fun to be around.' Maryanne rose from her chair and walked into the pantry and walked out with a rifle over her shoulder. 'If you come here again, I'll use it.'

'What the fuck, Maryanne?' Emma moved towards the door, but stopped when she heard a noise upstairs. 'What's that?'

Maryanne looked towards the stairs. 'Biscuit. Come here, boy.'

A bedraggled dog that looked like it had once been a Maltese Terrier came bounding down the stairs. Maryanne bent down and scratched it under the chin.

'I'm sorry for what happened, Maryanne.' Emma offered.

Maryanne walked towards her, the rifle dragging on the ground. 'Get off my property.'

Emma slipped out the door and back out to the street. Whoever Maryanne used to be was long gone.'

Emma stopped at a hardware store. She didn't know exactly what she was looking for, but bought some cable ties and a small mallet she could fit inside her handbag. She had a six-hour drive ahead of her if she took the Canberra route. She wanted to avoid the coast road. That was for lovers and families, not lone women trying to find a psychopath from their past.

Emma never wanted to be mother. She'd watched her own mother fail time and time again, why would she be any different? Emma was nineteen when she met Neil. She'd crashed a party at the local church with her friend Toby. It wasn't much of a party; no booze, no drugs, and no-one was trying to hook up with anyone.

'Who the hell are you people?' Emma asked one of the young men.

'I'm Neil.' He talked about the church in a way she'd never seen anyone talk so passionately about something, not even Toby when he was on drugs, and Toby loved drugs.

'This is your pain,' he said, 'the acting out, but you can't escape yourself.'

Emma laughed. 'You really believe this stuff?'

He nodded. 'It's the only way we can heal. Let me show you.'

Neil had picked her up at nine am the next morning and drove them to the river.

'You need to see this,' Neil said pointing to a woman with long black hair that hung past her waist. 'That's Maryanne. She was abused by her stepfather, beaten by her mother. Look at her now.'

It didn't take a genius to figure out he was in love with her. The woman walked into the water, accompanied by two men. When they were waist deep, she disappeared beneath the water. The two men held her head under water for a full three minutes.

'They're going to kill her,' Emma said, her voice shaking.

Neil smiled, and when Maryanne emerged, she was luminescent. Everyone cheered. Maryanne was their rockstar.

'I want to try that.'

Maryanne walked over and stared her down. 'What are you waiting for?'

She trusted Neil back then. Even when he told her to stop seeing her friends. They were a bad influence. Or the night he pushed her into a public toilet block and forced himself on her.

'You are temptation.' His breath was hot on her neck, and she was too frightened to push him away in fear that he might exclude her. By then the church was all she had. 'There is too much of the Devil inside you, and He is testing me.'

A test he failed time and again.

When Emma married Brent, the church felt suffocating, it had rounded her edges. She drank and took Valium, but at least she felt like herself again.

The GPS took her through a winding road that made her stomach churn. She'd Googled Pastor Nicholas at Canberra and set the GPS to his church. When she found Neil, she was going to tear him apart.

Pastor Nicholas welcomed her inside the church and made her tea. The church overlooked the sea, a small seaside township full of families in tents and cabins enjoying the sun. Eden was midway between Sydney and Melbourne, but as picturesque as it seemed, there was something about the place that made her skin crawl. Pastor Nicholas was good looking and charming, as were most of the pastors she had known, but there was something darker about him too; a narcissism that made him think he was God-like enough to lead a church.

"I'm looking for Neil Carter. I'm an old friend.'

Pastor Nicholas said a quiet prayer and then opened his eyes. 'I hope Maryanne finally finds her peace. Neil said he's seen a change.'

Pastor Nicholas led her outside and they walked down a path where a dozen tiny houses were dotted around a clearing.

'It looks like a commune,' she said, her chest tightening.

He smiled. 'More like an intentional community.'

A euphemism for a cult.

Pastor Nicholas pointed out the tiny house that belonged to Neil and excused himself. 'I'll let you two catch up.'

The door was open. She let herself in and found Neil sitting in the lounge reading the Bible. 'What have you done with my daughter?' Ivy!' she called. But there was no answer.

Neil sat on the ottoman, unmoved.

Emma sobbed. 'I'm sorry about Charlie, but please–'

'Don't fight me on this, Emma. Or I'll tell the police about Alicia Bently.'

Alicia's family had worshipped at the church. She was thirteen years old and impressionable. Emma wanted to be a role model, but Neil kept telling her she wasn't ready..

One morning before church, she and Alicia snuck down to the river and took turns holding their breath under the water. Emma couldn't have known that Alicia was epileptic, nor that she would start convulsing when it was her turn. Emma dragged her onto the riverbed but had no idea how to do CPR or get the water out of her lungs. When Neil arrived, he didn't seem surprised. 'Dig a hole and bury her.'

'It was an accident.'

Neil was adamant that his church would receive no bad press, and because it was Emma's DNA all over the body, she didn't argue.

'I saw Maryanne.'

Neil's eyes turned dark. 'Why would you do that?'

'Did you think I was just going to let you take my daughter without a fight?'

'She's unwell.' His voice uneven.

Emma knew that Maryanne was his weakness. 'Tell me where Ivy is, or I will go back to Surry Hills and burn the house down with her inside it.'

'I wouldn't do that if I were you.' He leant towards her and pressed his thumb against her forehead. 'You've always had the devil inside you.'

'Where is my daughter?'

'Where she needs to be.'

Where she needs to be. An idea struck her. She couldn't provide she was right, but what other options were there?

'I need a glass of water.' Emma moved to the kitchen, where Neil's back was to her. He started babbling on about how Emma had never been able to expel the darkness that dwelled inside her.

'Are you suggesting an exorcism?' Emma asked, but she didn't give him the chance to reply. She took the mallet from her bag and whacked him at the base of his skull. The sound made her nauseous, but Neil was right. Only someone with the Devil inside them could do what she had done. He made a gurgling noise and his head fell forward at a strange angle. For a moment, she thought she'd killed him, but then she heard a breath. Shaking, she bound his wrists and ankles with the cable ties and went to get the car.

Neil has heavier than she expected. There was no way she was getting him inside the boot without some help. She splashed water in his face and his eyes snapped open.

'Get in the boot.'

Saliva fell out of his mouth. There was a lump on the back of his head and blood coming out of his ears. That wasn't good.

'You told me that I had too much of the Devil inside me, Neil. It's about time I showed you how much.' She took the mallet out of her bag. 'Get in the boot or I will smash your brains in.'

Back on the road, she jumped at the sound of her phone.

'This better be important, we haven't slept in days.' This is how Brent answered the phone these days.

She wanted to ask if he'd expected fatherhood would be any easier in his forties, but she swallowed her words. 'Neil Carter took Ivy last night.'

'What? What do you mean?'

Emma explained what had happened, leaving out the part where she'd whacked Neil in the back of the skull with a mallet and the fact he was lying in the boot of her car.

'Meet me at home. Millie is there with the kids.'

'Do you think we should call the police?' he asked.

'What do you think? Would you like me to go to gaol for Alicia's death? Or perhaps you'd like to go for helping Neil rip off charities or tax fraud?'

Brent grunted.

'I think I know where Ivy is. I'm going to get her.'

Brent had no other option but to go along with her plan. Neil started making noises in the boot, like he might be kicking out a taillight.

'What's that noise?' Brent asked.

'I have to go.' Emma hung up the phone.

Emma didn't knock on the front door this time. She took the mallet and smashed the sliding glass door open. Maryanne stood in the centre of the room, shaking.

'I don't know why I didn't put it all together when I was here, but Neil kept saying that you'd be better soon, as if Charlie was coming back. But it wasn't Charlie, was it?' Emma knew Maryanne had always pulled the strings in her relationship with Neil. 'Did you make him bring her here? Are you replacing your son with my daughter?'

'I wouldn't want your boy. He's just a cheap copy of my son,' Maryanne hissed.

Emma paled. 'You know about Jack?'

Maryanne scoffed. 'It was my idea that Neil sleep with you until he and I were married, but then you got pregnant, so we married you off to Brent who was too stupid to figure it out.'

'You're sick.'

'It should've been Jack that drowned that day. Not my boy.'

'It was an accident.' Emma shouted.

'You were responsible for him. If you'd hadn't been drunk and drugged up to the eyeballs, he would still be alive.'

'The noise upstairs this morning. It wasn't the dog, was it?' Emma walked towards Maryanne with the mallet. 'What have you done to her?'

'You don't want her. She has the Devil inside her too.' Maryanne paused. 'We know what she did.'

There was another noise upstairs, as if someone was trying to kick open a door. Emma ran up the stairs two at a time.

Ivy was gagged and tied to a chair in Maryanne's ensuite. She must've heard voices and started kicking the door. She was dressed in what must've been Neil's clothes and Maryanne had shaved her hair. Ivy's eyes filled with tears at the sight of her mother.

Emma freed her, and she fell into her arms.

'I'm so sorry, mama. Forgive me.'

'You're safe now.'

Emma heard a chair scraping across the wooden floor downstairs, then the sound of it being flung across the room. Emma lifted Ivy into her arms and went downstairs.

Maryanne had hung herself from the exposed wooden beams, a rope around her throat and her body jerking mid-air. I could save her, Emma thought, but she didn't move. She remembered how fierce Maryanne had been when they'd met, how much Emma wanted to be like her and how she had lost every ounce of that person when Charlie drowned. The life drained for Maryanne's face. 'Let's go,' she whispered.

Strapping her daughter in the front seat of the car, she handed Ivy the half-eaten chocolate bar she had in her handbag. 'Give me a minute.'

She opened the boot of the car and cut the cable ties around Neil's wrists and ankles. He struggled to climb out of the car then fell onto the driveway.

'Maryanne is dead'

He shook his head and blinked and for the first time in her life, she saw fear in his eyes. Emma watched as he opened the front door and went inside. He screamed, and Emma felt a cold shiver run down her back. As she reversed out of the driveway, there was a gunshot. Something settled inside her. The Devil was dead.

Brent, his new wife Tanya, and their newborn daughter Bianca were sitting in the lounge room when Emma and Ivy arrived home. Millie was making toasted sandwiches.

'Thank God.' Brent hugged his daughter to his chest and started to cry. 'Are you okay?'

'She will be.' Emma assured him.

Millie took Jack and Clarabel next door to watch movies and eat pizza. She was no longer buying the whole appendicitis story but there would be plenty of time for that. Emma kissed Clarabel on the forehead and hugged her son, his likeness to Neil becoming more obvious over the years. Something Brent failed to notice.

'Why don't you hold your baby sister while the three adults go outside and talk for a bit.' Tanya suggested to Ivy.

As much as Emma had tried to dislike Tanya, she was kind to their kids and she hadn't been responsible for the end of their marriage. That was all on them.

The three of them went outside, leaving Ivy to hold the baby on the lounge. Emma explained everything. Brent shook his head in shock, but Tanya patted Emma's hand.

'I'd do the same for my daughter.'

Emma thanked her and went inside to check on the Ivy and her half-sister. At first Emma couldn't quite see what Ivy was doing. Was it a game of peek-a-boo or another game she had invented to amuse her.

'What are you doing?'

Ivy removed her hand from the baby's face and the baby cried. 'Nothing.'

Emma took the baby from her daughter and patted her back as she had done with all her children.

'Did you tell Neil to take me because I'm bad? He said I had the Devil inside me, like you.' Ivy bit her fingernails.

Emma shook her head. 'I didn't send you away. Neil came here with a gun and took you.' She put her arm around her daughter's thin frame.

'Maryanne said she knew what I did.'

'Knew what?'

Ivy avoided her mother's eyes.

Emma remembered how hot it had been that afternoon, five years ago. Brent and Neil were cooking sausages on the BBQ, while Emma nursed a wine and Maryanne was drinking a soda water. Clarabel just turned six months old, and all Emma could think of was that she was grateful to be drinking again.

'Damn it.' Brent said. 'We've run out of gas for the BBQ.'

'I'll run you down to the servo,' Neil offered.

'I'll come.' Maryanne said, 'I want an ice cream.'

Neil offered to buy her one, but she insisted on going with them. Things had been tense between Emma and Maryanne. Maryanne didn't approve of Emma's drinking, or the way she parented, or anything, really.

'I'll watch the kids.' Emma said filling up her wine glass.

Clarabel was asleep, and Jack, Ivy and Charlie were in the pool, diving to the bottom to find the toys they'd thrown in. Finally, alone in the house, Emma started drinking from the wine bottle. While searching for something to eat in the pantry she found the packet of Valium, Brent had hidden from her. She swallowed two and settled on the couch. When she opened her eyes again, Ivy and Jack were standing over her, wet and shivering in the lounge.

'What are you doing in here?'

Jack was pale.

It was Ivy who spoke. 'Charlie isn't moving.'

'What?' Emma lifted herself from the lounge and went outside. Charlie was face down in the swimming pool.

'Oh my God.'

Emma dragged him out and started CPR while calling out to Ivy to call triple zero.

Ivy stood watching with a blank expression. The paramedics arrived minutes before Brent, Neil and Maryanne returned.

'What happened?' Brent asked.

'Mummy took some pills and fell asleep on the couch.' Ivy offered.

'What did you do that day, Ivy?' Emma asked.

Ivy squinted at her and pouted. 'You told me to protect Jack because he was special.'

Emma rocked Brent and Tanya's baby in her arms, and felt her legs turned to water.

'Charlie was teasing him. He wouldn't stop even after I asked him nicely, so I made him stop.'

'What did you do?' Emma's breath was uneven.

'I held his head under the water.'

The air left Emma's body. 'What were you doing to Bianca when I walked in?'

'Stopping her from crying,' she said, 'it's so annoying.'

'By putting your hand over her face?'

Emma thought back to all the times she had found bruises on Jack's body and dismissed him as clumsy, or the reason why Clarabel never wanted to be alone with her older sister. Ivy was a monster.

'You held Charlie's head under the water until he drowned?'

Ivy tilted her head. 'You weren't watching, mama.'

'No, I wasn't.'

'Everything okay?' Tanya asked coming back inside.

Emma's thoughts raced. If Ivy could hurt Charlie, was she be capable of harming her siblings? She knew what it was like to have darkness inside her, it was what had driven her to drink, what had led to the death of Alicia Bently, and why she had watched Maryanne die this afternoon rather than help her. It wasn't Ivy's fault. Whatever was wrong with her she'd inherited from her mother, and now it was Emma's job to protect her daughter.

Ivy looked up at her mother. 'Can I go to bed, mama?'

Emma nodded. 'Of course, baby.'

'Will she be okay?' Brent asked, when Ivy had disappeared up the stairs.

I would do the same for Bianca. Tanya's words echoed through her. A mother did whatever it took to protect her children, even when their children were wrong.

'She'll be okay.' Emma said, her voice shaking. 'I'll make sure of it.'

THE FLEMISH BOND

MICHAEL BOTUR

My flight from Christchurch up to Auckland is supposed to land at 3pm but delays push it back to 4, then 4.30, and by the time I'm squeezing into the back of this Uber fella's souped-up boyish Honda outside the terminal, I'm seriously watching the clock.

If I don't get up to Warkworth for the show at 7.30pm, I don't get paid. It's that simple. I chuck my overnight bag in the boot, not that I'm staying the night. We have to get out of Auckland Airport and into mainstream traffic by 4.35pm. I want to yell at Uberman *You could've squeezed into that gap there behind the tanker, or that gap, or that one. It's a roundabout, man: just go for it.* I drum my thick blunt fighting fingers impatiently on the glass. Hopefully he'll take note of my scarred knuckles, my thick arms. *These hands get results – so you need to hurry your arse.*

Uberman gets the car a few hundred metres along but it's slow as fuck and every car seems welded together into a train. No gaps. We're dealing with Friday afternoon traffic here – every cunt in Auckland's on the motorway heading to their fancy bach. We can expect this one-hour drive to take two and a half. Or more.

Air New Zealand made me late, the incompetent wankers. Story of my life, honestly, people taking what they want from me.

The deal is I'm expected at the Warkworth Masonic Community Hall for 7 o'clock. 7.15 is juuuust doable; 7.30 is when the actual bell rings for my wrestle. If I miss the bell, I'm in breach of contract, which means no pay, which means I've paid for a flight for nothing, which means I'll miss my credit card repayments, my rent, my child support. My car could get repo-ed. Everything will fail.

We finally screech into a space and point north and I relax a fraction and get a chance to study my driver: Hawaiian shirt, gelled black hair, messy black goatee. Jesus on the dash, rasta air freshener hanging from the rearview in the shape of a weed leaf. He's my age, more or less. His biceps are interesting. Bit of muscle on him.

'Vili,' he goes, offering me an upside-down handshake over his shoulder as he changes lanes.

'Tone.'

The fella looks Tongan, I reckon, and I'm about to strike up a little small talk about Tonga's chances in the World Cup when the driver goes, 'You're Tony Timaru of the Timaru Two, right?'

'Just the Timaru One these days. My partner got himself a house and a spouse. Shoulda followed suit, really.' I snort. 'God knows why I chose to fight for a living. Cheers for noticing, though.'

'I know my fighters.' His eyes in the rear-view are serious. Unlaughing. Some kind of stalker. Great.

My driver suddenly overtakes a BMW and we start leaving hotels behind us. He's 20 kays an hour over the speed limit, but it feels good to dodge the traffic.

My fight is strictly 7.35 to 8.05pm. After that the Warkworth Community Hall is being used by the country music club at 8.30. I'll need a ride back to the airport to fly home to Christchurch at 9.50 pm because the $110 flight is cheaper than paying for a meal and a mattress in Auckland. Wrestling, kickboxing, Muay Thai, bareknuckle, MMA – none of the disciplines pay much so I have to haggle to find a taxi driver who'll do the drive cheap and fast to cut down my costs. Being a journeyman sucks.

Auckland is oozing by my window now at a good pace. The driver tells me he's taking the route past Middlemore. He's gonna connect with

Highway One then we'll be sorted. I relax one percentage point but I can't trust this motherfucker completely. I learned a long time ago never to let your guard down even when a man seems solid.

'You said you know your fighters?'

'Hard. MMA, UFC, bareknuckle, Golden Gloves. I keep up. This fight tonight's AAWA, right?'

'Aotearoa Amateur Wrestling Association, indeed. These jokers are a lot less prestigious than they act, I gotta tell ya. Bastards wouldn't shout me a flexi ticket for the plane.'

Vili flits between lanes then zooms up an onramp and settles in the centre of the motorway where the flow's pretty good. I look at the cars on either side to gauge whether we're slipping. I notice us lose a couple places then Vili veers left, races up then veers right again.

Vili stares at the car in front's bumper, deadly serious. 'It's all bullshit, behind the glam. Oi: you see this right here?'

We're passing a new housing development called Mangrove Waters that doesn't seem to end. Linked by new black asphalt are all these McMansions held up by pillars rising up from freshly-poured concrete sitting in brown dirt with sprouts of grass. At the end of the subdivision is a brick house on a tiny paddock with a dozen cows. It's completely circled by new roads.

I don't know why the driver's singled out some standard brick build.

'Typical Dorkland expansion?'

'Nah, G,' my driver tells me, 'Brick, bro, brick. Built to last. And you know how come? No plaster, no steel– '

'Flemish bond.'

'Damn, Tone,' he says from the front. 'How'd you know about the Flemish bond?'

'You lay the bricks, fuck, what's the word... perpendicular? Looks like they're goin' different directions but they hold together better than anything.'

Vili the driver gives me deep eye contact in the rear-view. 'My man. You lay bricks?'

'When I was a kid, a bit, yeah. Couple of my stepdads were bricklayers. Made sense to go to work with them after I dropped outta school. Guess Mum had a type.'

Driver Vili is nodding deep and long and slow. He cuts to the right, across two lanes. I watch the needle creep up and hit 140. I don't care if we die. My life started off shit; let it have a symmetrical end.

'You got the government tryna vaccinate little kids, you got homos gettin married: while the rest of society crumbles, decent masonry holds tight, my brother. I wish more people appreciated it.'

My driver is positively grinning into the mirror now. He thinks he's found a friend.

'One brick watches the other brick's back,' he continues. 'That's why it's strong. Get a brick on its own, it can be susceptible. But two united, nothing can hurt it.'

'You married, Vili?'

'Nah. You?'

'Used to be. I was an arsehole to live with.'

'I'd live with you, bro. Watch fights on YouTube all day, am I right?!'

He's getting a little serial killer-y for me now. Vili punches the dashboard, steps harder on the gas. I study the fascinating billboards we don't have down south. Wendy's, St. Pierre's Sushi, Rainbow's End...

'Bro, layin bricks was meeeean money when I was tryina get out of the hood. Wasn't much else work in Aranui, eh.'

'Aranui? Mate, I went to Hornby High. I'm old school Christchurch too.'

'So you're a westside whiteboy eh? East Side Bloods over here.'

He passes his hand over his shoulder again for a fist bump while he holds the wheel with his pinky finger.

We blaze past a city-sized shopping mall called Sylvia Park, then a bend in the road where there's a Tip Top ice cream factory, then a Mercedes dealership and a gigantic church and this smokestack billowing melted Pink Batts, then my driver's pointing out brick buildings left right and centre as we put Newmarket behind us.

He won't stop running his mouth, this guy. Tells me his whole life story – after his old man got shot by the Harris Gang he tried to find an alternative dad in church elders, Scout masters, and rugby coaches before settling on boxing pretty much because he wanted to punch people constantly from the age of 14.

It's gotten a fraction colder in the car. I put my bag on my lap for warmth. We're in a tangle of curled concrete bridges now. Traffic is bunching up and the Sky Tower appears between buildings. My driver looks for a different lane but everything's slowing.

'FUCKIN' SPAGHETTI FUCKIN' JUNCTION.' He thumps his door.

'So you like to get some punches in,' I chuckle, 'I used to box at Dutchy's in Cashmere, dunno if you know the place.'

Vili hauls the steering wheel left and settles in a nicely-flowing rapid. He's got an anger management problem but my man knows how to hack traffic. My phone tells me it's now 5.05pm. We might actually make the venue on time.

'I was a Dutchy's boy myself,' Vili mumbles. 'Don't recall seeing your photo on the wall.'

'I don't let anyone take my picture unless it's marketing shit. How old are you? Maybe we were a couple years apart.'

He tells me he's 34; I tell him I'm 37. About 17 years too old to be fake-fighting for minimum wage, I want to add. Couldn't stick with boxing though, not after what happened.

We reach the top of the Harbour Bridge. Halfway. I've got white noise in my ears.

I've hardly thought about Dutchy's Boxing Gym in ages. When I was 18, 19, I doused my brain with so much weed and crack and bourbon my memories of Dutchy's got pushed wayyyyy down. I found myself smashing people on Colombo Street, jumping on the bonnet of some cop car in Cashel Mall. Can't even remember how half the fights started.

Dutchy's was so refreshing at first. We used to have Fight Club at school with a few uppercuts and king hits but Dutchy's was a hundred times more disciplined. My mum drove me there one afternoon just before dinner time cause her boyfriend had pinched my ear and I'd busted his nose and my mum was shrieking if I wanted to fight so bad I could at least get some exercise while doing it.

She dumped me on old Coach Dutchy's driveway. Coach Dutchy came out in his white singlet and flip flops. Springy curly white chest hair stuck out around his tits. His eyes were 100 percent on me. Didn't ask to meet my mum or anything. No fees, no paperwork, no names, no nothing – just shoved these sweaty, manky leather gloves in my arms, tossed a roll of cotton bandage on top and told me to glove up and get in the ring. We'd sort out money later. He didn't have a wife or kids anymore; we didn't have dads.

The boys at the gym were skinheads, Crips, gingers, Māoris – the only thing we had in common was Dutchy – like a father, punishing our arses, making us soldiers. We had to do sit-ups while he dropped heavy leather balls on our stomachs. He made us skip for 10, 15, sometimes 20 minutes. He blasted these corny Irish resistance songs with violins and big rousing choruses and cause Coach's ears were warped and puffy like fungus he wouldn't hear his shitty 1980s CD player skipping and all us boys would be haemorrhaging sweat, looking for sympathy from the photos of shirtless graduates smiling on the wall, praying for the skipping and the CD to end so we could snatch a quick sip of soothing water.

When we got in the fuckin ring though, by God. We had incredible leg work from all the skipping. Plus the combos he'd force us to practice a hundred times paid off. I was shit-scared going to my first Golden Gloves but a 1-6-3-2 combo won me my very first fight. My mum was at the casino and didn't see it but the boys were all hugging me and shit. It was all thanks to the fitness – Dutchy's people had gone through famine around the Second World War and he was obsessed with self-denial. Pain makes you strong, he'd tell us.

The first dude I fought saw right from the ding of the first bell he was in for a long, hard dance instead of a quick knockout. I made him drain himself chasing me round the ring till he let his guard down then I pummelled the cunt and got me a medal.

I started to love Dutchy's after that. He offered three sessions every week and I took them all up. Other fights in life had brought me only trouble but Dutchy's was a place to turn your anger into gold. Every dude that turned up for training was from a different clique but we all bowed down to the god of discipline.

That discipline took a lot of forms not even related to boxing. We weren't allowed to smoke or drink or eat pizza. He'd use forceps on your stomach. He whipped you with a skipping rope if you had any fat on you. If we wanted an energy snack it had to be sunflower seeds. Some days there was zero boxing and Dutchy had us laying bricks. We built something called a heat wall where the bricks face north to catch the sun so Ol' Dutch could grow kumara around his house, which was on the same section as the gym. And he was proud, don't get me wrong. For a few minutes a week he'd be all mushy, nuzzling your hair and telling you he loved you. Then he'd whack you in the guts for not standing up straight.

I boxed all through 14, 15, 16. At 17 I was still going hard. Partly I was waiting for a chance to earn a one-on-one session with Dutchy on some rainy Friday night when he'd get all fatherly, dust off the camera and take a photo for the Wall of Fame. Dutchy didn't give all the boys the honour of being photographed with their medals dangling between their pecs. His head was as banged-up as his ears and he'd go months forgetting to take a new photo before quietly leading a boy aside to arrange a photo sesh. *Kom met mee, jongen*, he'd always go. A few days later there'd be a picture of a boy on the wall, freckled with sweat, neck flared, chin upthrust. The heroes. The favourites. I woulda given anything to have my picture on that wall.

One night we witnessed Coach Dutchy face down a whole carload of Road Knights out in the blue and orange woodsmoke of a Christchurch winter night. The gangsters were calling out little Hori for a one-out and our coach, bro, he mighta had vegetables in his head but he knew how to win a scrap, woo whee. It was obvious Hori wasn't being called for an actual one-out — a buncha bearded 40 year olds were planning to stomp his face into the gravel. Dutchy went over to the car, cocked his finger like a gun, pointed at the passenger then each of the two goons in the back of the Holden and shouted, 'YOU FIRST, THEN YOU, THEN YOU, JA, COME OOOOOOOOOON.'

The little toerag prospect calling out Hori got the fuck back in the car reeeeal quick and disappeared. Dutchy hadn't even thrown a single punch.

That was one of my last memories of Dutchy, actually. I dropped out of the gym not long after then.

'Dutchy died real sudden, eh.'

'That he did,' Vili says.

God, I've drifted off. She's after 6pm now. We've moved up the map. We're passing a huge glittery spire sticking up out of Takapuna. The motorway is wide and generous. Saints be praised, we may just make it to Warkworth on time.

I'm about to ask what happened to the gym, how long it kept going after I dropped out, when Vili goes, 'How much you weighing these days?'

'Eighty. Reeeeal good fighting weight. Lets you be nimble if you keep yourself at 80 kilos. You?'

We're passing a KFC beside something called North Shore Stadium. God I could go for some fried chicken. I hate having to stay paleo.

'Me, I don't weigh myself any more,' Vili goes, swearing at a Mini as he moves around it. In the mirror I notice Vili gritting his teeth. He's pissed about something.

I'm getting a flashback of when Coach Dutchy used to weigh us boys. Dutch started doing weigh-ins at 7am. The gym was always cold, nobody moving, nobody speaking. Hardly anyone showed up to the before-school sessions, actually. I would've appreciated some of that Irish music but the first half of the day was just warming the air up. Wiping the dribble off the windows. Dutchy'd told me we were here to scrub the gym clean. After I'd mopped and hung the knuckle-bandages on the clothesline to dry he had me strip naked and stand on the scales. Coach Dutchy then asked me, 'Do you think you are weighing more if you are having a piece of wood on you, yes?'

'What wood?'

Dutchy reached between my legs. I froze. Dutchy peeled the foreskin off my diddle and started stroking it. He was close enough a few of his chest hairs tickled my arm. I felt static electricity. He got down on his knees and put his crusty lips on my cock and moved his tongue and his gums. Then he pulled his mouth off and told me to jack myself til I got a "schtiffcock." I said I was scared.

'Son, I will knock you out lickety split. You are doing what I am tellingk you, ja?'

I did what he said. I could've smashed just about any cunt in Christchurch back then. Anyone except Dutchy.

The car is silent as we put Auckland behind us. We gobble up farmland with mist settling on it like bedsheets. Overpasses, roadside turkeys, sheep, Snowplanet, Silverdale. I grab the headrest of the passenger seat that's in front of me and crush it, fingers digging into the foam. Maybe I'll dig out an eyeball in my fight tonight. I'm pissed about everything. These McMansions we're hooning past? Fuck those people. Fuck their luck. They never got pulled out of the mainstream for a private photo session. All them homeowners in Millwater, Auckland's most expensive development, all them cunts had daddies and mummies to hand them a fuckin' chequebook and say Here ya go, son. Take as much support as ya want. It's bottomless.

Me? My life is layin' bricks and takin' hits. I can't get a straighto job. I've got convictions for, God, you name it – GBH, assaulting a female, assault with a blunt instrument, armed robbery, drug utensils. Put your body on the line for a dime. This fuckin' world didn't give me many alternatives.

As we come up to some tunnel near Puhoi, we pass under a bank of cameras.

'What's with all the photos?'

'They snag your licence plate. Government's always watching citizens, bro.'

'I fuckin' hate being photographed. Dutch, the bastard, he took... Never mind.'

I don't say anything while we're in the tunnel. We emerge and race past the Puhoi turnoff. There's a billboard saying you can get oysters and chips for ten bucks. I could use a feed. No time tonight, though. Pay the driver, fight, get dressed after, scoff some sunflower seeds, hop a taxi to Auckland Airport. Catch the late flight back down south. Eat white bread and margarine to balance the books. Keep my phone in hand til the next gig lands.

'He took photos of you, I'm guessing,' Vili the Uber Driver goes, 'Said he was weighing you then started taking your photo and shit?'

'Mind your business.'

A sign says Warkworth is 35 kays away. The time is 6.49 and the sky is indigo. Hurry, driver, hurry.

'I quit the gym, god, 2003-ish,' Vili goes.

'Good for you.'

'Lemme finish.' He's looking at me hard in the rearview now. Can't be long til we hit Warkworth. May as well hear the weirdo out. Dude seems to think we're some kind of equals.

'So I dropped out of my apprenticeship. Drinking, burgs, fuckin' gangs, Tone. That was the life. Anyway one night I got really wasted on BZP. Member that shit? That was just after the 90s, cuz. I used to pushbike everywhere back then, I didn't give a fuck, and if my bike got nicked I'd just boost another one. Anyway I wound up at Dutchy's house when I was real baked. This was like four months after I'd stopped showing up to training cause Dutchy'd taken those bloody photos of me, on the scales of course, butt naked, as ya do – and he tried the old "got wood" trick on me too, the unoriginal cunt – so anyway, it's summer when I bike round for a catch up, I'll never forget that. Cicadas in ya fuckin' ears. Bugs crawling on the light on his porch. And I'm high as a kite, right, and I pedal from Aranui all the way to Cashmere on autopilot. It was 8 o'clock on a Saturday night, I remember cause they were drawing the Lotto and one of my aunties had my birthday as her numbers. But you don't wanna... ah, sorry man. I shouldn't've... never mind.'

'Bro: finish.'

Vili matches my eyes in the mirror. I can feel the car slowing slightly. This better be good.

'Anyway I bang on his door and Dutchy's real happy to invite us into his warm lounge, even though I'm looking rough as guts. I've got an NBA singlet on and gumboots. Dutchy lays two cocktails on the coffee table and sits beside me on the couch azif we're on a date. The movie was *E.T.*, I'll never forget that. Classic Saturday night family shit in front of a roaring fire, nice drink, everything's happy endings.'

A sign says Warkworth is five kilometres away now. The clock has just spilled past seven. We're going to make this.

'God knows why but Dutchy got a stiff from *E.T.* He was real engrossed in the movie, the fucking paedo, and it was only when the ads came on he put his hand on the back of my head and kinda nudged my face down towards his cock. I whacked him with a left hook to the jaw, of course, all while sitting down. He was stunned, right, sitting there in his old man robe. I didn't wanna get a hiding so I put the cunt in a sleeper hold. Lights out, old man. Then I kneeled on his shoulders and held a cushion on his face. Musta choked him for a good ten minutes, eh. Made it look like an accident. Then I went through this box under Coach's bed and I found all photos of diddles and boys crying and standing on the scales naked and shit. Burned those fuckin' photos in his fireplace, eh. Oi: here's Warkworth. We did it.'

We bend through a couple streets and find a parking lot. The

Warkworth Masonic Community Hall is a brick building beside a low muddy river. Palm trees and wrought iron lamps and paving stones. Cars everywhere. Bass and treble and voices on the breeze.

'I'm a good guy,' I tell my driver, 'A babyface. Just so you know. In the ring, I mean. Not one of the bad ones.'

I pay my driver, pull my gear from the trunk and head for the green room. 7.13pm. A respectable time, all things considered.

'I'll find a taxi back,' I tell Vili as I slam shut the trunk of his car and prepare to go put my body on the line. 'I don't expect you to wait for me, man. Laters.'

The small crowd cheer and whistle as I stride through them. Amateur wrestling brings joy and escapism to your life, if you think about it. I replay a charade I've done over and over – Tony Timaru the superhero. People rip my epaulettes off, firstly, then the cuffs of my shirt, then some of my buttons. Souvenirs. People have always taken a piece of me.

The Beehive is a heel in a beekeeper suit whose signature move is The Sting. Backstage we plan our battle, synchronizing a couple of choke slams then go out and smash each other round the ring for half an hour. After our fight, everyone poses for photos with me. I escape after four minutes, sweaty, struggling to breathe. I've knocked fans unconscious in the past. I can't always control my fists when I get anxious.

In the parking lot beside the salty river, a shitty Uber is waiting for me. An elbow is pointing out of the driver side window. The radio is playing Bob Marley. Vili is giving the Eastside with his fingers and grinning, waiting to take me home. This hall is built of 120-mil bricks. I knock on the masonry and wink at him. Call it shitty, call it shabby, but the Warkworth Masonic Community Hall has stood since 1895, cause nothing can bring down the Flemish bond.

THE LOKKAS

HELEN FITZGERALD

FOR MY BIRTHDAY I GOT A DVD (*THE FLY*), A BOOK (*FRANKENSTEIN*), a cupcake (chocolate), a jar of jam (Davidson Plum), and a monitor, which was the best present of all.

It's not the window I dreamt about and prayed for, but I know a window is impossible down here. I have always known that, ever since I arrived. Hard to believe that's a whole nine years ago now; hard to believe my world has been this one room for all that time. The monitor is better anyhow because everything up there is further away. I am so lucky to be safe and sound underground with every comfort I could hope for, thanks to Mumma. I can turn the monitor off when I want, which is what I did pretty much straight away. Mumma set up a camera outside the house and that's what I see on the screen, the real world, and it's even scarier than I imagined, and for years I imagined flying monsters and fires and floods and earthquakes and a dead mummy and a dead daddy and a dead little sister and a dead big brother. I've switched it on every day in the last week and it makes me jump every time and I hide my eyes with my hands and fumble to switch it off again and I shake for ages which isn't as bad as it sounds. Shaking is something I've always done and I've always found it kind of exciting. I appreciate Mumma's present though, as I begged her to let me see the outside for so long and she found a safe way to show me at last. It's such a relief that I can switch it off. And even though it's been scary every time, I know I'll want to take a look at least once a day. Maybe something will change. Maybe God will made things right again up there. Maybe next time I look the Lokkas will have gone away.

It's time to have another look.

They have big eyes, the Lokkas. They're like tigers and vultures and dinosaurs all rolled into one. They're green and brown and have razor sharp wings and sword-like pincers. And they eat anything. Mumma says they grow to full size – six feet long and almost as tall – in just one week, and then they have lots of tiny babies. Their pincers prick and spurt poison so potent one drop will kill a saltwater crocodile. And did I mention that they eat anything, and by that I mean *anything*?

I just looked and I saw three Lokkas. The up-close one seemed skewwhiff, magnified, with eyes that were too big. It was the same size as the dusty old car out there, the only thing that's visible other than rubble and dust and Lokkas. The skewwhiff Lokka flew away from the camera and seemed to bang something above it that I can't see on my screen. It fell to the ground and wriggled. I wonder what it banged into. Maybe I'm going crazy but the bottom right corner of the screen is weird, like wobbly, and there is something shining and bright down there that I haven't noticed before, like a reflection.

It's off now and I'm supposed to be asleep but I'm waiting for Mumma to say night night so I can check on my jar. It's the first secret I've kept from Mumma since the day she saved me and it feels wrong and bad of me. But I know she'll be worried if she finds out about the jar and I don't want her to worry. There's enough for her to worry about as it is.

Mumma's come and gone. We looked at old photos of my family that's in heaven like we always do when I get scared. I wish we didn't always have to speak in French when we do this. I don't feel myself in French, and it's emotional, looking at photos of my dead family in our dead kitchen with its ginormous pantry, or in our front garden with the gigantic purple bottlebrush, or in our street with the roundabout and the huge statue of the man in uniform with the strange hat bent up on one side who did something important once.

I think Mumma likes speaking in French. It makes her feel productive when she is educating me, and I prefer it when she is happy.

I've been fourteen for seven days now. By day seven, a Lokka should be fully grown like the ones I can see on my monitor, according to all the books Mumma has read. It should be much bigger than me and spiky and hairy. It should be having babies and be pricking people with its poisonous pincers.

Mumma must never find out, but there's a baby Lokka in my room. He's seven days old and still teeny tiny and I don't know why. Maybe he needs more food than the breadcrumbs I've given him, more air than the three holes I have pricked in his lid. He's not scary to me anymore, he's kind of cute. I don't know if he's a boy or not. I call him Lokky.

Lokky got inside on the night of my birthday. Mumma had just given me the monitor and was comforting me because I'd just taken my first look outside then we both saw it: a tiny Lokka, small as a finger, scuttling across the floor. I screamed and jumped on the bed. Mumma stamped on it and swore at the same time. After that we looked through my photo album and talked in French for a while then Mumma went up to her bed.

A while later I heard a scratching sound coming from the floor and everything inside me got really hot. It wasn't dead, the baby Lokka. Its pincers were twitching on the concrete. I jumped on my bed and then up on the top of my chest of drawers and I stood there for ages, my face burning, my whole body shaking. I couldn't reach the intercom to get Mumma. All I could do was try and breathe until the shaking turned into adventure. Eventually, I jumped off the chest of drawers and onto the bed, where I gobbled all my plum jam and watched in case he wriggled again.

A few hours later he wriggled again. He was alive! I was ready. I pounced off the bed and trapped him in my jar.

Lokky has lived in the jam jar ever since and I have waited to be scared of him again; for him to grow so big his pincers smash through the glass, for him to suddenly expand to full size at high speed, like in my American Werewolf DVD, but he is still a teeny thing. He should be ginormous. I have had no need to stamp on him with my boots or squidge him with my heavy bible. He hasn't grown at all.

I just turned the monitor on and had another look at the outside and I am shaking again. Up there is like a desert with fully grown Lokkas coming every which way. This time one flew in to view from the side then three jumped down from above and I'm sure one of their pincers squirted poison on the camera. They move really fast, the Lokkas out there, and when they do I close my eyes and switch off the monitor. But the thing is, there is something strange about my camera view. This time I saw more lights at the bottom-right of the screen. They were moving, bobbing about, like the lights on my dead family's car. I saw a flash of red too, maybe some green, and I think some yellow. I've never seen any colour out there, not till today. I wonder if I'm seeing things, hallucinating. I'm too scared to look again. I'll check tomorrow.

I couldn't wait. I got up and stared at the screen for ages and ages. I watched the lights reflecting on the bottom right corner. White, green, yellow, red. I drank in the colours. I miss colours so much. I saw a Lokka flying sideways then smashing into something and dropping to the ground where it wriggled and writhed. I do think I was hallucinating because of what I saw next. It's the middle of the night and I am never awake at this time, so maybe my eyes were playing tricks on me. I was staring at the wobbly rainbow reflections on the bottom right when a giant hand came into view from above. It was ten times bigger than the car, ten times bigger than the six-foot Lokka. I nearly died of fright. I had to rub my eyes before looking again. Definitely a hand, palm outstretched with a wriggling Lokka on it. The hand moved to the brown ground and placed the Lokka down beside the car. I nearly fainted. I have never been so scared. Are there giants out there now? Not just floods and fires and plagues but enormous people with terrifying hands?

No, I am definitely seeing things. Gonna sleep now. Gonna close my eyes and not think of fully grown Lokkas and giant fingers. Instead I'm gonna think about the morning before Mumma saved me and about bottlebrush.

I'm five. It's my first day of school, at last. I'm wearing my sunhat, koala backpack, a brand new red-checked uniform, and white runners that make me bounce when I run which is great because I love running. I don't think I'll be able to stop myself and I am not going to let Leo stop me either. Leo is taking ages. He doesn't want to walk with his little sister to school. He doesn't want to hold my hand all the way there and all the way back like Mummy and Daddy are making him promise over and over as they put on my sunscreen. He wants to talk footy and cricket and big-boy stuff with his friend.

There are bottlebrushes at the side of our driveway. They have bright purple heads and live in bunches. Sometimes they're beautiful and make me smile and other times they're mean and make me look down at the ground and rush by as fast as I can. I like them this morning. I am out in the big world and I am so excited. Leo holds my hand till we reach the roundabout with the statue of the man with the funny hat who did something very important once. I will not look at the statue of the man. He's grey and hover-y and he's not going to frighten me, no matter what he did that was so important.

Mummy and Daddy can't see us anymore. Leo has caught up with his friend and they are talking about things I wouldn't understand. At last, I can run.

I don't make it as far as I thought I would and am out of breath when I reach the horses. Leo and his friend aren't taking any notice of me. I am free. I can go any which way I like. But it's St Patrick's I'm heading for and I know how to get there. I say hi to the horses and I walk along the dirt track. I can see other red-checked dresses ahead. St Patrick's! My backpack is getting heavy but I will not wait for Leo and his friend and I will not ask for help. It is my independence day. I am my own boss. What I need is the opposite of help.

All the way there is colour: purple and yellow and blue and green; bright, fresh, smile-making colour.

I run again, to a line which has formed on the concrete outside the school. A bell is ringing and there are children everywhere and they are all amazing. One has the bluest eyes I have ever seen and I don't stop looking at her all day. She's beside me when I stand in line, my hand on the shoulder in front of me. She's beside me in the brightest happiest room I've ever seen, sitting at her desk as if she knows everything about school; like that we must sit up as straight as we can with our arms crossed. I copy what she's doing because of her blue eyes and because Sister Mary Pauline says she is the best at sitting up straight. My back is so straight it hurts. I look at the blue-eyed girl and her back is getting even straighter and her arms are so crossed they are rising before her. She is lifting them higher and higher, inch by inch, and I do the same until they are above my head and Sister Mary Pauline is telling me that's enough and to stop.

In the room there is chalk and there are pencils of every single colour and there is paper if you need it and I do need it and there is a radio playing *London Bridge is Falling Down*, falling down, and I learn all the words to it and so does everyone and I am in heaven.

At playtime the blue-eyed girl asks if I want to come to her place after school to see her white cockatoo with its yellow spiky hair and to play with her puppy and I say yes, like duh, course I do. The rest of the day is a blur of crayons and paint and stories and learning to put my hand up if I want to say something and of sitting up straight but not as straight as before.

A bell goes and I can hardly breathe. The blue-eyed girl takes my hand. We exit the school from a different door and everything on the other side looks really strange. The sky is dark and the ground is brown. We skip for a while and then we walk to her place which isn't far, she says. There's no bottlebrush and no statue and no horses and no dirt track and no Leo and no Leo's friend and no smile-making colours. I am in a whole other universe and I am exploring it.

The blue-eyed girl's house is tall and so is her mother, who is standing at the door but not letting me in. The blue-eyed girl has gone in, though. I can't see her now but I can hear her cockatoo screeching and her puppy barking and I really wish I could go in. Her mother is looking down at me and telling me that no play date has been agreed and that I should go home. Before I know it, the enormous white door is shut and I am looking at it.

Right, I will go home then, I say to myself, heading for the biggest road I can see. Trucks are roaring along it and lots of cars too. Everything is even browner than it was before and it's so windy that I can taste dirt. Suddenly, a huge cloud happens, dark and noisy. It is moving towards me and I am wondering if I should turn around and go the other way. There are still no colours and it dawns on me that I might be going the wrong way. I am about to turn around when the cloud gets darker and zooms in on me and I see them up close, huge scary dinosaur insects. They are coming to get me. There are millions of them, each one so big and ugly that I close my eyes and my mouth and stand as still as I can, which isn't very, because I am shaking hard. I can feel them bashing into me but I will not look.

'Hey,' I hear someone say. I open my eyes to see Mumma's smiling face. I have never met Mumma before but I can already tell she is kind and is saving me. Her car door is open. 'You'd better get in,' she says.

As we drive she tells me all about the Lokka plague. She says not to worry. The world might be ending but I'm not. She is going to keep me safe. She says prayers as we drive, prayers for my family who will be dead by now, prayers for St Patrick's which I will never go to again. Lokkas are smashing into the windscreen. I have my eyes closed. I am shuddering and crying, especially when we drive past the statue on the roundabout, especially when we pass the purple bottlebrush in the driveway.

THE BIG LIE

PETER CORRIS

ROBERT ADAMO WAS A SLENDER, MEDIUM-SIZED MAN WITH A SLOW, disconnected way of speaking. 'Mr Hardy, I hope you can help me,' he drawled. 'I've never hired a private detective before.'

'There's a first time for everything, Mr Adamo,' I said. 'I don't ask as many questions as an accountant or cost as much as a plumber. What's the problem?'

He glanced around my office for a moment, which is all the time it takes to register the minimal furniture and non-existent decoration. 'I want to find someone. That is, I saw her yesterday, but–'

'Hold on. Who're we talking about?' I'd already written Adamo's name and address on a foolscap pad, along with the fact that he ran a picture framing and art restoration business in Paddington. Now I wrote MP for missing person, and drew the male and female symbols and a question mark.

'Valerie Hammond. She's my fiancée. We were going to be married in two months.'

I scratched out the male symbol. It took a bit of hacking and slashing through Adamo's reticence and shyness, but I eventually got something I could put down in point form on the pad. Adamo and Valerie Hammond had met when he'd come to collect a painting she wanted framed. They got engaged after six months. The date was set; then Valerie Hammond disappeared. She moved out of Adamo's house, where she'd been living for three months, quit her executive job with Air France and dropped out of sight.

'So you had an argument?' I said. 'What about?'

'No argument. Nothing. I asked her to marry me. She said yes. Then she was gone.'

'What did you do?' I said.

His long, bony hands were in his lap now, twisting and flexing. They were strong-looking hands, and Adamo himself was a strong-looking man – straight dark hair, firm chin, high cheekbones. 'I... I looked for her, but I didn't know what to do. She took her clothes and she got a reference from Air France. She's very good at languages.'

It was a better start than some. Adamo was a very well organised guy: he had a recent photograph of his girl, who was a blonde with a high forehead, big eyes, and a sexy mouth – 165 centimetres, 55 kilos. I did the conversions to the old system on my pad. Valerie was twenty-five to Adamo's twenty-nine; she'd learned French, German, and Italian from her Swiss mother, and she and Robert had had a lot of fun in Leichhardt restaurants.

His people were Italians who'd come out in the sixties when Roberto was a small boy. He was Robert now, and his Italian was rusty. I got the rest of the dope on Valerie – parents both dead, no siblings, only friends known to Adamo were Air France people he'd already talked to with no result. Valerie Hammond seemed to lead a quiet, very constrained life.

'Sorry to have to ask,' I said, 'but does she have any peculiarities? I mean does she smoke a lot, or drink, or gamble?' I gave a little laugh to help the medicine go down.

Adamo shook his head. 'Nothing like that. She is very quiet, a very private person. That's why I'm dealing with you rather than the police.'

'What does she spend her money on? She'd be on a good salary with the airline.'

'Don't know. We never talked about money. I'm very careful about money. Running a small business isn't easy.' His eyed flicked around the office again and I could sense him weighing up incomings and outgoings the way I did myself, periodically. 'All I can tell you is that she's careful about it too.'

I made a note on the pad. 'She must have saved a bit then. You don't know what bank she used?'

He shook his head. 'She didn't have any money'.

'Excuse me, Mr Adamo, but you don't seem to know a lot about the woman you were going to marry.'

'Am going to marry,' he said fiercely, 'when you find her.'

I nodded. His firmness deflected me from that approach. 'Tell me about seeing her yesterday.'

'In Terrey Hills, Mona Vale Road.' He checked his watch. 'At half past three. She got in a Redline taxi and drove away. I was in my van. I'd been delivering a picture I'd restored.'

It turned out that he'd tried to follow the taxi but couldn't do it. I'd have been surprised if he could; following taxis is a lot harder than it sounds. He also didn't get the taxi's number, which was disappointing but not fatal. I took the photograph and got addresses and phone numbers and two hundred and fifty dollars from him – two days' pay – and told him I'd phone him within forty-eight hours.

'I love her,' he said. 'No matter what'.

'There could be problems you haven't anticipated, Mr Adamo,' I said. 'Emotional things.'

He shook his head. 'I deal with artists every day. I know about such things. They're a part of life. I want Valerie for better or for worse.'

He was serious and I was impressed. He lived in Lilyfield, only a hop, step, and a jump from Glebe, where I live. I could always drop in on him and take a look at the coop Valerie had flown. Unlikely to be necessary; people can be hard to find, but it's a matter of categories. Clean-living, good-looking quadrilingual blondes who get references from their employers aren't as hard to find as some.

It's not often in a missing persons case that you have the luxury of two clear, fresh trails to follow. As I get older, luxury appeals to me more. I rang Redline Cabs and spoke to a guy I know there who helps me because I once helped him. He undertook to find out from the service dockets which driver had picked up a fare in Mona Vale Road, Terrey Hills, approximately twenty-four hours ago, and to put me in touch with him, or her.

Then I rang an employment agency which had once provided me with a typist when I needed one to make up a long and largely fictitious report. Amy Post was the typist; we'd had a brief, non-title, sexual bout and had remained friends. Amy was an executive in the company now.

'Amy? It's Cliff Hardy.'

'God, so it is. Let me guess – you need a physiotherapist who can do bookkeeping and house repairs.'

'I don't need anyone. I–'

Amy's voice went smoky. 'We all need someone, Cliff.'

'Sometimes,' I said. 'Right now, I've got a profile of a person who's left a job and is looking for another. I'll give you the details, and you tell me where she goes looking. Okay?'

'Okay. She, eh? Hmmm.'

'It's business. A man's paying me to find her.'

Amy's voice went professional. 'Shoot.'

I gave her the details, such as I had, of Valerie Hammond's age, appearance, qualifications, and experience. Amy said, 'Fluent in all of 'em?'

'So I understand.'

'Half her luck. She wouldn't need to be out of work a minute. And with a good reference? Shit, she could walk in anywhere and ask for top dollar. Got your pencil sharpened? No joke intended.'

Amy gave me a list of eleven likely employers – airlines, travel agents, convention organisers, consultants. I noted down the addresses and numbers and the names of her contacts at each place. Efficiency was Amy's god, and that was one of the things that had kept our affair light – she'd sensed that my ramshackle operation ran the way I liked it, and in a manner she couldn't bear. I drew a line under the last entry and thanked her.'

'Glad to help. Are you sure this chick's a job of work for you?'

'Yes. Why?'

'Nothing. Just that she sounds interesting, and she'd be earning a hell of a lot of money. Bye, Cliff.'

I hung up and thought about what she'd said before dialling the first number. I'd made a dollar sign on the pad when I'd been getting information from Adamo. I underlined it and put another question mark beside it, and the word 'bank'.

The next hour was a minefield of answering machines, indifferent secretaries, hostile underlings, and the occasional cooperative person. My spiel was that I was representing a legal client who needed to contact Ms Hammond, and Amy Post's name was my calling card.

I positively eliminated eight of the organisations and was left with just three – Air Europe, a new charter flight operation that could get you anywhere as long as you could pay the freight; a package holiday outfit which specialised in booking clients into off-the-beaten-track hotels; and a consultancy that arranged computer linkups and interpreters in certain European locations. I could expect calls from these three when Amy's contacts were available and their commitments permitted. I made a separate note of the addresses – my time is important too.

Then I felt a little stir-crazy and went out for a drink and the afternoon paper. It was a cool, early November day, and the city seemed oddly quiet. There was nothing of interest in the paper, and I had to get out of the pub fast after one drink – it was the sort of afternoon you could easily spend in a pub, hanging around until the afternoon became the evening and the evening night, and all you'd get out of it would be a headache. It wasn't so far to the Redline depot in Surry Hills, and I decided to walk it and tell myself I was working.

'You missed him,' Bernie, my satisfied ex-client, said. 'Name's Wesley.' He waved at the phone on his desk. 'Be home now. Call him if you like.'

I sighed and called the number he gave me. Wesley had a deep, tuneful voice and sounded very tired. He remembered the fare.

'Where did you drop her?' I asked.

'Lindfield, I think. Yeah, Lindfield.'

'At a house, block of flats, what?'

Wesley's deep yawn came down the line. 'In the street, brother, just across from the railway station.'

I swore, apologised to Wesley and got his address in case I needed to talk with him about his impressions of the woman. Another question now and I was sure I'd hear him start to snore.

'No go, Cliff?'

I put down the phone. 'Tougher than I thought it'd be.'

Bernie clucked sympathetically and went back to his work.

That's the way it goes, one minute you think you can solve the whole thing between lunch and afternoon tea, and the next it's all questions and no answers. I went back to the office and looked at the three illuminated zeroes on the answering machine. No calls. I sat down and wrote up my notes on the Hammond case so far, the way the *Commercial Agents and Private Enquiry Agents Act* of 1963 requires you to do. I also completed the notes on a couple of other cases which had either been resolved or had petered out.

Full of virtue, I drove home to an evening of TV news, spaghetti, red wine, and Len Deighton. I worried on Len's behalf about the effects on his fiction of the Berlin Wall coming down. But not too much. Len could probably have more fun without a wall.

The calls came in the next morning, two of them with a little urging. At Conferences International, the outfit that set up the computer links and interpreters, I hit the bull's-eye. Yes, Ms Hammond was an employee and yes, certainly, the message to call me would be passed on to her. I sat at my desk and thought about cigarettes and mid-morning drinking, two habits I'd reluctantly abandoned, while I waited for the call. As a result, I was edgy when the phone rang.

'Mr Hardy?' A crisp, businesslike female voice. A voice used to cutting through the shit and getting things done. 'This is Valerie Hammond. I'm returning your call.'

'I'll be honest with you, Ms Hammond. I'm a private investigator. It's not a legal matter. I'm working for Mr Robert Adamo. He hired me to locate you.'

'I see. And you've succeeded.'

'He needs to talk to you, very badly.'

The voice started off flat, dull almost, and rose in pitch and intensity, losing control. 'No. Positively not. Tell him I don't want to see him or talk to him. I don't want to marry him – or, or have children or have anything to do with him. Do you understand?'

'No,' I said.

'That's all. Leave me alone!' The line buzzed and then went dead; she must have fumbled cutting the connection. Very upset. Very intriguing. Very unsatisfactory. How do you tell a client you scored a bull's-eye but the arrow fell out of the target? You don't. I hung up and ran down the stairs and along the street to where my car was parked. I drove straight to the Conferences International office in Bent Street and parked almost outside. Totally illegal, but I didn't expect to be there long. I got out of the car and circled the tall building on foot – smoked glass windows, imposing entrance but no car park. I lounged in the street enjoying luxury again – I'd recognise her and she wouldn't know me from Harry M. Miller.

She came out fast, taller and blonder than I expected, but still Valerie H. as per the picture in my pocket. Her business clothes were smart and looked medium-expensive. No car. She stepped into a taxi, which had drawn up seconds before. The parking Nazi was just rounding the corner as I got back into my car and pulled away from the no parking zone. I jockeyed the Falcon into the traffic, a couple of cars behind the cab. I had my sunglasses on against the glare and a full tank of petrol; I had to hope that the driver was a sober type who signalled early and stopped for lights.

He was. The drive to Lindfield was almost sedate. I had no trouble keeping the cab in sight and staying unobtrusive myself. It was a little after eleven, with a fine, clear day shaping up. I squinted hard trying to read something from the woman's demeanour. She sat in the back the way most women passengers do. Nothing in that. She seemed to be sitting very rigidly, but it might have been my imagination. The cab turned off the main road just past the railway station and pulled up outside a small block of red-brick flats. For the area, very low-rent stuff. There was no mistaking her distress now; she rushed from the cab, leaving the door open, and almost fell as she plunged up the steps towards the small entrance.

Shaking his head, the cabbie got out, closed the door, and drove away. I parked opposite the flats; the sun was shining directly through my windscreen and my shirt was sticking to my back. It was suddenly very hot and still. The highway was noisy, and I heard a train rattle past. This little patch of Lindfield seemed to have missed out on the trees and the quiet and the money. I sat in the car and looked at the flats. It didn't figure. Amy said she must be earning a bundle. Adamo said she had no vices. So why was she living here? Like other people in my racket, I've been known to trace someone, phone the client with the address and bank the cheque. Not this time. I had to know more.

It wasn't nearly as hot out of the car. I flapped my arms to unglue my shirt, and put on my jacket. A sticker over the letter box told me that Hammond lived in flat 3. That was one flight up, a narrow door at the top of a narrow set of stairs. Ratty carpet, cheap plastic screw-on numbers, flimsy handrail, no peephole, no buzzer. I knocked and held my licence folder at the ready. The door opened more quickly than I expected. A big man stood there. He was moon-faced, with thinning fair hair. He wore a white T-shirt and jeans that sagged under his bulging belly. He was well over 180 centimetres tall and must have weighed over 90 kilos, much of it fat.

'My name's Hardy,' I said. 'I'd like to see Ms Hammond.'

Valerie Hammond shrieked, 'No', from behind the fat man and he reacted by brushing the folder away, putting a big, meaty hand on my chest and pushing.

Fat can be a problem if it comes at you fast. This guy was serious, but he wasn't fast. I stepped back, surprised but balanced, and he swung a punch. I'd almost have had time to put my licence back in my pocket before it got anywhere near me. As it was, I moved to one side and let the punch drift away into thin air. That upset and angered him. He lowered his head and bullocked forward, trying to crush me against the brick wall a few feet back. Couldn't have that; I jolted the side of his head with a short elbow jab and pushed at him with my shoulder as he blundered past. He hit the wall awkwardly with his knee and head, groaned and went down.

I looked through the open door. Valerie Hammond was standing there with a shocked, dazed expression on her face. Her eyes were full of terror, and her hands were fluttering like lost birds. I couldn't think of a thing to say to her. I took out a card, bent and put it on the frayed carpet just inside the door. Behind me, the fat man was struggling gamely to his feet.

I pointed to the card. 'I don't mean you any harm. Robert Adamo is concerned about you. Call me when you feel calmer. I don't know what your trouble is, but maybe I can help. I didn't want to hurt this guy.'

Her hands stopped at her face, almost covering her eyes. I stepped clear of the man trying to make a grab at me and went down the stairs. I realised that I was breathing hard but not from the mild exertion. Valerie Hammond's fear had shaken me more than anything Fatty could have done. I peeled off my jacket and sat sweating in the car, wondering what to do next. It was one of those times when the distress you run into seems to outweigh the distress of the person who hired you. It happens and it's confusing. The only way to cope is to get more information. I started the engine and drove away, grateful for the breeze created by the movement and feeling an overwhelming need for a drink.

I had the drink in a North Sydney pub and reviewed my options. All very well to want more information, but where to get it? I couldn't give a work-in-progress report to Adamo as things stood, and I didn't see Conferences International as a promising source. The only other person who'd dealt with the lady was Wesley, the taxi driver with the tuneful voice. *What the hell?* I thought. *He sounded bright, and she might have said something useful.* I had another glass of wine and a sandwich and rang Bernie at Redline, who told me that Wesley would be signing off at the depot about three o'clock. He'd tell Wesley I'd be there for a quick talk, but he warned me not to be late because Wesley would be buggered after his shift and wouldn't wait around.

Wesley was a Tongan, short and wide with a bushy black beard. He rubbed at the small of his back and flexed his shoulders as he spoke. 'Remember the lady well. Very upset, she was.'

'How d'you mean?'

'Crying. That's not so unusual there, you understand.'

'What? Where?'

'Where I picked her up – there in Mona Vale Road. Outside the place.'

'What place?'

'Some kind of institution for, you know, people with something wrong – mental cases, spastics and like that. Very sad place. But they treat them real good there. Looks very pricey – nice grounds, nurses in uniform, all that. But the visitors don't come away laughing. That all, brother? I'm bushed.'

I thanked him and Bernie and drove away with more questions in my mind but also some of the answers, maybe. I stopped at the Post Office in Glebe and located the Terrey Hills Nursing Clinic in Mona Vale Road in the phone book. Then I called in at the surgery of Ian Sangster, who is a doctor and a friend, and a lover of intrigue. I waited while Ian disposed of two patients and then went into his light, airy consulting room. Ian is a jokester: he poured two measures of single malt whisky into medicine glasses and lifted his in a toast. 'Good health.'

We drank and I told him what I wanted.

'It's a top-class joint. Very good, very expensive. But it's for serious defectives, Cliff. I doubt you're ready for it yet.'

'You'll beat me to it if you keep knocking this stuff back the way you do,' I said. 'When will you know anything?'

'Tomorrow, late morning. I'll call you.'

That left me with another evening to kill. I went to a fitness centre in Balmain and hung around until someone turned up willing to play table tennis with me. The deal is, you hire one of the squash courts, a table, net and balls for an hour at an exorbitant price, and play as hard as you can to get your money's worth. I played against a police sergeant from the Balmain station and let him win, four matches to three. In my business, you never know when a friendly police sergeant might come in handy.

I went into the office in the morning, paid a few bills, requested payment for the third time from a faithless client and generally waited for Ian's call. I plugged in a recording device and activated it when I heard Ian's voice on the line.

'Cliff,' he said, 'I've got good news and bad news. There's a patient named Carl Hammond who fills your bill. Aged twenty-three; the contact is his sister, Valerie Ursula–'

'That's it,' I said.

'Poor chap's in a very bad way.'

'What is it?'

'It's called kernicterus. This is the most severe case to come the way of the people there, and the worst I've ever heard of. Put simply, it's brain damage caused by jaundice at birth. The baby's red blood cells are broken down to such a degree that the liver can't cope with the by-products and this stuff called bilirubin is released into the blood stream. Are you making notes or something?'

'I'm recording it, Ian. Go on.'

Sangster cleared his throat. 'Well, as I say, in a severe case a part of the brain is damaged and you get deafness, palsy, loss of coordination. Usually, in a case this bad, the baby is born prematurely and dies. That's called a *hydropis fetalis*, for your information. Carl Hammond should have died. Some freak of nature kept him alive. A cruel freak, I'd call it. Not everyone would agree.'

'Can he–'

'To almost any question you can put, the answer is no.'

'Jesus.'

'Not around when he was needed, nor his dad. I'm sorry mate. This is grim stuff. He's there until he dies, which could be tomorrow or ten years away. He requires complete care. The fees must be astronomical. Is that all you need?'

'Yes. No. What causes it?'

'The Rhesus factor.'

'What's that?'

'God, you laymen are so ignorant. No wonder we get so much money. It's an incompatibility between the mother's blood group and that of the foetus. The mother's metabolism sort of creates antibodies against the foetus, which pass through the placenta and fuck everything up. Get on to it early and you can do a transfusion and avoid the whole mess. Not in this case.'

'Why not?'

'Sorry, I don't know. It's a chance in a thousand sort of thing. Harder to detect twenty-odd years ago than now.'

I thanked him and rang off. I wound back the tape and played the conversation through again. Then I got out a dictionary and looked up some of the words while I made notes. I had an answer to one question now, at least: what Valerie Hammond did with her money. And, remembering her outcry on the phone, I had inklings of other questions and other answers. I resisted the impulse to go out for a drink before attempting to call Valerie Hammond. The only number I had was at work. Maybe she hadn't gone in today. I was almost hoping she hadn't when I heard her voice, crisp and confidence-inspiring, on the line.'

'Valerie Hammond?'

She'd pulled herself together and sounded in better emotional shape than me. But what do you say? How do you tell someone you know their secrets and their nightmares?

I tried to keep my voice level and calm and I spoke very quickly. 'Ms Hammond, I don't want to distress you, but I know about your brother and your problem. I'm working for Mr Adamo, but I want to help you. Please talk to me. Please don't hang up.'

I heard the sharp intake of breath, could sense the struggle for control.

'I have to tell you I'm taking Valium which is the only reason I'm able to talk to you like this. What do you want, Mr Hardy?'

'To talk to you for a few minutes, face to face. If what I have to say doesn't make any sense to you, I'll back off, report to Mr Adamo that I couldn't find you.'

'Very well. If it'll get rid of you. I don't mean to be rude, but you're a violent man.'

'I'll meet you outside your office building. We can talk as we walk. Play it by ear.'

'Did you follow me from work yesterday?'

Uncomfortable question, but it felt like time to play everything straight with her. 'Yes. I hope I didn't hurt your friend.'

'He's all right. He...   he's just sharing the rent with me. It's an arrangement. I'm not... oh, what does it matter?'

This response was my first glimmer of hope; the first indication that she had some awareness of things outside the prison of her problems. 'In about an hour, Ms Hammond?'

'Yes. I'll see you in an hour, Mr Hardy.'

She was on time and so was I. I walked up to her and we shook hands. It seemed like the right thing to do. She was wearing the same clothes she had on yesterday. So was I, as it happened. We walked along Bent Street past the government buildings, in the direction of the stock exchange. There were very few people about. We walked slowly. She said that she hoped this interview would be brief.

'Were you fond of Robert Adamo?' I asked.

'Very,' she said. 'Very, very fond. That was the trouble. I hadn't even allowed myself to feel as much for anyone before. It was a mistake.'

'Why?'

'Robert wanted to marry me and for us to have children. I can't possibly do that, and you know why.' She quickened her pace slightly and spoke more quickly, as if she wanted to get the talk over. 'Oh, I know he loved me and he might have agreed not to have children. But that wouldn't have been fair to him. Or I might have weakened, or there might have been an accident. Anyway, my first duty is to Carl. I should never have got involved with Robert. He's too intense, too... good. His hiring you proves how serious he was. It was an awful, cruel thing for me to do.'

'I know this is painful for you, Ms Hammond, but I'd be glad if you could just answer a few questions. Why do you say you can't have children?'

Her high heels tapped faster. 'Because there is severe mental and physical disability in my genes.'

'Who told you that?'

'I didn't have to be told. Take a look at my brother, Mr Hardy.'

'Who told you?'

'My mother.'

'Did you ever inquire yourself about his condition, ask a doctor?'

'No. I love Carl, strange as it may seem. I just want to make sure he's as happy as he can be. That's all. That's my life.'

'When did your mother die?'

'Six years ago. She left Carl in my charge.'

We'd reached a row of benches outside a new steel and glass tower. I steered her towards one which was shaded by a tree growing in a large wooden box. 'Sit down, Ms Hammond.'

She sat. The tension in her body was visible in every line; also the slight buffer zone, created by Valium, between her and the world. On close inspection, she was a little too heavy-featured to be really good-looking, but she was impressive and there was energy and intelligence behind her sadness. 'I can't imagine what you have to say to me,' she said.

'Your mother lied to you,' I said. 'I suppose she was afraid that if you led a full, normal life you'd neglect your brother. She told you a very cruel lie. Perhaps she was ashamed.'

'That's impossible! My mother was never ashamed of anything. She was immensely strong.'

'I imagine so. Nevertheless, the disability your brother suffers has nothing to do with genetics, at least as far as you're concerned.'

'What do you mean?'

I had to resort to my notes, but I pride myself that I gave it to her clearly and accurately. I explained the medical terms and stressed that the whole Rhesus tragedy could be easily averted by today's technology. She sat perfectly still and absorbed it all. Tears were running down her face by the time I'd finished. She pulled a tissue from a leather shoulder bag and blotted the tears. Through all her distress her mind was razor sharp. 'If what you say is true, how is it that I was born normal, and Carl had this terrible thing?'

'I'm not very sure of my ground here,' I said. 'It could be a matter of chance, but if not, I think you know the answer.'

'Different fathers?'

I nodded. 'And the reason for your mother's behaviour. Guilty people can be strong, and vice versa. When did your father die?'

'A few years after Carl was born. They were very unhappy, my mother and father. They fought terribly. I was very young and didn't understand much. I thought it was because of Carl, or the money. But perhaps...'

She was sobbing now. I put my arm around her shoulders, and she rested her head against me. 'You've got a lot to think about,' I said. 'Most of it's very painful, but not all. You don't have to think of yourself as cursed or tainted. I don't want to push things, but Adamo's a good man. I don't see many, but I recognise one when I do. I think you'd find him understanding and sympathetic.'

She lifted her head and sniffed. 'He's very smart, too, isn't he?'

I remembered Adamo's firmness of purpose, his confidence that he could set things right if he just got a little help.

'Smart enough to run a small business profitably,' I said. 'I'm here to tell you that's tough. And he's smart enough to be in love with you and to hire me. Yes, I'd say he's pretty bright.'

THE CASE OF KORO'S STONE

RENÉE

HANA HAD NOT INTENDED TO PRACTISE HER FOLLOWING AND observation skills today but when she saw Ra Rolleson pushing the scooter very quickly – almost running – she did a U-turn and followed him.

Could there be two red scooters with the same little bear hanging from the handle?

Alice Cain had written about this in her blog, *Becoming a Private Eye*. She said: *If the odds are questionable, it's worth investigating.*

Hana knew about this hut because her nan had told her. He Kākano. The seed pod. A place of beginnings, a place of safety. She'd told Nan about wanting to be a PI and Nan had said, 'Good one.'

Then she said, 'You'll need someone to report to so you can report to me.'

Hana crouched down behind the clump of wavy grasses at the side the hut. She should look up grasses. They all looked the same, but she was pretty sure there were differences.

The wooden outside of He Kākano was weathered to the same pale bluey-grey colour of the stones on the beach, which today merged with the grey of the sky so if Hana shut her eyes to *fix the impression* (as Alice Cain instructed), all she could see was a grey blob. She opened her eyes, smiled at the gulls swooping and diving, calling *where where* as they looked for their breakfast. Probably lots of different kinds of gulls too. Alice Cain was right. *A private investigator's job is never finished. Always something new to learn.* First-aid skills, observation, collecting facts, processing facts, online expertise, self-defence.

Should she go and knock on the hut door, ask Ra about the scooter? She was only up to part six of *Becoming a Private Eye* – hadn't got to *Approaching a Suspect*, yet.

Over the rise of the dunes came a boy in jeans, red jersey, track shoes.

Jase Morris.

So the trolley was definitely his.

Jase walked to the door of the hut and knocked.

The door opened immediately like Ra had been waiting for that knock.

'I've come for my scooter.' Jase was trying to sound cool and firm but Hana thought he sounded nervous too.

Ra said, 'Give me back my stone and I'll give you back your trolley.'

'Millions of them out there.' Jase nodded towards the beach. 'Take your pick.'

'My one's special.'

Jase shrugged. 'That's where I chucked it. Bet you can't even tell which one. That's how special it is.'

He got out his phone, said, 'I'm gonna count to five. If you haven't given me my trolley back by then I'm ringing the cops.'

Ra stared at Jase. 'Last time my koro was on the beach, he gave me that stone. You throw away the stone, you throw away my koro. Give me back the stone, I'll give you back your scooter.'

Jase shrugged, lifted his phone.

Hana stood up, walked towards the boys. Alice Cain said: *A PI has to deal with anything the job throws at you.*

'I'm Hana,' she said. 'I'm good at finding things. She looked at Jase. 'Where did you throw it?'

The two boys stared at her then Jase shrugged.

Habit, thought Hana.

Jase sighed but he walked around to the back of He Kākano, pointed to the beach.

'Describe it to me,' said Hana to Ra.

'Size of my palm, round, kind of flat.'

'Any special marks?'

Ra's turn to shrug. 'Black specks on one side?'

'Okay,' said Hana, 'We'll divide the area into three and we can each take a third.'

'Huh,' said Jase, 'you're crazy. I don't even know what I'm looking for.'

'A stone the size of your palm, flat, round, with a few black flecks on one side.'

Jase looked up at the sky and rolled his eyes.

The three of them walked down to the beach.

'Where?'

Jase thought for a minute, pointed.

'Okay,' said Hana, 'Ra, you take the middle. Jase, take the other side. I'll take this side. Start from the sea and work up to the dunes.'

The boys stared at her like – *who did she think she was*?

'Look,' said Hana, 'If you know where a missing object is then it's simply a matter of finding it, right?'

Jase shrugged.

Hana thought someone should speak to Jase about his shrugging.

Hana walked over to her area. She crouched down, began looking. After a second, Jase walked to the other outside bit, got down on his knees and stared at the stones. Ra shook his head but walked to the middle, bent over, picked up a stone, stared at it, put it down again.

Apart from the gulls crying *where where* and the waves going *swish swish*, it was very quiet.

Hana kept thinking. *It has to be here. Jase threw it here, has to be here.*

Her knees and legs got sore so she stood up, but it was hard to see the stones properly, so she crouched down again. At first all the stones had looked the same but when she looked closer some were fat, some were thin, some had chips out of them, some had streaks of white, some had black flecks. It wasn't until she'd really started looking that she'd realised just how different they all were.

Hana, Jase, and Ra all kept looking. The clouds got greyer; a few spits of rain fell.

In some cases, failure is part of the job. When this happens we have to accept it.

Just as Hana was about to say, 'This was a crap idea – we won't find it,' there was a loud shout and Ra held his arm up high, 'Got it, *got it.*' And he jumped and down, holding up the stone and laughing.

Hana ran over and she and Ra jumped up and down, shouting, 'We got it, *we* got it,' and Jase forgot to be cool and jumped up and down and shouted too.

Hana looked at the stone on Ra's hand.

Palm size, flat, some black specks.

She didn't know whether it was Koro's stone or not, but it certainly looked like the one Ra had described. What were the odds? Private investigators were always working against the odds, according to Alice Cain.

Hana watched Jase walk off with his trolley, saw Ra go the other way with Koro's stone, got out her phone. Made a new file.

Hana Porohiwi, Private Investigator. Case 1. Koro's Stone.

She thought for a moment then added a word.

Solved.

Hana smiled.

Time to go home. Time to report in to Nan.

Editor's Note: This short story was originally written for the Urban Hut Club arts project by Renée (1929-2023), a force of nature and storytelling taonga (treasure) of Aotearoa New Zealand, and a much-loved contributor to our first volume of *Dark Deeds Down Under*.

One of the events curated by Academy Award-winning comedian, actor, musician Bret McKenzie (*Flights of the Conchords, The Muppets*) for the 2020 Aotearoa New Zealand Festival of the Arts, the Urban Hut Club saw miniature backcountry huts crafted by visual artists Kemi Niko & Co installed along the Kāpiti Coast; each including a story from a New Zealand writer that hut visitors could read or listen to once they found the hut.

Renée's story was included in a driftwood miniature hut placed near the Ōtaki Beach dunes.

Hana Porohiwi later became the basis for the character of Bella Rose, a young girl who wanted to be a private investigator, in Renée's second crime novel, *Blood Matters*, which was a finalist for the 2023 Ngaio Marsh Award for Best Novel. This story is reprinted here as a tribute to Renée, with the kind permission of her estate, her family, and publisher.

THE AUTHORS

CHARITY NORMAN

Born in Uganda, Charity grew up in draughty vicarages in Yorkshire and Birmingham. After working as a criminal and family law barrister she emigrated to rural New Zealand in 2002. Also a mediator, Charity is passionate about the power of communication.

She published her debut, *Freeing Grace*, in 2010. Her books have been Richard & Judy and Radio 2 Book Club selections, and she's a three-time Ngaio Marsh Awards finalist. Charity's seventh novel, *Remember Me*, set among the Ruahine Ranges in rural Hawke's Bay where Charity lives, won the 2023 Ngaio Marsh Award for Best Novel.

ANNA DOWNES

Anna is a bestselling author living on the NSW Central Coast with her husband and two children. Before emigrating to Australia in 2011, she attended the Royal Academy of Dramatic Art, appeared in BBC dramas *EastEnders, Casualty* and *Dalziel and Pascoe*, and West End production *The Dresser*.

Her novel, *The Safe Place,* was inspired by her experiences working as a live-in housekeeper on a remote French estate and was shortlisted for the Davitt Awards. Her thrillers have been translated into more than 10 languages. Her third, *Red River Road*, set on Western Australia's Coral Coast, published in 2024.

JACK HEATH

The #1 bestselling author of 40 books for adults and young adults, and published in nine languages, Jack began writing his first novel while studying at Lyneham High School in Canberra and working at a fish and chip shop. That manuscript became his first international bestseller. The 2009 ACT Young Australian of the Year, Jack's mission is to create books that inspire a love of reading in children and adults.

Author of the Timothy Blake series, Ned Kelly Award-shortlisted *Kill Your Brother*, and the recent release *Kill Your Husbands*, Jack lives with his wife and their children in Gungahlin, on Ngunnawal/Ngambri land.

JENNIFER LANE

Jennifer is a Wellington novelist and short story writer who grew up in the tiny town of Cambewarra on the South Coast of New South Wales, where she won a school creative writing competition.

After moving to New Zealand's capital as an adult she won the NZ Book Month Six Pack Two competition with a story that later grew into her debut *All Our Secrets*, which went on to win the 2018 Ngaio Marsh Award for Best First Novel. Her second novel *Miracle*, also set in a small Australian town, was shortlisted for the 2023 NZ Book Awards for Children and Young Adults. Jennifer's story in this book has since evolved during her Masters in Creative writing into a novel tentatively titled *She Loves You*.

ROBERT GOTT

Robert is a Melbourne author of more than 100 books, fiction and non-fiction, for children and adults. He is also the creator of the long-running newspaper cartoon, *The Adventures of Naked Man*, which he drew the old-fashioned way: with a nib pen dipped in ink.

For crime fans, he's written two Ned Kelly Award-shortlisted series set in wartime Australia: the Will Power mysteries starring a failed Shakespeare actor turned wannabe sleuth, and the Holiday Murders series set in Melbourne during the dark days of the Second World War. 'Spike' is a Will Power story.

SHELLEY BURNE-FIELD

Shelley (Ngāti Mutunga, Ngāti Rārua) writes fiction, creative non-fiction, and poetry. An alum of the University of Auckland's Master of Creative Writing, her stories have appeared in local and international literary journals and anthologies, and on major media sites. Shelley's work has been shortlisted for the Commonwealth Short Story Prize, the Voyager Media Awards, and won a poetry category at the 2023 Pikihuia Awards. She is the IIML Emerging Māori Writer in Residence for 2024. Her first children's novel, *Brave Kahu and the Porangi Magpie*, is published in 2024. Her story in our book, 'The Barber', was originally published in *takahē* magazine.

NATALIE CONYER

Natalie is a Sydney author who has a lifelong love of crime fiction, from childhood reading to completing a PhD in Creative Arts in the subject, to writing award-winning stories and novels. She is a serial winner of the Scarlet Stiletto short story awards run by Sisters in Crime Australia, including the Viliama Grakalic Best Art and Crime Story Award in 2022. Natalie's debut novel *Present Tense* is a hardboiled police procedural set in her native Cape Town, which was shortlisted for the Davitt Awards, and won the 2020 Ned Kelly Award for Best Debut Crime Fiction. A collection of her short crime fiction will be released in 2024.

ASHLEY KALAGIAN BLUNT

Originally from Canada, Ashley is a bestselling thriller author, award-winning speaker, podcaster and writing tutor and mentor who now lives on the lands of the Gadigal people of the Eora Nation.

Her first book, *My Name Is Revenge* was a thriller novella and collected essays, initially inspired by her great-grandparents' survival of the Armenian genocide. It was shortlisted for the Woollahra and Carmel Bird Digital Literary Awards. Ashley followed her memoir, *How to Be Australian*, with her first psychological thriller, *Dark Mode*. Her story 'Shock Waves' is a fictionalised retelling of true events.

JEAN BEDFORD

Born in England and raised on Victoria's Mornington Peninsula, Jean helped build and propel the modern era of Australian crime writing as a writer, editor, critic, awards judge, and creative writing teacher. Her novels include an early 1990s trilogy starring private eye Anna Southwood, and standalone thriller *Now You See Me*.

Jean is co-founder and editor of The Newtown Review of Books, and in 2019 edited *See You at the Toxteth*, a posthumous anthology of her late husband Peter Corris's Cliff Hardy stories and columns. Her Anna Southwood story 'I Know Where You Go To, My Lovely' was first published in *Moonlight Becomes You*, a crime anthology Jean edited in 1995.

CHAD TAYLOR

A master of neo-noir, Chad is an Auckland author whose novels either side of the millennium, such as *Heaven, Shirker, Electric*, and *Departure Lounge*, embraced and upturned crime and thriller tropes and saw his writing feted by US and European critics as 'ambitious and hypnotic' and 'original, surprising, and about as cool as a novel can get'. Chad has also written four screenplays, including *REALITi*, which was nominated for five New Zealand Film Awards. After a 13-year hiatus, he published his seventh novel, *Blue Heaven*, which was a finalist for the 2023 Ngaio Marsh Awards.

MALLA NUNN

Malla is an award-winning Sydney filmmaker and author. Born in Swaziland (now Eswatini), she moved to Perth with her parents in the 1970s. Her first novel, *A Beautiful Place to Die*, was set in 1950s South Africa and introduced Detective Emmanuel Cooper. Winning a Davitt Award, it kickstarted a terrific four-book series that was shortlisted for multiple Davitt and Ned Kelly Awards, as well as a CWA Dagger (UK) and Edgar Award (US). Malla's YA novel *When The Ground is Hard* won an *LA Times* Book Prize and was shortlisted for the Australian Prime Minister's Literary Award.

DOROTHY PORTER

Dorothy was an iconic Australia poet who created 18 poetry collections, verse novels, libretti, and YA fictions before her death in 2008. A rare proponent of the verse novel, Dorothy won *The Age* Book of the Year, and the National Book Council Award for her extraordinary *The Monkey's Mask*; and was twice shortlisted for the Miles Franklin Award, for *What a Piece of Work* and *Wild Surmise*. In 2001 she received the Christopher Brennan Award for Lifetime Achievement in poetry. 'Poems from El Dorado' are selected extracts from Dorothy's final verse novel *El Dorado* (2007), about a serial child killer, which was nominated for several prizes including the Ned Kelly Awards and inaugural Prime Minister's Literary Award.

STEPHEN JOHNSON

Stephen is an Australian-born TV news and sports producer who swapped the studio for a writer's garret overlooking the Tamaki Estuary in Auckland. His debut, *Tugga's Mob*, was inspired by his time guiding on double-decker European bus tours in the 1980s, and blended crime, TV journalism, and the classic antipodean 'Big OE'. It was a finalist for the Ngaio Marsh Award for Best First Novel. The investigations and (mis)adventures of the Melbourne Spotlight TV crew continued in *Boxed*, set in Melbourne and rural Victoria, then in *Kaikoura Rendezvous*, set mainly in New Zealand, and again in Stephen's short story herein, 'The Cadaver Crew'.

PETER PAPATHANASIOU

Peter is a Canberra author who was born in northern Greece and adopted as a baby by an Australia family. His writing has been published in major media outlets including the *New York Times, Guardian, Daily Telegraph, Sydney Morning Herald*, and *The Age*.

He began writing his debut outback noir, *The Stoning*, while completing an MA in Creative Writing in London. Peter has also written a memoir, *Little One* and competed a PhD in Biomedical Sciences from the Australian National University. His DS George Manolis crime series continued with *The Invisible* and *The Pit*.

ANDI C BUCHANAN

Andi lives among streams and fault lines just north of Wellington. Their forthcoming novel *Sanctuary* is about found family and haunted houses. Winner of a Sir Julius Vogel Award, their genre-blending novella *From a Shadow Grave* explores a historical murder, the legends surrounding it, and what might have been. Andi is also the author of the Windflower series – five witchy mystery novellas – and their short fiction has been published in *Fireside, Cossmass Infinities, Apex*, and more. When not writing they enjoy cheese, knitting, and winning disputes with the neighbour's cat.

BEN HOBSON

Ben is an author and English and Music teacher in Brisbane. In 2014 his novella, *If the Saddle Breaks My Spine*, was shortlisted for the Viva La Novella prize. Three years later his debut novel, *To Become a Whale*, was published, and longlisted for the ABIA Debut Fiction award and shortlisted for the *Courier Mail*'s People Choice Award.

Ben followed that with a superb literary thriller, *Snake Island*. He interviews authors for Ben's Book Club, an online book club for libraries, and his monthly podcast *Burgers, Beers, and Books*. Ben's third novel is *The Death of John Lacey*.

EMMA VISKIC

Emma is an award-winning Melbourne crime writer and classical musician. Her superb series starring Caleb Zelic, a profoundly deaf private investigator, has been shortlisted for multiple Davitt Awards as well as CWA Daggers (UK) and Barry Awards (USA). Emma learned Auslan to help create and understand the character of Caleb.

Her first novel in the series, *Resurrection Bay*, won the Ned Kelly Award for Best Debut, three Davitt Awards, and iBooks Australia's Crime Book of the Year. Emma's story herein, 'Web Design' began as a deleted chapter of what would become her first Caleb Zelic novel, before evolving into the current standalone story, which won the SD Harvey Award.

DANI VEE

The host of popular literary podcast *Words and Nerds*, which has surpassed one million plays, Dani is a Sydney-based children's author of *My EXTRAordinary Mum* and the *My EPIC Dad!* series. A longtime crime and mystery fan, Dani has interviewed an array of Australian and New Zealand crime writers on her podcast and been a judge for both the Ned Kelly and Ngaio Marsh Awards. 'Not My Daughter' is Dani's debut crime story. She is currently working on more picture books, junior fiction and middle grade novels, and an adult crime novel that draws on her Dutch-Indonesian heritage.

MICHAEL BOTUR

Michael is a prolific, award-winning Northland writer, journalist, and poet who has published several short story collections and two novels. His short fiction and poetry has been published in several leading New Zealand literary journals including *Landfall, Takahe, Poetry New Zealand,* and *Reading Room*. His first horror collection, *The Devil Took Her: Tales of Terror* (2022), was a finalist for both the Sir Julius Vogel Awards and the Australian Shadows Awards. Michael's writing has won several awards, including the 2021 Robert N Stephenson AHWA Short Story & Flash Fiction Competition.

HELEN FITZGERALD

Helen is a screenwriter and bestselling author of sixteen novels, including *The Cry* (2013), which was adapted into a hit BBC drama, and *Worst Case Scenario* (2019), which was shortlisted for the Theakston's Old Peculier Crime Novel of the Year, and won the CrimeFest Last Laugh Award.

She grew up the second youngest of thirteen children, in Kilmore, Victoria, and now lives in Glasgow, where she worked for many years as a criminal justice social worker. Helen's domestic noir thrillers have also been nominated for multiple Davitt Awards. Her latest novel is *Halfway House*.

PETER CORRIS

Known as the Godfather of Australian crime writing, Peter was a prolific Sydney author, historian, and journalist who kickstarted the modern era *Down Under with The Dying Trade* (1980), a distinctly Aussie take on hardboiled fiction that introduced boxer and soldier turned private eye Cliff Hardy. In 1999, Peter became one of the earliest recipients of the Ned Kelly Lifetime Achievement Award, and ten years later he won won Best Fiction for Deep Water, the 34th of his 42 books featuring Cliff Hardy.

Sadly, Peter passed away in 2018, but he remains a giant on whose shoulders many authors have stood. 'The Big Lie' is a Cliff Hardy story originally published in *More Crimes for a Summer Christmas*, edited by Stephen Knight, and is republished here with the permission of Peter's estate.

RENÉE

Renée ONZM (Ngāti Kahungunu) was one of Aotearoa's storytelling *rangatira*, a lesbian feminist, dramatist, poet, and author who lived her later years in Ōtaki. She left school aged 12, during the Second World War, to work in Hawke's Bay wool mills and the printing factory, and later wrote her first play aged 50, kickstarting four decades plus of storytelling on stage and page that featured women in leading roles and humanised the working class.

In recent years, Renée received the Prime Minister's Award for Literary Achievement, the Playmarket Award for significant artistic contribution to New Zealand theatre, and – at the age of 89 – wrote her first crime novel, *The Wild Card*. Both it and *Blood Matters* were finalists for the Ngaio Marsh Awards.

Renée, a much-loved contributor to our first *Dark Deeds Down Under*, passed away aged 94 on 11 December 2023. Her story, 'The Case of Koro's Stone', a precursor to her Porohiwi mysteries, is published in this volume in her honour.

OUR ARTISTS & ARTWORK

MĀHINA ROSE HOLLAND BENNETT

Māhina is an exciting young Māori (Te Arawa, Ngāti Pikiao, Ngāti Whakaue) multimedia visual artist and creative who lives in Tāmaki Makaurau (Auckland). Her practice includes solo and collaborative pieces. She has crafted silk visual artworks with her siblings, poet Matariki and composer Tihema, for the Auckland Pride Festival. She also works in the Costume Department for television series and film, and creates original book cover artwork inspired by traditional Māori art and patterns.

For our *Dark Deeds Down Under* series, Māhina's original design incorporates the endangered Kiwi, New Zealand's national bird, with several traditional patterns. The koru design running up the Kiwi's legs and through the centre of its body represents growth and community. The Mangopare (hammerhead) and Te Mako patterns signify strength and fighting spirit. The koiri pattern running from the Kiwi's head to its back represents self-reflection and nurturing.

SEANTELLE WALSH

Seantelle Walsh is a contemporary Noongar artist, born and raised in Boorloo (Perth), Whadjuk Country. The eldest of six children, she loves creating work that showcases the energy and essence of culture and exploring these connections through creative storytelling.

Under her trade name Kardy Kreations she's worked across Western Australia, creating bespoke and commissioned pieces in a diverse practice that includes studio-based paintings, digital work, murals and public art. She also delivers painting workshops to various schools and organisations, encouraging cultural diversity with a contemporary perspective on Aboriginal art and culture. She draws inspiration from what she sees and feels around her, through her spirituality and her connection to Boodja (Country).

Seantelle designed the First Nations jersey for the Wallaroos – the national women's Rugby Union team of Australia – which depicts the connection between women and their spirit, as well as the connection with the Dreamtime and overcoming barriers.

For our *Dark Deeds Down Under* series, Seantelle has created an original platypus design.

ACKNOWLEDGEMENTS

NGĀ MIHI NUI

So here we are, a coda of our second *Dark Deeds Down Under* anthology, and chance to say 'thanks mate' to some of the people who've helped along the way, whether they knew it or not. First up, a huge 'good on ya, mates' to the ever-growing Aussie and Kiwi writing communities – crime and thriller and beyond – who continue to inspire and make it easy and fun for this sports-loving book nerd from the prow of Maui's canoe (Top of the South Island of Aotearoa New Zealand), to keep shouting all over the world – on page, stage, and airwaves – about the treasure trove of storytellers we have.

This time around, a particular *kia ora rawa atu* (thanks heaps) to all our wonderful contributors for *Dark Deeds Down Under 2*, who provided not only superb stories but plenty of patience and understanding as this one stretched out far longer than any of us anticipated, due to some heavy duty away-from-the-page stuff I had going on.

Huge thanks to Charity, Anna, Jack, Jennifer, Robert, Shelley, Natalie, Ashley, Jean, Chad, Malla, Stephen, Peter, Andi, Ben, Emma, Dani, Michael, and Helen. I'm a big fan of each of you. Thanks for picking up the baton from our 20 fabulous contributors in the first volume, and running with it so strongly. Even if we had a few false starts along the way. You all rock.

Thank you to Seantelle and Māhina, brilliant young First Nations artists who've blessed us with their beautiful artworks created especially for our *Dark Deeds Down Under* series.

Thanks to the family and estates of Dorothy, Peter, and Renée for being keen to showcase their stories for a new audience, here. To Claire Mabey for first alerting me to Renée's story as we all battled with grief and gratitude following the loss of such a writing rangatira in December.

And thanks in particular to the powerhouse that is Lindy Cameron, publisher at Clan Destine Press and long-time National Co-Convenor of Sisters in Crime Australia. What a gift you've given me, to collaborate with you and so many of our wonderful antipodean storytellers on these anthologies. Despite the stresses and frustrations of publishing, who's got it better, eh?

Thanks mate to all the wonderful booksellers, libraries, readers, and authors in Australia and New Zealand who have supported our project over the past couple of years.

Special thanks to the Queen of Crime, Val McDermid, for the kind words and cover quote for our first volume – and holding up a pre-release hardcover onstage at Theakston Old Peculier Crime Writing Festival in the UK, telling 1,000 people in the audience to go get it (if only we'd had it in the festival bookshop!) Thanks also to the amazing Ann Cleeves for reading and enjoying our new volume and providing *Dark Deeds Down Under 2*'s cover quote.

To the family, friends, and supporters of all our contributors, thank you.

My love of stories was started by my parents and stoked by librarians and teachers. Kia ora to Mrs Gately, Mr Joyce, Mrs Sivak, Mr Ledingham, Mrs Hall, and Mrs Clouston. Thank you to all my amazing, crazy, cool mates spread across the world who've made my life infinitely better, in various moments and eras and overall. To Geoff, Nathan, Dale, and Kirstie for being there in late 2022, when I really needed it; and Matt, Ange, Andrea, and all those who checked in from afar. *Aroha nui.*

Finally, to my family. Mum, Dad, and Claire, much of the good in me comes from you. Any mistakes are all mine. I'll always be grateful, and always driven to do you proud. Dad, I hope I can be half the father to Madi that you were for me. And to Helen and Madi, the two girls who've forever changed my life in adulthood. *Aroha nui ahau ki a koe.*

Craig Sisterson

CLAN DESTINE PRESS CRIME ANTHOLOGIES

A vibrant showcase of modern Aussie and Kiwi crime writing with a star-filled southern constellation of antipodean crime writers.

The first volume of this ground-breaking anthology series has 19 short stories from the brightest storytelling talents from Australia and New Zealand: including award winners, international bestsellers, and a host of fresh voices.

Brand new stories, many starring some of crime fiction's most beloved series characters, share the pages of our Down Under world with edgy standalone tales, all of which range far and wide across our unique rural and urban landscapes.

A crew of beloved characters: Corinna Chapman, Hirsch, Sam Shephard, Rowly Sinclair, Nick Chester, and Murray Whelan, will lead you down dark alleys to meet our newer series heroes, the Nancys, Penny Yee and Matiu, Alex Clayton, Kate Miles – and the stars of some cracking standalone tales.

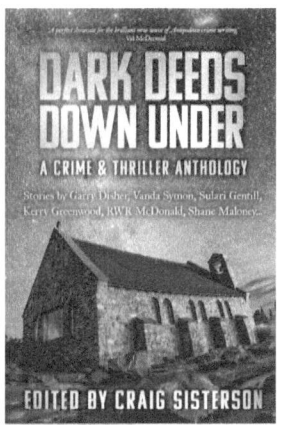

ISBNs: 9780645316780 (pb)
9780645316803 (eb)

These dark deeds are perpetrated by: Alan Carter, Garry Disher, Kerry Greenwood, Sulari Gentill, Nikki Crutchley, Aoife Clifford, Shane Maloney, Vanda Symon, Lisa Fuller, Helen Vivienne Fletcher, Narrelle M. Harris, Renée, Katherine Kovacic, R.W.R. McDonald, Dinuka McKenzie, Fiona Sussman, Lee Murray & Dan Rabarts, Stephen Ross, and David Whish-Wilson.

Who would the Great Detective be if Sherlock was a woman?

That's the question posed in *Sherlock is a Girls' Name*, an anthology imagining Sherlock Holmes as female, in fabulous mysteries that follow the great detective across time and even space.

The eleven stories in this book, selected by Holmes and Watson tragics – aka long-time Sherlockian writer-editors – Narrelle M. Harris and Atlin Merrick, imagine Holmes in deep space, 1990s Russia, Victorian London, contemporary USA, worlds of magic, and more.

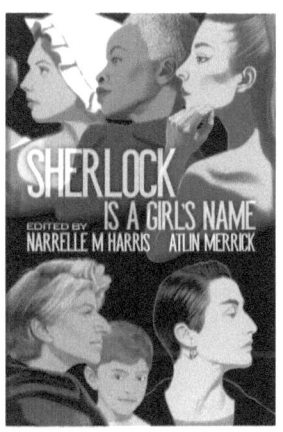

Of course Holmes is not Holmes without Watson, and the many Watsons herein include ghosts, robots, a boy who doesn't speak, a teenage tuba player, a stranger on a plane. In each story Holmes and her Watson do what they do best: solve crimes and have adventures!

Stories by: Tansy Rayner Roberts, Eugen Bacon, Sarah Tollok, Verity Burns, Dannye Chase, Kenzie Lappin, JD Cadmon, Stacy Lawhorne, Karen Carlisle, Katya de Becerra, Narrelle M. Harris, and Atlin Merrick.

ISBNs: 9781922904713 (pb)
9781922904720 (eb)

Cats and dogs, birds and bats
Squirrels and monkeys, spiders and rats
Humans, a penguin, a fox and some pigs
All share the limelight on detecting gigs.

Who Sleuthed It? is dedicated to all the animal-loving mystery readers who know their furkids and their feather, fin and tailed ones would definitely help solve all the crimes – when not perpetrating them.

Who Sleuthed It? is an anthology of fabulous tales in which animals help their animal friends, or human sidekicks, solve diabolical crimes and whimsical mysteries.

It features 19 riveting stories by a cohort of Australian, Irish and American authors.

Despite appearances, this perplexing collection of mysteries is NOT a children's book... although it can be read to or by them.

Fingers and feelers and paws and wings
Solving thrillers and chillers and secretive things

ISBN: **9780648848769** (pb)
9780648848776 (eb)

Possibly in cahoots with a creature of some kind, the stories herein are by: Kerry Greenwood, Vikki Petraitis, Meg Keneally, Lindy Cameron, Elizabeth Ann Scarborough, Atlin Merrick, Jack Fennell, Tor Roxburgh, David Greagg, Craig Hilton, Louisa Bennet, LJM Owen, Narrelle M. Harris, Kat Clay, Chuck McKenzie, GV Pearce, CJ McGumbleberry, Livia Day, and Fin J Ross.

Since his first appearance in 1887, Sherlock Holmes has been the quintessential English sleuth, alongside his loyal companion and biographer, Doctor Watson.

But what if they had come from some other place in the world, or another time? How would they differ from Conan Doyle's creations? How similar might they remain?

Holmes and Watson are herein re-imagined in new cultural contexts, different genders and sexualities, and in stories rich in foreign detail that still reflect their origins.

Thirteen writers from around the world, with cultural or historic expertise, explore the possibilities with stories set in Germany, C17th England, Ireland, Australia, Russia, South Africa, India, Poland, USA, Ancient Egypt, Viking Iceland, and even the entire world.

You'll discover Holmes and Watson are not only unique in original canon, but the Great Detective remains singular in every world!

ISBNs: **9780648848783** (pb)
9780648958635 (eb)

Stories by: Kerry Greenwood & David Greagg, Greg Herren, Atlin Merrick, Jack Fennell, Lucy Sussex, Jason Franks, Natalie Conyer, Lisa Fessler, Katya de Becerra, LJM Owen, Jayantika Ganguly, Raymond Gates, and JM Redmann.

www.ingramcontent.com/pod-product-compliance
Lightning Source LLC
Chambersburg PA
CBHW031156050726
47495CB00019B/1882